Romance and intrigue on the Norfolk marshes

Boot Camp Bride
by
Lizzie Lamb

Lizzie Lamb is now on my list of authors to look out for!

ISBN 978-0-9573985-3-5

For Sir Roger de Bushby
A dear friend who is sadly missed.
Meet you at the Coal Shed, Thornham Staithe on the morning
of the high tide,
Dodger.

To Celia,

Lots of love

Lizzie

Table of Contents

Chapter One
No, No, No

Charlee was listening to Amy Winehouse on her iPod in the large walk-in cupboard that doubled as a storeroom for copier paper, last year's Comic Relief publicity material and those computers even the techno-geeks couldn't fix. The sign on the door read 'Photo Archive'. But looking round the room crammed with filing cabinets and office detritus - and with the sour smell from an abandoned mop bucket wafting towards her - Charlee decided that a spell in rehab was beginning to look an attractive alternative. Trying to keep her spirits up, she sang along with Amy at the top of her voice.

No one ever came down to the basement of *What'cha!* Magazine of their own volition and the photo archive was rumoured to be haunted. But Charlee guessed that was just a story put about by the post boys to scare her. She glanced once over her shoulder in the windowless twilight, shivered, and then continued with her task. Editorial wanted 'before/after' photos of celebrities whose facelifts had gone wrong. And, as a lowly intern who had seriously pissed off the fashion editor, Vanessa Lloyd, Charlee had been given the task.

Listening to the iPod was a small act of rebellion on her part. Out of sheer vindictiveness - and just because she could - Vanessa had banned the use of iPods and mobiles during office hours. However, Charlee's defiance couldn't compensate for the crumminess of the task. Or the fact that she'd been sitting in a cramped position for two hours, flicking through photos of lopsided celebrities, dying to use the loo.

Her - that is - not the celebrities!

Cutting-edge journalism? Hardly.

It all seemed far away from the heady day last summer when she'd graduated with a first in Modern Languages and Political Studies. Then she'd imagined herself reporting from a war zone above the rolling titles of a breaking news story on the Beeb. Instead, here she was, wondering if it was possible to get dowager's hump from sitting hunched over a low desk for hours on end while all feeling left her lower limbs.

'Montague,' a voice growled. 'Is that an iPod I see?' A pair of hands clamped over her knotted shoulders.

In one well-practised move, Charlee put her hand up her sweater, pulled out the earphones and hid the wires from view. She spun round expecting to find Vanessa Lloyd standing there ready to give her a ticking off for not being on task. Instead, she found Poppy Walker - daughter of *What'cha!*'s editor-cum-proprietor - her best friend and confidante.

'You've just shaved five years off my life, Walker, know that?' Charlee said, now she could breathe easy again. Poppy ignored her, looking round the dinginess of the photo archive and wrinkling her nose instead.

'What is that smell?'

'I've been down here so long I've become immune to it. But I think it's coming from that mop bucket over there.' Charlee collected the 'before/after' photos together, making sure that she'd left markers in the filing cabinets to show where they'd come from. She knew exactly who'd be putting them back once Editorial had finished with them.

'Poor Charlee,' Poppy sighed. She reached into an oversized designer handbag, pulled out a bottle of perfume and sprayed a suffocating cloud of some exclusive, spicy scent in Charlee's direction. 'There, sweetie; that ought to stop dogs running after you in the street.'

'Thanks, mate.' Charlee put a sarcastic stress on the word, but the irony was lost on Poppy. She wasn't the sharpest knife in the drawer and was only kept on at *What'cha!* because her family owned the magazine. And no one - not even the almighty Vanessa - dared to complain to Sam Walker about his daughter.

Charlee regarded Poppy with fond exasperation.

Last summer, she'd written to every newspaper from *The Times* to *Pigeon Fanciers' Weekly* in an attempt to get a toehold in the world of journalism - but none of them had bothered to answer her letters or emails. As the weeks stretched into months, Poppy had spoken to her father on Charlee's behalf, brushing aside Charlee's half-hearted protests that she was cashing in on their friendship. The result was a year's internship at *What'cha!* during which time Charlee had to prove herself worthy of Sam and Poppy's belief in her.

'Why can't you do this online?' Poppy asked, waving a hand in front of Charlee's face and breaking her dream.

'That's exactly what I asked - dared to ask - Vanessa.'

'And your head is still attached to your shoulders?' They exchanged a look of fellow feeling. Vanessa's high-handedness with interns was legendary, but her dislike of Charlee verged on the pathological. It was Charlee's avowed intention to make Vanessa review her low opinion of her and eat her caustic words. All she needed was a chance, an opportunity to show everyone her mettle. She had it in her to be a great journalist; she felt it in her water. One day her lucky break would come along and when it did, she'd be ready.

Dreaming of being handed the Pulitzer Prize for Journalism, Charlee locked the door of the photo archive and put the key in her pocket.

'I don't know why you're bothering to lock the door. I mean, you'd have to be a very desperate thief to break in at dead of night and steal a Windows 95 computer or a Betamax video recorder. Wouldn't you? 'Bout time Daddy consigned half this junk to the techie-graveyard. I would tell him so myself, but he might give me the job of sorting it out.' Poppy glanced at one of her manicured nails and pulled a glum face.

'He says I've got to work harder or he's halving my salary and some of the horses will have to be sold off.'

Charlee laughed at her woeful expression. Poppy was an excellent rider, it was one of the things she excelled at. Despite *What'cha!* Magazine having been in her family for three generations, journalism came a very poor second to eventing, in her opinion.

'Corners are being cut and sails trimmed, Miss Walker,' she said with mock-severity. 'We're in the middle of a double-dip recession in case you hadn't noticed. Apparently, we own the copyright to these photos, and have to use them instead of buying new ones from the usual agencies. Editorial's budget has been slashed in view of last month's disastrous sales figures.'

'In view of Vanessa's long lunches and fiddled expense account, you mean,' Poppy added, before giving herself another squirt of perfume and returning it to her bag. 'If there's another cull in the office you can bet old Teflon Knickers will come out of it unscathed.'

As style editor, Vanessa was highly regarded because of her address book and contacts with the rich and famous. She kept an army of not-so-rich-and-famous waiters, hairdressers and stylists on retainer to ensure that she had first pickings of the juiciest items of celebrity gossip. She was almost untouchable, feared as much as revered. Her nickname: Teflon Knickers, referred to some of the less scrupulous things she'd done in pursuit of a scoop.

At *What'cha!* Magazine, the end, in most cases, justified the means. Its tagline said it all - *what'cha want is what'cha get!*

'So what brings you down here?' Charlee prompted, wishing she could get a glance in Vanessa's famous little black book. Just once.

'Oh yes. Fear not, for I bring you glad tidings of great joy,' Poppy said, waving her arms about and striking a pose.

'Oh yeah?' Charlee asked suspiciously.

She remembered Poppy peeing herself in excitement at their first nativity play whilst waiting to deliver the same line, but wisely didn't remind her of it. Christmas was only a few days away and clearly Poppy was already in the party mood whereas Charlee's Christmas spirit was languishing in the doldrums.

'You are so going to love me for this, Montague. Most of Editorial's gone down with the norovirus. Chief wants stand-ins for the book awards tonight. Sort of rent-a-crowd,' she tailed off, perhaps sensing that her sales pitch wasn't having the desired effect on its target audience.

'And?'

'And. You're one of them. I got you a ticket. Ta-da.' She gave a little twirl, clearly relishing her role as fairy-godmother-cum-archangel and waving the precious ticket under Charlee's nose.

'I don't believe it,' Charlee said, showing sudden interest.

What'cha!'s Book of the Year Award was legendary and invitations were coveted, even among the rich and famous. It was the celebrity/style magazine's token nod towards 'The Arts' and the prize money was so generous that even the most donnish professor was keen to be nominated. Apart from the money and the kudos, the winner was guaranteed mega sales and an appearance on all the major chat shows. Something not to be sniffed at when purse strings were being tightened.

Charlee had only been at *What'cha!* a few months but knew it was more than her life was worth to accept a perk like this. She had no illusions about her place in the pecking order: one step above the cleaning staff, but well below the boys who brought round the mail, sandwiches and takeaway cappuccinos from Pret A Manger. The only perks likely to come her way were a few bent paperclips and dried-up biros. Or, if she was lucky, organising Secret Santa or the sweepstake for the Grand National next year - always supposing she was kept on at the end of her internship.

Book launches? Champagne receptions?

She didn't think so.

By accepting the invitation, she'd probably offend some old dinosaur who'd worked at *What'cha!* for at least a thousand years, and be bludgeoned to death with the lid of the photocopier for her temerity, her corpse hidden in the photo archive and -

Maybe that's what the smell was. An intern who'd got above herself.

'Thanks; but no thanks,' Charlee sighed. 'I'm going straight home. There's an M&S chilli in the fridge with my name on it. I'm going to have a long bath with lots of candles, slurp a bucket of wine and then start writing Christmas cards.' Even to her ears, it sounded dull, with a capital D.

'Christmas cards? Are you mad - the last date for posting them was two days ago. Tonight's for fun. You're coming to this award ceremony, or I'll get Daddy to stop your Christmas bonus.' Poppy grinned to show she was joking. But judging from the way she was blocking Charlee's access to the stairs, it was clear that she wouldn't take no, or even maybe, for an answer.

'Norovirus, you say?' Charlee asked, her spirits lifting once more.

'Synchronised - Projectile - Vomiting. ' Poppy emphasised each word with a shudder. 'But good news for you and the other little elves in Editorial.'

'I'd be doing Chief a favour, then?'

'It's your duty to attend, Montague,' Poppy said sternly. 'And don't tell me that you haven't been sitting in that health hazard that passes for a stock room wishing for something - or someone - to whisk you away?' Clearly sensing Charlee's weakening resolve, Poppy walked backwards up the stairs, dangling the invitation and singing: 'We Three Kings of Orient Are'.

'Okay, okay, I give in. On one condition.'

'Anything.'

'You stop singing or I'm going back into the photo archive.'

'Very amusing.' As Charlee reached out for the invitation, Poppy turned and ran ahead of her, openly delighted that she'd finally caved. 'Be ready by seven o'clock. And Montague -'

'Yes, Walker?' Charlee caught up with her and snatched the heavily embossed invitation out of her hand.

'Do something about that awful smell, sweetie.'

Then she ran up the stairs with Charlee close on her heels, threatening retribution.

Chapter Two
The Devil Wears Primark

Charlee stepped out of the taxi around about eight o'clock and pulled her pashmina around her, warding off the wind that came straight off the Thames. Sharp and cutting, it whistled round her exposed legs and ankles and she wished now that she'd worn a coat. But, she was young and reckless and not even the threat of double pneumonia could dampen her enthusiasm for tonight's event. In fact, learning to suffer the cold without complaint would stand her in good stead when she worked on a serious newspaper and not a celebrity-driven magazine. Slipping into one of her customary daydreams, she imagined herself in Afghanistan where the wind scoured through the Khyber Pass. She'd suffer it all without complaint as she hunkered down in her fatigues, staking out the Taliban with a platoon of soldiers. Ready to report what the living conditions were like for our Heroes out there.

No privation was too great for Charlee Montague, the pundits would say, her dedication to the job is legendary.

Totally wired, Charlee skipped up the marble steps of the art gallery where the event was being held. Christmas was just around the corner and if that meant a groan-inducing stay at her family home, at least she was free from the dungeon of the photo archive. As she waited for Poppy to pay the driver and give him a generous tip, she was determined to make the most of this God-given opportunity. Tonight she would make her mark or die in the attempt. Journalism was as much about luck as talent; about being in the right place at the right time and getting the scoop. This could be her chance to mingle with people who would spot her potential and offer her a place on a team of talented young writers. Editors and subs who would give their eyeteeth to -

'Charlee, snap out of it. While you're dreaming of winning the Pulitzer Prize - again - I'm freezing my assets off,' Poppy complained, teetering on heels guaranteed to wreak havoc on the natural wood flooring in the art gallery. 'Come on, let's pard-ee, girlfriend.'

The huge glass doors swung open and as Charlee crossed the threshold, she gave a little shiver that had nothing to do with the cold. Squaring her shoulders she stepped into the overheated atrium which was filled with the hum of voices and a hundred clashing perfumes.

'Invitation?' An impatient voice stopped Charlee and Poppy in their tracks. Sally, Vanessa Lloyd's familiar, was collecting the stiffies and checking for gatecrashers. When she clocked Charlee, she pulled a face and snatched the invitation out of her hand. Her laser beam eyes subjected it to a thorough examination as though she suspected it was a counterfeit, manufactured in true Blue Peter fashion at Charlee's kitchen table that very afternoon and the ink was wet. 'How did you get this, Montague?' She glanced at Poppy standing just out of earshot. 'Oh, I get it. Friends in high places.' Her acid tone made clear exactly what she thought of those interns who'd made it here by default and courtesy of the norovirus.

'Better than friends in low places, or no friends at all,' Charlee responded, so cheerfully that it took a few seconds for Sally to register the put-down.

Charlee didn't know what she'd done to antagonise Sally Taylor, but she never missed an opportunity to remind Charlee of her lowly status at *What'cha!* or to emphasise just how precarious her position was. However, one thing was certain. Charlee might have to kowtow to old Teflon Knickers but she could be as rude as she liked to her PA and get away with it. And, like the other interns, Charlee took a perverse delight in baiting Sally.

Charlee certainly wasn't going to allow her to ruin a once-in-a-lifetime invitation to *What'cha!*'s prestigious book award.

'You know us interns, Sal. Rent-a-crowd. Go anywhere for a free glass of champagne and a chance to climb the greasy pole.' That statement, and calling her 'Sal', touched a raw nerve and drew a quick response.

'You're not climbing any pole; greasy or otherwise, Missy,' she snarled, revealing newly veneered teeth so brilliant white that Charlee and Poppy were temporarily dazzled. 'Vanessa wants you wannabes in the side room over there.' She pointed with the invitations in the direction of a small room off the main art gallery. 'The catering staff's been hit by the same sickness bug as Editorial. You and the others are to serve the champagne and canapés.'

'What? Even me?' questioned Poppy, joining in with the conversation and giving the PA a quelling look.

Momentarily wrong-footed, Sally checked her list of guests and then came back with a flustered, sycophantic: 'Are you here as Miss Walker, daughter of the proprietor and friend of Mr Fonseca-Ffinch. Or an intern and employee of *What'cha!*'

'Don't be such a fuckwit, Sally. Figure it out for yourself.'

Acting daughter-of-the-boss, Poppy sashayed into the crowd air-kissing people as she headed towards an exhibition of photographs from the award-winning book: *The Ten Most Dangerous Destinations on the Planet.* She picked up a glass of champagne clearly expecting Charlee to follow her, but Charlee suddenly thought better of it. Poppy's position at *What'cha!* was ambiguous to say the least and she could wrap Sam Walker round her French manicured finger. But Charlee didn't have that luxury. She sighed and her earlier euphoria evaporated, leaving her depressingly aware of her lowly status.

She should have known there was no such thing as a free lunch - or a baksheesh invitation to an exclusive book launch, come to that. Realising she'd been sold a pup, Charlee headed for the side room Sally had indicated, the glitter, glamour and promise of the evening receding with every step. She entered the room just in time to hear Vanessa's uplifting team talk.

'I don't care how many episodes of *Ugly Betty* you've seen, or what your pathetic little dreams are. Tonight is not about promoting yourselves or your dubious writing talents.' There was a general shuffling of feet as this venomous barb struck home. Like Charlee, everyone present had aspirations and hoped one day to write their own column or at least be given a by-line in the publication of their choice. An optimism Vanessa clearly did not share - if her scathing glance over the assembled interns was anything to judge by.

'Sorry I'm late,' Charlee began. Vanessa squinted at her short-sightedly, but after realising it was Charlee - a person of no importance, she ignored her and carried on.

'Tonight you are invisible; here to act as cater-waiters. Do well and you'll be rewarded. Screw up and you'll be counting paper clips and kissing your Christmas bonus goodbye. If you're lucky, you might get to hear the author's acceptance speech and buy his book at the end of the launch. I've negotiated a generous staff discount,' she added magnanimously, as Sally entered and gave them all a supercilious, pitying look.

With a nod from Vanessa, Sally put in her two pennyworth, just in case they didn't get it. 'Anyone seen doorstepping the author or any VIP will be disciplined and summarily dismissed.' She shot a little dart of wishful thinking in Charlee's direction.

Vanessa, hearing the siren call of chinking glasses and catching the flash of cameras as publicity shots were taken, clearly decided that she had bigger - and more important - fish to fry. With a 'let's get this over with' nod to Sally, she left the interns under no illusion what she thought of them.

'For the love of God, Sally, check out what each of them is wearing before you let them loose on the unsuspecting guests. Most of them look like extras from the "Devil Wears Primark". I've never seen so many synthetic fabrics together in one room. A carelessly positioned candle and the whole place could go up.' Her cold blue eyes treated them to one, last hypercritical sweep before she left the room, leaving a trail of her signature lung-clogging perfume in her wake.

'Yes Vanessa!' Sally almost clicked the heels of her fashionable shoes together, openly terrified that Vanessa would glance her way and find her wanting, too. After a moment's silence, everyone began to mutter. However, working for Vanessa had turned Sally into one tough little cookie, because other than a tell-tale wobble she didn't even blink in the face of such voluble resentment. 'Here are your aprons,' she gestured towards a table stacked high with white linen. 'Put them on before you leave the room and then head over to the kitchens where you'll be given name badges and further orders.'

'Hang on a minute.'

'Are you having a laugh?'

'I'm not wearing this!'

Apparently more frightened of disobeying Vanessa than upsetting a troupe of junior reporters, Sally swatted their objections away as if they were particularly bothersome flies. 'Any complaints, take them up with Vanessa.' At the mention of her name, the rebellion was quashed. But Charlee wasn't giving in that easily. Believing that fortune favours the brave, she marched up to the table and took an apron off the pile. She tied it around her waist French waiter style with the bib folded under, leaving her new Jigsaw top clearly visible.

'Look at it this way, guys,' she addressed her co-workers, putting a positive spin on the situation. 'At least we'll be able to get up close and personal to some seriously famous authors and agents - do a bit of networking.'

'You heard what Vanessa said about doorstepping, Montague,' Sally screeched as a muted cheer went up from the demoralised troops. 'You can't … you wouldn't dare!' She stood in front of the door in an attempt to bar Charlee's way out of the room. Such was the terror Vanessa engendered in her staff.

'Don't. Push. It. Taylor.' Charlee enunciated with just the right degree of menace and none too gently moved her size zero bones out of the way. 'You have no idea who you're messing with -'

'You'll pay for this,' Sally hissed. The other interns took Charlee's lead, tying on their aprons with a smile as they realised the evening wasn't a complete disaster. 'I'll make it my business to see that you do.'

'Of that I have no doubt.' Charlee shut the door and walked away, leaving Sally standing on the other side of the glass mouthing threatening words and looking like a fish in an aquarium demanding food. Pulling back her shoulders, Charlee put on her best smile, tied her apron more securely and prepared to rub shoulders with the rich and famous.

She'd turn this debacle round and make the evening a success, if it was the last thing she did.

Chapter Three
Rock, Paper, Scissors

After an hour of smiling pleasantly and counting how many guests actually bothered to crack their surgically enhanced, botoxed faces with 'yes, please' or 'no, thank you', Charlee's optimism was wearing thin. She glanced round the gallery and exchanged cheesed-off looks with her fellow cater-waiters.

The award ceremony was drawing to a close and cosmopolitans and tiny chocolate brownies were being served. All very *Sex in the City*, but she felt less like Carrie Bradshaw and more like an invisible will-o'-the-wisp as she helped guests into their coats and watched them leave for trendy after-parties and members-only clubs. Even the author who'd won the Elfreda Walker prize - named after Poppy's grandmother - had abandoned the table where he'd spent most of the evening signing copies of his book. Every time Charlee had walked past he'd been obscured by punters eager to buy a copy of *The Ten Most Dangerous Destinations on the Planet*.

He must have raked it in this evening.

Charlee wondered how many guests would actually read his book and not simply leave it on the coffee table gathering dust. A trophy from another champagne reception.

And talking of champagne …

She slid away from the yawping, air-kissing crowd and collected her clutch bag from the staffroom. After retouching her make-up, she headed back into the exhibition hall a free woman. She caught sight of herself in one of the mirrors. She had the determined - if slightly deranged - look of a woman on a mission. A woman determined to have a good time and to establish her credentials with authority to anyone who was willing to listen. Even if she was still wearing the hideous apron foisted on her by Sally.

Untying the apron, she deftly kicked it under the table. Having spent all night handing out glasses of the 'Widow' to the undeserving rich and trying to engage them in conversation, Charlee felt the need to redress the yin/yang balance. She went in search of the glass of Veuve Clicquot she'd stashed behind a pile of unsigned books. Like her, the champagne had lost some of its effervescence. But - champagne was still champagne, even when slightly flat. Cramming a miniature chocolate brownie in her mouth, she glanced over her shoulder to check the whereabouts of the ever-vigilant Sally. When she turned back, someone was reaching out for her glass of champagne.

'That glass is spoken for,' Charlee growled, in a tone that would have won her the lead in a remake of *The Exorcist*. Irrationally annoyed at the thought of her well-earned glass of bubbly being appropriated, she was in no mood for dalliance.

'I think you'll find it's my glass,' countered a voice that was well-bred and with a husky edge to it. Charlee got the sense that rather than be intimidated by her glowering look, the champagne thief was amused by it - by her. Irritated beyond all reason at a further downturn to her evening, she reached for the glass at the exact moment he did and their fingers touched. A spark of electricity crackled between them, like in a department store when you touch the clothes rail and attract static from the carpet. Charlee gasped at the strength of it and drew her hand back, feeling as if her fingers had been scorched.

Perplexed, she glanced down at her feet. But, here's the thing - she was standing on expensive wooden flooring the colour of dark sand and there wasn't a carpet in sight. She didn't have time to speculate what had generated the static, or whether the stranger had experienced the jolt, too, because he took a step closer. So close that his expensive leather shoes were now toe-to-toe with her sale bargain wedges.

'As I said - that's my glass of champagne. However … Chelsea,' he continued, 'I'm prepared to act the gentleman and let you have it - if you'll be a good girl and fetch me another.'

Good girl?

Good God!

She wasn't ten years old and this wasn't a playground tussle over a bar of chocolate. She was twenty-three, had a first class degree and this was a glass of Veuve Clicquot Premier Cru. More to the point, her glass of Veuve Clicquot Premier Cru, which she wasn't about to give up without a fight. Then another, more pressing thought struck her - how come he knew she was 'staff'? A quick glance at her Jigsaw top solved the mystery. A sticky label, torn off a roll and scrawled on in black felt-tip pen, identified her as CHELSEA MONTARGUE, a member of the catering staff - semi-literate and incapable of spelling her name.

Very different from the innovative journo she longed to be.

Misnamed and shamed, she stammered out a hot:

'Here. Have the bloody champagne.' She had the uncomfortable feeling that she was being patronised and oh-so-subtly put-down, and in that droll way posh boys do. 'It's flat anyway,' she added, taking the edge off his victory.

That should have been her cue to exit stage left with what dignity she had left. But her elbow was held in a firm 'you're not going any-where' grip. Unable to move without engaging in an unseemly struggle and spilling the champagne all over clothes bought specially for the award ceremony, Charlee gave Posh Boy the benefit of her practised, Medusa-like stare. The one that deterred potential gropers and would-be suitors at ten paces; it'd never failed her yet.

Just as she was about to deliver a scathing put-down, she raised her head and their gazes locked. It was then that she noticed him - really noticed him - and she was forced to admit, he ticked all the boxes.

Lean athletic build, fashionably dishevelled dark hair, straight black eyebrows above slate-grey eyes and full of confidence and assurance. The way he held himself, the angle of his head and the set of his shoulders made it plain that he thought - no, knew - he was the hottest ticket in town. He looked like a man used to stretching out his hand and having everything he wanted fall into it.

Evidently unfazed by her Medusa-like stare, he allowed the seconds to lengthen. Charlee gained the impression that he was not so much assessing her, as waiting for her reaction to all the aforementioned attributes. A response he apparently regarded as no more than his due. But it would take more than dark good looks and eyes the colour of wet slate to have her falling at any man's feet, her dampening look informed him.

She gave him one last 'get over yourself' withering glance, pulled her elbow free and prepared to leave.

She'd been raised with four handsome, talented brothers - arrogant, self-assured men like the champagne thief just didn't float her boat. Catching her uncompromising look, he took a step back and with a kind of brisk nod inclined his head, as if in tribute to her for standing her ground. Charlee wanted an apology from him for behaving like he was the master and she was the hired hand. However, further scrutiny suggested that if she wanted an apology it would be a long time coming.

That imperceptible nod was it.

She didn't have time to give the idea further thought because she wanted to join the other interns who were fetching their coats and heading for the bright lights of the bars and clubs in the West End of London. Evidently aware that he been dismissed and not ready or willing to concede defeat, the champagne thief barred her way and held out a knuckled fist towards her.

Charlee sent him another derisive look. Did he really expect her to touch knuckles and mutter: respect, dude? Like she'd spent her life hanging with her homies in the 'hood instead of on a large veterinary

practice-cum-farm in the Home Counties? Giving him one last un-
swerving look she neatly sidestepped him and was about to walk away
when he called after her.

'Rock, paper, scissors, Chelsea?'

'What?'

'Rock, paper, scissors - the game. A challenge. For the champagne?'

As soon as he uttered the word 'challenge', Charlee was hooked.

She'd grown up in an unruly household of brothers and male cousins and was competitive to a fault. She could withstand any amount
of practical jokes involving frogs in beds, Chinese burns and eye-wa-
tering wedgies. She'd spent long summers becoming expert at rock,
paper, scissors and it would be her pleasure to beat him, knock back
the glass of flat champagne and dent his arrogant self-belief. Suddenly,
falling out of a taxi and into a bar where she could hardly afford more
than two drinks took second place to teaching him a life lesson.

Don't judge a book by looking at its cover.

Chelsea Montargue, she seethed inwardly, sending him a coy Princess Di look through her blonde fringe.

'I'm not quite sure of the rules,' she faltered. Amused, and with a
slightly condescending smile, he explained them. Charlee glanced at
the champagne flute, saw the condensation beading on the outside and
the last of the bubbles bursting on the surface. That was her glass of the
Widow and she wanted it - badly; badly enough to play rock, paper,
scissors with a total stranger.

'Ready?' he asked.

'Yes.' She squared her shoulders. He counted to three and it was
game on.

After their first moves, he glanced at his open hand and at her 'scis-
sored' fingers as though he couldn't quite believe he'd lost. Or, to put it
more accurately, that she'd won. Giving him a triumphant smile, Charlee reached out for the champagne.

'Best of three?' he countered, manoeuvring himself between Charlee and her exit. The playful, teasing light left his eyes and his body language became more determined, resolute. Charlee experienced a frisson of unease. She was dealing with someone who, on the surface, looked charming and urbane, but seemingly had a steely core he was at pains to hide. For all she knew, he could be a serial killer who picked out his victims at classy parties, lured them back to his penthouse and then -

'Best of three?' He cut across her wild imaginings, seemingly unwilling to let her go - as if she had something he wanted. Something other than the champagne. More to reassure herself than for any other reason, Charlee gave him a more thorough, second look. With his casual but expensive clothes, unseasonable tan and 'nothing can touch me' air, he didn't look like he was at the top of Scotland Yard's most wanted list.

But a girl could never be too careful.

Even serial killers wore designer suits these days - probably with a secret pocket in which to stash their supply of Rohypnol.

'If you like.' She smiled up at him, thinking she'd string him along and then make a dart for the cloakroom when his guard was down. Reining in her overly vivid imagination, which had got her into trouble on more than one occasion, she concentrated on her next move. 'I've already chosen scissors ... that leaves rock, or ...' she said, just loud enough for him to hear and anticipate her next gambit - giving her the opportunity to slip him a dummy.

He counted to three and this time they both chose rock. Dead heat. He counted to three again. Clearly believing that she'd go for 'paper', he chose scissors. But Charlee played the double bluff and went for rock, again.

Game over. She'd won!

Poleaxed, he stared at her clenched fist as if he couldn't believe what had happened. Charlee wanted to punch the air in triumph and give out a loud 'Yuss!' and down the champagne in one ladette-like gulp. Instead, she watched with some satisfaction as he replayed the match in his head, puzzling over how he'd lost. She knew that look. It was the one on her brothers' faces before they chased her into the orchard threatening retribution, and she hid in the barns until the heat died down.

She thought it unlikely that he would do that exactly. But just in case - and to show how magnanimous she could be - she picked up the flute and handed it to him. 'Here. Have it. Champagne is the perfect antidote for shock.'

With that, she abandoned her decision to join Poppy and the other interns, took a cosmopolitan off the tray of a passing waiter and moved towards the first photograph in the exhibition. She sipped at the cock-tail with a glow of triumph, knowing that the game she'd perfected as a girl had stood her in good stead this evening. She also suspected, with-out glancing back at him, that he wouldn't be happy until he'd evened the score.

Chapter Four
Mad, Bad and Dangerous to Know

Feigning indifference and sipping her cosmo in front of a huge photograph of the Brazilian rainforest, Charlee strained to catch her antagonist's reflection in the glass covering the photograph. What would his next move be? She smiled as, predictably, he made his way over, confident and assured - acting as if he'd won the game, not her.

However, even as her smile broadened, her sixth sense kicked in and cautioned her that it would be unwise to let her guard drop, even for a second. She had a hunch that his apparent interest in her went beyond rock, paper, scissors. Although what that 'interest' might be, she had no idea. The idea was scary, yet oddly exhilarating.

Sobering, she vowed to take things slowly. Think before she spoke. Not indulge in the flippant, off the cuff remarks that were her stock in trade and usually got her into a mess of trouble. He was just another alpha male, wasn't he? And she knew all about those. There had been so much testosterone around when she'd been growing up, it wouldn't have surprised her to find that her voice had broken. Or, that she'd taken to wearing her jeans so low-slung you could see her knickers. She pulled a wry face at the thought and recalled with some satisfaction the way he'd fallen for her double bluff.

Maybe she'd caught him on a bad day.

Maybe she was just cleverer than him.

Or - maybe that'd been his objective all along?

She regarded him through her glass, darkly, and gained the impression he was purposely taking his time to reach her. As if it was a ploy to redraw the boundaries; to establish who had the upper hand. But if - as she was beginning to suspect - it was all part of some hidden agenda, what could be the reason behind it?

Eyes narrowing, she gave him another, more thorough, second look.

There was a certain something about him; an air, a manner of just being, that intrigued her and compelled her to stay. It set him apart from the other men in the room wearing Paul Smith suits and two-hundred-pound shoes. It was almost as if, like her, he was here under false pretences. Then she assured herself that it was his clothes - battleship grey linen and silk mix trousers, loose-fitting jacket and white Sea Island cotton shirt - that made him stand out. Nothing more. Except - perhaps - his Byronic good looks. Charlee grimaced. If she was beginning to think in clichés, it was time for her to put down the empty glass and head for the cloakroom.

However, she was intrigued and wanted to know more.

'You walked off without giving me a chance of a rematch,' he said smoothly, looking over Charlee's shoulder at the photographs. His warm breath stirred the tendrils of hair on the nape of her neck and a tiny shiver of reaction travelled the length of her body. Ever practical, Charlee put the frisson, and the goose bumps in its wake, down to the fact that the gallery was cooling now that the evening was almost over and the big doors were wide open.

'Rematch? Dream on,' she said, with a mix of asperity and incredulity. 'You lost, mate - take the shame.' Laughing, she turned a victorious face towards him just in time to catch the displeased frown before it was hidden behind another charming smile. The smile of a snake towards a mongoose, she thought, experiencing another shock wave of response.

Now she wanted to take back the careless words.

What if he wasn't an employee of the gallery?

What if he was an important guest and she'd offended him?

Much as she longed to take the wind out of his sails and the swagger from his walk, she reminded herself that she was the hired hand this evening, whereas he, apparently, was a VIP or well known to the gallery. Sobering, her heart plummeted - this would probably be her first and last chance to represent *What'cha!* at a prestigious award ceremony. Even as part of the catering staff. After tonight, sifting through the photo archive would be regarded a career move.

'So no chance, then?' he persisted, seeming more amused than annoyed by her outburst.

'None.'

Relieved that he wasn't going to report her for overstepping the mark, Charlee relaxed. Her self-assurance and sassiness reasserted themselves and she soon forgot her misgivings about his identity and apparent interest in her. She took a few steps towards the next photograph; more to give herself some thinking time than to look at yet another yawn-inducing shot of the rainforest.

'So, Chelsea ...' He barred her way, inclining his dark head as he peered down at her name tag. Oh, that firmly put her in her place. 'When does your shift finish?'

'My name's Charlee by the way. Short for Charlotte? And my shift - as you so quaintly put it - is over when I say it is. I don't work down t'pit until my canary keels over; nor - in case you're wondering - do I take floors in to scrub. You've got me all wrong, mate.' She sent him a scathing look. Wasn't it plain that she'd come dressed to party, not to hew coal - or man the cloakroom? Didn't she have aspiring journalist written all over her? Clearly not! She removed the offending label, screwed it up, tetchily. 'What's it to you, anyway?'

'I was going to ask if you would -'

'Would what?' In that second, everything slotted into place and she had his back story all figured out.

Of course.

He worked for the gallery in some vague capacity because the owner was a chum from boarding school. He was probably called Binky or something else equally ludicrous and had fagged for the gallery owner at Eton/Harrow/Winchester. Delete as appropriate. His definition of a hard day's work would be directing men in brown overalls to move the display boards a few more centimetres to the left. Sweetie. And - on a really exacting day, he probably ensured that the author/artist didn't run out of pens during book signings/exhibitions. However with the natural authority of his class, he was past master at swanning around looking busy, taking long lunches and delegating jobs to people like her.

Or, at least, the person he thought her to be.

She'd met his type before and avoided them at all costs. Dull, boring, predictable and up their own arses. She gave him a look that said: prepare to be disappointed, and followed it up with a curt:

'Forget it. I have plans for tonight. And they don't include stacking chairs, sweeping floors or any other menial tasks you can dream up. I'm not spending another minute in this gallery.' She encompassed the room with a dramatic sweep of her arm. 'Places to go; people to see. Champagne to drink, it's almost Christmas Eve, after all.'

'So you're not impressed by the exhibition of photographs?'

'I might have been impressed if I'd had a chance to look at them. Properly, that is.' She struggled to keep the aggrieved note out of her voice. Under normal circumstances, she'd have loved to look round the exhibition and discuss the photographs, sip champagne and go clubbing with the other interns. But thanks to Vanessa that had all gone down the toilet, along with any dreams she nurtured of schmoozing her way to an introduction to someone influential.

'So why don't you look round now?' he asked reasonably, summoning a passing waiter and taking two glasses off his tray. But the moment had passed and Charlee wanted to get away from him and out of there. Hang with her friends in a bar and have a bitching session about Vanessa and Sally over several glasses of bone-dry, white wine.

'Look,' she glanced towards the cloakroom where Poppy was making 'get a move on' signs and pointing at her watch. 'I don't want to be rude, but …'

'That's not the impression I get, Chelsea,' he said smoothly, as he replaced her cocktail with a fresh one. 'I think you enjoy being rude. You're a bit of a rebel, aren't you? A rebel without a clue.'

'Now, hang on a minute. Mate.' Putting an emphasis on the word, she attempted to reduce him to the level of an ordinary Joe. But even as she sprang to her own defence, a nagging voice reminded her that it wasn't the first time this particular charge had been laid at her door.

'Hey, don't get me wrong,' he held up his hands as if to protect himself from her wrath. 'I like rebels.' He grinned, a boyish, charming grin. No doubt the one used to melt implacable female hearts and weaken their resistance. 'Even rebels who aren't quite sure what they're rebelling against.'

'Oh, I know exactly what I'm rebelling against, thank you very much.' Charlee could feel her veneer of sophistication slipping and knew that soon she'd say something she regretted. Words that couldn't be called back.

'And what might that be?'

Over the course of the evening, the list of grievances had stacked up. The hours she'd spent getting ready, the new clothes she'd bought on her MasterCard but couldn't really afford, the fun she and Poppy had planned on their way over in the taxi. The fact that her Christmas flash and glitter had been hidden behind a grotty apron, the misspelled label which had marked her out as a ditsy, Essex Blonde. And now, Mr-friend-of-the-gallery-owner was about to ask her to stay behind, to count the takings and help with the clearing up. Well, he could go hang.

'It's personal,' she said with all the hauteur of a grand duchess. 'So if you'll excuse me?' She turned on her heel and stepped away from him.

'Something tells me there's more to you than a waitress and a grand master at rock, paper, scissors.' He paused, giving her the chance to put the record straight.

'And you'd be right.' Charlee not only took the bait but snapped it right up. 'Actually,' she drew the word out, arching her eyebrows and giving him a haughty look that dared him to laugh. 'I'm a journalist.' He didn't need to know that she spent most of her life in a rank smelling cupboard or collecting Vanessa's designer clothes from the dry cleaners.

'Really?' He looked impressed. 'In that case I really would value your opinion of the exhibition.' He took her by the elbow and steered towards a large photo of an indigenous South American female with a fierce expression and three porcupine quills threaded through her nose.

Charlee's brain was in danger of complete meltdown as she thought of something clever to say. Something that would mark her out from the crowd and indicate what an amazing journalist she would, someday, become. A pithy phrase, some witticism which would show Posh Boy that he was dealing with a sophisticated, articulate professional.

'Now that's what I call an extreme makeover,' she blurted out.

Chapter Five
Your Starter for Ten

Within moments, Charlee realised that instead of putting him in his place she'd made a complete arse of herself. She gave the woman in the photograph a considering look while she searched for a telling phrase to undo the damage. However, judging from his boot-faced expression, the time for damage limitation had passed.

It was plain that he thought he was dealing with a total flake.

And, as the seconds drew out, Charlee imagined she could hear the slow, sonorous tick of a grandfather clock marking time; feel the chill wind of disapproval whistling round her ankles. In fact, she half expected clumps of tumbleweed to come rolling across the gallery towards her, like in an old cowboy film.

She suppressed a groan of dismay. He was right. She was a complete flake.

Now that she looked at him more closely, it was evident that he belonged to the moneyed, metropolitan-artsy-fartsy world of gallery openings and first nights. He probably had a mantelpiece bristling with exclusive invitations. He wouldn't appreciate the flippant, throwaway remarks that passed for humour in the subs' office where she worked, the facetious one-liners used to deflect the sarcastic comments considered fair game for newbies like her.

Time to move on, head off into the night before she made another gaffe.

First, she had to leave him with a more favourable impression; you never knew where a casual encounter at a party could lead. Five years down the line, his opinion of her could mean the difference between an exclusive scoop and a libel suit. She simply had to shatter the cringe-making silence stretching out between them.

Thinking on her feet, she read the tiny inscription at the bottom of the photograph. Then, as casually as possible, she cleared her throat and regurgitated the information with all the aplomb of an expert at the Natural History Museum; the BBC's go-to anthropologist.

'Ahem - Not everyone knows that, due to the characteristic whiskers the women place in their noses, the Matsés Indians are often referred to as the Cat People.' For effect, and to add gravitas, she drew inverted commas round the words: Cat People, and whiskers in the air using her fingers.

'Amazing.'

At last - he spoke!

'Cater-waiter, journalist; and now,' he paused for effect, a smile lighting his smoky grey eyes, 'anthropologist.'

Charlee glanced to see if she could detect irony in his expression. His disapproval had vanished and in its place was an appreciative look that suggested he was impressed by her knowledge. Crossing her fingers behind her back she prayed he wouldn't realise she was making it up as she went along.

'Well, I wouldn't quite go that far …' She dipped her head modestly and - with her earlier gaffe forgotten - bounced back with customary chutzpah, full of dangerous self-confidence which usually preceded her descent into deeper dung.

Now in full daydreaming mode, she was no longer Charlee Montague, cupboard dwelling troglodyte. She was Dame Charlotte Montague; blue stocking, Amazon explorer and doyenne of the late-night television circuit. In her mind's eye, she saw Ant and Dec pleading with her to go on *I'm a Celebrity* in order to teach the contestants how to survive in the rainforest. Naturally, she would refuse. Nothing could distract her from penning her next learned article, which she would present at the Natural History Museum on the anniversary of Darwin's birth - to a packed audience of envious peers.

'Tell me more about the ...' he dragged her out of the daydream and back to the present.

'Cat People of the Amazon?'

'Precisely.'

Glancing down at the inscription, she realised there was no information there. So, like a good journalist, what she didn't know, she made up.

'They revere the cat as a god,' she began, regarding him with an expression she hoped was both serious and profound. It wouldn't hurt to let him know there was more to her than rock, paper, scissors, being paid minimum wage, and an unguarded tongue. But she was edging her way forward. She had the unnerving feeling that everything she said was being filed away for future reference and he was just waiting for her to drop another clanger. Then, he would have her ejected from the gallery and fired from her job.

'Rather like the ancient Egyptians?' he added helpfully, moving the conversation along.

'Exactly like the ancient Egyptians. Except ...'

'Except?'

'Except, you can't build pyramids in the rainforest ... All those trees.' Charlee's alter ego, Dame Charlotte Montague, slipped alarmingly for a moment. 'Although, I do believe that the Incas built ziggurats in the rainforest?'

'Oh, quite.' He took a sip of his cocktail and was beset by a coughing fit and Charlee had an awful suspicion that he was laughing at her. But when she looked again, he was straight-faced and serious - so she guessed she had him all wrong.

'Let's move on shall we? I find your erudition fascinating. Quite illuminating, in fact.' He took her by the elbow and then stopped in front of a large photograph of an atoll. A long crescent of sand set in a turquoise sea so blue it almost hurt to look at it. 'And this?' he asked.

'Ah, yes.' A quick glance at the title in the bottom left-hand corner provided her next clue. 'This is Mururoa Atoll in the Pacific Ocean. You may have heard of it?'

'You know, I don't think I have.' Engrossed, he turned to face her, and waited politely for her to continue.

Now this Charlee did know about.

When she was in primary school, her brother Tom and some of his uber cool sixth form mates had protested with Greenpeace outside the French Embassy in London because the atoll had been used as a nuclear testing ground. Inspired, Tom had gone on to study Environmental Sciences at Uni, and now worked as a lobbyist for various green pressure groups.

'Well, let's just say I wouldn't advise you to 'Thomas-Cook-it' for a few thousand years, until the radiation subsides.' Charlee laughed to demonstrate that she could be light-hearted and amusing as well as knowledgeable.

Experience had taught her that an intelligent woman generally frightened men. She'd lost several boyfriends because of her quick wit, sharp tongue and intelligence, so she reined herself in. However, she wasn't about to let him off the hook just yet. When they did part, it would be on her terms and with him left wondering what'd hit him. Although, with his air of 'I can do anything I damn well please', he looked like it would take more than her off-key ramblings to make an impression on him.

She was intrigued by him, by his mood switches and sudden change of tack. There was a story here, one the journo in her wanted to learn. Why, for example, did he have a long, grey cashmere scarf wound loosely around his neck in this overheated room. Affectation? How come his eyes were dark-circled beneath his tropical tan - as though he was recovering from a long illness? Why, despite his obvious youth and vigour did he look world-weary - as though he'd been there, seen it, done it - and had worn out the tee shirt.

Her desire to escape was overridden as her journalistic antennae started to twitch. She gave him one more sidelong glance and made mental notes to dissect later. His suit had obviously been tailored but no longer appeared to fit him; it hung loose on his rangy frame and the jacket seemed too wide for his shoulders.

'Quite,' he agreed, leading her onwards, as if he sensed her sudden interest in him and was keen to deflect it. They paused by a photograph of an ancient Romanesque temple burning white beneath an unforgiving desert sun. Once more, the titles came to Charlee's rescue.

Hatra, Iraq.

Charlee knew Iraq was formerly ancient Assyria and lay along the fertile crescent of the east. Then - out of nowhere - she remembered that the opening scenes of *The Exorcist* had been filmed there. She'd watched the DVD with her brothers years ago when her parents had travelled north for some family wedding and she'd been left behind in the un-tender care of Tom, Wills, Jack and George.

For months afterwards, she'd had nightmares about the girl with the green face and revolving head. She'd taken to creeping into Tom's room when she was too frightened to sleep, knowing that she couldn't go to her parents' room without landing her brothers in a heap of trouble.

'Ah, yes. Hatra. Where they filmed *The Exorcist*. A dangerous place to go,' was all she managed as memories crowded in, thick and fast. Remembering how it'd felt to bask in her brothers' approval, knowing that they appreciated her not dobbing them in. How, briefly, she'd been admitted into their gang of four. But it hadn't lasted. Within days, she'd reverted to being 'Shrimp', fit only for retrieving cricket balls from the long grass and running errands to the village shop.

Seemingly sensing that she'd zoned out, he moved her onto the next photograph. It was then that the penny dropped. Of course!

The Amazon Basin ... A contaminated atoll in the Pacific ... Iraq.

The photographs were taken in some of the most dangerous places on the planet. Places where only the most intrepid or foolhardy travel-ler dared to tread.

'And this?' he asked, drawing up at the last one: Darien Gap, Colom-bia and Panama. He positioned himself so that she couldn't read the entire label, and she suspected he knew she'd been blagging. But she'd seen enough photos for one evening and so she abandoned her alter ego - Dame Charlotte Montague, darling of the lecture circuit - and reverted back to plain old Charlee Montague, bloody-minded intern, full of half-baked opinions and careless who she shared them with.

'Well … clearly, only a complete idiot would go there,' she pro-nounced with all the conviction of someone who knew nothing of the sort. Other than what she'd read in the Sunday papers about drug smugglers, kidnappers, Contras - all working deep in the impenetra-ble rainforest. She gave him one last assessing look. Sure, he was good looking; but she'd had a lifetime of being put in her place by gorgeous, exasperating males.

The opinion of a man she'd probably never see again didn't matter to her, either way.

Now, did it?

'An idiot?' he pursued.

'Oh yes. You know the type - ' Charlee was so anxious to join Poppy over by the door that she didn't register that his wry, slightly patronis-ing smile had morphed into something considerably more tight-lipped and not quite so amiable.

'I'm not sure that I do. But something tells me I'm about to find out.'

Chapter Six
Fools Rush In

Charlee was only too happy to elaborate. 'It's like those extreme bush tucker trials/wildlife programs you see on TV. Bear Grylls and Ray what's-his-face -'

'Mears?' he helped out.

'Exactly. Everybody knows those places are dangerous. So why go there?' Charlee shrugged, like a hard-bitten journo. 'It's all been done before. We geddit, right? Move on.'

Taking that as her cue, she made her way over to the table where the unsold books were stacked. Overtaking her, he barred her way and prevented her from leaving. It was plain that she'd ruffled his feathers, but for the life of her, she couldn't understand why. Surely, after her gaffe about the cat woman, disagreeing with him over some celebrity author was small fry?

But apparently, it was a big deal. To him.

'Let me get this straight. You don't think that the author deserves some credit for donating the royalties from the book to provide a hospital boat for the remote region of the Amazon where he was rescued?'

'Rescued?' The word leapt out and suddenly he had her full attention. She sensed that a tale of epic proportions was about to unfold; a scoop, maybe. A world exclusive that she, Charlee Montague, would snatch from more experienced journalists. Naturally.

'Surely you know the story?' he asked, implying that either she'd been living on the moon or was a total idiot. The cool, autocratic look that swept her from head to toe made it clear he thought her capable of fitting into either category but probably the latter. Charlee gave him a thin-lipped smile, inwardly smarting as she struggled to hide the depth of her ignorance. She'd been too busy studying for her finals this summer and working to pay off her overdraft to notice what'd been happening in the real world.

Luckily, he was very happy to fill in the gaps. 'The author -'

'Rafael Fonseca-Ffinch?' Charlee read the name on the spine of one of the books piled high on the signing table. She was just about to make some sarcastic comment like: 'is that name for real', when some instinct for self-preservation stopped her. She'd already seriously pissed him off twice this evening, time to quit while she was ahead.

'You've heard of him?' he asked.

'Who hasn't?' she lied. Then she frowned. Actually, the moniker was vaguely familiar. But, maybe she was confusing him with Rafael Nadal, tennis-god and all-round hottie. Or perhaps it was an echo from childhood … one of those Ninja Turtle things had been called Raphael. Hadn't it? Then there was the Renaissance painter … In danger of being carried away again, Charlee reined herself in with the mantra: Concentrate. Focus. Centre.

She sensed that the validation of this author was very important to him. Perhaps he wanted to ensure that the gallery sold shedloads of books and he got his juicy commission. Maybe she looked like she had money to spare.

'He wanted to raise peoples' awareness of some of the most hazardous places on earth,' he went on. 'Places where ordinary people live in poverty and disappear without a trace … where even the aid agencies daren't go. South America seems to have slipped below the radar and peoples' consciences, despite Brazil hosting the next Olympics and the Pope originating from Argentina. Perhaps the deprivation there isn't as cool or fashionable as Africa.'

Sensing that a lecture was about to follow, Charlee cut him off with, 'Like I said, we get it. What I don't get is why Mr double-barrelled-explorer had to go there - physically, I mean. There are stock images of these places. He could have downloaded those, written his copy and the book wouldn't have been any different. He could have given the money it took to mount the expedition to the Cat People of the Amazon. Or, whatever.'

She sensed that her dismissive 'whatever' riled him because he struggled to keep his cool.

Ha! That'd teach him to patronise her. She gained the impression that he was trying to redress the balance of power between them. She'd won their game of rock, paper, scissors, but clearly he was going for the world series. Maintaining a bright, friendly expression and not wanting him to guess she was intent on scoring further points, Charlee prolonged the conversation.

It wasn't over until the fat lady sang, or she said it was.

'What if the author felt compelled to go? What if he wanted to show the poverty? Tell the world what he'd seen with his own eyes?' he asked, clearly trying to convert her to his cause. Not to mention the incentive of selling more books, a cynical but knowing voice whispered in her ear. He had a point, and she actually agreed with him; but she wasn't going to let him know. Matters had gone too far for either of them to back down now.

The game wasn't over and there was everything to play for.

His passionate defence of the author and his campaign made him look strikingly attractive.

Charlee gave her head a little shake and sublimated her instinctive reaction to his sheer maleness even as she made a covert inventory of him. Sexy little frown that creased his forehead (tick) - the combative light in his blue-grey eyes (tick) - the appealing downward curve of his mouth as he sought the words that would win his argument and convince her she was wrong (tick). Even the way he ran his hands through his dark hair as if she drove him to distraction drew an unwanted response from her.

However, she swallowed hard and carried on. The only way she'd managed to hold her own with her brothers was never to back down. And this was no different …

'Yeah, I can just imagine how tough it was with a backup team and a documentary crew every step of the way. The whole expedition must have cost a bomb. Money that could - should - have been given directly to the Cat People.' She gestured towards the photograph of the woman with the body piercings and continued. 'And, by the way, have you ever noticed how the people behind the camera never get a mention? For all I know, he could have had Fortnum and Mason hampers parachuted into the jungle and his own personal stylist with him, while his team lived on berries and drank rancid water.'

'Now you're being bloody ridiculous,' he snapped, and reached for one of the books.

Charlee experienced a moment of triumph because she'd broken through the ennui that men of his class affected. A world-weariness that she didn't find in the least bit attractive. She liked her men bright-eyed and enthusiastic, burning with the rightness of their cause; wanting to make a difference. Um - rather like him in fact, her more rational self pointed out. For one wild moment she thought that he was about to bring the weighty tome crashing down on her head and she cringed.

Instead, he opened it at the dedication page and read aloud. 'To my wonderful crew. For leading you where angels fear to tread; apologies and sincere thanks for everything I put you through. Rafa Ffinch.' She took the book from him and read the inscription. Then she flipped back to the front dust cover flap and gave a slow, appreciative whistle.

'Finally,' he managed through gritted teeth. 'She's impressed.'

'More astounded, actually.'

'Astounded?'

'Yeah. That anyone would part with thirty quid for a book like this.'

Charlee closed it with a loud snap before handing it back. 'Anyone who actually had to work for a living, that is.' Her tone implied that he was a stranger to hard work. 'Thanks; but no thanks. I'll wait for it to be three for two at Waterstones, or reduced on Amazon. Unless you want to give me a free copy before they're taken back to the warehouse and pulped?'

He looked torn between a desire to say something cutting and original and the need to finish his tale. Like it really meant something to him, something more than just another book launch at a swish London gallery. 'Let me tell you more about the rescue and then you can decide if the book's worth a whole thirty pounds.' He said it like the amount was small change and Charlee was one of those lowlifes who watched *Comic Relief* without reaching for their credit card at the end of the evening.

'Okay.' She parked her derriere on the book-signing table and waited for him to begin.

Under different circumstances, she'd have loved nothing more than to hear tales of the author's derring-do and rescue in the Amazon Basin. She could just imagine herself as Fonseca-Ffinch's right-hand woman ... no, strike that ... his equal partner. Standing shoulder to shoulder with him on some peak in Darien, machete at the ready, prepared to hack through virgin rainforest. Facing danger together, working as a team, overcoming obstacles ... nothing behind them but miles of impenetrable jungle. Only the blue of the Pacific before them as they trod in the footsteps of Cortez and the conquistadors ...

Eldorado. The City of Gold.

Instead, the mood was broken as staff stacked chairs and swept the floor. She looked over his shoulder and saw Poppy advancing towards them, obviously fed up with waiting. He caught her distracted look and half-turned his head, clearly sensing that time had run out and he wouldn't be able to finish his story, or persuade her to buy a copy of the book.

'One of your friends?'

43

'Best friend. Actually.'

'I see she's bought one of the books.'

'Poppy's minted. Maybe I'll borrow it off her and read it this week-end.'

'And maybe you won't.' He shrugged, as though he'd had enough of her posturing.

'I -'

Suddenly the rebel without a clue had no mocking words left in her arsenal. With one cold, dismissive look he managed to make her feel petty, small-minded and parochial. As though, in her attempt to best him, she'd disparaged something significant and worthwhile. She wanted to tell him that her posturing was just that. An act: a role she had to play in order to survive the sniper fire in *What'cha!*'s offices.

That she was on his side.

There was a slight commotion as the staff took the unsold books off the table and whipped the linen cloth from under her with a magician-like flourish. Not wishing to land on the floor in an ungainly heap, Charlee stood up, but when she turned around Poppy was at her side and her adversary had gone.

'Hey.'

'Hey,' Charlee returned Poppy's greeting, trying hard to act cool and not swivel her head through 360-degrees, like the girl in *The Exorcist*, in search of him.

'You two were getting on well,' Poppy began, like it mattered to her. Then she gave Charlee a bright smile, tucked the book more securely under her arm and gave her watch another look. 'What was the thing with the hands?'

'It's a long story ...' Charlee let out a long breath, feeling as if she'd run a marathon. It no longer felt like the night was young and she was up for some fun. She wanted to be quiet, reflective and to think over her encounter with Gallery Guy.

'Here. Hold the book while I find my mobile and call one of the firm's taxis.' Poppy handed the heavy book to Charlee. Curious, she turned the book over to read the blurb on the back cover, and then let out a long:

'Nooooooh.'

Staring back in full technicolour was a head and shoulders portrait shot of the author. The man she'd just spent the last twenty minutes with.

Rafael Fonseca-Ffinch.

The man who now believed she was a complete pain in the arse and the rudest woman on the planet. She returned the book to Poppy as though it was burning coals. Hoping, once it was no longer in her hands, that she could disassociate herself from it, her behaviour - and its author.

'Nooooooh,' Charlee repeated the keening cry as she glanced towards the doors and saw Fonseca-Ffinch in deep conversation with Sam Walker, Vanessa and Sally. Ominously, they kept glancing in her direction and frowning, with Sam Walker shaking his head in apparent disbelief. She just knew she was being dropped in it, big time, by the intrepid explorer.

'What's the matter?' Poppy followed Charlee's gaze and appeared to sum it all up in a trice. It wasn't long before Sally came mincing over, an evil parody of a Cheshire cat's grin all over her face.

'You are sooo in trouble, Montague,' she informed delightedly. 'You've really cocked up this time. Insulted the guest of honour; dissed his book and accused him of defrauding the charity he founded. Classic, Montague, classic.'

'Really?' Charlee tried to wrong-foot Sally with a show of nonchalance. But her stomach was churning like a cement mixer full of rubble as the realisation of what she'd done hit home.

'Yes. Really. Chief wants to see you first thing Monday morning.' She delivered the *coup de grâce* with relish. 'And this time? Not even being Miss Walker's best friend is going to save you.'

She turned on her designer heels and went back to join the group by the door. For once, Poppy could offer no words of comfort and Charlee was left trembling with anxiety and wondering where she was going to find another job two days before the world shut down for the Christmas holidays.

Chapter Seven
The Unwilling Apprentice

Two days later on December 23rd Charlee was at her desk emptying her drawer before the rest of the office arrived. Being fired was bad enough. But having to run the gauntlet of the office wags, as she packed her belongings into a document box, scattering emergency supplies of tights, tampons and fused together Kit Kats in her wake would be even worse. She shut the drawer with a decisive snap.

Time she stopped dithering, drew the threads of her argument together and prepared the case for the defence before Sam Walker called her to his office for a well-deserved dressing down. She'd spent the weekend holed up in her bedsit deciding the course to take. She'd appear contrite - naturally; sorry for all the offence she'd caused Mr Big Author, and promise never to do it again. But, taking the rap for Friday night's debacle wouldn't be easy. She couldn't get it out of her head that somehow Fonseca-bloody-Ffinch had deliberately goaded her into behaving badly.

Not that she'd ever needed any encouragement to go just that step too far. The unguarded remark, the unasked for comment were her stock in trade. She was rash and unthinking - and this time she wasn't going to get away with it. Rebel without a clue he'd called her. Rebel without a job was nearer the mark this morning.

She resisted the urge to clear her desk and focused instead on rearranging items of stationery in serried ranks, like war game figures. She sighed. News of her dismissal would put a damper on the Montague family Christmas and bring a whole load of recriminations down on her head. Her parents' censorious faces swam into focus; they'd been dead against her becoming a journalist in the first place. With her double first in Languages and Politics, they reasoned, she could become a political lobbyist, a parliamentary research assistant, a translator at The Hague or coach foreign students desperate to enter a top-notch English university. Taken a second or even third degree - gained her doctorate; she had the mental capacity for it, they were constantly telling her … but her heart wasn't in it.

She wanted the thrill of the scoop, the lure of the exclusive. She longed for danger, the knowledge that she was on the trail of the BIG ONE. Why, even Sam Walker at his most acerbic had recognised she had a nose for a story, an instinct for sensing when the great white whale was about to surface and everyone else was headed off in the opposite direction following a false lead. Maybe that was the reason he'd overlooked some of her minor gaffes since she'd joined *What'cha!* Shrugged off Vanessa's complaints about her copy, which she knew was better than anything the other interns handed in.

Equally, Sam knew that she was the only reason Poppy came to work every morning when she'd rather be off eventing or hunting with her mother. However, that was another story and Charlee pushed it to the back of her mind. She knew that one day she would make her name and earn the respect of her peers. Then she'd no longer be the add-on in the Montague family. The menopausal baby who'd arrived unexpectedly after four strapping boys and announced her presence with a squalling red face and a shock of white-blonde hair. To them, she'd always be 'Shrimp', the runt of the litter - but it was time she rewrote her entry in the family bible.

She snapped out of her reverie when a couple of party poppers went off at close range. Their contents shot through the air and came to rest on her head, draping her in multicoloured dreadlocks. Charlee glared at the two post boys who swaggered in wearing Santa hats making a racket with party blowers.

The post boys were flirty, impudent and rather overdid the whole cock-e-nay geezer act in an attempt to make the day-to-day grind of their job bearable. Usually Charlee gave as good as she got; but today she wasn't in the mood for their Del-Boy-Meets-Chas-and-Dave routine.

'You're here a bit bleedin' early, ain't cha, Charl.' One handed her a stack of jiffy bags. 'Don't want to overdo it, you've gotta save your energy for dancing wiv us tonight at the knees-up. I've been practising my Salsa, just for you.' He laid a hand over his heart like a lovelorn swain and danced a few steps.

'Sure. Whatever,' Charlee responded unenthusiastically and started to rip open the jiffy bags

They noticed her mood straightaway: 'You are going ain't cha?'

'Dunno. It's complicated,' she gave a half-hearted shrug.

'Yeah. We 'eard.'

Their exchanged look confirmed her worst suspicions. Her hours of gainful employment were drawing to a close. The post boys knew everything that went down at *What'cha!* They eavesdropped shamelessly as they made their way round the building and were very good at stringing pieces of seemingly unconnected gossip together to make a story. They spread rumours faster than the Ebola virus.

'Upset Chief and his mate, didn't cha?' He nodded towards Sam Walker's office. 'Don't worry, Charl. You know Chief. He'll give you a bollocking and forget ...'

'Not this time,' she cut in, unable to draw any comfort from their words. Sighing, she took the rest of the mail from them and pretended to deal with it. Getting the message, they gave one last toot on their party blowers and trundled the mail cart down the corridor towards the Features Office. No doubt to gossip about her to a more than receptive audience.

Not this time … the words haunted her.

She'd humiliated the guest of honour and let down the magazine. It didn't get any worse. Pressing the palms of her hands onto the desktop, she practised some deep breathing exercises. However, being as she'd quit yoga after two sessions, she wasn't entirely sure how one attained spiritual enlightenment in under ten minutes. The best she could hope for was a state of despair underwritten with mild terror.

Thinking back to everything that had passed between herself and Fonseca-Ffinch, Charlee decided there was no point going into the meeting spoiling for a fight. It was her stubborn, combative streak that had got her into trouble in the first place. No. She'd have to take full responsibility for acting unprofessionally and offending his lordship - no matter how much it stuck in her craw. Sam Walker's punishment, when it came, would be swift and harsh.

But maybe - if she swallowed her pride and grovelled low enough - she'd get away with a verbal warning. Momentarily, hope fluttered in her chest and then reality kicked in. Who was she kidding? Fonseca-Ffinch was man of the moment; she was an intern. No amount of slick talking was going to get her out of this one.

Of course - now it was too late, she remembered everything about him. His reputation as the photographer who captured the zeitgeist: the politician with the rent boy, the celebrity snorting coke at his daughter's wedding, and the stand-off between police and G8 protestors last summer.

Through his connections - she'd read somewhere that his parents were career diplomats - he had an access to the rich and famous that other journos could only dream of and weep over. While they had to settle for pushing telephoto lenses through the bars of remote controlled gates and the second best shot, he commanded the front page and earned colossal syndication rights.

Now there was this book: *The Ten Most Dangerous Destinations on the Planet*, which had received glowing reviews in most of the Sundays. The book she'd refused to spend her hard-earned cash on was being hailed as 'one man's mission to bring hope to the hopeless'.

Because of his experiences in the Amazon, he'd chosen to devote himself to improving the lot of the people there. The very tribe, as Charlee had learned from yesterday's article, who'd found him unconscious on the bank of a piranha-infested stretch of the Amazon, carried him to their village and brought him back from the brink of death. She burned with shame as she recalled how she'd derided them with a smart-arsed remark: 'Now that's what I call an extreme makeover.'

Using his advance, he'd established a fund to provide a hospital boat to ply the long stretch of the Amazon and bring much needed medical aid to the people who lived there. The journalist who'd written the piece in the colour supplement had added to Charlee's wretchedness with every well-chosen word. "Fonseca-Ffinch is an antidote for all that is cynical and self-serving in the world; a template for those who give so freely of their time and money to help those less fortunate. He has travelled the road to Damascus and the scales have fallen from his eyes."

How had she put it?

Oh yes: 'I'd be astounded that anyone would part with thirty quid for a book like this.'

She deserved to be fired - instead of planning her defence, she should write her resignation and leave it on Sam Walker's office desk. Jump before she was pushed. Charlee groaned as her mood swung between belligerence and despair. Fonseca-Ffinch was in danger of becoming a living saint, whereas she ...

The hands of the office clock made a large clunk as they reached the top of the hour and Poppy Walker strolled into the office wearing a shearling coat and a pair of to-die-for boots, looking just like Cameron Diaz in *The Holiday*, one of their favourite films. She was carrying two coffees in a cardboard holder and almond croissants wrapped in a napkin. She gave Charlee a worried look and then put the drink in front of her.

'Have you eaten?' she asked.

'I don't think I can,' Charlee said unconvincingly. The aroma of coffee wafted over to her and the croissant shed its delicious flakes on her desk, making her stomach rumble.

''Course you can. You're the condemned prisoner the original hearty breakfast was created for. Get that down you, girl. You don't want to face Chief on an empty stomach, do you?'

They pulled a face, both well aware of Sam Walker's volatility and Charlee's spirits plummeted even lower. Within the confines of this building, Walker was God Almighty, with a team of shit-hot, hand-picked subs acting as his vengeful archangels. When he called you into his office, you were never sure if it was for a decapitation or a pat on the back. He kept his staff in awe of him, his daughter Poppy included.

'What mood's he in?' Charlee asked Poppy. It'd been through her persistent lobbying that she'd landed the job in the first place and she felt she'd let Poppy down, too.

'Strangely calm.' Poppy frowned as she took the lid off her cappuccino and stirred the coffee with a pencil. 'He's been shut up in his study all weekend. Mostly on the phone to his old Fleet Street cronies. Mummy was furious because we had friends staying over and he hardly passed the time of day with them. Then Rafa … '

Charlee frowned. She didn't want to hear, read or learn anything more about Rafael Fonseca-Ffinch unless it was that he was leaving the country, for good! There was a loud bang on the office door and both girls started, Charlee spilling coffee all over her white shirt. Poppy leapt away from her. That coat looked like it would need dry cleaning at least once a week and coffee stains are pretty unforgiving.

'Montague.' Sam Walker strode past her office without seeming to glance her way. 'My office. If you please.' Well, it didn't please her, but Charlee guessed that wasn't quite what he meant.

'Chief.' She pulled herself up smartly and almost saluted.

'And, Montague,' he paused. And without turning round added, 'I don't know what the fuck you've done to your hair. But sort it. Now! '

Closing her eyes, Charlee groaned and remembered the party popper dreadlocks.

'Sorry,' Poppy whispered and helped her to pick the last bits of stretchy, multicoloured plastic out of her hair. 'I thought you knew.'

'How do I look?' Charlee asked, seeking reassurance.

'Scared?' Poppy ventured, apparently not quite grasping the concept of giving moral support to a friend.

'Thanks.' Wiping her hands down the sides of her skirt, Charlee walked down the corridor and prepared herself for execution.

Chapter Eight
An Offer You Can't Refuse

Steeling herself, Charlee knocked on Chief's door. Usually, he shouted: 'Fuck Off', in an aggressive Sarf Lunnon accent and sent hapless staff members scuttling down the corridor until he was in a better mood. Or, he gave a long drawn out: 'Co-ome', like he was the headmaster of a top independent school and you'd been summoned to his office for a caning. This morning it was the latter and, as Charlee pushed the heavy door open, she half expected him to address her as Montague Minor.

Fixing a bright, optimistic smile on her face, she walked into his office.

'You wanted to see me, Chief?'

'Actually Montague, I don't want to see you. In fact, I never want to see you again.' Charlee's heart bungeed down to her boots and she found it hard to breathe. The last of her chutzpah disappeared when she saw Vanessa - looking for all the world like the boot-faced woman on *Dragon's Den* - seated at Sam Walker's right-hand side.

Charlee half expected Vanessa to say: 'I'm out.' But apparently even she knew that Chief would demand the first (and probably last) word on this matter. So she pursed her lips and settled instead for sending Charlee a scorching look. Charlie knew that Vanessa would relish seeing Sam Walker dismiss her without a reference and would regale anyone who cared to listen with the story of her downfall.

Charlee's hopeful smile slipped in the face of such negative vibes coming her way. However, deciding that she wasn't going down without a fight, she started to present the case for the defence. 'Chief, if you give me a moment, I can explain ...'

'I doubt that very much, Montague. As I say, I never want to see you again.'

Charlee pretended that she hadn't heard and ploughed right on. 'You see, I didn't realise that I was talking to Mr Fonseca-Ffinch. I thought I was talking to some random friend of the gallery owner's who'd -'

'Shut it, Montague. We're not interested in what you thought,' Sam fixed her with a beady stare. 'In fact, you'd be better off not thinking at all. Clearly, your brain's not equipped for the job. As I said - before you interrupted me - I never want to see you again, but for reasons I won't go into, I've been prevailed upon.'

'Prevailed upon?' Charlee frowned and a little spark of hope ignited deep within her. 'Does that mean -'

'Which bit of shut it, don't you get Montague?'

'Sorry Chief,' Charlee said automatically and earned another basilisk stare. Aware that she'd spoken out of turn, again, Charlee clamped her lips together and cast down her eyes in a convincing show of penitence. But all the while a single thought was going through her mind. He's been prevailed upon; maybe he isn't going to fire me, after all.

'That's better. Remind me, how many languages are you fluent in?' he asked, coming from left of field. He scribbled some notes on his desk pad in shorthand - a hangover, Charlee supposed, from his days as a Fleet Street hack. The 'glory days' as he referred to them, bemoaning the day they moved to Wapping in the eighties as the beginning of the end. Now everyone had smartphones and tablet computers; Sam foresaw the day when the presses would stop running altogether.

'Five - six if you include Portuguese.' She faltered, her pulse was racing as she wondered where this was leading and how honest she should be. 'Although my Mandarin isn't quite up to scratch,' she admitted candidly.

'Well, luckily you ain't being asked to act as a tour guide on the Great Wall of bleedin' China, so we'll gloss over that - shall we?' he asked sarcastically. 'Speak Russian?'

Charlee thought of coming back with a sassy: '*dobraye utro*' - good morning - but upon catching his expression, thought better of it. Banking down her curiosity, she wondered exactly where this conversation was leading. The Moscow office? The salt mines? She'd entered the room expecting to be fired. Instead it looked as if Chief's Machiavellian instincts were on overdrive, and she could smell a story in the air.

She recalled what Poppy had said about him not coming down to dinner the previous evening, about Fonseca-Ffinch being in their house. Had that something to do with his attitude this morning? Had something reawakened the newshound in him?

'Montague. A simple yes or no. I'm waiting.'

'Yes, I speak Russian,' she replied quickly.

'And can you read their alphabet?'

'I can read, write and translate Cyrillic script, yes.'

'Okay. Don't milk it, Montague. No one's asking you to translate the fuckin' Rosetta Stone.'

Sam Walker's bark was worse than his bite and cringing or sycophantic members of staff irritated him, so Charlie added for good measure: 'The Rosetta Stone is written in hieroglyphics and Demotic Greek, Chief.'

He searched for something scathing to add, finally settling for, 'Don't be a smart arse, Montague, this isn't a job interview. You're in trouble and don't forget it.' Then Vanessa coughed and they exchanged a pointed look, after which they glanced over Charlee's shoulder and to her left. Charlee shivered. What had they seen, the ghost of interns past? She dismissed the idea as ridiculous, but even so, a shiver of prescience made the hair on the nape of her neck rise like the hackles on a dog.

Then a familiar voice chimed in. 'Although, Sam, in a way this is an interview, isn't it?' Charlee spun round on one foot, saw who was sitting in the chair behind the door and groaned. She was unaware that she'd groaned out loud until he came back with, 'Lovely to see you again, too, Chelsea.' He stood up and extended his right hand. Charlee looked at him, at it, suspiciously. Was this a trap? Surely, he hadn't gone to all this trouble to organise a reunion because he wanted a return match of rock, paper, scissors.

'My name,' she hissed through clenched teeth, 'is Charlee.'

'Your name is anything Mr Fonseca-Ffinch wants it to be, Montague,' Vanessa snapped. She gave Charlee a little shove in the back and pushed her closer to Fonseca-Ffinch. 'Manners, Montague.' Forced into a corner, Charlie extended her hand and shook fingers with him. A full hand clasp was out of the question, if, as she suspected he was responsible for her losing her job. She also remembered the shock of electricity which had passed between them on Friday night and didn't want to experience it again.

'Mr Fonseca-Ffinch,' Charlee greeted him. With her back turned towards Vanessa and Sam she was able to glare at him as much as she dared.

'Young people, Rafa, honestly ...' Vanessa simpered, coming round to his side of the desk. Then, as if realising she'd made herself sound like some ancient maiden aunt she hastily smoothed down her business suit - this season's Burberry Prorsum - and gave a seductive little wriggle.

Then she was at Fonseca-Ffinch's side - noiselessly, like a shape shifter. But he neatly sidestepped her, offered her his vacant chair and then he and Charlee were standing in front of Chief's desk.

'I want to speak to you,' he began, and then glanced between Vanessa and Sam Walker. Clearly, what he had to say was for her ears only.

'Look. I'm sorry about the other night. I didn't know you were someone important.' Even as she said it, Charlee couldn't help her lip curling slightly, which gave lie to her words. 'I thought you were ...'

'Never mind all that, now, Montague. Ffinch wants someone to help him out on an assignment and - Gawd help us - has asked for you. Specifically.'

'Me?' Charlee gave him a suspicious look. Chief pulled a wry face.

'My feelings exactly, Montague, but he says it has to be you. When he could have Vanessa, Sally or any of our more experienced members of staff.' Chief shook his head and Vanessa - who hadn't ventured further than the few yards from a taxi to the front door of the Ivy or Quag's in years - gave a little moue of regret.

'What's the assignment?' Charlee could smell freshly cooked rat and wanted more details before she was dispatched to fetch the barbeque sauce. Her less than gracious acceptance speech earned her a severe look from Chief.

'What Montague means, Rafa, is - yes; she'll be delighted to help in any way she can. That's right, isn't it, Charlotte?' Sam used her given name with an expression close to pain. Surnames were de rigueur at *What'cha!* if you were one of the lesser beings - aka, staff. Only Vanessa and her team of harpies were referred to by their first name.

'Of course.' Charlee gave Ffinch a bright smile, though her narrowed eyes told him to take a running jump if he thought she would be willing to spend Christmas Eve translating back copies of *Pravda* into flawless English for him. The other afternoon in the photo archive and a whole weekend spent stressing over what Chief was going to say to her had awoken her inner rebel. Now, despite Ffinch's snarky observation at the book award, this rebel had a cause. She'd had enough of being patronised and given the worst jobs on the magazine. She wasn't prepared to go down without a fight, even if that meant leaving *What'cha!* and hunting for another internship.

Ffinch looked at Sam and then back at Vanessa, making it plain that he wanted to talk to Charlee alone. Sam shook his head at what he obviously perceived to be Ffinch's folly and escorted Vanessa towards the office door.

'Five minutes, Montague, and then I'll return to flesh out the details. Right?' he growled.

'Yes, Chief,' Charlee replied smartly. Ffinch waited until they'd shut the door behind him and then turned towards her. They looked at each other warily, like dogs spoiling for a fight and changed position on the carpet, circling each other.

'Let's get it over with, Montague. Drop the pretence.'

'Pretence; what pretence?' Charlee schooled her features, realising she'd fallen at the first hurdle and cursing her inexperience. In this job, you had to be poker-faced, play your cards close to your chest. Instead, she'd given herself away, made it plain that she couldn't stand the sight of him - and he'd picked up the vibe. She was so vexed with herself that she almost missed his amused:

'Now we're alone, Chelsea, you can kiss me.'

Chapter Nine
Just Another Frog

'I can what?' Charlee spluttered, thinking she'd misheard.

'I said you can kiss me,' Fonseca-Ffinch repeated patiently as though dealing with a simple-minded child. He leaned back against the window ledge and folded his arms - waiting!

Blushing, Charlee gave him a 'get over yourself' look. If he thought for one minute she was so grateful over not being sacked that she'd be willing to -

'And why on earth would I want to do that? You almost got me fired and now you have some spurious assignment up your sleeve and want me on your team. For reasons you've yet to explain.'

'Ever heard of looking a gift horse in the mouth?' he asked.

'Of course. But the saying also covers Trojan horses and warns me to beware of Greeks bearing gifts,' she said bluntly. 'So you'd better make it clear why you want me and not one of the more experienced journalists. And, just to be clear, I have no desire to kiss you,' her tone made it clear that she found the whole idea repellent. 'Nor have I any intention of working late, missing the last train back to town and "staying over" in some country house hotel with you. Where I'll be shown to a suite of rooms which - surprise, surprise - have conveniently interconnecting doors ...'

He gave her a considering look.

'Don't think you'd be able to keep your hands off me, eh Chelsea? I quite understand; you're only human, I guess.' He looked amused rather than put out by her show of indignation. That made Charlee bristle; she'd had a lifetime of being patronised by her brothers. What she didn't need in her life right now was another alpha male who found her 'amusing', and thought her a push over. She didn't like the way he was looking at her, as if trying to weigh her up. Or the way he kept referring to her as Chelsea, when he knew damned well what her name was.

He cocked his head on one side and his grey eyes darkened to blue and Charlee sensed he was assessing whether her reaction to his proposal was genuine. Charlee guessed that he didn't get many refusals … ha!

'I might,' she replied with a snap in her voice, 'have trouble stopping myself from strangling you. If that's what you mean. You are the most -'

'Okay, relax. I was just testing.'

'Testing?' Her voice rose to an almost inaudible shriek.

'This investigation will mean us working in close proximity. Think you can handle that?' Again, the long look, but this time his eyes had a faraway look as if he was remembering another time, another place. A different woman.

'I can handle it,' Charlee said. And *you*, her look assured him.

'You see,' he continued as though she hadn't spoken, 'I need a female assistant who won't go all mushy on me. Who won't be hearing wedding bells, dream of being a June bride or think of registering our wedding list at John Lewis and expecting more than I have to offer.' As expected, that drew an extreme reaction from Charlee.

'And I don't want you going all mushy on me, either. There's no room for a man in my life - I have my career to think of,' she added, grandly. 'And if I was looking for a life partner - which I'm not - you'd be the last man on earth I'd …' Then she clammed up. Five minutes ago, she'd thought she was heading for the Job Centre and here she was with Mr Award-Winning Author, about to throw her second chance away. 'Sorry. What I meant to say was -'

'No. Hold onto that thought, and that expression. I rather suspect that being penitent isn't exactly your bag.' Closing the distance between them, he grasped her by the shoulders. Charlee took a step backwards and turned her head to the side, thinking he meant to kiss her after all. He surprised her by turning her to face the mirror on the wall. Left with little choice, Charlee raised her head and stared back at herself - with Ffinch standing at her right shoulder.

She was hardly the picture of glowing health. Her blonde, asymmetrically cut hair was sticking up like she'd had her fingers in an electrical socket. After a troubled weekend, her winter pale skin was blotchy and she looked in dire need of a facial. And - although her bright blue eyes stared back at Ffinch defiantly - her cheeks were flushed, making her look flummoxed and out of her depth.

However - to her credit - she also looked angry and not in the least bit mushy.

She was about to wriggle free but hesitated, became aware that some part of her actually relished the feel of his chest lightly pressed against her shoulder blades. The touch of warm hands on knotted shoulders; the way his lime-scented aftershave fused harmoniously with her perfume as the temperature rose and they radiated body heat. A frisson travelled her length and reminded her that over six months had passed since she and her boyfriend had parted amicably after their finals. Six months since she'd shared her bed and her body with a man.

The thought was enough to cool her ardour. Wriggling free, she shrugged off his hands, hoping her lowering expression made it plain that she found the physical contact unwelcome. She put some space between them and leaned against Sam Walker's desk, something she would never have done under normal circumstances. But needs must, because her legs felt strangely boneless and her heart was racing.

'Okay, what's the assignment?' She straightened her clothes and tried to look hard-bitten, like she'd just come back from a war zone and had copy to file for tomorrow's headlines. Not a rookie with too much attitude and too little experience to warrant it.

'I don't know how much you know about me,' he began. She was about to make polite noises when he cut her off. 'That doesn't matter. All you need to know about this assignment is that it's one last favour for Sam. He gave me my big break when no one could see past my name and my antecedents - my parents, my background,' he amended.

'I know what antecedents are, thanks,' she bit out. 'A first in languages does tend to build up one's vocabulary.'

'Of course. Sorry. It's just that I'm used to -' then he pulled himself up short. 'Never mind what I'm used to. It's you I want.' A shiver ran up her spine and this time she tried to pass it off as a shiver of distaste. 'I hope to God I haven't made a colossal blunder.' For a moment, his face took on a bleak expression and remembrance seemed to swamp him. He rocked back on his heels and Charlee was reminded of the night at the gallery when she thought he looked ill and his eyes were dark-circled beneath his tropical tan.

'Why me?' she demanded suspiciously, looking the gift horse firmly between the eyes.

'You're ballsy, opinionated - and clearly not too enamoured of me.' He held his hand up when she began to protest, feeling it was incumbent upon her. 'That's okay. That's how I want it to be. At the end of this assignment we'll dissolve our partnership,' he pulled a wry face at the word, 'and go our separate ways.'

'No moon in June. No roses round the door. No happily ever after. Got it.' Charlee summed up the terms of engagement succinctly and he nodded. That being settled, he then continued in a businesslike tone.

'Sam wants snaps of a young royal playing away from home while his girlfriend's in Africa, working for Save the Children. It's for the Valentine's edition of *What'cha!* Romantic, huh?' She pulled a face. 'I know what you're thinking - more celeb stuff - but if this works out, you show your mettle and I can trust you, there's a bigger story to cover. Sam reckons you're a bit green, but you've got what it takes. Is that enough, for now?'

Judging from his guarded expression she guessed it would have to be.

Bigger story? That was more like it.

'Sure,' she shrugged with a great show of nonchalance but her brain was on overdrive. It was common knowledge that *What'cha!* was haemorrhaging money and that Sam Walker had had it with featuring D-list soap stars on the front cover. He wasn't getting any younger and the rumour was that he wanted to retire. But he wanted a good story to retire on, to go out in a blaze of glory. Perhaps the bigger story was his last hurrah.

'Now that's settled, I've got a Christmas present for you.'

'A present,' she stammered, completely wrong-footed. 'But I haven't got you anything. I didn't know - oh, ha-bloody-ha, very funny.'

Ffinch handed her a copy of his award-winning tome: *The Ten Most Dangerous Destinations on the Planet.*

'I thought you'd find a use for it.'

'As a doorstop,' she quipped, and then bit her lip. But luckily he laughed at the joke and leaned back on the window ledge once more, arms folded across his chest, watching her. As if trying to decide if he'd made the biggest mistake of his life or taken a gamble that might just pay off. She squirmed under his scrutiny and, as was her way, made light of her feelings. 'You know, you should have called your book *Where Angels Fear to Tread* or, *Fools Rush In.*'

'Do you have an opinion on everything?' he asked. 'No, don't answer that, I have a feeling that you do.'

'This assignment, when is it?' she asked, ignoring the last.

'Tomorrow night.'

'But tomorrow's Christmas Eve …'

'I'm sure Father Christmas will deliver your presents whether you're there or not, Chelsea,' he drawled, his lip curling at the sentiment.

'Okay. Time out. My name is Charlee, as you well know. Or Montague, if you must. Call me Chelsea once more and I'll …' She raised his book above her head and he held up his hands in defence.

'Okay, Char-lee,' he replied with a nod of acquiescence. 'Although something tells me that you're known as *The Full Monty*, too?' he said, and his lips quirked in a so-far-so-predictable half-smile

'That, too,' she nodded, giving a look that said if he had a problem with her name, he should just come out with it. 'Just, enough with the Chelsea thing - okay? It wasn't funny first time around and it isn't funny now. So, what do I call you Mr Fonseca-Ffinch? You're a bit of a mouthful, aren't you?' He raised his eyebrow and she realised what she'd said. 'I didn't mean - I mean, I wouldn't, I don't.' Charlee had a horrible suspicion that her cheeks were flaming again.

'Relax, Charlee. I'm Ffinch, plain and simple.'

Charlee suspected there was nothing plain or simple about him. 'And Rafa?' she asked and earned one of his dark looks for her presumption.

'For the use of friends and family only,' he said firmly. Feeling well and truly put in her place, she hid her humiliation behind an insouciant shrug. In that instant, she vowed she'd make it her business to impress him enough with her skills as a journo that he'd be begging her to call him Rafa.

'Okay, Ffinch it is. I -'

At that moment, Sam Walker came back into the office with Vanessa. He was less than pleased to see Charlee perched on his desk.

'Montague - arse off my burr walnut, if you please.'

'Yes, Chief.' She got to her feet and tucked Ffinch's novel under her arm. Sensing she was dismissed, she headed for the door. She paused there with one hand on the door jamb and turned to ask Ffinch one last question: 'Where and when?'

'I'll pick you up around eleven. Sam's given me your address.'

'Around eleven, fine. Dress code?'

'A little black dress - assuming you have one. Wear a thick coat and thermal underwear. You do have thermal underwear, I take it?' he asked, straight-faced, and earned another glare from her. What was his game - what exactly were the rules of engagement? To flirt or not to flirt; he really should make his mind up.

'Doesn't everyone?' she said, chiefly to show that nothing he could say or do could faze her. 'It that it?'

'No; bring food, enough for two of us. None of that low-cal, high protein rubbish females eat. I want doorstep sandwiches containing meat, slabs of cake - and oh, a flask of coffee.'

'Thermal underwear, man food, flask of coffee. Got it … anything else?' she asked as sarcastically as she dared with Sam Walker and Vanessa listening.

'Tell Father Christmas you'll be home in time to open your presents. But warn your legion of boyfriends that you'll have to put the kiss under the mistletoe on hold.'

Boyfriends? Did he think she was sweet sixteen and never been kissed. She was just about to make a suitable retort when Vanessa put in, ever so helpfully:

'Montague doesn't have a boyfriend, Rafa.'

'Good, that makes things less complicated,' Ffinch murmured, almost as an aside.

Before Charlee had time to ask him exactly what he meant by that, he pushed himself off the window ledge, ushered - almost pushed - her out of the room and closed the door behind her. Standing in the corridor, Charlee could hear their muffled voices and knew they were talking about her. She suspected none of it was complimentary.

'Charlee? You okay?' Poppy appeared at her side and gave her a shake. 'Come on.'

'Why? Where are we going?' Charlee asked as Poppy steered her back into the office and whipped their coats off the backs of their chairs.

'Pret A Manger.' She took Ffinch's book out of Charlee's slack fingers, put it on Charlee's desk, replacing it with a notepad and a pen. 'Daddy says I have to bring you up to speed on Rafa to prevent you from making a monumental cock-up tomorrow night. His words not mine,' she rolled her eyes as they made their way towards the lifts. 'And

I agree with him; this is your big chance and I'm not going to let you blow it.' Poppy pressed the buttons and they waited for the lift to arrive on their floor.

Chapter Ten
Are You Writing This Down?

Fifteen minutes later, Charlee was in their local branch of Pret, watching the pre-breakfast crowd grab their lattes and croissants. Tomorrow, as she'd pointed out to Ffinch, was Christmas Eve and she'd planned to finish work at noon, load her overnight bag and presents into the Mini and then head for home. Now she was going on this assignment with him!

She didn't much care for the sarcastic way he'd said: tell your boyfriends they'll have to put the kiss under the mistletoe on hold. Or how his lip had curled as if he doubted her capable of being a go-for-it trainee journo and full-time girlfriend. It annoyed her to admit that he was right. Since leaving university last summer, she'd been on a couple of abortive dates with some of Poppy's male friends - braying Hoorays for the most part. Or, dated men she met in the wine bars where she hung out with the other interns after work. But the men only seemed interested in a quick fumble and the chance to tell her how wonderful/successful/talented they were - and how lucky she was to be dating them.

Not that she was in any hurry to find a soul-mate. As she'd been quick to assure Ffinch, she was wedded to her career - love, marriage, babies and all that jazz could wait as far as she was concerned. And, in any case, she doubted her ideal man existed other than in her dreams:

artistic, brave, funny, and as hungry for the exclusive - the scoop - as she was.

'I thought double espressos, in the circumstances.' Poppy plonked two small cups of extremely strong coffee in front of them and a couple of cheese and ham toasties. She pushed her thick black French plait over her shoulder and looked at Charlee expectantly with eyes as bright and darting as a robin's. 'Okay, give. What happened in Pa's office?'

'Don't you ever stop eating?' Charlee asked, already knowing the answer.

Poppy ate like a man but was stick thin because she spent half her life riding horses and the other half mucking them out. Charlee guessed that Poppy'd been up before it was light, helping with the tack and feeding routine at her mother's riding school. When she got home this evening, she would exercise her mother's hunters in the indoor ménage and practise her dressage. And on Boxing Day, Poppy would be out with the local hunt while Charlee stayed in bed and nursed a hangover. 'Okay, Popps; Fonseca-Ffinch. Give.'

'Rafa,' Poppy began, biting into her sandwich with straight white teeth. She gets to call him Rafa, Charlee thought, but held her peace until Poppy finished chewing. 'Rafa is an old friend of the family. I've had a massive crush on him for years, all the girls have - he's totally gorgeous ... but regards me as the younger sister he never had, or even worse - a cute pet, like a Labrador.'

They pulled a face at that and then laughed because their expressions exactly mirrored one another.

'Go on,' Charlee commanded.

'Chief gave him his first break when no one could see past his name and his family connections. His family are diplomats and their present posting is Paris; I've been over there to stay with them loads of times. Okay, don't give me that look - I'm waffling, I know. Back to Ffinch; everyone thought he was just another posh boy playing at photo journalism, cashing in on his connections until something new or more exciting took his fancy.'

'He's told me that, already,' Charlee put in, sipping her strong coffee and toying with the corner of her toastie. Last night, the same thoughts had gone through her mind.

'He was writing the last chapter of his book: *The Ten Most Dangerous Destinations on the Planet.*'

'And?' Charlee was anxious for Poppy to cut to the chase. Her explanations were notoriously long-winded and the copy she presented nearly always ended up being 'spiked' by the subs as unusable. But Sam Walker insisted that she come into work every day because, as he rightly suspected, she'd fritter her time away at that 'bloody money-draining riding school,' and never forge a career for herself.

Poppy paused and then asked severely: 'Are you writing any of this down, Montague?'

'Filing it away,' Charlee grinned and tapped her temple with a fore-finger. 'In my bank vault. Carry on -' An aptitude for language had given Charlee the ability to remember what was said, who said it and when. On top of that, she had a phenomenal recall of faces, facts and figures; she guessed that's what had gained her a double first when she'd graduated last summer.

'His last trip was to Darien, Colombia, where he and his team of local guides, plus two young research assistants from the University of Colombia, were kidnapped by a guerrilla group and held to ransom.' Charlee moved to the edge of her seat - this was more like it! 'The guerrillas - or whatever they are - got wind of how rich Ffinch's family is and saw dollar signs. Ker-ching,' she made a noise like an old-fashioned cash register.

'So how come -'

'He lived to tell the tale and write this book?' For once, Poppy stayed focused. 'I don't know all the ins and outs, and I don't ask. He's very touchy on the subject but who can blame him?' She rifled in her pocket, brought out a piece of folded A4 lined paper and pushed it across the table to Charlee. 'Chief knew you'd have lots of questions, so he's drawn up a list of topics that are off limits when you're out with Rafa.'

That struck a raw nerve with Charlee. Who did Rafa Frigging-Ffinch think he was? And why was Chief so ready to agree to his every request?

'But I'm a journalist,' Charlee protested. Then, catching Poppy's expression amended it to 'Okay, trainee journalist. How can I not ask questions? Anyway, what's verboten?' She took the paper off the table with the utmost reluctance and read down the list. 'Ffinch's family; his capture and subsequent release; the death of his two research assistants. Death?' That struck a chord with her; she imagined their families, the guilt Ffinch must feel at not keeping them safe. 'His rescue by an indigenous tribe; the ongoing investigation by the Colombian Drugs Agency.'

'Pretty comprehensive, huh?' Poppy asked, pulling a face as Charlee read on.

'The assignment; his plans for the future ... yada, yada, yada. The list's endless,' she complained. Then she put on a false, bright smile: 'Oh, wait - we can discuss the weather and whether he's having turkey or roast beef on Christmas Day. Bloody marvellous.'

'You'll be great together,' Poppy soothed. 'Just do as you're told - you are capable of doing that, aren't you? No wait, don't answer that question.' She pulled a face and then started to eat Charlee's almost untouched toastie. 'Chief had his reservations but I told him that you were the girl for the job ...'

'How do you mean you told Chief I was the girl for the job? Put down my toastie and explain yourself, Missy,' Charlee said, suspecting another one of Poppy's matchmaking efforts.

'Look,' Poppy said, clearly picking up the vibe. 'Rafa isn't interested in you in that way, he probably hasn't even noticed that you're a woman.'

'Thanks for that!'

'He wants an assistant, someone he can trust to go on this assignment and not cling to him or be difficult. You want an adventure, the chance of breaking out of the photo archive and into the big time. The scoop. He wants a no-nonsense partner who won't throw her arms around his neck sobbing at the first obstacle. It's a win-win situation, he gets the scoop and you get to bask in reflected glory.' Charlee didn't much like the sound of reflected glory but let it pass.

'What about Vanessa?'

'Too old?'

'Or Sally?'

'Too stoop-id.'

Charlee acknowledged there was truth in Poppy's statement. After fifteen minutes in Sally's company Rafa would be wishing himself back in the bug-infested jungle or a piranha-infested stretch of the Amazon, anything to escape her simpering. As if of the same mind, Poppy put down Charlee's toastie and propped her chin up on the back of her hands, like a Victorian maiden.

'Oh, Rafa, you are so brave. Oh, Rafa you are so clever. Oh Rafa …' she mimicked the unfortunate Sally. 'But you're different. You two will be great together.'

'Somehow I doubt that. Just as I suspect I'm only being told half the story. Why would a journo of Ffinch's repute be interested in a royal playing away from home? Why would he need a rookie like me to ac-company him?'

'See - you're curious and that's what makes a good journalist. That's why I'll never be any good.' Poppy sighed and polished off the last of the sandwich. 'I just don't care enough.'

'Sweetie,' Charlee put her hand over Poppy's. 'Your weekly 'Life in the Country' column's great …'

'Only because, more often than not, you and Mummy write it for me!' Poppy grinned unashamedly. 'Chief would drop it from *What'cha!* if he thought he'd get away with it. But Mummy would raise blue mur-der. It's all that's left from the original magazine he took over when they married. More coffee?' She went to join the queue. Charlee sank back in her seat and watched Poppy sashay up to the counter like the thoroughbred she was: long limbs, slender ankles, hair in a French plait interwoven with a red ribbon.

And what was she? A bit of a pocket Venus - with unruly thick blonde hair and a generally thrown together appearance. She had the feeling that Poppy longed to take the curry comb to her - lick her into shape, maybe even rub hoof oil into the ancient, cracked boots she'd bought in a vintage shop. Smiling, she tucked the piece of paper into the expandable wallet at the back of her Moleskine to read over before Ffinch picked her up.

Then she frowned.

She had a gut feeling that the stone, paper, scissors interlude two days ago had been a set-up, a test to see if she was equal to the role Sam and Ffinch had earmarked her for. Not to mention Poppy putting her forward ... But, what if she'd been picked for her size rather than her journalistic prowess. She pulled a face in concentration: what was it Ffinch had said? This assignment will mean us being in a confined space together. Think you can handle that? She pulled out the piece of paper and read down the list again. No mention of spaces, confined or otherwise. Frowning, she turned over the sheet of paper and saw more writing, this time in Sam's unmistakable handwriting.

'AND WHATEVER YOU DO, MONTAGUE, DON'T ARGUE WITH FFINCH OR ASK ABOUT THINGS THAT ARE NONE OF YOUR BUSINESS ...'

Charlee allowed herself a mirthless smile. Didn't Sam know her after all these years? Asking her not to do something was guaranteed to make her do just the opposite. Now, of course, she wanted to know all about what had happened in Colombia and it would be burning a hole through the synapses of her brain until she found out.

Feck, she thought, as she read the list again. Being with Ffinch would be like being granted an audience with the Queen. Don't speak until spoken to. Never ask a direct question. Curtsey. Address him as 'Your Majesty' in the first instance and 'Sir' thereafter. She gave an ironic sniff - as if that was likely. She was already feeling mighty irritated by him, the secrecy surrounding the assignment and Chief's list of forbidden topics. If the object had been to put distance between them and make her find him as attractive as a case of boils, the plan was working fine.

By the sounds of it, one assignment together and then she'd be glad to see the back of Rafael Fonseca-Ffinch.

Chapter Eleven
This One's a Classic

B ang on eleven o'clock on Christmas Eve, the intercom buzzed
in Charlee's bedsit and she picked up the handset.

'Ffinch,' he said without preamble.

'Montague,' she replied, feeling absurdly like she was in a rerun of
the classic TV show, *Cagney and Lacey*. Ffinch's brisk tone shook her
from her daydream.

'Get yourself down here, Montague. Clock's a-ticking.'

'Yes sir, no sir, three bags flippin' full sir,' she said, under her
breath.

'I heard that,' he replied. She pulled a face and mouthed 'good' as
she put the receiver back on the intercom, grabbed her bag, coat and
the two carrier bags containing the midnight feast he'd ordered.

Then she pulled the door of the bedsit behind her and took the
stairs two at a time. She skidded to a halt in the scruffy hall and allowed herself a little happy dance. 'I'm on my first assignment - with
an award-winning journalist,' she shouted at a pile of takeaway leaflets
littering the doormat. And a monumental pain in the arse, her brain
added as a coda for good measure. But nothing could dampen her
enthusiasm or crush her high spirits and she smiled as she stepped out
into the street. Ffinch was waiting by the side of a classic VW camper
van with his arms folded and a wry smile twisting his lips.

'Oh, wow,' Charlee exclaimed as she walked towards the classic 1960s camper van with navy and cream coachwork and split windscreen. 'A splitty and a left hooker. I've always wanted one.'

'I thought for a moment the wow was for me, Montague,' Ffinch observed dryly as he opened the passenger door and signalled for her to climb in. 'But I can see from your expression that isn't the case.' He closed the door, shrugged as though it was of no consequence, and walked round to the driver's side.

'It isn't,' she informed shortly. 'It's for your gorgeous camper van. 1966, isn't it? I love Vee Dubbya camper vans, especially pre-1970 models. When I land the scoop of the decade, I'll buy one just like this - with navy-blue and white coachwork.' She turned towards him, her eyes shining as she fastened her seat belt, forgetting for a moment that she was annoyed with him (and Sam Walker) for the list of forbidden topics. And, if she was being totally honest, for his no flirting rule - which he seemed to bend when it suited him.

'I hope you won't forget who gave you your big chance,' he commented as they moved out into the traffic. Then he slanted a sideways look at her as she pulled down the sunshade and started fluffing up her hair. 'Is this how you're going to be all night,' he asked. 'All bouncy and lit up? Like it's Christmas or something?' His mouth quirked in one of his mirthless smiles.

'It is Christmas, in case you hadn't noticed, and yes; I might be bouncy and lit up all night. But when I need to be I can be still and calm and - Oh. My. God!' Charlee exclaimed, causing him to slam his foot on the brakes.

'What the - Jeezus, Montague, we were nearly rammed from behind by that taxi,' he said, plainly beginning to have second thoughts about choosing her as his partner.

'You've installed the Porsche engine!'

'Well, the guy who imported the camper from California did. Not me.'

'California? Oh, just imagine where this camper has been,' she sighed and stroked the dashboard like it was a favourite pet. 'The road to Malibu, Sunset Boulevard, the Hollywood Hills.'

'Walsall,' he added crushingly.

'Walsall?'

'That's where I take her to be serviced. The guy there's a Vee-Dubb enthusiast and a genius at making old girls like this one run as sweet as a nut.' He looked at her quizzically, as if she wasn't running true to form and he was revising his opinion of her minute by minute. 'Anyway - how did you ...'

'... know it was a Porsche engine? I'm interested in such things,' she said simply and turned to look out of the passenger window. Damn. Now he'd think she was some kind of butch tomboy who excelled at stone, paper, scissors, knew all about car engines and arm wrestled men in bars. 'My brothers ...' she muttered by way of an explanation. She might not harbour romantic feelings towards Rafael Fonseca-Ffinch, but she wanted him to know - should he be in any doubt - that she was all woman.

'Ah yes - your brothers.' Then he gave an 'I know all about you and your family' sort of laugh. Charlee was prepared to bet good money he'd done his homework and that Sam and Poppy had filled him in on the rest ... the family of high achievers; the great disappointment she was to all concerned because of her chosen career.

Tinker. Tailor. Soldier. Sailor. Rich Man. Poor Man ...

Or, as was the case with the Montagues: two veterinary surgeons. Retired HMI. Political lobbyist. Research chemist. Greenpeace activist - and, last and very much least - a wannabe journalist. All she had to measure him against was a list of proscribed questions currently burning a hole in her handbag. And a shedload more questions burning a hole in her brain.

'What does that mean: your brothers?' she demanded, turning towards him and giving him a scorching look. But the effect was lost because the interior of the camper van was in shadow apart from the orange glow of the street lamps.

'You're like Cinderella, aren't you? Only, instead of ugly stepsisters, you have the Brothers Grimm.'

'I'm nothing like Cinderella. And, I'll have you know, my brothers are clever, talented, uber handsome and … and think the world of me.' She crossed her fingers as she said the last bit, not entirely sure if it was true. It was one thing for her to bemoan her lot regarding her brothers and the way they'd teased her almost unmercifully while she'd been growing up: nearly drowning her in the lake at the bottom of the farm and hanging her dolls and teddies from the apple trees in the garden. Then, as she grew older, scaring off potential boyfriends with glowering looks, folded arms and a hundred and one questions about their intentions. The way they kept harping on about 'men are only after one thing, Charlee, and we should know.' It was all too embarrassing; too mortifying. She flushed in the shadowy darkness of the camper van.

But she wasn't going to allow Fonseca-Ffinch to cast aspersions on her family. It was none of his business.

'So where does that leave you, Little Miss Intern?' He managed to give her another swift, assessing glance as the traffic built up and the camper van crawled along.

She made as if to answer but then clammed up; she'd trade information with him on a quid pro quo basis. She wasn't going to answer his questions when she wasn't allowed to ask any of her own. Why, for example, had she been chosen for this assignment - apart from her assertion that she wouldn't go all mushy on him and her declaration that she was prepared to die an old maid clutching the Pulitzer Prize for Journalism to her scrawny bosom? If that's what it took to make her mark.

'It leaves me in a camper van with you on Christmas Eve, wearing thermal underwear and cooking on gas,' she answered. 'Could you turn down the heat before I expire?' She fanned herself with a magazine she'd found in the glove compartment. There were all sorts of notebooks in there and a top of the range camera.

'I'll remind you of that when you're freezing cold in half an hour's time,' he said, reaching across and rearranging the parcel shelf to his liking. Something else out of bounds? No surprise there, Charlee thought, unfastening her coat and unwrapping the pashmina from her neck.

Patronised and demoralised - this was turning out to be a very un-equal partnership - she slunk lower in her seat and folded her arms across her breasts. God, he'd had more mood swings in fifteen minutes than was entirely attractive in a grown man. She'd be more than happy to walk away from tonight's assignment without exchanging Christ-mas cards, let alone email addresses and mobile phone numbers.

Something was eating him. But what?

On their previous encounters, she'd sensed an undercurrent, no-ticed the way his eyes looked dead, even when he smiled. Like he was grieving over something - or, someone. Yet, on both occasions, he'd pulled himself out of his dolour and appeared to enjoy sparring with her. As if she drew him away from dark thoughts that haunted him. But tonight was different, he seemed driven, almost unaware of her presence until she annoyed him - then he looked surprised to find her sitting next to him in the passenger seat.

Nothing like being made to feel invisible to build up one's confi-dence on a first assignment, Charlee thought.

'Anyhoo, Ffinch,' she began.

'What now?' he asked in exasperated tones. Charlee could tell that he wasn't in the mood for conversation or company and that made her all the more determined to needle him.

'I thought you might have had our names stuck on the windscreen. Fonseca and Montague; Rafa and Charlee. Frankly, I'm disappointed - we are partners, after all.'

'Temporary partners,' he said crushingly. 'With an emphasis on *temporary.*'

'Were you this grumpy with your last partners?' Then she remem-bered that his partners had drowned in the Amazon and he'd only just escaped with his life. She could have bitten her tongue off but laid a hand on his arm instead. 'I - I'm sorry Ffinch, that was unforgivable of me. I forgot.'

'It doesn't matter,' he shrugged off her hand. 'Nothing matters except getting through tonight without being spotted. Okay?' He let out a shaky breath and when Charlee glanced at him in the orange city lights, his brow was furrowed and he looked unbearably sad. Deciding she'd said more than enough, she folded her arms across her chest and said nothing more until they drew into a side street in Mayfair. Ffinch parked the camper van on the darker side of the street and killed the engine.

'We're here.'

'Here?' Charlee looked around at the discreet hotels with their doormen, the armed policemen from the diplomatic protection group walking together in pairs, machine guns slung across their chests. The upmarket designer shops with their subdued lighting and wares visible through the grilles.

'Not here, exactly. Close by. Come on.'

He seemed to have regained some of his good humour because he came round to her side of the camper van, opened the door and held out his hand with a gracious bow. Charlee ignored his hand and slithered out instead, glancing over at Berkeley Square and wondering if nightingales had ever sung there. Ffinch looked down at his open hand and shrugged as if Charlee's show of independence was of little consequence to him.

He locked the camper and strode out towards Piccadilly with his camera bag slung over his shoulder. Charlee had to break into a trot at his heels in order to match his long strides. She rather suspected that he was giving no quarter after she'd so ungraciously refused to be helped down from the camper van.

The evening was wet but mild. Well dressed, affluent partygoers drifted in and out of doorways which were flanked by Christmas trees or hung with lights and garlands. Most of Charlee's friends had returned home for Christmas and it hadn't gone down well with her parents, her mother in particular, that she wouldn't be travelling down to Berkshire until early tomorrow morning.

'Don't disturb any of your father's patients when you arrive late, Charlotte,' her mother's aggrieved tone echoed in her head. And, as she followed Ffinch down a side street, she thought it quite ridiculous that her mother referred to the animals requiring overnight care at her father's veterinary practice as patients. And she wondered, not for the first time, why her mother couldn't be more relaxed and accepting of who she was. She sighed, and pressed her hand to her side where a painful stitch was developing. She was getting quite out of breath and Ffinch showed no sign of slowing down. In fact, it looked as if he'd forgotten she was at his heels.

Then he ducked down an alleyway between tall, elegant buildings, stopped in his tracks and held his hand up for silence, like an Indian scout. Turning, he put his finger to his lips and indicated, by nodding his head, that she should follow him - quietly. Charlee stayed true to the promise that she'd made in the camper van, that when push came to shove she could be quiet as a mouse. But excitement bubbled up inside her as she wondered what was in store.

Ffinch led the way to the back of one of the houses where dustbins were discreetly hidden behind wrought iron screens and a tarpaulin-shrouded skip stood in one corner of the yard. Outside the back entrance of what was clearly a private club, there was a canopied smoking area with sturdy wicker chairs and a table. Crouching low, he went over to the skip, deftly raised up one corner of the tarpaulin and nodded towards it.

'Your coach, Cinders. Get in.'

'What?' Charlee mouthed, sensing the need to be quiet, circumspect. Ffinch came over, removed the two Waitrose bags from her slack fingers and repeated his instructions.

'I said, get in. Do it now, without arguing and I'll explain ...'

It was the thought of the explanation rather than his hissed command that made Charlee comply. She gave a shudder of distaste, envis-

aging sitting among rotting fish tails and the remains of last night's dinner. At his earlier insistence, she was wearing her little black number
and she did not intend ruining it, not even in the line of duty. But
needs must; the experienced journo had to be prepared to put personal comfort aside and get on with the job. But the skip sides were quite
high and she was rather on the short side so she raised an enquiring
eyebrow at Ffinch.

Giving an irritated tut, he put the bags containing the food and his
camera equipment on the floor and swung her easily into the skip,
as if she weighed no more than a fly. He held her in his arms briefly
and his warm breath fanned her temple. For a moment, Charlee felt
like a bride being carried across the threshold, but then pulled herself
together and put a stop to her wild imaginings. He might be the hottest ticket in town, but this was a skip for God's sake - and hadn't she
promised not to go all mushy on him?

He deposited her gently into the skip, followed close behind and
pulled the green tarp over their heads. Using a pocket torch, he illuminated the interior which was loaded with offcuts of wood and indicated that she should sit. Then he took up position next to her on a
sturdy plank and started to examine his photographic equipment.

Feeling dismissed, Charlee said nothing for a few moments. When
she did finally manage to say: 'Okay, level with me, what are we doing
here?' her voice was hoarse from being route marched through Piccadilly. Although she'd spoken no louder than a whisper, he made a
throat cutting gesture with his forefinger, raised a corner of the tarp
and poked his camera lens through it. He fired off a few rapid frames
and then withdrew the camera and sank back on the makeshift seat.

'We're here,' he offered, rifling through the bag of food until he
found some doorstep sandwiches oozing brown sauce, 'to photograph
a prince who, it turns out, is less than charming, Cinders. He's playing
away from home while his girlfriend is -'

'Over in Africa in a drought zone with Save the Children. Yeah, I've
seen the photos,' she drawled cynically, 'of her holding starving babies,

all perfectly made-up and in crease proof fatigues.'

'The babies are wearing make-up and fatigues?' he asked innocently, biting into a cold bacon and tomato sandwich.

'You know perfectly well what I mean,' she replied haughtily. 'And it's not funny to make fun of starving children in the Horn of Africa.'

'About as PC as referring to one of the Cat People as having had an extreme makeover?' he came back with, HP sauce dribbling down his chin as he ate his sandwich.

'Touché,' she remarked as she handed him a piece of kitchen roll to use as a napkin. 'That was a stupid of me and I'm sorry - but you were goading me -'

'I don't think I was. I rather get the impression that you pretty much act on impulse and do and say what you want.'

His assessment of her was so unnervingly accurate that Charlee changed the subject.

'I smell a rat; one wearing a crown and ermine, but a rat nonetheless. Not much of a story, though, is it: PRINCE PLAYS THE FIELD WHILE FIANCEE IS IN AFRICA DOING GOOD WORKS? I mean, it's hardly breaking news that HRH is poor husband material, but if she wants the big wedding and the title then she'll have to get used to him playing away from home. It runs in the blood. So, cut the bullshit and give me the truth, Ffinch.' She took the bag of food away from him. 'Food seems to be the only bargaining chip I have and I'm prepared to use it. No cranberry muffins, or coffee, until you come clean.'

'Montague, you're beginning to make me wonder if I did the right thing in choosing you. Sam assured me that you were ambitious but biddable.' He had reverted to the same light, bantering tone he'd used the night of his book launch and in Sam's office. Whatever demons had been haunting him when he'd picked her up at her bedsit seemed to have vanished into the darkness the moment they had climbed into the skip. Maybe, like her, the stake-out and the story had pushed everything else to the edge of his consciousness.

'One out of two ain't bad,' Charlee laughed and fetched her own sandwich out of the bag. 'Don't change the subject. Give.'

'Okay, this isn't about the prince and the showgirl. That was just a smoke-screen for the team back at *What'cha!* There's a story unfolding here tonight, one which I'm on the trail of.'

'I knew it. And?'

'That's as much as I'm prepared to divulge at the moment.'

'Even to a partner?' she asked pertly, knowing that their partnership only existed in her imagination. 'Montague and Ffinch - sounds good to me.'

'Ffinch and Montague you mean. Not that we are partners,' he corrected, 'you are my assistant - nothing more.' He reached for the bag of food but Charlee held it away from him.

'Then this assistant needs to know what's expected of her or she's leaving and taking her sandwiches with her. Then you'll have the whole skip to yourself. Capice?'

Ffinch shone the torch on her face. 'You are trouble, lady. Not only that, you've been watching too many episodes of *The Sopranos*. Capice, indeed,' he pulled a face but she could see that he was figuring out that she was no pushover. And, quite possibly, trying not to laugh. 'Okay, Montague, here's the thing. You've heard of Anastasia Markova, the model who's marrying the Russian plutocrat?'

Just in time, Charlee stopped herself from saying, Duh! She knew she had to play this one poker-faced and hide her excitement. 'Sure.' She shrugged and put the bag of sandwiches between them on the plank.

'I've had a tip-off that she's holding her hen night, here.' He pulled a face and left Charlee wondering if it was the whole concept of marriage, weddings and the attendant brouhaha that cheesed him off. Or the expression 'hen night' with its connotations of soon-to-be brides tied to lamp posts and wearing L plates while their attendants were sick in the gutter. Dancing on tables and staggering out of nightclubs wearing pink Stetsons was so not what she would do when/if her moment arrived. 'Montague! Are you listening to a word I'm saying?'

'I don't have to look adoringly into your eyes to prove I'm concentrating. Okay? Not that I can see them in this light,' she added in a more conciliatory tone just in case she was seriously pissing him off and blowing her chances of being taken on another assignment. 'Okay, so where do I fit into your plan, apart from being in charge of catering?' She pushed the bag of sandwiches closer to him.

'I need you to go over to the smoking area and stand there until they come out.'

'Who comes out?'

'Anastasia and her laydees,' he explained patiently. Charlee bit her lip; the flaw in the plan was blindingly obvious - wasn't it?

'But I could be standing there all night, freezing my assets off waiting for her to put in an appearance. Or, when we spot her I can hardly clamber out of the skip, walk over and start passing round the Silk Cut, can I? And, besides, I don't smoke and don't carry ciggies round with me on the off-chance that - '

Ffinch leaned forward in the semi-darkness and put two fingers on her lips.

'Montague. It's all been taken care of ... Now, are you going to shut up and listen?'

Charlee knocked his hand away and nodded her head, fuming that he had acted so patronisingly towards her. She wasn't a doll to be manhandled as and when he thought fit, and the sooner he realised that, the better.

'I'm listening,' she said.

'Here's how it works. I get a text from my contact inside the club to say she's coming out. That gives us time to get you out of the skip and station you at the back door looking like you've been there all night.'

'What am I supposed to do when she comes out? Secretly film her, or what?'

'No,' he sighed heavily as though she just didn't get it. 'You are to do nothing.'

'Nothing?'

'Although,' she felt rather than saw his moody grey eyes directed towards her like laser beams in the darkness, 'I suspect that doing nothing might not sit easily with you.'

'I told you back in the van. I can be anything you want me to be - if it results in getting the story.' As she uttered, I can be anything you want me to be, she wanted to call back the words. She rather suspected that too many women had been just a little too keen to please Rafa Fonseca-Ffinch. Apparently finding the idea of her pleasing him in a non-work related capacity repellent, he shifted uneasily on the uncomfortable plank. As he did so, his knee grazed against the inside of her thigh where her dress had ridden up, the hardness of bone meeting soft, yielding flesh.

Anything you want me to be? Now he'd think she was coming onto him and ... as if of one mind they sprang apart, scalded and embarrassed by the unexpected, intimate touch.

Then Ffinch's iPhone buzzed twice, the screen lit up and he grabbed it as if it were a lifeline. The light illuminated the planes and angles of his face, emphasising the dark circles of fatigue beneath his eyes and the shadows beneath his cheekbones. He seemed far away, as if he was remembering Christmas Eve in a different place and time, and the remembrance saddened him. Then he shrugged off whatever was haunting him, and became suddenly focused and businesslike.

'Okay. We're on.' He looped a velvet evening bag over her head. 'Cigarettes, lighter and a mobile phone. Switch the phone to voice recorder, leave it on the table and record everything they say. Everything. Got it?'

'But, what if -'

'There's no time for ifs. You were chosen by Sam specifically because you can speak Russian, you're full of bravado and - correct me if I'm wrong - can blag your way out of most situations.' If there'd been time, Charlee would have felt almost flattered by the description; but, as it was ...

'Okay. Here, help me off with my coat. I can't ...'

In the confined space of the skip, Ffinch managed to winkle her out of her coat and scarf. Keyed up by the thought of what lay ahead, Charlee almost didn't notice the way his fingers grazed her collarbone. Or that his hand had brushed against her breasts in the darkness. She'd remember all of that much, much later when she was alone in bed. Now she concentrated on divesting her outdoor things and smoothing the wrinkles out of her black hold-up stockings. Then she shuffled past him, losing her footing and almost sitting in his lap as she tried to avoid laddering her stockings on the side of the skip.

'Oof, Montague, have a care. You almost flattened me,' was his gallant response as she rested the flat of her hand on his thighs and pushed herself off. Strangely, without her coat, instead of freezing to death, she felt uncomfortably warm. Her cheeks and forehead burned while goose pimples travelled the length of her arms. Excitement, she guessed, hurriedly dismissing the conflicting sensations of hot and cold. That's all it was. What else could it be?

'Ready?' he asked in a hoarse whisper, like he was in dire need of the drink she'd packed, possibly with an added shot of rum.

In one swift movement, he threw back the corner of the tarp, lifted her up and over the high sides of the skip and deposited her on the ground. The back door of the nightclub opened and light streamed out over the smoking area. Charlee froze - then a member of staff poked her head cautiously round the door and placed a glass of red wine on the table. She glanced, once, towards the skip and then withdrew.

'That's your drink. Go and get it - and remember … voice recorder. Go!'

As Charlee staggered across the space between the skip and the calico framed gazebo strung with fairy lights, she wondered how he'd organised all this. If he could survive capture by a guerrilla group in Colombia, she supposed that paying a member of staff to do his bidding was small fry by comparison.

Three tables, comfortable sofas and chairs were positioned inside the decorative corral trimmed with winter foliage and berries. Huge scented candles spiked on sconces at the corners of the enclosure sent out a perfume of oranges, cloves and winter spices towards Charlee. The smoking area was warmed by overhead heaters, and onyx ashtrays filled with sand were positioned strategically on the tables. All quite different to the pub yards where her friends did their smoking. Usually there was a bucket of sand for stubbing out cigarettes, if you were lucky. Mostly, the stubs were crushed underfoot on the pavement.

There was little time for reflection or one of her usual flights of fancy. She had to be in position, glass in hand and puffing away at a cigarette before the bridal party came out. She allowed herself one backward glance at the skip and then stationed herself under the nearest heater. She was anxious to prove that she was the woman for the job and ready for whatever fate sent her. A chill wind blew into the yard and cut through the fabric of her little black shift dress. She searched in the quilted velvet bag and did a double take when she saw the label - it was vintage Chanel. Whose was it? An ex-girlfriend's? His mother's? Did he have a wardrobe of props for occasions such as this? It wouldn't surprise her to learn that he did.

Hands shaking, she extracted a solid silver cigarette case and lighter; the case was just the right size to hold six long cigarettes. Inside the lid it was engraved with signatures in different handwriting and Charlee suspected it was a family heirloom. She turned it over and saw the intertwined C's - Cartier, what else? Why couldn't he have given her an ordinary pack of cigarettes? It'd be just her luck to drop the heavy case down a drain or damage it, and then spend the next six months working to pay it off.

Voices.

Stiffening, she concentrated on carrying out the task to the best of her ability.

With her ear for languages, she detected the cadence of upper-class vowels overlaid with Estuary English. Posh kids, trying to disguise the Received Pronunciation considered so uncool nowadays. Not her intended mark, clearly. Pulling the mobile phone out of the bag, she turned away and pretended to talk to someone on the other end, but not before registering the young prince surrounded by his circle of trusted friends. Then she practically singed her eyebrows as she inexpertly put the cigarette in her mouth, tried to light it one-handed and take a long draw without choking. Eventually, she was beneath their notice and looked just like another young woman out enjoying the Christmas Eve buzz. They carried on talking about driving down the M4 to Wiltshire to stay on their parents' 'estates', and how they would need to meet up if they were to survive the ordeal.

Then the door opened again and a troupe of long-legged beauties wearing minimal clothing but some serious jewellery walked out of the back entrance. Well, not so much walked as covered the ground in long, languorous strides with legs that looked like they belonged on thoroughbred racehorses - all bone, sinew and slender ankles. Charlee looked at her definitely average legs and wondered how it would feel to have those added inches. Or to be able to walk on five-inch Jimmy Choos without falling over. But there was no time to give full rein to her neuroses, she could feel Ffinch's eyes boring a hole in the back of her skull and hear him saying: What are you playing at, Montague - get closer. Move in for the kill.

The models joined the prince and his friends and they air-kissed and schmoozed each other big time. The blue bloods happy to rub shoulders with the supermodels, and the models glad of the validation they gained from mixing with the prince and his entourage. Then Anastasia Markova spotted Charlee's mobile.

'No photos. No photos', she shrieked, holding her hands over her face. Charlee gave a shrug and put the phone on the table, after making sure the voice recorder was activated.

'Whatever, darling', Charlee drawled, picking up her drink and moving away from them. She drank the red wine in several thirsty gulps and then as the bouquet hit her taste buds suppressed a wow of delight. Whatever bottle it had come out of had spent long years in the darkness of a temperature regulated wine cellar.

Vin de Pays it was not.

Some desultory conversation passed between the disparate group, mostly about how this was Markova's hen night and how close her wedding was. Then the prince and his friends stubbed out their cigarettes and went back into the nightclub. Charlee, sitting on the large sofa, made a great play of letting her cigarette burn down and flicking the ash onto the ground. The models slipped into Russian and she looked away from them while the recorder did its business and captured every word. She was trying so hard not to look in their direction that, when Anastasia Markova touched her on the shoulder, she almost jumped out of her skin.

'Is vintage Chanel, no?' Markova said pointing at Charlee's bag and reaching out to stroke it. 'You permit?' She didn't wait for an answer but un-looped the bag and without more ado looked inside. Flaming cheek, Charlee thought, but smiled sweetly - had she left her manners on the Russian Steppes along with her impoverished background? Markova was checking out the stitching with all the thoroughness of a customs officer looking for drugs. 'Is real deal,' she declared and gave Charlee a beatific smile, admitting her into their circle. 'Cartier,' she pulled out the cigarette case and lighter and showed the other models who cooed over it. They spoke in rapid Russian and Charlee gleaned that they loved vintage but it cost too much, even on their wages. 'Lucky girr-ll.' She passed the bag and the cigarette case round her girlfriends. 'Your man buy this?' she asked directly, slanting Charlee an envious look.

'Oh nawr,' Charlee affected an upper-class drawl, 'It belongs to Mummy.' She thought about her man sitting not so many metres away, watching, taking photos and no doubt getting ready to mark her performance out of ten. Low marks, like Craig Revel Horwood in *Strictly* - a big, fat five probably. They returned the bag and cigarette case back to her and the phone on the table rang. Smiling apologetically, she reached for it.

'Darling, we were just talking about yow,' she said, in an accent no one had used for at least fifty years. Not even the Queen.

'Okay, you've got what we need …'

'But darling, I don't want to come home just yet,' she protested, and laughed one of those tinkling laughs she'd read about in novels. 'Don't send the chauffeur round for me, sweetie, I'm going back in for a nightcap.'

'Montague, you've done well, don't overplay your hand.' Charlee pulled a petulant expression and gave a large sigh.

'Honestly, sweetie, you can be such a party pooper.' She turned towards the models who were openly listening to her conversation, no doubt hoping to improve their English. 'He's such a pain in the a-r-s-e,' she spelled out, pointing at her own derriere. 'But he loves me to bits! Can't wait to marry me. But I'm in no hurry to get tied down, or have babies,' she informed them, pulling a face. Nodding sagely, they stubbed out their cigarettes and made their way back towards the nightclub.

Anastasia Markova turned. 'Get married soon. Looks fade. Men change, grow cold. You join us for drink? It is my hen's nights.' She smiled uncertainly at Charlee, looking like a child in the playground, anxious to make a new friend.

'Of course. Go ahead, I'll just finish talking to my fiancé and join you.'

Her fiancé in the skip was less than impressed. 'Don't even think it Montague. Wait until they've left and then make your way down the alley and towards the camper van. Don't glance at the skip - wait in the street for me, and don't forget the bloody phone …'

'Relax, darling, remember your blood pressure,' she said sweetly before cutting him off. The models walked back into the nightclub as graceful as borzois. She waited until the door closed and then made her way down the alley and into the side street towards Ffinch's camper van - the theme from *Mission Impossible* playing in her head.

Move over Ethan Hawke - there's a new kid on the block.

Chapter Twelve
Hand Over the Phone, Ma'am, and No One Gets Hurt

F ive minutes later, Ffinch joined her by the camper van carrying his camera case and the Waitrose bags.

'Here,' he said shortly, shoving them into her arms while he fumbled with the keys. 'In, Montague.' He climbed up into the driver's seat, drumming his fingers impatiently on the steering wheel while Charlee put the bags behind the passenger seat and fastened her seat belt. 'Right?'

'Right,' she replied in equal tones.

She let out a sigh of anger and frustration; if she'd been expecting a pat on the back for a job well done, it obviously wouldn't be forthcoming. Somewhat randomly, she remembered a documentary about how the birth pill had passed through millions of women's kidneys and into the water supply overloading it with oestrogen. It must be true, she thought, because Ffinch manifested all the classic symptoms of PMT - mood swings, irritability and signs of depression. As for bloating - if anything he was too thin and looked like he could gain a couple of stones in weight without losing his chiselled features and appealing physique.

She gave a huff of annoyance when it became apparent that he had nothing to say to her. Folding her arms tightly across her chest, she stared moodily into the traffic and worked herself up into a strop.

'That was well done, Charlee. I couldn't have managed without you, Charlee. You are destined for great things, Charlee,' she mocked. But he concentrated on the road ahead and ignored her.

'It wasn't well done, as you put it,' he finally snapped back. 'You put the whole mission at risk with your ridiculous play-acting. "He loves me to bits. Can't wait to marry me". What was that all about?'

'Just staying in role, Ffinch, just staying in role. And it worked, didn't it? Another couple of minutes and we'd have been BFFs,' she said, goading him. This was a game she excelled at. Her brothers might have been able to wrestle her to the ground but, verbally, she could tie them in knots.

'BF - what's?' he demanded. He narrowly missed a cyclist as he turned sideways to look at her. The cyclist gave them the bird and snarled something that didn't quite fit under the heading: festive greetings.

'Best Friends Forever,' she explained and gave him a severe look. 'Don't you think it's about time you got down with the kids, Ffinch? You're only about - what - thirty? Yet you act like an old man.'

'Sorry if I don't go round behaving like Pollyanna on crack cocaine every minute of the day,' he snarled back. 'Time spent in your company, Montague, is exhausting.'

'Well, time spent in your company is - depressing. Lighten up for God's sake ...'

'By the same token, I might ask you to tone it down. Maybe I have things on my mind; things to sort out - that you know nothing about, Montague.'

'Yeah, yeah - spare me the wounded hero act, cos I ain't impressed.' Charlee knew she had to say her piece even if it meant she'd never accompany him on another assignment. Judging by his grim expression, no one had spoken to him like this in many a long year. 'You have a foul temper, but you're not taking it out on me. Not after I've done everything you asked and the mission is a success. Bastard,' she muttered under her breath, tossing the evening bag into the back of the camper van. It hit the quilted side panels with a resounding thunk. Sod his vintage Chanel - and sod him, too.

After the exchange of pleasantries, they remained silent and lost in thought as London decked out in all its Christmas finery slipped past them. Soon they were outside Charlee's bedsit and she was slamming the door of the van behind her with scant regard for its provenance. Leaving the two bags of food in the van - she hoped it would go mouldy and give him a gippy tummy over Christmas - she headed for the front door. As she searched for the key in her handbag, she heard the camper van door open and close and then Ffinch was by her side. She turned round to face him, her back pressed against the door, waiting for his apology.

'Phone,' he said shortly. He held out his hand, making it plain he believed she'd deliberately held onto the phone to gain leverage. She slapped it into the palm of his outstretched hand like she was glad to be shot of it - and him. 'Thanks,' he managed, as if at last remembering his manners and the fact he was the experienced partner, she was the rookie and deserved some praise.

'No problem,' she snarled, glaring at him under the porch light. When he made no attempt to leave, she looked him up and down. 'Was there something else? If you think I'm asking you up for a coffee, think again. As of now I'm on holiday and I don't have to be nice to you.'

'That was you being nice?' he asked, but this time a flash of humour lit up his eyes. He looked down at the iPhone and then back up at Charlee as if realising what they'd accomplished that evening. And that, in some way, their arguing had, fleetingly, proved cathartic and chased away whatever demons haunted his waking hours.

'Believe me, you don't want to see me when I'm really pissed off ...'

'That I can believe,' he butted in, a smile quirking at the corner of his mouth. 'Good work, Montague.'

'No problemo, Ffinch.' Charlee opened the door, walked into the dingy hall and her mood of excitement and euphoria evaporated. She swung back to face him, feeling absurdly as if he'd walked her home after a date and that it would be the most natural thing to lean forward and kiss him.

'Goodnight, Montague.' He made his way towards the camper van shaking his head, as though she took some fathoming out.

'Ffinch?' Charlee called from the door.

'Yes?' He half-turned and looked at her expectantly, clearly believing she was going to apologise for being so confrontational.

'Don't forget to return my flask after the holidays, will you?' With that, Charlee closed the door on his bemused expression. 'Merry Christmas, pardner,' she said softly as she climbed the stairs to her apartment, 'rock beats scissors, every time.'

Church bells ringing the Christmas morning changes seeped into Charlee's subconscious and she dreamed she was walking out of the village church on the arm of the man she loved. Then, as always happened in this recurring dream, she looked up at her new husband only to discover that he had no face. Her moment of complete, sublime happiness evaporated and she was fully awake, heart pounding and with a hollow feeling, as if all the love and happiness had been scoured out of her. She longed to fall back into sleep, to recapture the high, which was so intense it was a wrench to wake from it.

But her mother had other ideas.

'Char-lotte.' She knocked on the bedroom door, entered and drew back the curtains with an exaggerated sigh. 'It's Christmas morning; I hope you're not going to lie in bed all day.'

Johnny Depp - in full *Pirates of the Caribbean* mode looked down from the wall, his gorgeous brown eyes rimmed with kohl. Charlee had had many an angst-ridden conversation with Cap'n Jack during her teenage years, but he'd never once come up with a practical solution to the problem that was her mother. Time he was taken down off the wall and she arranged her bedroom into something more befitting her age and status as a working woman.

'Cut me some slack, Mum, I didn't arrive until after three this morning. I've been on a very important assignment with an award-winning journalist.' Charlee quickly dismissed the memory of their argument on her doorstep. She sat up in bed, her unruly mop of blonde hair sticking up at all angles and last night's make-up smeared across the pillow. She'd been so exhausted after arriving home in Berkshire that she'd parked her Mini under the carport and fallen straight into bed without brushing her teeth or removing her war paint.

'That's no excuse arriving so late,' her mother remonstrated, dismissing Charlee's very important assignment with an award-winning journalist as if it was no more than a trip to the supermarket. 'So, let's have you downstairs, everyone's waiting to open their presents. Slip on your dressing gown, no time for anything else. You can get dressed afterwards. Miranda's making breakfast.'

At the mention of her son's wife, Barbara Montague smiled. Charlee groaned, crossed herself underneath the duvet and irreverently paraphrased the scriptures: This is my beloved daughter-in-law in whom I am well pleased. She wasn't looking forward to spending Christmas with her brother, George, or his bloody wife. Time spent in their company would be a further affirmation of how marvellous they were at ... well, just about everything. What high achievers the Montagues were in general and how hopeless she appeared by comparison, despite her academic achievements.

'A double first is so much easier to achieve these days,' her brothers had informed matter of factly when her results were in. 'And of course, your Uni isn't even in the Russell Group, let alone the top five ... you'll find it hard to get a job as a researcher or a translator in a top-notch establishment with those credentials.'

But Charlee had never wanted to be a researcher, or, as her mother kept suggesting, a language teacher. She wanted excitement, the thrill of the chase - like last night, only with more danger. And perhaps, not sharing a skip with a bad-tempered journo such as Ffinch.

'Are you listening to me, Charlotte?'

'Yes, Mum,' Charlee dragged herself out of another daydream. Why, she wondered, were dreams so much more satisfying than real life?

'Well, downstairs with you. Quickly now.' Her mother spoke to her like she was a teenager and not a grown woman of almost twenty-four.

After her mother closed the door, Charlee scurried round pulling on an ancient dressing gown that was way too short for her and searched for her slippers. She'd left her presents in the hall last night and, as was family tradition, her father would have put them under the tree in the sitting room. She'd also noticed that the house was fully trimmed for Christmas; that was usually her job. But, clearly, those days were over. Miranda had usurped her position as daughter-of-the-house and she and Barbara had decked the hall with boughs of holly without Charlee's help.

'Tra-la-flippin'-la,' she said, in front of the mirror. She attempted to rub some of the blue eyeliner from under her eyes and rake a comb through her uncooperative thatch of hair. She stuck out her tongue; it was white and coated and unattractive. She grimaced, she looked a total wreck but maybe there was time for her to brush her teeth …

'Charl-ee,' her father called from the foot of the stairs.

'The world's not going to come to an end and the four horsemen of the apocalypse come galloping across the lawn if I keep Miranda's egg en cocotte waiting. Is it?' she asked Cap'n Jack. Slipping on a pair of slippers fashioned like oversized cows' heads, Charlee squirted herself with perfume and made her way downstairs. She was still buzzing from last night's mission and was desperate to ring Poppy and talk it over, but she wouldn't see Poppy until tomorrow evening when the Montagues and the Walkers met up for Christmas drinks.

Crossing the large, square hall, Charlee entered the farmhouse kitchen to find Miranda stationed by the Aga serving some ghastly vegetarian, low-fat version of the 'full English' to an adoring George.

Charlee's other three brothers weren't expected until just before lunch and she was glad of it - Miranda's health food kick would put a damper on everyone's Christmas.

'Quorn sausage, Charlotte?' Miranda waved a spatula in Charlee's direction with missionary zeal. 'George and I are vegans now,' she informed her parents-in-law. 'I do hope that doesn't affect Christmas lunch? If so, we're quite happy to eat the vegetables, as long as they haven't been cooked in goose fat. And, of course, no Christmas pudding, eh, Georgie. Suet,' she explained to her mother-in-law and patted her flat stomach.

For a moment, George's besotted smile slipped and he looked quite glum. He loved his food and Charlee could have sworn he looked longingly at the dog's bowl, which was full of leftovers from the Montagues' Christmas Eve roast dinner. She hid a smile and poured herself a coffee. George had married Miranda for her family connections and to further his ambition of becoming an MP. She rather suspected that Miranda had given him a hair shirt as a wedding present and he'd been forced to wear it ever since.

'We're hoping to get pregnant very soon and a healthy diet will aid George's sperm count,' Miranda informed as she took her place at the table. 'We want good, strong swimmers, don't we Georgie?' Charlee's father winced, and she imagined little spermatozoa in stripy Edwardian bathing costumes and mob caps, coated in goose fat, preparing to swim the gynaecological equivalent of the English Channel.

'Quite,' was all Henry Montague managed and then changed the subject, 'So, Charlotte - what were you up to last night? Hanging with your friends?' He used the word like he'd just plucked it from a well-thumbed copy of the English Jive Talking dictionary.

'Actually,' Charlee said, and waved her toast at them. 'I was on a stake-out ...'

'A stake-out,' George mocked. 'In the real world or in Charlotte World?'

'I was this far away from a certain member of the royal family ...'

She ignored the put-down and demonstrated the distance with her hands. 'But if you're not interested, it's your loss not mine.'

'Royal family?' Miranda squawked. 'Not Prince ...' she pointed at a photograph on the front page of the *Telegraph*.

'One and the same.' Charlee realised that she was being too free with her information and tapped the side of her nose, knowingly. 'Better not say any more. My partner,' this time she crossed her fingers behind her back, 'wouldn't like it.'

'Well, that's a good thing, Charlotte,' her father observed. 'If this partner of yours teaches you restraint then working for Sam Walker won't be a complete disaster.' The rest of Charlee's family nodded wisely, but instead of coming back at them in her usual confrontational style, Charlee sent them a Mona Lisa smile. They'd all be singing from a different hymn sheet when they saw her by-line in *What'cha!* in a few weeks' time. Accompanied, maybe, by a head and shoulders shot of Charlee Montague: budding journalist.

'Surely Poppy Walker isn't your partner?' George observed. 'The girl's just filling in time until she bags herself a rich husband who'll fund her horse habit,' he explained to Miranda.

'She snorts cocaine?' Miranda asked, surprising them all by knowing the street name for the drug.

'No-oh, Miranda, horses - plural; animals with a leg at each corner. Used in eventing?' Charlee flashed George a *do you really know what you've married* look. Miranda blushed and said no more and, for a moment, Charlee felt guilty for bating her; she was easy prey. Then she remembered the number of times Miranda had brought up the subject of her lack of career prospects, and/or a 'serious boyfriend'.

'I don't suppose,' Charlee began, turning innocent blue eyes on Miranda and George, 'you'll be attending the Boxing Day meet at the Walkers. With your being vegan, I mean.' Conflicting emotions crossed their faces: disapproval at blood sports, but an awareness that most of the best families in Berkshire, and potential political sponsors, would be attending the meet.

'Well, it would be rude not to,' Miranda answered for her husband. 'We will have to compromise our principles, for George's career,' she sighed, as though she was making a great sacrifice.

'We will all be there - as usual,' Henry Montague said, making plain this wasn't up for debate. 'Charlee - and the boys, too, when they arrive. Folly Foot Stud keeps my practice afloat. Apart from which, the Walkers are old friends ...' he growled, and poked his vegan sausage around the plate as if it were radioactive. 'Barbara, could you please cook me some bacon?' he asked in despair.

'At least they follow an aniseed trail nowadays and there isn't a kill at the end of it,' Miranda observed, as though justifying the whole idea of hunting with hounds to herself.

'Not what the sabs say,' Charlee said. Perhaps sensing the undercurrent, Henry Montague suggested that they each open one present while they waited for the other Montagues to arrive.

'Good idea, darling,' his wife concurred. 'Charlotte. Fetch them from the sitting room and we can open them at the breakfast table.' As she crossed the hall, Charlee muttered that it was time they stopped using her as the family gopher. She was a grown woman with a burgeoning career. What part of that didn't they get?

She returned with the presents and experienced a slight twinge of guilt as George ripped back the paper to reveal a copy of Ffinch's award-winning tome. The very copy Ffinch had given to her the night of the award ceremony. Then she relaxed. Ffinch would never know that his book had been recycled, would he? She didn't feel quite so guilty when Miranda and George handed her mother, father and herself an envelope, explaining that they wouldn't be giving presents this year. They would be donating money to worthwhile causes in their names, instead.

'Typical,' Charlee heard her father mutter under his breath and they exchanged a conspiratorial look across the table. As a vet, he had raised thousands in his practice for worthwhile causes and didn't appreciate a share in a cow in some Indian village as a Christmas present. He'd been hoping for a bottle of ten-year-old malt whisky.

'Is it like a pantomime cow, George? Do I have the front half or the back half?' Charlee asked, looking at the gift card. 'Perhaps Daddy and I have shares in two different cows. Is that how it works?' Barbara Montague sent her a reproving look.

'Well, thank you for the book, Charlee. I've wanted to read this for ages.' George's resigned expression acknowledged that Charlee and his father would be ribbing him for months to come over their shared cow. 'Fonseca-Ffinch, quite an adventurer,' he turned the frontispiece over. 'And signed, too. Do you know him, Charlee?'

In the past, Charlee would have blurted out the whole story of their meeting; how she'd spent Christmas Eve in a skip with a man everyone rated - apart from her - but she now kept quiet.

'Sort of.' Then she handed her mother the pashmina she'd bought for Christmas. And waited ... she knew what was coming, and steeled herself for each hurtful word.

'Thank you, Charlotte, but it's not quite my colour. Have you kept the receipt? Ah, it's from Harvey Nick's, I'll exchange for something more suitable next time I'm in town.' And with that, the present was put back in its tissue paper and left discarded on the large welsh dresser. Thanks, Mum, Charlee thought silently but maintained a stiff smile. It was the same every year; no present she ever bought remained unchanged for long. Sometimes she thought that a gift voucher would do just as well and save them both time and effort.

'I think it would suit you very well, Barbara,' her father put in, giving Charlee an affectionate look. Charlee shrugged away the hurt and handed her father a soft, cashmere scarf.

Where, once, her mother's indifference and open preference for her sons had had the power to wound - now it no longer mattered. Charlee's skin (and her heart) had hardened over the years and now the barbs bounced off, almost painlessly. Knowing that her mother had suffered badly with postnatal depression after her difficult birth and that they'd never bonded, held no water with Charlee. It was all so long ago, but somehow Barbara Montague could not forgive her daughter for putting her through the hell.

Charlee started as the Victorian doorbell, worked by a series of pulleys and levers and with its own distinct sound, rang out over the kitchen door.

'Who can that be?' Henry Montague wondered. Charlee was glad that she looked too disreputable to welcome a visitor and returned to her coffee. Her father closed the kitchen door behind him and muffled male voices were heard in the hall.

The kitchen door was pushed open and her father returned with a visitor.

'Charlotte; a work colleague - for you.'

'Work colleague?' Charlee licked marmalade off her fingers. 'Who?' When Henry brought the unexpected guest into the kitchen, Charlee leapt to her feet, galvanised. 'Ff - Ffinch. What are you doing here?'

Fonseca-Ffinch's gaze swept the room, taking in the family gathering, the copy of his book lying half out of its wrapping paper, and gave Charlee one of his knowing half-smiles. It was obvious that she'd recycled his gift and offering him a quarter share in a sacred cow wouldn't go even part way to repairing this new rent in their partnership.

'Merry Christmas, Mr and Mrs Montague,' he greeted courteously, nodding towards Barbara, George and Miranda. 'I'm sorry to call unannounced on Christmas morning but I need an urgent word with Charlee.'

'Oh my God,' Miranda exclaimed. 'You're him, I mean he - I mean Rafa Ffinch, the author ... of this book.' She held it up so the family could see Rafa's portrait on the back cover. 'You need to speak to Charlotte?' she asked incredulously and they all turned to look at Charlee like she'd sprouted horns and a tail. 'George is a prospective parliamentary candidate, I'm sure that -'

'I'm sure of it, too,' Ffinch said in a conciliatory voice that didn't fool Charlee for a second. 'But unless George speaks Russian ...' He shrugged and looked admiringly in Charlee's direction. 'He wouldn't really be of much help. It's Charlee or no one I'm afraid.' He pressed his lips together.

'Of course,' Barbara and Miranda almost fell over themselves in their eagerness to push Charlee forward. Ffinch, looking every inch the go-to photojournalist in black jeans, boots, scarf and vintage flying jacket, turned back to Charlee. His slow sweep of her made her blush to the roots of her hair. He did a double take when he saw the cows' head slippers and, lips twitching with ironic amusement, he coughed and brought himself under control.

'Merry Christmas, Charlee ... nice slippers.'

Charlee looked down at the threadbare cow's heads and then back at Ffinch. The last time she'd seen him she'd been wearing her LBD, sheer hold-ups and five-inch heels. She could tell he was thinking - who is the real Charlotte Montague; the rebel without a cause, the up for anything rookie journo, or the grown woman wearing night attire from her teenage years?

'What do you want?' she hissed at him, pulling down her pyjama jacket while her family burbled on, innocent of the atmosphere between them.

'A word.'

'It'd better be a good one. It's Christmas morning and as I told you last night, I'm on holiday,' she said, fiercely. 'And before you tell me that a good journalist never sleeps and the news waits for neither tide nor time, let me remind you that this is my home and I didn't invite you in.'

'Perhaps,' her father intervened, 'you would like some breakfast and a cup of coffee, Mr Fonseca-Ffinch ...'

'Ffinch; please,' Rafa smiled at Henry Montague.

'... that would give Charlotte a moment to have a shower and get changed?' And get in a better mood, his censorious look implied.

'Of course,' Ffinch nodded and sat down at the table, pushing his book to one side while the women fussed around him. Half-turning in his chair he said, 'Don't take too long ... partner, I'll be waiting.'

Chapter Thirteen
Speak Russian to Me

Charlee showered in record time, pulled on a pair of skinny jeans and a big shirt, slapped on some war paint and searched round for her shoes. She remembered kicking them off in the hall last night so, in lieu of anything better being at hand, slipped on the cow's head slippers and was back in the kitchen before Ffinch was on his second mince pie. Clearly, he was a big hit with her family because they all protested when he left the table. At Henry Montague's suggestion, Charlee led the way across the hall and into his study to continue their conversation in private.

Charlee shut the door behind them and then rounded on Ffinch.

'What do you want?' she demanded, dropping any pretence of civility.

'And a Merry Christmas to you, too, Montague. Okay - I can see that you're not in the mood for pleasantries, so down to business. I'm returning your flask because you seemed quite attached to it last night. And I can see why.' Putting his leather messenger bag on the floor he pulled out a flask covered in Mutant Ninja Turtles. 'Family heirloom?'

Charlee knew she had to explain quickly, otherwise he'd have the upper hand once more. 'If you recall, you were most insistent I bring a flask of coffee on our stake-out. Mr Hansrani who runs the corner shop didn't have any flasks for sale. And, so, to help me out, he loaned me the one from his son's lunch box. Okay? I don't really own a Ninja Turtle flask. What do you take me for?'

'The kind of woman who wears massive slippers shaped like a cow's head?' he suggested. Charlee suspected he enjoyed needling her, but it was hard to know for certain because he was poker-faced and giving nothing away.

'Those are my old slippers, from before I went up to university. So you can stop being so amused at my expense. And, anyhow, I don't have to justify myself to you, Ffinch. Just tell me what you want and then I can get back to my Christmas breakfast.'

Finch folded his arms, tilted his head on one side and gave her a searching look. 'I know I warned you not to go all mushy on me Montague,' he observed wryly. 'But you needn't take it to the other extreme. Anyone would think you didn't like me.'

Charlee chose not to answer that, but her silence spoke volumes. 'What does my opinion of you matter either way? You made it perfectly clear last night that I almost ruined the mission by going off-piste, couldn't wait to get your phone back and didn't even bother to thank me for a job well done.'

'But I did thank you …' Ffinch put in, moving round to her father's desk and making himself comfortable in Henry's swivel chair. Then he started rotating slowly, annoyingly, and very much at his ease.

'Yes, you did. Ironically. Sarcastically. Pollyanna on crack cocaine is how you described me,' Charlee reminded him.

'I think at one point you told me to lighten up? That wasn't polite or friendly, now was it?' Almost absent-mindedly, he started to rearrange her father's fly-fishing equipment on the desk. Charlee walked over to the desk, put her hands flat on the top of it, leaned forward and gave him a 'don't bullshit me' straight look.

'Okay, Ffinch. The truth. Why are you here? Today of all days.'

He got up from the chair and moved over to the window where he stared over the ha-ha and towards the Berkshire downs. Then he turned round, put the iPhone on the table next to the window and pressed the voice recorder app. Charlee listened to a reprise of the models speaking Russian and then their discussion about the vintage evening bag. At the end of the conversation, Ffinch stopped the recording.

'So?' Charlee asked.

'Do I need to spell it out?'

'Apparently,' Charlee responded and waited for an explanation. She did not intend to make this easy for him - seemingly, he needed her help. Needed it badly enough to turn up unannounced and uninvited at her family home. He must be pretty keen to learn what was on the phone …

'I don't speak Russian.'

There. He'd said it!

'However, I do? And you'd like a translation?' She couldn't resist a triumphant smirk, knowing what it must have cost him to come here on Christmas morning and ask for her help. 'Why is it so important?' she asked, taking a step back and looking at him suspiciously.

'You don't need to know that.'

'Oh, I think I do.' Ffinch looked at her for several long moments, his expression suggesting that he would be giving Sam Walker a less than flattering account of her.

'Very well, you tell me what they said and I'll tell you why it's important.'

'Partners?' she asked, holding out her hand.

'Partners …' Ffinch repeated under his breath, as if the word transported him to a place and time a world away from Berkshire on a frosty Christmas morning. He no longer seemed aware of her presence. The colour had drained from his face, leaving him pale, wan and with the look of a man recovering from a long illness. Or, from an experience he couldn't - wouldn't - share with her. Standing quietly, Charlee tried to get the measure of him, to work out the reason behind his sadness.

'Partners?' she persisted, holding out her hand to shake on the deal.

With a visible effort, Ffinch pulled himself back into the room.

'Partners,' he conceded. Then, quite unexpectedly, he took her hand in both of his and held on to it, giving Charlee the impression that he drew some kind of emotional strength from the physical contact. Before she had time to give the idea further thought, he snapped out of his reverie and sent her a lopsided smile that didn't quite marry up with the darkness behind his eyes. 'Although, I'd say that someone who owns cow's head slippers and a Ninja Turtle flask is hardly in a position to make any kinds of demands.'

'Montague and Ffinch,' Charlee couldn't resist going the extra mile. 'It has a certain ring to it.' She gasped as he tightened his grip on her hand, pulled her towards him and held her close. Remembering her response when he'd stood behind her in Sam Walker's office looking into the mirror and she'd almost made a fool of herself, Charlee tried to pull free. Her heart was beating like a mad thing, her breath had caught in her throat and she was blushing like a schoolgirl.

The very epitome of mushy.

'Montague and Ffinch? Don't. Push. It. Montague,' he growled with mock-ferocity and then released her. 'Translate, now.'

'Okay, okay. No need for the *King Kong* routine,' she protested, flexing her fingers as though he'd crushed them during the handshake. 'You're the alpha male, the pack leader, I get it. Okay? But what they discussed is so insignificant, I think you're going to be majorly disappointed.'

'Let me be the judge of that.'

Sending him a defiant look, Charlee did as asked. 'Anastasia and her bridesmaids have checked into a boot camp for brides in just over three weeks to lose weight and get toned for the wedding. Although there isn't a spare ounce of fat on any of them. She probably weighs as much as my left leg.' When he didn't laugh at her self-deprecating joke, Charlee felt rather deflated. This could turn out to be a very short-lived partnership she reflected as she switched off the voice recorder and handed the phone to him.

'Boot camp for brides? Is that it, nothing else? '

'She mentioned her fiancé, that Russian financier Yevgeny Trushev and how she could have anything she wanted, no expense spared. Then they all admired her diamond ring, which was practically a supernova, and talked about girly things.'

'Hmm,' Ffinch returned to staring moodily out of the window. 'Girly things?' he persisted, jangling loose change in his jeans pocket.

'Yes, like she'd wanted to book into a boot camp nearer London for the weekend, but her fiancé insisted on booking her into one in Norfolk … near Brancaster, or Thornham; somewhere like that.'

'Norfolk?' He whipped round, looking suddenly very interested. 'Are you sure?'

'Of course I'm sure,' Charlee snapped back. 'Anastasia pronounced it Nor-fol-k. I thought it was rather sweet at the time and … What is it?' Her antennae had started to twitch. Judging from Ffinch's expression he was onto something, although why a boot camp on the edge of the Norfolk marshes should interest him wasn't clear.

'Nothing, it doesn't matter,' he responded, the shutters coming down. Charlee felt the bonds of their partnership straining before they'd been tested under fire. 'You look disappointed - did you think there was more to it? That you'd be working under cover like a latter-day Miss Marple?' he asked with unwarranted harshness.

'Yes, only sixty years younger and with better clothes,' Charlee snapped back to cover her disappointment. That's exactly what she had thought; now all her hopes and dreams had turned to dust. Story of her life …

'This was a simple mission and you've fulfilled the brief - there's no need for me to monopolise any more of your valuable time.' Ffinch put the iPhone in his messenger bag and then slung it across his body. 'Thanks, Montague, you've been a great help - see, I remembered to thank you properly this time. And look on the positive side, you've proved to your family - and Sam - that you've got what it takes to make it as a journalist.'

'You don't know anything about me or my family, so spare me the amateur psychology. And as for Sam, I think he already knows my worth otherwise he wouldn't have chosen me for this investigation. So don't patronise me - you, you ...' Charlee couldn't bring herself to use an expletive on Christmas morning and settled instead for pointing towards the door like a gothic heroine dismissing an unworthy suitor. 'There's the door - I suggest you use it. Partner.'

He crossed the study and paused briefly with his hand on the door-knob. His eloquent look made it clear he wanted to say more but was deterred by her uncompromising expression.

'Go back to your family and wish them Merry Christmas from me, Montague. I'll see myself out.'

Chapter Fourteen
I Didn't Know You Cared

Momentarily, Charlee was rooted to the spot. But once the front door closed, she unglued her feet from the carpet and ran across the hall to watch Ffinch's camper van spin the gravel and zoom off down the lane.

Just who did he think he was? Some second-rate cognitive behavioural therapist dishing out strategies to help her deal with her family and move herself forward? Maybe he should concentrate on confronting whatever demons haunted him instead of giving her advice and tossing platitudes around. Demons! With a flash of insight, she wondered if his sudden interest in brides, boot camps and Norfolk was in some way connected to what had happened in Colombia.

Damn! Now she'd never know; she'd given him everything without gaining any guarantees she'd have further involvement in the story.

'Charlotte Montague, Ffinch has played you for a fool,' she berated herself.

Instead of returning to the kitchen, she went back into the study, flicked on the iPad and logged onto Google Earth. Typing Thornham, Norfolk, in the search bar, she waited as the app loaded and then zoomed in on the topography. Thornham appeared as a village divided by a road and surrounded for the most part by cultivated fields. The larger portion of the village lay to the right of the road and beyond that there was the blue-green expanse of the sea. Pinching the image between her thumb and fingers Charlee rotated the view through one hundred and eighty degrees and homed in on Thornham Beach. In front of the beach lay marshes, mudflats and sandbanks. The satellite had obviously taken the photograph at low tide and in high summer because tiny boats leaned against the bank of the creek waiting for the tide to turn and take them out to sea.

The whole place looked wild, abandoned and yet at the same time, unremarkable.

Unremarkable?

Charlee moved the image around and located Thornham Boot Camp for Brides. To the unpractised eye, it looked like any other large manor house set back from the road and surrounded on three sides by trees. The marshes butted right up to the other side of the property and a couple of small boats, moored by a large boathouse, were visible.

Charlee frowned. What wasn't she seeing?

There had to be something more; something that had made Ffinch light up with excitement when she'd mentioned Norfolk. On impulse, she typed Boot Camp for Brides + Thornham into the browser bar and a website opened up. One shot showed Amazonian women in fatigues and baseball caps trudging through the wooded area that led to the marshes. In another, a blushing bride gazed dewily at her hand tied bouquet of lilies and roses.

'Get rid of bloated tum, fat arms and chubby back,' it read. 'Enhance your pelvic floor muscles in anticipation of THE BIG DAY - Learn how to cope with the mother-in- law.' Charlee'd settle for learning how to cope with her mother! She read on and learned that the bride-to-be and her bridesmaids could also participate in aqua-aerobics, morning PT, Fartlek Training and stretcher runs.

Stretcher runs?

'Sounds like they're preparing for war - not their wedding day,' she remarked as she scanned further down the web page. 'And what the hell is Fartlek Training?' Refraining from making the obvious joke, she typed Fartlek Training into the browser bar and discovered that it was Swedish for 'Speed Play'.

'Fartlek,' she read aloud in an accent that was pure Sara Lund from *The Killing*, 'allows you to run whatever distance and speed you wish, varying the pace and occasionally running at high intensity levels.' Sounded like her idea of torture. As far as she was concerned, Fartlek Training, Boot Camps for Brides and everything they entailed, could feck off.

When it was her turn to get married, she'd take off on a long girly weekend with Poppy and a couple of other good mates to some gorgeous spa in Italy - Positano or Portofino, for choice. Relaxation, rude jokes about the wedding night and promises never to let anything break their friendship were more up her strasse. Boot camp brides, Russian models and secretive journos could all go hang, she decided, flipping the protective cover over the iPad.

It was Christmas Day, after all.

And yet, she couldn't let it go.

Why was stick thin Anastasia Markova and her skeletal BFFs so keen to attend the boot camp? They needed to lose weight about as much as a fish needed a bicycle. What was there about this seemingly non-story that made every journalistic instinct she possessed stand to attention? She'd read how divvies in the art and antique world could tell if a painting or object was a fake simply by looking at it. Just imagining what Ffinch was keeping from her sent a shot of adrenalin coursing through her veins, leaving an unsettling echo behind.

The scrunch of tyres on gravel drew her back to the window and her stomach gave an excited lurch; maybe Ffinch had had second thoughts and was returning to renew their partnership. She'd make sure that she pinned him down this time.

She smoothed down her shirt and raked her fingers through her hair. Not that she cared what she looked like; she simply didn't want Ffinch to think for one moment that he'd bested her. She'd play it cool and let him do the running, she decided as she went back in to the hall.

Her whole body slumped when she discovered that, instead of Ffinch, it was the other three Montague brothers Jack, Tom and Wills arriving for Christmas lunch.

Damn Christmas Day and all it entailed. She longed to be back at work snooping around the offices, finding out what was behind Sam and Ffinch's sudden interest in boot camps in Norfolk. However, the next edition of *What'cha!* had been put to bed and was ready to print at the press of a button on January 2nd. Until then, a skeleton staff would man the offices and she had no legitimate reason for calling in without arousing suspicion.

Frowning, she walked back into the kitchen. Something was going down, the divvy in her was sure of it. She deserved to be in on it after everything she'd done. And if Ffinch thought he'd shaken her off, then he'd seriously underestimated her.

After Christmas lunch, the four Montague brothers cleared up and loaded the dishwasher before joining the rest of their family in the sitting room by a roaring log fire. They entered, pushing and jostling for position on the large squashy sofa just as they had done as teenagers. Charlee, relegated to sitting on the padded needlework fender as usual, noted her mother's indulgent expression as she half-heartedly remonstrated with them for their boisterous behaviour.

'Boys. Boys! You'll break something. Henry, tell them,' she commanded her husband who was happily cracking Brazil nuts with an ancient wooden nutcracker.

'Boys, you'll break something. Do you have to revert to childhood every time you come home? You're getting the dogs overexcited; stop before your mother's prophesy comes true.' Barbara Montague cast her eyes up to the heavens as George, Wills and Jack squashed onto the sofa and Tom sat on the other end of the fender to Charlee - rocking it like a seesaw and trying to unseat her.

'So, Charlotte,' Tom began, using her Sunday name. 'Who was that driving down the lane in a classic VW camper van?' He reached across and ruffled her hair. 'Don't tell me young Charlee's got a boyfriend,' he raised an eyebrow and the others laughed.

'Actually,' Charlee said, moving beyond his reach and smoothing her hair. 'It was my partner - in the non-boyfriend sense of the word - if you must know.'

'Non-boyfriend sense of the word?'

'Oo - Charlee's got a partner,' Wills and Jack chorused in camp voices, elbowing each other in the ribs. 'Get 'er.'

'He's Rafael Fonseca-Ffinch,' Miranda put in, seemingly not enjoying Charlee being the focus of the brothers' attention. 'Charlotte has given his bestseller *The Ten Most Dangerous Destinations on the Planet* to George as a Christmas present. Signed, too.' She held the book out so Tom could inspect it.

'Signed?' Tom left his place on the fender to examine the book more closely. 'Do you really know him, Charlee?' he asked, giving his sister a serious, and very uncharacteristic, respectful look.

'Noo-oh. He was lost, drove up to the house to ask for directions and dropped a signed copy of his book - ready-wrapped in Christmas paper and with George's name on the flyleaf - onto the kitchen table. Of course I know him you idiot. Didn't I say we're partners?' Surreptitiously, Charlee crossed her fingers behind her back to counter the lie.

'Ouch, you've grown teeth since you left home, Charlee. Hard-bitten hack these days is it? God, I wish we'd arrived earlier,' Wills, a green activist, said to Tom. 'I would give anything to discuss his journey along the Amazon with him.' Wills spent most of his life trying to conserve the rainforest and prevent governments from clearing it for logging or to raise cattle to provide beefburgers for food chains around the world.

'Wouldn't have done you much good,' Charlee replied, fondling the black lab's ears. 'He refuses to talk about it. I expect he wants you to buy his book instead.'

'Cynical as well as waspish,' Tom put in. 'I'm with Wills on this one. If I remember the story correctly he contracted dengue fever after his team were kidnapped and held to ransom.'

'Yes; I remember now,' trainee vet Jack added. 'Trouble is, the story was in the headlines, briefly, and then sank without a trace - overshadowed by the Queen's Jubilee and then the Olympics.'

'I wonder if he'd consent to giving me some blood samples,' Tom added. A registrar at the Hospital for Tropical Diseases in London, he hoped to become a consultant specialising in parasitic diseases acquired in the tropics. Perhaps an armful of Ffinch's blood would clinch it for him. 'I believe he was treated by an indigenous tribe and hidden from the drug smugglers who patrol the area, before being transferred to a hospital boat. Just thinking about the homeopathic remedies they've tried and tested over the years and which the west knows nothing about, makes me long to go there.'

'They took a great risk helping him,' Wills observed. Charlee was reminded of her crass remarks on the night of the book launch and hoped they'd put her burning face down to the heat of the fire - not shame and mortification.

'It says on the dust jacket that all royalties from the book are being donated to raising funds to help the people who helped him,' Miranda said, clearly not wishing to be excluded from the discussion.

'The Cat People,' Charlee said. 'The Cat People found him on the banks of the Amazon and nursed him back to health.' She vowed to take the iPad upstairs and get up to speed on Ffinch's lucky escape in Darien. She'd always left revising for her exams until the last minute. Now she was in the real world that attitude would have to change ... thoroughness would become her watchword.

'Oh,' Miranda sat bolt upright. 'You don't think he's still infectious, do you? George and I are trying for a family.'

Barbara Montague patted Miranda's arm while the other Montagues rolled their eyes. Miranda had been like a broken record all through

Christmas lunch, banging on about George's parliamentary ambitions, or their reproductive trials and tribulations.

'The disease is transmitted by mosquito, Miranda, so I think it's safe to assume that you're not in any danger,' Henry Montague said dryly. 'Although, naturally, I bow to Tom's superior knowledge in this matter. Charlotte?'

'Yes, Dad?'

'Partners? You haven't mentioned Fonseca-Ffinch before.'

'It's a recent development,' Charlee prevaricated, sensing her father's unease and not wanting to reveal just how recent it was. Or how he'd terminated their partnership earlier in Henry's study.

'Do you think we ought to ask him for dinner? Get to know him better?' Barbara suggested, her look of concentration suggesting that she was already planning menus in her head.

'For goodness sake, Mum! He's a work colleague, that's all - not a potential boyfriend. I really can't say any more at the risk of ruining our scoop.'

The four brothers exchanged another look, one that conveyed Charlee was living in cloud cuckoo land. A rookie and someone as experienced as Rafa Ffinch working together - how likely was that? Catching their look, Charlee stood up and the two Labradors looked at her expectantly.

'Think I'll take the dogs for a W-A-L-K.' Hiding her bruised feelings beneath a bright smile she spelled out the word so the dogs didn't go ballistic. It rankled that her family treated her like she was still in primary school and in danger of losing her sweets to sharper kids in the playground.

'Sit down a minute, Charlotte,' her father forestalled her. 'I'm a little concerned, to be honest. If what Wills says is true, Mr Fonseca-Ffinch ignored Foreign Office advice to give Darien a wide berth due to the risk of kidnap by drugs gangs plying the Amazon.'

'Maybe it was his casual regard for safety which put his team at risk.

Weren't two of them thrown overboard when they became too ill to travel and only Mr Fonseca-Ffinch made it to the shore?' Barbara Montague actually looked concerned for Charlee's welfare. 'Charlotte?'

'Rest assured I - we - won't be travelling the length of the Amazon any time soon.' Charlee looked round at their anxious faces and wondered what was going on. They'd always made her feel the runt of the litter, treating her enthusiasms and projects with: 'Oh, Charlee's chasing rainbows, again,' accompanied by condescending, exasperated smiles. This was the first time in her life she'd been taken seriously, so perhaps she had something to thank Ffinch for after all.

'Sam Walker seems to think he's kosher,' Charlee put in, standing her ground.

'Sam would sell his own grandmother for an exclusive,' Tom said. 'I think we all know that.' He looked to the others for corroboration.

'None of it has anything to do with you, so I'll thank you all to butt out of my life.'

'Charlotte, really, manners. Henry, reason with her,' her mother cut in. Charlee folded her arms across her chest. As far as she was concerned, their concern for her welfare stemmed more from a desire to interfere and control rather than from love. At almost twenty-four years of age she was too old for playing this game, and it was time they knew it.

'Teal, Marley - walkies.' Upon hearing the magic word, the two black labs headed for the kitchen where their leads hung on a hook behind the door.

'You're not going out now, are you Charlotte? You'll miss the Queen's Speech,' her mother protested. 'We always watch it together; it's in 3D this year,' she added, indicating a basket of 3D glasses by way of a clincher.

'I'm going out, because if I stay I'll only end up arguing with you all and spoiling Christmas. This discussion is closed.' She crossed the hall, took down a Barbour from the bentwood coat stand and pushed her feet into a pair of wellingtons. Retrieving their leads from the kitchen, she whistled to the dogs and left the house, heading for Poppy's home, two fields away.

Much to their delight, the labs put up a couple of pheasants and went chasing after them as Charlee trudged across the ridges and furrows of the ploughed field. She could see lights on at the Walkers' and she knew she'd receive a good welcome and a glass of something warming if she turned up uninvited on Christmas Day. She began to relax for the first time that day.

The Walkers and the Montagues had been friends for years and Poppy and Charlee inseparable since nursery school. That was the main reason Charlee hadn't approached Sam, initially, to ask for an internship. She wanted to make her own way and not have everyone say she'd won her position because of family connections. However, after offering to work for no wages at various newspapers and still unable to land a job, Charlee had been glad of Poppy's suggestion that she speak to her father.

And, to be fair, it was no more than Charlee calling in a favour. Indirectly, she must have saved the Walkers thousands of pounds in school fees when, at seven years old, she'd refused to attend boarding school as her brothers had before her. And, Poppy had declared, if Charlee wasn't leaving home, neither was she.

Instead, they'd both been educated at the tiny village school where Barbara Montague was teaching head, before finally transferring to an independent school as day pupils at eleven. Charlee had always felt that her mother's attitude towards her was that of an exasperated teacher towards a bright, but recalcitrant, pupil; big on lectures but short on love. When she'd been in her mother's class, she'd referred to her as Mrs Montague like all the other children and it neatly summed up their distant relationship. Later, as her mother pursued her ambition to become one of Her Majesty's Inspectors of Schools and her father focused on building up his veterinary practice, Charlee had been left to her own devices.

If it hadn't have been for her Montague grandparents, she would have been brought up by a succession of nannies and au pairs. It was ironic, really, now she was on the verge of her big break that the family should close ranks and come over all protective towards her.

Whistling the dogs to heel, she climbed the stile that marked the boundary between the two properties. From her vantage point on top of the stile, she looked down on the Walkers' house fast disappearing in the late December afternoon. It wouldn't be the first time she'd marched out of her home in high dudgeon and gone over to Poppy's house seeking solace, reassurance and a slab of home-made cake.

However, just as she raised one leg to climb down, someone came round the side of the house and set off the Walkers' security lights. There was no mistaking the distinctive navy and white VW camper van parked next to Sam Walker's Range Rover.

'Ffinch!' she exclaimed, her breath snagging as she almost toppled off the stile. 'Why are you still here? What's he up to, boys?' she asked the dogs waiting at her heels. 'Sorry old chaps, change of plan. Home. We've got some thinking to do.'

Chapter Fifteen
A Blooding

After a night spent tossing and turning, trying to guess Ffinch's motives for staying on at the Walkers' when he should have been halfway to his family home in Scotland, Charlee woke up, woolly headed. She knew she was capable of fashioning mountains where previously there had only been molehills - but she couldn't get the picture of Ffinch, snapping to attention when she'd mentioned the boot camp in Norfolk, out of her mind.

Something linked the two events, but what?

Pushing herself out of the warm cocoon of her duvet, Charlee glanced at the iPad on her bedside table. She'd lain awake until well after two o'clock delving into the background of Ffinch, Markova and her shadowy Russian fiancé until the battery had run down. She'd been so enamoured with the idea of being Ffinch's partner that she'd been less than thorough in finding out exactly who he was. But, thanks to the internet, she was now fully up to speed with his backstory. Even if it was an uncorroborated version of it gleaned from several different sources.

And it didn't make for pretty reading.

'Charlotte, Boys, breakfast! Come on, we'll be late for the meet,' her father called from downstairs. It was a familiar scenario, all the Montagues together under one roof and faded posters of Buffy, Cap'n Jack and Aragorn looking down from the bedroom wall. She'd take them down today - she was no more the girl who'd pinned them up there, than Johnny Depp was captain of the Black Pearl.

That thought in mind, she leapt out of bed and headed for the shower.

Later that morning, Tom, Wills and Jack would borrow horses from Daphne Walker's stud and make utter fools of themselves chasing after the hounds across the furrowed fields. As usual, her mother and father would follow the hunt in their Land Rover with Miranda and George.

As for Charlee - she had a quarry of her own to pursue.

Two hours later, Charlee clambered out of her father's Land Rover County, and pushed through hunt followers, villagers, saboteurs and animal rights groups massing at the closed five-bar gate to the Walkers' stud. She'd stopped attending the Boxing Day meet when she was old enough to realise what happened when the dogs caught the fox. However, now the hunt followed an aniseed trail across the countryside, she'd started attending again - much to her family and Poppy Walker's delight. Charlee's philosophy being, if the riders wanted to dress up like something out of a nineteenth-century print and risk their necks over bush and briar that was entirely their affair. Being a spectator was as far as she was willing to go.

It wasn't long before she located Ffinch sitting on the sill of his camper van eating fruit cake and drinking a traditional stirrup cup of port. Like her, he was dressed casually but for warmth - woollen trousers tucked into fur-lined leather boots, a thick jersey, scarf and scuffed flying jacket. The wind ruffled his thick dark hair, which was held off his forehead by a pair of pushed-up Ray-Ban Aviators. The low sun caught the angles of his cheekbones and the line of his nose and mouth - all very photogenic to be sure, Charlee thought, unaffected by the beguiling picture he presented.

She wanted to go up to him, shake him by the lapels of his sheepskin jacket and demand to be told what was going on. Anger fizzed inside her chest like an out of control firework as she made her way over to him.

'Not hunting, Ffinch? I'd've thought chasing a quarry halfway across the county and then moving in for the kill was right up your street.'

Ffinch's slate-grey eyes narrowed and his expression became wary. Charlee sensed that he'd been waiting for her, guessing that she'd show up today after their acrimonious farewell yesterday. And she'd have plenty to say!

'A metaphorical quarry these days, surely,' he said, handing his empty port glass to a waitress and getting to his feet. He sent her another sharp look, evidently sensing her pent-up anger and aware that he was the cause of it. 'I don't ride to hounds,' he pronounced 'hounds' as 'hinds' in a mock upper-class accent. 'To be honest, it's all too *Downton Abbey* for my tastes.'

He dropped the Ray-Bans over his eyes as protection against the low sun glittering over the frost-rimed fields - and, Charlee suspected, to hide his expression. Standing with one foot on the VW's sill and with his head turned slightly to the left so his face was in profile, he looked quite the man. Charlee harboured the uncharitable suspicion that he was aware of just how good he looked and wanted to ensure that he stood out among the red-coated huntsmen. Much to her annoyance, he managed to look more macho than any of them, in spite of the fact they looked like they'd stepped out of the Cecil Aldin print: *A Hunting We Will Go.*

'*Downton Abbey*?' She gave a derisive 'I'm so not impressed by your posturing' snort. She'd spent her life surrounded by handsome, photogenic men - it would take more than dark good looks and a high opinion of oneself to float her boat. Hearing her contemptuous snort, Ffinch turned towards her, unsmiling, very much aware that her displeasure was nothing to do with his reference to *Downton Abbey* but everything to do with how he'd walked out on her yesterday. He gave her a long look as if her unpredictable temperament gave him pause for thought and made him aware he'd have to proceed with care.

He came over, his body language suggesting there was something he had to say to her - something for her ears only. But he couldn't have a private conversation with her without appearing to whisper in her ear, and she guessed that was too intimate given the way things stood between them. Instead, they stood side by side watching the local vicar, wearing a surplice over his hunting gear, bless the hounds and wish the riders safe passage over the hedges and fields.

'More Jilly Cooper than *Downton Abbey*, I'd say.' Charlee said, more from a desire to fill in the awkward silence stretching out between them than to be sociable.

Huntsmen and women in black or red jackets bent down from their saddles, handed their empty glasses to waitresses bearing silver trays and brushed crumbs from their breeches. Poppy Walker, looking gorgeous in full riding gear and with her hair tidied away in a net, waved her crop at them. Charlee waved back and Ffinch gave one of his sardonic smiles, though what was so amusing she couldn't imagine. From what she'd learned of his background last night - he came from an Anglo-Brazilian family of coffee growers who'd used their money and influence to move into politics - he was used to mixing in the higher echelons of society and she guessed this wasn't the first Boxing Day meet he'd attended.

Following his line of sight Charlee soon discovered the source of his amusement: her brothers - looking undeniably handsome in hunting gear, examining their borrowed horses' girths and stirrups and tapping their whips against their boots - anxious to be off.

'Do you have to look a dead spit for Rupert Penry-Jones to be a member of your family?' Finch asked as her brothers exchanged a collective purposeful look and walked over to them. 'Do you think I'm in danger of being beaten by the Ruperts?' He leaned against the camper van in a relaxed attitude as though he found the whole idea ludicrous. 'You know, I was wrong when I said your brothers were the male equivalent of Cinderella's ugly stepsisters.'

'You were?' Charlee braced herself for the killer punch line.

'Yes, they're more like an illustration from a history primer I had at prep school. Pope Gregory seeing Anglo-Saxon children in the slave market in Rome and commenting: "Not Angles, but angels." That's what your brothers put me in mind of - although, I'd imagine all that blonde magnificence gets rather tedious after a time.'

Charlee raised a hand to her blonde hair and gave his naturally olive skin and dark hair a severe look. Then she caught the gleam in his eyes and realised he was enjoying himself. What was behind his uncharacteristic buoyant mood, she wondered? Perhaps now would be a good time to ask some pertinent questions about what the big deal was with Anastasia Markova and Norfolk - and what, if any, part she had left to play in it.

He owed her that at least.

'I hope you'll have time to introduce me to the Ruperts before they beat me to a pulp for whatever they think it is I've done to their little sister.'

'Shut it Ffinch. I'm not their little sister any longer and I don't do what they - or you - tell me to.'

'I had noticed,' Ffinch remarked sardonically as the Montagues reached them.

'Everything all right, Charlee?' Jack asked, giving Ffinch a flinty look.

'Why shouldn't it be?' Charlee snapped, making it plain that their concern wasn't necessary or welcome. 'This is Rafael Fonseca-Ffinch,' she began as way of an introduction. 'Jack, Wills and Tom Montague.' The manner in which she fired out their names made it plain that they should get out of her face and back on their horses.

'Jack, Wills, Tom - pleased to make your acquaintance.' The four men shook hands, but Charlee suspected that, if they'd been the hounds milling round the whippers-in, they'd have been circling each other, tails high and teeth on show.

'I gather you're Charlee's partner?' Jack asked Ffinch, looking towards Charlee for corroboration.

'Charlee's partner?' Ffinch hesitated, just long enough to make Charlee squirm. She waited for Ffinch to deny the connection and humiliate her in front of her brothers. Instead, he pushed himself away from the van and put his arm round her shoulder. 'Oh, much more than partners, I'd say - wouldn't you, Carlotta?'

Ffinch's use of Carlotta suggested an intimacy that didn't exist but was enough to put her brothers on alert. He smiled down at her and then whispered seductively in Portuguese: *'Isso limpou o sorriso da cara deles.'*

'Carlotta?' Jack repeated. 'And what does - what has he just said to you? ' Charlee thought it diplomatic not to tell them it translated, roughly, into 'that's taken the smug looks off their faces'. Jack took a menacing step towards Ffinch. 'Are you two -' he baulked at finishing the sentence.

The word HAVING SEX hovered in the air between them.

'You'd better ask Charlee that hadn't you?' Ffinch said, dropping a kiss on the top of her head.

'Charlee?'

'My relationship with Ffinch is professional and has nothing to do with any of you. This is my life and how I conduct it is my affair.' Charlee was glad that the rest of her family were in the Land Rover waiting for the hunt to set off. To have them questioning Ffinch as if he'd robbed her of her virginity would have been too provoking for words. 'Why don't you get on your horses, follow the hounds across the field and make complete idiots of yourselves?'

'Thanks for that, Charlotte,' Wills replied, using her given name. Carlotta, indeed! He tapped his riding crop against his boot like a villain in a B-movie as if he'd like to submit Ffinch to a good horsewhipping. The other two Montagues gave Ffinch and Charlee a more thorough glance. Charlee was desperate to wriggle free of Ffinch's arm but knew she had to maintain the pose until her brothers were on their horses. Then she could round on Ffinch and ask him what the bloody hell he was playing at.

As her brothers were about to walk off, shooting warning looks at Ffinch and 'what have you got yourself into this time' looks at Charlee, the vicar made his way over. Knowing what was coming next, Charlee steeled herself.

'Greetings, Montagues on this fine day. No sign of the Capulets?' He laughed uproariously at his own witticism and then spotted Ffinch with his arm around Charlee's shoulders. He gave them a professional once-over. 'What have we here … Romeo and his Juliet? Most excellent.' He rubbed his hands together and then extended his right hand towards Ffinch.

'Jeremy Trevelyan, pleased to meet you. But please call me the Rev Trev, everyone else does.'

'Rafael Ffinch - without one Capulet gene in his body,' was Ffinch's dry response as they shook hands. The vicar's hearty laugh made heads turn in their direction. Charlee squirmed and felt hot with embarrassment. She hadn't seen her neighbours since the summer and turning up with a new man who had his arm draped over her shoulders in such a proprietary manner would set the tongues wagging.

Ffinch was right - it was too Downton-bloody-Abbey for words.

'Church is getting pretty booked up for the summer, Charlotte,' the vicar came back with another unwanted observation. 'If you lovebirds have a date in mind, don't leave it too late.'

'But, we're not …' Charlee began. Ffinch's arm slipped from her shoulder and snaked round her waist. His grip tightened warningly and Charlee had the sense to say no more, very much aware of her brothers' furious expressions. There would be a family conference tonight when the hunt was over, and she'd be interrogated. Ffinch had better come up with some good reasons for this absurd play-acting.

'We won't, thanks,' Ffinch replied as the vicar stripped off his surplice to reveal full hunting gear, boots and spurs. 'A fox hunting vicar, how very *Tom Jones*. The novel, not the singer,' he added for the benefit of Charlee's brothers - as though he thought them incapable of getting the literary reference. It was clear that they were torn between joining the hunt, which was preparing to move off, and finding out what was going on between Ffinch and Charlee.

'*Tom Jones* - Henry Fielding. Marvellous, simply marvellous,' the vicar butted in, openly pleased at the comparison. 'Come, Montagues, we must away!' he said in a fruity voice as the Master of Foxhounds blew his hunting horn in short, sharp toots and the pack prepared to move off. Left with no other choice the Montague boys followed him.

'I think your vicar has overdosed on P.G. Wodehouse as well as Fielding,' Ffinch bent down and whispered in Charlee's ear with all the tenderness of a lover. 'Wave; smile, that's the way.'

'I think you've overdosed on banned substances,' Charlee said, wriggling out of his grasp the second the hunt and its followers had disappeared behind the high hedges lining the lanes. 'Was that charade just to wind my brothers up - not that I'm adverse to that - or is there method in your madness?'

Ffinch looked at her long and hard, his eyes uncertain - as if he couldn't quite make up his mind how far to take her into his confidence. Charlee read the conflict in his face, knew he couldn't quite bring himself to trust her and was annoyed that it mattered. At the first opportunity, she'd let him know that the feeling was mutual.

'Let's go indoors,' he said, steering her towards the house with his hand in the small of her back. Charlee skidded to a halt like a cartoon character, dug her heels in and waited until he'd removed his hand. 'My God, you're prickly this morning. More so than usual,' he breathed as he shoved his hands into his trouser pockets.

'And with good reason,' she returned, tossing her head like one of the thoroughbreds heading off down the lane. 'I don't know what game you're playing but you can stop your play-acting now, there's no one around to fool or impress.' Her sparky look was designed to remind him she was no pushover.

They entered the Walkers' house and Charlee led the way into the kitchen, the heart of the house. Here she'd wept on Daphne Walker's shoulder - in lieu of her mother's - when at the tender age of thirteen her first romance had broken up. It was in this kitchen, among the equestrian paraphernalia draped over chair backs and a welsh dresser covered in rosettes, that she'd opened the letter offering her an unconditional place to read Politics and Modern Languages. In the same untidy room, Sam Walker had conducted an informal interview for her internship at *What'cha!* with Daphne at his shoulder, beaming encouragement at her honorary daughter and daring him to turn her down.

On all of those occasions, her parents had been unavailable, too busy pursuing their careers and deaf to her insistence that she wanted to become a journalist. They weren't being deliberately obstructive, Charlee knew that. They simply didn't get her in the same way that Daphne did - and that's what hurt the most. She suspected her mother was only half joking when she referred to her as their 'Little Changeling'.

'No, not the kitchen - Sam's study,' Ffinch stalled her, holding up his hands to show that he wouldn't touch her again without her permission. He waited for her to precede him into the holy of holies and Charlee's brain shifted up a gear. This was the only room in the house, apart from Sam and Daphne's bedroom, out of bounds to Charlee and Poppy when they were growing up. To be ushered in there by Ffinch made Charlee realise that Sam Walker, at least, recognised she was no longer a child.

The acknowledgement made her heart swell with satisfaction.

'Charlotte,' Sam greeted, looking up from his laptop. He preferred to leave all that 'horsey nonsense', as he put it, to Poppy and Daphne and never rode to hounds. He had a glass of whisky by his right hand and Charlee guessed he was happy in his own company. And Ffinch's, she thought, eying him surreptitiously and wondering if he'd spent the night in the camper van in these freezing temperatures, or in the guest room.

'Sit down, Charlotte. You, too, Rafa.'

They moved copies of the week's newspapers and back issues of *Horse and Hound* off chairs. Ffinch, with a gallant little bow, allowed Charlee to choose the most comfortable seat - a French bergère chair with deep cushions, rattan sides and matching footstool.

'Saw your brothers and that idiot of a vicar talking to you,' Sam said, pointing out of the window with a paper knife.

'Yes,' Charlee replied, careful of what she said, not sure what this was all about. 'The Rev Trev now thinks Ffinch and I will be visiting him at the vicarage to book St Peter's for a summer wedding.' She smiled weakly at Sam, hoping for enlightenment.

'Oh, that?' Sam laughed, winking at Ffinch. 'Just sowing the seeds, Montague. Just sowing the seeds.'

'What seeds? Will one of you please tell me what's going on?' Charlee demanded, leaning forward in her chair. 'Am I in, or out? Ffinch's partner or not?'

'Sam?' Ffinch raised an eyebrow, waiting for Sam to give him the go ahead. 'Okay, here's the thing.' Ffinch moved the cat off the window seat and perched there in its place. 'Sam wants photos of Anastasia Markova taken at the Thornham Boot Camp for Brides.'

'What kind of photos?' Charlee asked glancing from Sam to Ffinch.

'Her looking dishevelled, less than perfect, anything. Having a strop whilst covered in mud would be great. Rumour has it she's sold exclusive rights to *Mirror, Mirror* and we want to run a spoiler.' Sam looked positively gleeful at the thought of pulling the rug out from under *What'cha!*'s biggest rival.

Charlee had heard rumours that *What'cha!* was losing money and in danger of closing if sales didn't pick up. There were so many style/ celebrity lifestyle magazines that *What'cha!* needed to pull two-headed mutant rabbits out of the hat every edition in order to survive. The situation was discussed openly at the water cooler and Charlee had experienced a pang when she'd first heard the news. She'd hoped to stay on at the magazine when her internship was over, but that was beginning to look increasingly unlikely.

Perhaps pulling off a coup with Markova would keep them afloat a while longer. If she pulled it off and prevented *What'cha!* from becoming another casualty of the recession it would be her way of repaying Sam and Daphne for their many kindnesses over the years. Eyes shining, she imagined landing the scoop of the year and how it'd surpass her brothers' achievements. Why - she might even allow Ffinch a small role in helping her achieve this goal.

Glancing round, Charlee examined the framed front covers of *What'cha!* hanging on the panelled walls. The magazine had started life as an equestrian monthly - *Snaffle and Bit* - and had belonged to Daphne Walker's family. In the mid-eighties Sam had been brought in to boost *Snaffle and Bit*'s circulation and had ended up marrying the boss's daughter. By 1990, *Snaffle and Bit* had morphed into *What'cha!* and had become a cheaper version of *Hello*. Now little remained of the original equestrian magazine, apart from Poppy's 'Life in the Country' column, which was heavily edited by Charlee and Daphne. It was the remaining link with the old family magazine and Daphne was reluctant to see it disappear.

Daphne, like Poppy, was happy with whatever Sam did as long as the money to fund their horse fetish kept rolling in. By helping Sam, Charlee would be helping the magazine and two people she most cared about. Take a few snaps of Anastasia Markova getting wet and muddy - how hard could it be?

But her smile faded as the flaw in the plan became staringly obvious.

'The other night, outside the nightclub, when I got my phone out, Anastasia turned away and held her hand up to her face because she thought I was taking a photo. I can't see her letting anyone with a camera get that close,' Charlee reasoned. 'Can you?'

'You did brilliantly the other night, Charlee. I'm sure you'd be able to pull it off.' Sam poured out two glasses of his finest malt and came round to their side of the desk. Sam's home persona never failed to amaze Charlee. At *What'cha!* he was the hellfire and brimstone propri-etor/editor with a sharp tongue, strong cockney accent and unpredict-able temperament. Most of his sentences were peppered with four let-ter words and even Vanessa feared his mercurial moods. But at home, he spoke with a Home Counties accent and behaved like a neutered tomcat, totally under the sway of its mistress.

He'd never praise Charlee openly at the office, so she made the most of it.

'I'd certainly have a bloody good go,' Charlee said and clinked glass-es with Sam. 'But, wouldn't I have to enrol in the boot camp to get that close?'

'Yes, you would.' Sam exchanged a telling look with Ffinch.

'There is another flaw in this plan. I'm between boyfriends at the moment.' She glossed over her lack of success with the opposite sex and steeled herself for one of Ffinch's dry comments. She'd had plenty of boyfriends at university, but no one special. She hadn't thought about any of them since leaving, being too wrapped up in her internship. 'Even supposing the man of my dreams came galloping up the drive on a white horse at the end of the meet, I'd hardly have time to get to know him, let alone become engaged before the month is out. Anastasia will be at the boot camp during the second week in January.'

'Maybe you wouldn't have to look too far for a fiancé,' Sam sug-gested artlessly.

'When I carried out some research into the boot camp yesterday,' Charlee went on, 'I discovered that the owners require proof of the bride's forthcoming nuptials. Or, at the very least, evidence of the en-gagement.' She stopped swirling round the contents of her glass, raised her head and continued, 'You might not believe this, but some girls enrol in bridal boot camps just for a lark. Viewing it as some kind of psycho bridezilla alternative to a girly weekend in Dublin.' Charlee's pained expression made it plain that such behaviour was her idea of hell, with torture as a side order. 'The camp is a favourite with A-listers and they don't want to mix with ... well, the likes of me. Hence the strict security.'

'Not something you'd be up for then, Charlee?' Sam asked, pressing home his suit and topping up their glasses. Charlee held up her left hand and waggled her ring finger at him.

'I'd be up for it, sure, if there was a story to uncover. But without the requisite fiancé I'd fall at the first hurdle.'

'Or should that be climbing wall?' Ffinch asked, joining the conversation.

'I wouldn't have thought it was the kind of thing you'd want to get involved with, Ffinch. You're allergic to love, marriage and all it entails, aren't you? What was it you said in Sam's office - No moon in June. No roses round the door. No happily ever after. You - taking photos of a supermodel? Why am I not buying this?' she asked, giving them a direct look.

'Okay Charlee, we'll level with you,' Sam interjected. 'I told you Charlee'd need persuading before she'd agree to our proposal, Rafa.'

'What proposal are we talking about exactly?' Hoping that her partnership with Ffinch was back on the cards, Charlee adopted the persona of a hard-bitten journo.

'Sam, I don't think Charlee needs -' Ffinch began but Sam cut across him.

'Charlee, here's the deal. I want to sell *What'cha!*'

'Sell *What'cha!* But it's your life ...' Charlee said in shocked tones. Rumours circulating round the photocopier were one thing, but Sam admitting they were true was quite another.

'Maybe so, but it's losing money,' he said, simply. 'Now's the right time to sell, the time for me to bow out. But one last scoop ... that's all I ask.'

Looking far from convinced, Charlee frowned at both men.

'I'd hardly call a few photos of Anastasia Markova in the mud a scoop. Even if she is marrying a Russian billionaire,' she said, knowing she was talking herself out of a job. Sam might play the part of the benign husband at home but underneath he was still Sam Walker, always on the lookout for the killer story. 'And where does Ffinch figure in all of this? One minute he's writing *The Ten Most Dangerous Destinations on the Planet*, getting kidnapped and held for ransom. The next he's snapping girls in designer tracksuits abseiling down climbing walls or sliding across zip wires.'

'Well, to be absolutely accurate, Charlee,' Ffinch rejoined the conversation, 'you'd be the one taking the photos. Not me. And as to why I'm doing it? I'm doing it for Sam because - well, let's just say I'm repaying a debt.' Both men maintained deadpan expressions but a significant look flashed between them, one which excluded Charlee from their circle of trust.

'I - I.' Charlee felt like she was being pushed into a corner. Three days ago, she'd been sorting through photographs in a cupboard that was most likely a biohazard. Two days ago, she'd been in a skip pretending to be someone she wasn't. Yesterday, Ffinch had effectively terminated their partnership. Now they were stepping up the game and proposing to send her into a boot camp for brides - undercover.

Just to get it all straight in her head, she posed the question she'd asked Poppy in Pret A Manger a few days ago. 'Why not Vanessa?' Both men pulled a 'get real' face at her.

'Sally?'

'Sally is an organiser, good at logistics but unable to think on her feet. Or blag it. You're good at both, Charlee,' Sam said. Two compliments in five minutes! However, she wasn't so flattered that she couldn't smell a rat; a whole family of them, in fact.

'Look, Sam, if Charlee doesn't think she's up to this assignment, it's best she says so now. Save us trouble in the long run ...' Ffinch put in, his tone full of faux regret.

'Puleese, spare me the reverse psychology,' Charlee said. 'I didn't say I wasn't up for the challenge.' She could feel the assignment slipping through her fingers. 'I simply want to know what's involved.'

'Worried you might be out of your league? That's perfectly understandable. You are inexperienced, after all, but ...' Ffinch paused. Charlee knew Ffinch was playing her like a well-strung violin, but she'd go along with it - for now. There was another story here, one they were keeping from her. She smiled with deceptive sweetness as a prickle of journalistic sixth sense traversed the length of her spine and almost left her feeing numb. She hid her reaction from Ffinch and Sam; she wanted them to believe that she was taking their story at face value.

'Charlee?' Sam prompted.

'I'm in. But what about - I mean, who's going to pose as my fiancé?'

As if she didn't know!

'That's where Rafa comes in. I'll leave him to flesh out the details with you.' Sam said. 'I've been left strict instructions as to my domestic duties while Daphne's out with the hunt. Apparently, I'm to check on the casserole in the Aga, and put the apple pie in the top oven at the designated time. I ask you!'

Throwing his hands in the air, he left them alone in his study.

Chapter Sixteen
Charades

Charlee looked round at Ffinch, expecting him to share a joke at Sam's kowtowing to his formidable wife, but he looked grey, drained - as if he'd been bracing himself for her refusal. A great believer in the medicinal properties of good malt, Charlee reached for Sam's bottle of Scotch, poured out several fingers' worth and passed it to him.

She had the distinct feeling - as she had done on previous occasions - that Ffinch was constantly drawn back to the time when he'd lost two of his team. Did he blame himself for their deaths, she wondered? Judging by the downward droop of his mouth, the lacklustre light in his eyes - it was plain that he did.

'So, how's this going to work? Do I let my family in on the secret?' Charlie asked in a businesslike manner, hoping to jolt him out of his introspection. Becoming aware of her scrutiny, Ffinch pulled himself out of his dark mood and downed his whisky in one.

'No.' He was most emphatic. 'For this to work, we've got to play it for real.'

'But, Ffinch,' Charlee chose her words carefully, 'we've made it pretty plain that we don't like each other. Even if that's how most marriages end up, I think at the beginning a little romance is expected. Not real romance in our case, you understand,' she blushed a furious scarlet.

'But a close approximation of it.'

'You're a consummate actress, Montague, I've seen you at work. I'm sure you'll manage,' he said with an unflattering touch of cynicism, and downed his whisky with one deft flick of his wrist.

'I'm not sure that speaking Spanish and calling me Carlotta will cut it with my family.' Charlee nibbled at her lower lip. 'They'll expect an announcement in *The Times*, a small party at the very least. A ring?' She raised an eyebrow at him, expectantly.

'And they shall have them. Think of it as creating our legend, isn't that what the spooks call it?' Then he clammed up as if he'd let his guard slip and wanted it back in place, pronto.

'It's just like Gerard Depardieu and Andie McDowell in that old chick-flick *Green Card*.' Ffinch looked blank and she went onto explain. 'He needs a green card to stay in the US, she needs a husband in order to keep her apartment. They concoct a false past with photos etc., and …' she bit her lip, remembering how the film had ended.

'And?'

'They're found out and it ends badly. But don't worry, that won't happen to us.'

'Glad to hear it,' Ffinch observed with customary dryness.

Ignoring him, Charlee reached across Sam's desk for a pad and pencil. 'Okay, I think we need to iron out a few details before we go any further.' Ffinch relaxed against the window pane, folded his arms across his chest and gave her the floor.

'Fire away,' he said, as if he found the idea of her taking control somehow diverting.

Ignoring him, Charlee continued. 'One - Markova might be a model but she's no airhead. I googled her. She has a degree in psychology from St Petersburg University - brains as well as great genes, and cheekbones you could slice cucumbers with. She's bound to remember me from outside the nightclub, don't you think?'

'Possibly,' Ffinch agreed. 'Once seen, never forgotten I would imagine.'

'I'll take that as a compliment, though I'm sure it wasn't meant as one,' Charlee was learning to ignore his dark asides and to recognise that his default mode was set to cynical. 'Two. Gossip is rife at *What'cha!* If I walk in after the holidays and announce our engagement, you can imagine the furore. We'll have to make it look as realistic as we can.' For a moment, Ffinch lost his bleak look and a wicked light shone in his smoky eyes, making him appear younger and lighter-hearted. Charlee felt as if she'd just descended in a very fast lift from the penthouse to the basement, but managed to give him a stern look. 'Forget it, Ffinch; I'm only prepared to take the play-acting so far.'

'Spoilsport,' he replied. 'You know, Montague, if I didn't know better I'd say you take great delight in sending me "get over yourself looks" and putting me down. Anyone would think you didn't like me.'

'We've only known each other for a couple of days, Ffinch. I'm still at the trying very hard not to dislike you phase, so I wouldn't push it,' she advised, drawing a circle round a large number three.

'Carry on, Montague,' he said, putting up his hands behind his head and crossing his feet at the ankles.

'How and when do we break the news to my family and the Walkers? My brothers will be returning home tomorrow, I think it would be a good idea to announce our 'engagement' after they've gone. Mum and Dad will ask fewer questions with them out of the way. Which brings me to number four.' She drew the digit on the pad, circled it and added a bullet point for good measure.

'Yes?'

'We need a legend, as you put it. Photographs on Facebook, announcement in *The Times*, that sort of thing. Where did we meet? How long have we known each other? It has to be authentic. If it doesn't stack up, I won't get into the boot camp - let alone escape in one piece. From what I read on the website, they are very, very particular - over the top thorough where security's concerned.'

'Good point.' He looked at her admiringly and then began to enter into the spirit of the thing. 'Okay, here's what I think. Announcement in *The Times* - not a problem. Backstory we can work out over the next few days, I'm staying here and then returning to my flat in London. It might be an idea if you came back with me and we could concentrate on synchronising our stories. Also, it'll be a good smokescreen if you're seen living at my place.'

Charlee nibbled the end of the pen and looked covertly at him through her eyelashes. With any other man, she would have suspected a come on; let's play at nurses and doctors back at my place. But, Ffinch didn't give off that vibe, and apart from his secrecy over this investigation she found him straight as a die. It was as if he'd tried love, it hadn't worked out, and he was in no hurry to travel that road anytime soon.

'Or we could move into my bedsit,' she suggested and pretended affront when Ffinch pulled a face.

'I've seen your bedsit, so - thanks but no, thanks. We'll move you into mine. I don't intend spending the next couple of months sleeping on your sofa, stepping over drunks on the doorstep, or fighting my way past all the junk littering your hall floor, every night after work.'

'Oh, that's a bit harsh. And I suppose you live in an exclusive block in Mayfair, do you?' she asked with some asperity.

'Chelsea. A little backwater just off the King's Road.' He paused, as if he was expecting a reaction to the postcode of his des res. However, Charlee's mind was on a different tack, wondering if she could put up with him 24/7.

'Really?' she said, disbelievingly. 'I thought you lived in that camper van when you weren't abroad. Mind you - Chelsea? I'll be able to register our wedding list at the General Trading Company or Harvey Nicks - how cool is that?' she said, unable to resist the opportunity to wind him up. The last twenty-four hours had been a nightmare for her and she felt he deserved to suffer a little.

'I thought we agreed -'

'Only kidd-ing,' she said as his frown was back in place. 'Jee-zus, you really are allergic to weddings and happily ever after, aren't you? '

'Ring,' Ffinch began, obviously trying to rein her in. 'Is that on your list, Montague?'

'I've got plenty of dress rings we could use -'

'I'm sure you have, but I have no intention of this assignment falling at the first post because your ring looks like it came free with a copy of some supermarket magazine.' He shook his head and then went on more seriously. 'I'll provide the ring, but you'll have to look after it.'

'I'll sign a chitty, if you like,' she replied, pertly. He sighed and passed a weary hand across his eyes.

'This is going to be the shortest engagement in history, but something tells me it's going to feel like the longest.'

'Which brings me to another dilemma,' Charlee began, giving him a direct look.

'Which is?'

'When it's all over, Sam's got his snaps and we've saved *What'cha!* from bankruptcy, we'll go our separate ways, yeah?'

'Of course,' he said.

'Okay, let's establish up front. Who's the dumper - and who's the dumpee?'

'The what?' He looked at Charlee as if she'd sprouted horns. 'I swear, five minutes in your company and I feel like I belong to a different generation.'

'That's because you're over thirty and need to lighten up, Ffinch.' Her cheeks dimpled as she grinned unrepentantly at him.

'You said that to me, on Christmas Eve. I didn't need your unasked for advice then, and I certainly don't need it now.' Charlee looked at him and then saluted him, unabashed.

'Message received, loud and clear.' She thought about the rest of that cliqued phrase: *and* get laid. The way the women swarmed round him, it didn't look like he'd have any problems in that department. She pulled a face - so what was his problem?

'What was - that?' he asked.

'What?'

'That face.' He drew a circle in the air, which Charlee assumed represented her face.

'Nothing I need to share. The point is,' she stuck the pencil behind her ear, put the pad on her knees and leaned forward, 'I've got my reputation to consider.'

'You've lost me there.'

'We get engaged; we break off the engagement. People will want to know why. After I photograph Anastasia looking all dishevelled, you repay Sam for giving you your first break and he spoils *Mirror, Mirror*'s exclusive, what then?' She gave him an honest look. 'You'll go off on another one of your hazardous trips and I'll be left at *What'cha!* with everyone thinking you've dumped me.'

'And that would bother you, would it?'

'What do you think? Of course it would. I don't want people laughing at me behind my back because I couldn't hold on to a man like, well - like you.' She bit her lip; the way she'd phrased it made it seem as if she was punching above her matrimonial weight. That in the normal run of things Ffinch would be out of her league.

'Don't worry, when it's all over you can dump me as publically as you like. On the *Ten O'Clock News*, a plane trailing a banner over London that reads: Montague dumps Ffinch - and a plague on both their houses. Hell, you can even take out a double-page spread in *The Times* and I'll pay for it. Such things don't matter to me.'

'Well, they matter to me,' she said. He stood up, making it clear he was dismissing her. 'One more thing -' Ffinch groaned and glanced at his watch. 'Will you stop acting like a man on his way to execution and start looking like a man who's deeply in love?' she demanded with some asperity. 'Really, some of the looks you give me are far from flattering if you must know.'

'You do a pretty good line in withering looks yourself, Montague.' They looked each other up and down and she saw a rare flash of humour in his face before it disappeared.

'And that's another thing - Montague. I think you should get used to calling me Charlee when we're around my family. Smoke and mirrors, you see; or, Charlotte if you prefer. I know you told me back in Sam's office that only your friends called you Rafael, so ...'

'I guess you can call me Rafa, if you must.'

'I must,' she replied. She sensed that she'd worn him out with her objections, suggestions and plans. When she'd googled dengue fever last night, she'd discovered how potentially life-threatening it was. No wonder he often looked pale and drawn, his eyes dark-ringed with fatigue. But underneath she sensed steely purpose - as if some devil was driving him.

Whatever it was, Charlee suspected it had nothing to do with spiking *Mirror, Mirror*'s exclusive, and everything to do with Anastasia Markova's attendance at the boot camp.

Just then, Sam came back into the room wearing an Emma Bridgewater Christmas apron and a frazzled expression. Charlee and Ffinch exchanged a humorous look and then killed it, but not before Sam caught it.

'If you tell anyone that you've seen me wearing an apron, holding a wooden spoon in one hand and a page from a cookery book in the other, Montague - and you, too, Ffinch - I'll ...' he threatened, waving the spoon at them.

'Our lips are sealed, Chief.' Walking over, Charlee removed the spoon and the laminated recipe card from his hands. 'Let me help you. There's only room for one domestic goddess in the house, and for the moment it'd better be me.'

Chapter Seventeen
Granny's Ring

O ver breakfast the next morning, Charlee was subjected to the third degree.

'Your partner has a very high opinion of himself, doesn't he?' Jack demanded as their mother rustled up the 'full English' at the Aga. 'He was bloody rude to us at the meet, smirking away, his arm around your shoulder - as if he found us vastly diverting.'

'It's just his way. You get used to it.' She shrugged and spread her toast with butter. She resisted the urge to tell Jack that Ffinch did find them highly amusing and his mocking nickname for them.

'And what's with the whole Carlotta, thing?' Tom demanded, frowning into his breakfast. 'That was a bit, creepy, wasn't it? I mean, it's not as if you're Spanish.'

'There's an air about him, as though he's the cat who got the cream; like he owns you, or something,' Wills put in. In retrospect, Charlee now knew what Ffinch'd been up to before the meet and was pleased it'd worked. However, having had enough of their cross-examining she felt it was her turn to wind them up.

'Oh, don't worry, it's not as if I'm *virgo intacta* and being seen with Ffinch is ruining my marriage prospects.' Everyone round the table spluttered into their breakfast but Charlee carried on eating toast, calmly. 'Anyhoo, what time are you three leaving today? I promised I'd go over to the Walkers' Stud and watch the DVD of Poppy and Daphne at HOYS back in October.'

'HOYS?' Miranda questioned, eating the gluten-free muesli she insisted on making fresh every morning. No wonder she looked permanently miserable, Charlee thought. Having spent three days with George and her sister-in-law, she'd reached the conclusion that a little of the newlyweds went a very long way.

'Horse of the Year Show,' Charlee's brothers chorused, openly pleased to be moving on from a discussion of their baby sister's sex life.

'My Little Pony,' Wills said, picking up his bacon rasher and eating it with his fingers.

'Poppy Walker's obsessed,' Jack added, earning a glowering look from Charlee. 'I don't know how you can bear to sit through a DVD of horses knocking down poles and prancing sideways, Charlee. You don't even ride.'

'I can ride,' Charlee corrected him. 'I just choose not to.' She banished a childhood memory of her pony careering round the bottom field after Jack or Wills had slapped it on its rump with a willow wand. That event had scared the bejeezus out of her and she hadn't been on a horse since. 'I've told you - when they equip horses with a set of brakes and a gear lever, I might consider getting back on one. Besides, it's no different to you three watching rugger on Sky Sports. I don't think the Harlequins will be knocking on the door asking the Montague brothers to play for England any time soon.'

She had the satisfaction of seeing their faces droop at her honest assessment of their sporting prowess.

'Oh, can I come?' Miranda asked brightly, entering into the conversation.

'No, you can't,' Charlee replied. 'You'd be bored to tears and start droning on about George's political ambitions. Poppy and I are going shopping later. Just the two of us,' she added in a voice that left no room for negotiation. Truth was, Ffinch was still over at the Walkers' and there were one or two agenda items she wanted to go over with him.

'Charlotte, that was very rude,' her mother remonstrated, and then sighed as if it was no more than expected. 'Never mind, Miranda, you and I can go into Woking to see what's open. I'd better make the most of your company; the house will seem empty once you and the boys have gone.'

'And that's not rude, I suppose?' Charlee demanded. Coming home and staying for a few days seemed harder than ever. When she'd first returned from university during the long vac, her childhood friends were still living in the vicinity and she could hang out with them. Now, like her, they had jobs elsewhere and had dispersed. She had become a stranger in her childhood home and while she felt immeasurably sad about that, she acknowledged it was a rite of passage. One day she'd return to find that her mother had kitted her bedroom out as an art studio or a sewing room and she'd be pushed out of the nest forever.

The sooner she and Ffinch announced their engagement and headed back to London, the better. Fortuitously, the bell jangled above the kitchen door and she scraped her chair back on the flagstone floor.

'I'll go,' she said, glad of the excuse to escape.

Crossing the hall, she let out a pent-up sigh over the way things had turned out between herself and her family. But sadness and regret were pushed to one side when she spotted Ffinch's distinctive camper van sitting on the drive.

Bugger!

What did he want?

He wasn't supposed to turn up until after her brothers and Miranda had gone home. Convincing her parents their engagement was bona fide would be hard enough without the rest of the family asking one hundred and one awkward questions. She ran over to the door, wrenched it open, grabbed him by the sleeve of his flying jacket and dragged him into her father's study.

'You really are getting into the spirit of the thing, Montague. How romantic,' he grinned, 'my new fiancée can't keep her hands off me.'

But Charlee wasn't in the mood for his snarky comments or for what passed for humour with him. She closed the study door behind them and pressed her back against its thick panels as though keeping ravening wolves at bay. She gave him a searching and far from welcoming look.

'What are you doing here? You were supposed to stay away until this evening.'

'I couldn't stay away. The attraction between us is too strong.' He put his hand over his heart and gave her a longing look. 'I've come to see your father to ask him for your hand.'

'No, no, no. That's out of the question. Are you mad?' She closed the gap between them to make her point. 'We'll simply tell them that we've got engaged. That way, when we - I - break it off, it won't be such a big deal.' Chewing her lip, Charlee thought rapidly. 'Maybe we should wait until we've got the ring?' Things were moving too quickly and she had a sneaking suspicion that the reality of being Ffinch's fiancée might be more than she bargained for. More than she could handle, even. He seemed wired, in uncharacteristic jovial mood and keen to get the show on the road - and that started alarm bells ringing, too.

'I have the ring. I had it couriered from my parents in Edinburgh and it arrived this morning. Amazing what can be arranged if one is prepared to pay above the going rate.' He tapped his breast pocket with two fingers and then rooted in his wallet. 'I've cobbled together an announcement for *The Times*, the sooner we declare our undying love to the world, the better. See what you think.' Charlee took the piece of paper from him, not much liking the sound of cobbled together or his sarcastic undying love. 'I didn't know your middle name so I've left a space for you to fill it in, should you think it necessary. My feeling is: plain and simple is the way to go.'

Mr R. Fonseca-Ffinch and Miss C. Montague

The engagement is announced between Rafael, son of His Excellency Ambassador Salvio Fonseca-Ffinch and Mrs Richenda Fonseca-Ffinch of Killiecrankie, Edinburgh, and Charlotte, daughter of Doctor and Mrs Henry Montague of Highclere, Berkshire.

'Oh,' Charlee let out a shaky breath. 'That looks very … official.'

For some absurd reason she didn't want to think about, her heart felt heavy and the enormity of what they were about to undertake hit home. It all seemed a mocking step too far, now. Tears pricked her nose and the print swam in front of her eyes. Fingers shaking, she handed the paper back to him, stuck her hands in the pockets of her jeans and stood looking out of the window with her back towards him.

'Shouldn't it be?' Ffinch seemed genuinely puzzled by her reaction. 'I thought the idea was to present everyone with fait accompli and give them no time to ask searching questions. We might as well do the dirty deed while the Ruperts are here and get it over and done with in one fell swoop.'

'Over and done with? Dirty deed? One fell swoop?' Charlee spun round, her voice thick with emotion. 'Don't overdo the romance, will you Ffinch? We wouldn't want me to swoon and fall into your arms, would we?' She wiped her finger inelegantly under her nose, let out another shaky breath and then composed herself. 'And stop referring to my brothers as the Ruperts,' she snapped, and normal service was resumed.

'We're play-acting, aren't we?' he reminded her and then frowned and looked at her quizzically. 'Aren't we?' he insisted, as if sensing her hesitation.

'Of course we are. I remember the deal - I'm not to go all mushy on you. It's just … well, I've envisaged this day in my mind and it was nothing like this.'

Ffinch looked at her long and hard and then his expression softened and his grey eyes filled with compassion, understanding. 'I keep forgetting how young you are. I think you're hard-bitten like me - and love has no place in your life … Cheer up, Montague, think of it as a dry run for the day when the great love of your life walks through the door and sweeps you off your size fives.'

Charlee might have known he couldn't be soft-hearted or empathetic for long.

'Four and a halves, actually. And I suppose you've been engaged at least a dozen times? You probably have to fight women off with a cricket bat. It's all a formality to you. Well, I need a few moments to get used to the idea and then we can go into the kitchen and tell my family the "good news".' She enclosed the words in ironic speech marks; she didn't want him to get the wrong impression about her - or her dedication to the job.

'Okay, let's have a little breather,' he conceded. 'You sit and tell me about this room, your father, your relationship with your parents. The Ruperts … sorry.' He guided her over to the tweed-covered office chair by her father's desk and made her sit while he roamed the room looking at family photos on the wall. They were mostly sporting photos of her brothers at boarding school in various guises - cricket, rugger, football and even fencing. There was one rather unflattering photo of her wearing braces and holding a lacrosse stick and she hoped Ffinch wouldn't dwell on that one for too long. 'Charlotte - Charlee. I guess your parents were expecting another boy and out you popped.'

Charlee didn't like the offhand way he referred to her arrival into the world, or how close to the truth he was. Her parents had been anticipating the arrival of another boy and had Charles James all lined up for him and had hurriedly changed it to Charlotte Jane. She remembered his mocking 'Carlotta' and despite feeling put out with him, shivered. The name sounded like it belonged in a Latin country, where the sun always shone and the skies were unfailingly blue. Where romance flourished . . .

'How come there are twice as many photos of the Ruperts than there are of you?'

'Because there's four of them and one of me?' Charlee suggested, annoyed that he'd pricked her bubble. She didn't want him playing amateur psychologist for a second time and rushed on. 'Don't you know that in large families the law of diminishing returns comes into play?'

'I'm an only child; you'll have to explain,' he said, sitting on the end of the desk. Fearing for the safety of her father's precious fishing flies Charlee pointedly moved them out of his way.

'With the first born, album after album is filled with photographs of the precious babe. Then along comes the next and the next. The parents are exhausted, distracted and fewer photographs are taken to mark the rites of passage - first pony, first day at school and so on. Until, by the time the last child is born - in this case, me - no one bothers anymore.'

'I see,' Ffinch frowned.

'My brothers charmingly explained the lack of photos by telling me I was adopted. Their little joke, everything they could do to confuse me was regarded as fair game.'

Ffinch nodded, beginning to understand the family dynamic and Charlee's place in the pecking order. 'Go on,' he commanded. Charlee didn't like being ordered around by anyone, least of all Ffinch, but hoped that if she got her backstory out of the way he would stop bugging her about her brothers.

'Not much to tell, really. My mother had just accepted a post as an adviser on primary education after many years of trying and was devastated to find herself pregnant at forty-one. Promotion was much harder for a woman back then, remember,' she cut her mother some unaccustomed slack. 'With the boys away at boarding school I was practically handed over to my grandparents to bring up while mother and father pursued their careers. Mother suffered horrendous postnatal depression and my birth plunged her into an early menopause. She never really took to me, I guess ... the unplanned child.'

She shrugged away the hurt. Ffinch straightened the photo of her with the lacrosse team and when he turned round, the mocking, jib-ing look was gone from his eyes. He regarded her intently with that 'I wonder if I can really trust you' look she was beginning to recognise.

'We should form a club: "Brought Up By Their Grandparents"', he said, half-jokingly. 'I spent most of my life in boarding schools when not staying with my cousins on the family coffee plantation in Brazil. My parents travelled the world, from embassy to embassy, until they hit pay dirt with their posting to Paris. My grandparents had a large hand in my upbringing, too.' He reached inside his flying jacket and brought out a blue leather box. 'Hence, Granny's ring. Great-Granny's ring to be precise, on my mother's side - they're the Ffinches, not the Fonsecas. Here,' he reached over the desk and opened the box. 'It's yours for now; try it on.'

He removed the ring from its white velvet bed and held it towards her. Holding her breath Charlee extended her left hand, glad she now had a grip on her emotions and had stopped trembling. This was a game, she reminded herself, something she had to do in order to be taken seriously as a journo. Otherwise, she'd spend the rest of her life covering school fetes and guess the name of the prize pig at the county show.

She leaned forward slightly and Ffinch slipped the ring over her fin-ger. It felt cold to the touch but fitted perfectly. The setting was a little old-fashioned - a large, square-cut diamond, mounted on the shoul-ders of four of the darkest sapphires she'd ever seen. She suspected it was very, very expensive and looked up at him concernedly.

But Ffinch was looking down at the ring as if it had a special place in his affections. Perhaps even remembering his great-grandmother wearing it. All the more unusual then, she thought, that he'd chosen that particular ring to make their bogus engagement appear genuine.

'You know, we could order one of those diamonique rings off the shopping channel. I'm going to live in a state of terror in case I lose it,' Charlee said, genuinely anxious about misplacing a family heirloom.

'I trust you, Montague,' he said quietly. His fingers closing over her left hand, he pulled her to her feet and round to his side of the desk. He looked serious and more than a little thoughtful. Despite the fact that she was still smarting over the way he'd ended their partnership on Christmas Day, Charlee felt close to him and understood that photographing Anastasia Markova meant everything to him. Why that should be, and what his interest was in a boot camp at the end of the world on the Norfolk marshes, eluded her.

For several beats, he stood holding her hand and looking down at the ring. Charlee made the most of the opportunity to study him: the strong line of his eyebrows, unfairly long eyelashes, expressive mouth and his sculpted cheekbones that hinted at his Brazilian ancestry. He raised his head and Charlee shivered as the December light streaming through the window reflected in his eyes, making them appear grey-flecked with blue and very appealing.

He looked back at her quizzically and Charlee wondered what he took with him when his scrutiny of her was over. She had no illusions about herself - she was just about okay. The most remarkable thing about her was her almost white-blonde hair, pale skin that blushed far too readily, bright blue eyes that made her appear younger than she was - and a stubborn mouth that one ignored at one's peril.

'Diamonique?' Ffinch questioned, apparently not willing to let go of her hand, just yet. 'You have to flash that rock under Vanessa and Sally's noses on the first day back after the holidays. If we can fool them, the rest of the world will be easy. Those two could have a permanent slot on *Antiques Roadshow* and would spot a fake piece at fifty paces.'

'That's true,' Charlee acknowledged. She frowned, wondering how she could free her hand without spoiling this rare moment of détente.

'On which subject,' Ffinch changed tack and looked suddenly businesslike.

'Yes?'

'We should get the first kiss out of the way, too. It might make the play-acting a bit easier?' He pulled a droll face as if he suspected that Charlee was finding the charade hard to deal with and wanted to help her over this next hurdle.

'Really know how to sweep a gal off her feet, don't cha Ffinch?' she said archly, pulling her hand free and standing hands on hips, like Calamity Jane. 'Forget it.' Shooting him an 'I don't think so' look, she headed for the door, totally unaware that she'd issued a challenge no man could resist. Least of all an alpha male like Ffinch.

'In the interests of research, then?' Reaching out, he grabbed her hand and pulled her into his arms and dipped her with all the skill of a tango dancer. Charlee's breath hitched as soft breasts came up against hard ribs and musculature. She tried to wriggle free but that was impossible without her losing her balance and falling flat on her derriere. He straightened up and she felt the gurgle of laughter rise in his chest as he took in her affronted expression. 'Now stop struggling and take your medicine like a good girl.'

'I will n-nphm,' her last word was lost as his mouth came down on hers.

Briefly, she continued to struggle. Then she went limp in his arms, waiting for the moment when she could twist away from him - just as she had done with her brothers when they were play-fighting. But Ffinch's arm snaked round her waist and his free hand cradled the back of her head, prolonging a kiss that was warm, enticing and - despite the unusual test conditions - very pleasurable.

Expertly, Ffinch prised her legs apart with his right knee, pressed her back against the desk and drew her closer into his body. The scent of skin, soap and clean linen assailed Charlee and she closed her eyes, forgetting for an instant that she was supposed to leap away from him. Trembling, she gave herself up to the kiss instead; her treacherous right hand tightened on the lapel of his ancient flying jacket, her nails dug into the sheepskin lining and she pulled him closer.

'Charlee ...' Ffinch, evidently feeling the resistance ebb out of her, whispered her name against her lips and prolonged the kiss. Just as his tongue started to explore her mouth and Charlee felt their lovemaking crank up a notch, the study door opened and Henry Montague walked in.

Chapter Eighteen
Economical With the Truth

'Charlee - Mr Fonseca-Ffinch - I - Sorry. God - Sorry.' Henry Montague found himself in the unenviable position of watching his daughter being thoroughly kissed by someone who was, to all intents and purposes, virtually a stranger. 'Your mother wondered if ...'

Evidently sensing that Charlee was about to spring away from him, Ffinch spun her round and held her in front of him - with his arms crossed over her. 'Caught red-handed,' Ffinch said, kissing the top of Charlee's head. 'Well, darling, looks like the secret's out ...' Darling? Charlee squirmed under the look her father sent her, but Ffinch seemingly was just getting into role. Holding Charlee closer, he shuffled them both forward and held out his hand to Henry Montague without letting Charlee go. 'I've come here to formally ask for Charlee's hand in marriage, sir.'

'Have you indeed? Looks like Charlotte's made up her own mind,' Henry observed dryly, looking first at Charlee's wedding finger and then searching her face. 'I rather suspect that what I want doesn't really come into it.'

'Charlee is a force of nature,' Ffinch agreed, with an edge that only Charlee detected. She pressed the heel of her left foot down on Ffinch's toes, but that had no apparent impact as he was wearing leather boots

'I'm of an age to do what I want,' Charlee declared, pushing out of Ffinch's arms.

'She's always done just what she wants,' Henry observed dryly, sending Ffinch what could only be interpreted as a *caveat emptor* look. As if concerned that Ffinch, being in the throes of love, hadn't quite got a handle on how difficult Charlee could be. 'Well, if it's what Charlee wants - and you want - then who am I to stand in your way? Congratulations - ahem - Mr Ffinch, and welcome to the family.' He extended his hand and gave Ffinch's a vigorous shake.

'No Mister; just Ffinch, or Rafa - if you prefer,' Ffinch pulled Charlee back into his arms, as though he suspected she was about to do a runner. 'Think we'd better go and tell the rest of your family the good news, Sweetie. Don't you?'

Charlie twisted round in Ffinch's arms so only he could see her expression. She felt like she was running with a group of lemmings towards the cliff edge and Ffinch was running alongside to make sure that she went over the precipice. He seemed preternaturally keen to make the engagement official despite his aversion to anything rhyming with moon and June.

Now that she was recovering - slowly - from the experimental kiss, all the old suspicions came winging back.

'We were going to tell you and Mum after the boys left, but ... let's go into the kitchen and get it over with. Ready, Pumpkin?' Clearly that was an endearment too far, because Ffinch frowned and her father's expression morphed between disbelief and incredulity. Best not overplay her hand, Charlee decided as she led the way back to the kitchen.

'Oh, Mr Fonseca-Ffinch,' Miranda greeted Ffinch. He walked over to the Aga and, making himself very much at home, stood with his back turned towards it, warming his cute arse. 'What a lovely surprise.' She smoothed her cashmere sweater down over her non-existent breasts and looked between Charlee, Ffinch and Henry uncertainly. Then she caught sight of the engagement ring on Charlee's finger. 'Are you two - engaged?'

'Looks like it, doesn't it?' Charlee said. She extended her left hand in the time-honoured fashion and the diamond caught the sunlight. Her mother dropped the spatula into the frying pan and came rushing forward. She pulled Charlee's hand towards her, almost dislocating her arm from her shoulder, and looked at Great-Granny's ring in astonishment.

'Charlotte! Why didn't you say? Henry - champagne, now. We must celebrate,' she clapped her hands.

'It's all been very sudden,' Charlee said, going over to stand by Ffinch at the Aga. She put her arm in his and looked up at him with an expression of adoration. 'Hasn't it, Pumpkin?' Her brothers got to their feet and moved towards them in a manner that was more menacing than congratulatory.

'Sudden?' Jack inquired, giving Ffinch an evil look. 'Charlee's not ...' He bunched his hands at his sides and everyone looked down at Charlee's stomach, which was hidden by her baggy top. Charlee blushed to the roots of her hair and glared back at them.

'Well, of course, the only way I could get a man would be to trap him by becoming pregnant. Thanks a bundle, Jack.' This time Charlee's high colour owed nothing to her embarrassment and everything to being humiliated in front of Ffinch. Miranda put a protective hand over her own stomach and looked forlornly at George. Charlee was about to come back with a scathing return when Ffinch intervened.

'Naturally you're suspicious,' he said smoothly, putting his arm round Charlee's shoulders. 'We haven't known each other very long, but when a *coup de foudre* strikes it's best not to ignore it. Charlee is unlike any woman I've ever known.' Charlee winced, very much aware of the irony behind Ffinch's words. 'We're partners in every sense of the word and will be working closely together in the near future too.'

Henry Montague opened up the door of the lime-green Smeg fridge in the corner and drew out two bottles of Louis Roederer Cristal. 'A gift from a grateful patient. I was going to open one to see in the New Year, but this is a much better use for them. Now, out of you boys, who's driving? Only half a glass for whoever it is, I'm afraid.'

'Thank you, Henry,' Barbara Montague said as she took her glass of champagne and went over to have another look at the ring. 'It's beautiful, Charlee, I hope you'll look after it.'

'No, Mum, I plan on losing it at the first opportunity when I'm making mud pies over by the potting shed. For God's sake.' Ever-present tears threatened to overwhelm her - why did her family always make her feel stupid and insignificant? And in front of Ffinch, too, this time?

'Does the Queen know that the Cullinan Diamond is missing from the crown jewels?' Wills asked but took the sting out of his words by coming over and shaking Ffinch's hand and giving Charlee an affectionate hug. 'Congratulations, Shrimp, I'm sure you'll be very happy. When's the wedding?'

'Oh, I don't ...' began Charlee uncertainly, but Ffinch cut across her.

'Early summer, if everything goes according to plan.'

'That doesn't give us long,' Barbara said, consulting her husband with a look.

'It'll be very low-key. I'll be off on my travels and Charlee will be accompanying me,' Ffinch said firmly. His uncompromising look was clearly designed to curb Barbara Montague's enthusiasm for a BIG FAT HOME COUNTIES WEDDING.

'Oh, but I thought ... Charlee would give up all this journalism nonsense and settle down to a nice job in a language school. And George says that lobbyists and MPs are always on the lookout for good translators. She could work from home, too, when the babies arrive.'

'For goodness sake, Mum ... Change the record,' Charlee protested.

'The drudgery of housework would be a waste of Charlee's many talents. And we're both far too young to think about starting a family,' Ffinch stated, his smile taking the sting out of his words. 'You have no need to worry about any of that. I'll be taking good care of Charlee from now on.' He accepted the flute of champagne from Henry and removed his arm from Charlee's shoulders.

'Not,' Charlee emphasised the word, 'that I need anyone to take care of me, Sweetheart.' She took Ffinch's hand and gave it a warning squeeze. He squeezed her fingers in return and grey eyes locked with blue as a battle of wills took place, until Ffinch's straight look reminded her to play her part.

'Your other partners didn't fare too well, did they?' Jack asked, accepting a glass of Cristal from his father. 'From what I read about your trip up the Amazon - two never returned and you barely escaped with your life?'

'You don't want to believe everything you read in the papers,' Ffinch said, making plain that his tribulations in Colombia weren't up for discussion. 'I'm sure your work with Greenpeace isn't without risk? Trailing the whaling fleets in small dinghies and so on. And Wills takes a calculated risk every time he examines pathogens under the microscope.'

'Quite. But its Charlee's safety I'm worried about ...'

'Well, don't be,' Charlee spoke up. 'Raise your glasses and be happy for me, this is what I want.' The fact that she was referring to her chance to work with Ffinch and not their engagement was something she did not intend to share with her family. Ffinch, clearly picking up the vibe, moved closer until they were standing shoulder to shoulder by the Aga.

It was left for Henry Montague to redeem the moment. 'Well, I think enough's been said ... Let's raise our glasses and toast the happy couple. Charlotte and Rafael.'

'Charlotte and Rafael,' everyone repeated as they sipped their champagne. There was an awkward pause as the Montagues eyeballed Charlee and Ffinch over the rim of their champagne flutes. There appearing to be nothing else to say, Ffinch gently nudged Charlee forward.

'Time for you to pack, Charlee. I'm sorry Mr and Mrs Montague but we need to return to London tonight - something's come up.' Charlee downed her champagne in one and put the flute back on the kitchen table. She'd been wondering how she was going to handle her family once Ffinch returned to the Walkers'. That thought had also occurred to him, apparently. 'I'm assuming that you will want to post an engagement notice in *The Times* as soon as possible? Charlotte and I have put a few words together.' Charlee was relieved, as Ffinch handed the piece of paper he'd shown earlier to her father, that he didn't use the phrase cobbled together this time. 'I should just mention that Charlee will be moving in with me, so if you need to contact either of us, ring this number.' He handed them a business card with his name embossed on it. 'We'll be in touch in a couple of days.'

Barbara Montague looked like she wanted to say more but, stiff-lipped, held her peace. Everyone seemed at a loss for words and Charlee was relieved to scuttle out of the kitchen and run upstairs to pack her bags.

'That was awkward,' Charlee said with a fine touch of ironic understatement as Ffinch drove them away from her family home. Letting out a long breath, she sank lower in the seat and attempted to make herself as small as possible. She wanted to pull up the drawbridge, sink beneath the parapet and keep below the radar - and every other cliché that sprang to mind. She'd had quite enough emotion for one day - thank you very much - even before she examined her reaction to Ffinch's kiss in her father's study.

Get the first kiss out of the way, he'd said, coolly in control of the situation. And what had she done? Held onto his flying jacket like a drowning woman and returned the kiss for all she was worth. Now he must think her deranged, as though slipping Great-Granny's carbuncle of a diamond on her finger had unhinged her. Luckily, events had overtaken them in the form of the inquisition in the kitchen and Ffinch appeared to have put the embarrassing episode down to skilled play-acting on her part. Nothing more.

She'd be more careful next time. If there was a next time!

'Awkward?' he laughed and slanted a glance at her. 'I thought the Ruperts were going to call me out, or whatever Regency Bucks did when their sister's virtue was under siege by some undesirable rake.'

Charlee gave him a covert look. With his overlong hair, chiselled features and expressive mouth he could be a hero straight out of the pages of the Georgette Heyer novels she'd devoured as a teenager. But it was time that she made her position clear.

'Just as well they didn't or they would have received no thanks from me. I don't need any man's protection.' She paused to let her words sink in and she saw the corner of his mouth quirk. 'Least of all four brothers who practically drowned me when I was ten.'

'Practically drowned you?' Ffinch responded sharply and Charlee wished she could call the words back. It was plain that he was reliving the moment when his captors had tossed him into the Amazon.

'Oh, it was just a bit of fun,' she backtracked. 'They told me a Spitfire had been shot down over our land during the Battle of Britain and was at the bottom of the lake. All I had to do was take a deep breath, dive down and I'd see it. They jumped in and hauled me out when I didn't surface after a few minutes.'

He looked far from pleased by this further revelation. It was obvious that he had a low opinion of her brothers and she'd just made things worse. She guessed that, being an only child, Ffinch didn't understand the rough and tumble that brothers and sisters shared and that wanting to do harm to each other came with the territory.

'A story for another time,' Charlee said and pushed herself upright in her seat as they neared the Walkers' stud. 'I won't have to go through it all again, will I?' She hated the idea of deceiving Daphne and Poppy more than she worried about her family's feelings. After all, it was thanks to Poppy that she'd been put up for Ffinch's assistant/partner in the first place.

'Don't worry, I've already packed my things and Sam will have told Daphne the whole story. And Poppy as much of the story as she needs to know if she needs to cover for us back at *What'cha!*'

The whole story?

Whatever <u>that</u> was.

There were gaps to be filled, things to be revealed, but the people who held all the cards - Ffinch and Sam Walker - clearly had no intention of showing their hand.

Chapter Nineteen
The Homecoming

It was dark when Ffinch guided his camper van down a narrow street leading to a Victorian mews just off the King's Road. The cobbled roadway looked picture-perfect as most of the residents had trimmed the ornamental trees outside their front doors with baubles and hung them with lights. Thick garlands tied with satin ribbons and overflowing with winter berries adorned front doors, and window boxes were planted with tiny cyclamen and winter pansies. The temperature had plummeted in the last hour and a thin rime of frost was spreading over the roofs of the former coachmen's houses.

The mews had a magical look and Charlee felt that she'd stepped onto the set of the latest Richard Curtis movie: Christmas, Actually.

Ffinch drew up by a garage door, flipped down the driver's sunshield and revealed a remote control attached to it. When he pressed it, the garage door rolled up. 'You get out and I'll bring the bags. I have to park your side of the van close to the garage wall, otherwise it won't fit in. Here,' he tossed over a bunch of keys. 'Open up. The code for the alarm is: 1951. The year my mother was born; okay?'

'Sure.' Charlee leapt out and walked up to the front door. The security light came on and dazzled her as she dealt with both locks - a mortise and a Yale - and then quickly located the keypad and disarmed it. She had to push hard against the panelled door to gain entry as several weeks' post lay on the sea grass flooring. Ha - and Ffinch had complained about her entrance hall being flooded with takeaway leaflets. Bending down, she picked up the post, separating it from the junk mail and put it on the hall table next to a pile of unopened Christmas cards.

Ffinch came in after her, dropped their bags on the floor and reached for the phone on the wall. 'Hungry?' he asked.

'Yes. Yes, I am.' Charlee's tummy gave a hungry growl. Without bothering to consult a menu, or ask Charlee's preferences, Ffinch speed dialled the local Indian takeaway. 'Hi, Joginder, it's Ffinch. The usual please, times two.' He grinned as Joginder made some quip. 'A colleague, if you must know. Yes, female ... no, a different one. Merry Christmas to you, too, my friend.' He replaced the phone and pulled an apologetic face at Charlee who was standing there boot-faced. How many other dinners a deux had he ordered in, she wondered? None of your business, Ffinch's expression told her, although he did offer up a brief explanation. 'Sorry about that. Joginder's a great mate, but very nosy. Come on through.'

Ffinch opened an inner door that led into a large, square sitting room. An open tread staircase took up most of one wall and underneath it were sloping bookcases crammed with an eclectic collection of ancient Penguins, romances, crime novels and travel books. Ffinch went round switching on table lamps revealing more of the very masculine interior of the mews.

Rubbing her hands together to warm them, Charlee was glad that Ffinch had left the central heating on over Christmas, otherwise, it would have been freezing in there. But that was his only concession to winter and the season. The mews was bereft of baubles, streamers and the usual gewgaws associated with Christmas, and another pile of unopened cards lay cast aside on the floor near a gas fire.

'Sit, make yourself at home, Montague. I'll make us a coffee.'

He dropped the bags at the foot of the stairs and went through to a tiny galley kitchen. But Charlee was too inquisitive to sit still for long and the thought of seeing a domesticated Ffinch was too good an opportunity to miss. Getting up from the brown suede and chrome modular sofa, which looked like it had won some prestigious design award back in the day, she walked over to the kitchen door and leaned against its frame. The kitchen was tiny, with only just enough room for one person to pass between orange and cream Formica units comfortably.

Ffinch, obviously sensing her interest, laughed. 'Poky, huh?'

'Bijou,' Charlee corrected, watching as he deftly spooned coffee into the basket of a retro chrome and teak percolator. 'Very sixties - like something out of *The Avengers*. All browns and oranges and with huge circular, paper lampshades designed to catch your head. I can imagine Diana Rigg walking in, wearing her leather gear, or Steed throwing his bowler hat onto the coat rack. Does the mews belong to you?'

Charlee had lived in London long enough to appreciate property prices and guestimated that the mews with its Chelsea postcode would command a price tag of several million pounds.

'Yes - and no. Actually, it belongs to my grandparents who no longer have a use for it. It will be mine one day but for now it's a great pied-à-terre when I'm in town.' Charlee smiled at his use of pied-à-terre and was about to say that it looked more like Austin Powers's shag pad, but stopped herself. She didn't want to draw them back to the scorching kiss they'd exchanged in her father's study or to have Ffinch think she was coming on to him. Ffinch had been right to get the kiss out of the way, because now they could act normally towards each other without sexual tension muddying the water. She only hoped that Ffinch would put her response to the kiss down to enthusiasm rather than outright lust.

'Cool,' she said, blushing afresh as she relived the moment. Unaware of her wayward thoughts, Ffinch rummaged round in a tiny under-the-counter fridge looking for milk and then turned back to her.

'I could have it modernised but I like it as it is - cool and retro. Apart from the plumbing, broadband, widescreen TV and the docking station for my iPod, I haven't changed a thing.'

'Most people would give their eye teeth to live in a mews off the King's Road. You can imagine a Beatle, or Michael Caine living here,' Charlee enthused. Ffinch switched on the ancient coffee percolator and looked over at her, his head tilted on one side. 'Now what?' she demanded with some asperity.

'Oh, nothing. It's just that you're the first woman I've encountered who likes sixties camper vans and a mews last decorated in the early seventies. You're different, I'll give you that, Montague,' he mused, seemingly perplexed by the idea. 'Very different.'

'Unique,' she countered, moving to one side as he came out of the kitchen, picked up their bags and climbed the stairs. He paused on the fourth tread and looked over his shoulder at her. 'Oh, I see, yes; lead the way,' Charlee followed in his wake, full of curiosity. When they reached a narrow landing, he pushed a door open to reveal a small bedroom containing a single brass bed, rattan dressing table and a calico hanging wardrobe.

Ffinch placed her bag on the purple and magenta bedspread with white cotton fringing. 'I hope you don't suffer from migraines, the colour scheme in this room's enough to induce an attack. But at least the bathroom,' he crossed the narrow landing and pushed open another door, 'is pretty up to date. If there's one thing I can't stand it's creaking plumbing.'

Charlee poked her head round the bathroom door and spotted a double shower stall with state-of-the-art angled water jets. Unbidden, the image of Ffinch showering with some female, their bodies covered in soap as the jets lashed them with hot water, sprung into her mind. She reminded herself it was none of her business who he brought back here.

'Groovy, baby,' she laughed, copying the dance from *Pulp Fiction*. Strangely enough, despite the erotic images rocketing around in her head, she felt completely at ease with Ffinch in his grandparents' house.

'Oh, behave ...' he responded in an Austin Powers voice and smiled back. Briefly, the tension that was always there behind his smile, the way he held himself in readiness for something she didn't quite understand, vanished and he seemed almost happy. Then the frown that knitted his straight dark eyebrows together was back in place. 'I'll leave you to settle in,' he said, backing out onto the landing and walking downstairs.

'Thanks.' Charlee re-entered the bedroom and stood on a semicircular rug in clashing shades of pink and fuchsia.

Then she flopped back onto the brass bed and drummed her heels. She was overwhelmed by a great sense of release, thankful that she'd left her family home and her angst-ridden Christmas behind. Here, in this shabby mews she could wrap her professional persona around her like a comfort blanket. She could be herself, or at the very least the person she longed to be, knew she could become - Charlee Montague, investigative reporter and free spirit.

She held Great-Granny's diamond ring up to the light, polished it on her sweater and kissed it. After all the setbacks, she couldn't quite believe she was Ffinch's partner and about to embark on her first professional assignment. She closed her eyes and prayed she wouldn't screw up and let down everyone who believed in her: Poppy, Sam Walker and Ffinch.

But, especially, herself.

By the time she wandered downstairs, the Indian takeaway had arrived and Ffinch was spreading out foil dishes on some portable food warmers, heated by night lights. Each foil dish had a serving spoon in it and he flicked the tops off two bottles of Indian beer, handing one to her.

'Hope you like your curry hot,' he said.

'We used to have curry-eating competitions at Uni, to see who could eat the hottest vindaloo before reaching for water or beer. Madly bad for one's constitution; I'm sure I've given myself ulcers trying not to let the side down.' She spooned fragrant rice onto a vintage Denby plate, dark-brown and with orange and yellow swirls.

'Happy days?' he asked, sliding off the sofa and leaning against the cube of brown suede that was the matching footstool to the sofa. He waited for her answer. But Charlee, in spite of her earlier resolution not be sidetracked from winning the Pulitzer Prize for Journalism, was distracted by his long, slim legs and the silver-tipped cowboy boots peeping out from beneath his jeans.

Quite the gaucho, she thought.

'Very,' she replied, giving herself a mental shake. 'Naturally, I was sad to leave my friends behind but very happy to take up my post at *What'cha!* I was appointed thanks to my friendship with Poppy Walker, and some of the staff quite understandably resent that. I want to prove to Sam, to everyone, what I'm made of.' Her slight pause made it plain that she was aware that she had to prove herself to Ffinch, too.

'I guess we both owe our leg up in the world to Sam. He's very astute, and wouldn't have suggested you for this assignment if he didn't think you had what it takes.' He took a long swig of his beer. 'Neither would I.' He raised the beer bottle and chinked against hers. 'I guess you turning up after the holidays wearing Granny's ring will set the tongues clacking?'

'I think you can safely assume that,' Charlee said as she speared a piece of beef with her fork. 'So, what happens next?'

'We wait for the announcement to appear in *The Times*. Book you into the Thornham Boot Camp the same weekend as Markova and then we talk tactics.'

'Tactics?'

'The logistics of the operation. Build up our legend: let everyone at *What'cha!* know how much in lurve we are.' His expression made Charlee think he'd travelled this road before, it had ended in disaster and he was in no hurry to repeat the mistake. Then he changed tack.

'Shopping,' Ffinch said, giving her a quizzical look. As if he could hear the cogs in her brain whizzing round and wondered what was distracting her. 'Earth calling Montague, come in please.'

Charlee snapped out of her introspection. 'What about shopping?'

'I was thinking; we'd better kit you out in some designer running gear. I don't think the tracksuit you've had since sixth form and a pair of old trainers will cut it with the kind of women who attend these boot camps.'

'On expenses?' she asked innocently, her mind running to Juicy Couture or Stella McCartney.

'Of course. I wouldn't imagine your intern's wages would cover it. But don't go mad, you'll only be there Thursday to Monday. Oh, and you'd better buy a posh frock for the Gala Dinner on Sunday night. All the fiancés are invited to that.'

'You seem to know a lot about it,' she observed, tearing into a piece of peshwari naan and trying not to sound overly suspicious.

'I've made it my business to find out as much about the camp as I can. Preparation is all, Montague. Never forget that.' He held out his beer bottle and Charlee chinked hers against it again.

'I'll drink to that, partner.' They ate in companionable silence, Charlee guessing that neither of them was in the mood for conversation. She yawned. Now that she was relaxing properly for the first time since their evening in the skip and they weren't sniping at each other, tiredness overwhelmed her. 'Sorry,' she said from behind her hand as another yawn almost dislocated her jaw. 'I think I'm going to have a shower and then turn in, if that's okay?'

'Sure. I'll watch a movie, clear up and then do the same. See you in the morning, Montague. We need to hit the ground running - I'll give you a call around about half seven.' He swivelled round, reached for the remote and turned on the flat screen TV and began surfing through the channels, effectively dismissing her.

'Okay, goodnight then.' But he didn't answer; he had the distracted look she was beginning to recognise. Putting down her beer bottle, she climbed the stairs as the opening titles from *Die Hard* burst noisily on to the screen.

Chapter Twenty
Green Card

Charlee woke up in pitch blackness. Her sleep-addled brain took a minute or so to remember where she was. She pulled the bedcovers up to her chin, inhaling the fresh smell of fabric conditioner mingled with a subtle undertone of some long-forgotten fragrance; patchouli? sandalwood? Then the thousand and one questions she'd put to the back of her mind when she'd fallen into a dreamless sleep demanded answers.

They came at her in a random, illogical order.

Had Ffinch known she'd be coming back to the mews with him and made up the spare bed in advance before leaving for Berkshire? He struck her as capable but in no way domesticated. It was more likely, she reasoned, that he had many friends who stayed over and he kept the room in a permanent state of readiness. Maybe he had a cleaner who looked after the mews for him and kept everything spick and span for him. She pictured a homely lady who left casseroles and pots of soup in the fridge and did the odd bit of shopping, too, hence the fresh milk.

More thoughts rattled round in her brain like loose marbles in a biscuit tin.

While she totally bought in to being his partner and getting the photographs Sam wanted, she couldn't help wondering why it was necessary for her to attend the boot camp. Ffinch probably had every long-angled lens known to man and a few more besides. Surely, he could lay hidden in the reed beds until the brides came out for their early morning jog or - what was the word - Fartlek Training? Snapping Markova looking all hot and sweaty would be a piece of low-fat, gluten-free cake in those circumstances.

On Christmas Eve, he'd accused her of looking a gift horse in the mouth and here she was, doing it again. If she had any sense she'd complete the mission, impress Sam and Ffinch with her professionalism and hope they used her again sometime in the future. She had no desire to return to the fetid photo archive or spend the rest of her days walking Vanessa's pampered rat on a rope.

Now very much awake and feeling overheated, Charlee threw back the bedcovers. She reached out and touched the radiator on the left-hand side of her bed and then drew back her hand. Who, she pondered, left their heating on all night? A man recovering from dengue fever, who felt the cold and suffered recurring bouts of malaria-like symptoms. That's who.

Knowing she wouldn't sleep, she swung her legs out of bed and reached for Poppy's Christmas present - a white, fleecy onesie covered in black splodges. She smiled as she zipped herself into it, pulling up the hood with its floppy ears, to complete the transformation. Tiptoeing onto the landing, but leaving her bedroom door open because she didn't want to wake Ffinch, Charlie suddenly felt hungry. She'd been too excited to eat last night but now fancied the cold remains of their vindaloo and maybe a glass of water. Without switching on the light, she felt her way downstairs, squeezing between the back of the sofa and the under-the-stairs bookcases. Not knowing the lay of the land, she barked her shin on the corner of a brass-edged occasional table.

'Christ on a bike!' she blasphemed, rubbing her knee until the pain subsided.

'What the fuck?' Dracula-like, Ffinch rose from the depths of the sofa where he'd obviously been asleep. He took one look at Charlee in

168

her onesie, clearly believing he was hallucinating.

'It's me, Charlee,' she said a trifle unnecessarily.

She threw back the hood of her onesie while Ffinch struggled into a sitting position, propping himself up on his elbows and shaking the sleep from his brain.

'Of course it's you. Who else would be roaming around at silly o'clock dressed like a ...'

'Character from *One Hundred and One Dalmatians*.' Charlee didn't like his sarcastic tone so she pulled herself to her full height and brushed down her fleecy suit. 'If you must know, Poppy thought ...' She was about to explain the joke but stopped herself. Was Ffinch one of the boys or part of the management? Would he find their alternative nickname for Vanessa amusing or insubordinate?

'Poppy?' he prompted, as though he'd forgotten who Poppy was. Charlee didn't respond, but headed for the kitchen instead. 'I'll have a coffee if you're making one,' he said, like a man used to giving orders and having them obeyed.

'Will you now?' Charlee muttered under her breath. 'I'm not making coffee, but I'll make you one. Fancy some cold vindaloo?'

'Strangely, I'll pass,' he said. Getting up, he stood in the doorway watching her opening cupboards, locating mugs and plates. 'Tell me - do you have a whole wardrobe of dodgy sleepwear? On Christmas Day, you wore a dressing gown several sizes and several years too young for you. Not to mention the bovine-shaped slippers.'

'How kind of you to notice,' Charlee said as she switched on the kettle. 'For your information, I keep the sexy stuff for ...' Aware that this conversation was getting a little too personal and remembering her vow to keep everything on a professional footing, she stopped in mid-sentence.

'For?' he prompted, lounging against the doorframe, arms folded, looking like he was enjoying himself. 'Gentlemen callers?'

'Gentlemen callers! Where do you get your ideas from?' she asked. 'The sixties, like this house? You make me sound like Christine Keeler.

Here ...' She reheated the remains of the coffee in the microwave and passed a mug to him with ill grace. She then piled a plate high with cold rice and beef vindaloo. ''Scuse,' she said and waited for him to move so she could pass by without making bodily contact. She sat down on the brown suede cube footstool and tucked into her midnight feast. 'Wha?' she asked, crunching into a poppadom and getting shards all over herself and the carpet. 'Don't worry, I'll clean up.'

'I'm not worried,' he said, moving onto the couch and looking at her like she was a species he hadn't encountered before. Charlee munched on, feeling very self-conscious under his unblinking scrutiny. He looked as if he was about to treat her to one of his barbed comments when his mobile rang. She glanced at the clock on the wall next to the faded Hockney print. Two thirty. Who rang at this time of the night? He must have been expecting the call and that was probably why he hadn't gone to bed. Either that or he was an insomniac. Charlee watched his expression morph from amusement at her eating cold curry in a onesie, into something entirely different - muted excitement overlain with dark purpose.

'I've got to take this.' Giving an apologetic shrug, he went into the kitchen and pulled the concertina-style vinyl door closed behind him.

Charlee sat cross-legged on the footstool and chewed at her beef. Then she carefully put her plate on the floor and tiptoed over to the kitchen door. She could hear Ffinch's conversation quite clearly through the gap where the door and the catch didn't quite meet.

He was speaking passable, if not fluent, Spanish.

'*Sí, la noche de la marea alta, lo he comprobado en las tablas de mareas e Internet -dos veces. Deja de preocuparte, no va a pasar nada. ¿Vas a estar allí?*' Yes, the night of the high tide; I've checked the tide tables and the internet - twice. Stop worrying, it'll be fine. You'll be there? '*Bien. No, ella no tiene ni idea y así quiero que siga.*' Good. No, she has no idea and that's how I intend to keep it. Then he laughed and the rest of his conversation was lost. When he emerged from the kitchen,

Charlee was back on the suede cube innocently polishing off the remains of her vindaloo and reaching for a glass of water.

'Everything, okay?' she asked.

'Fine. I think I'll turn in ...'

'Were you waiting for that phone call?' she asked directly. 'Is it something to do with our assignment? Something you need to share with me?' There - she'd provided him with the chance to include her, take her into his confidence.

'Oh, no - that? Just speaking to one of my Brazilian cousins. Different time zone. You know how it is,' he added evasively.

'Not sure that I do,' she said. 'But I do know for a fact that they speak Portuguese in Brazil and you were speaking Spanish. I couldn't help but overhear.' She gave a small, unrepentant shrug and walked through to the kitchen with her plate. 'See you in the morning then, partner.' She put enough emphasis on the word to let him know that she was aware he was keeping stuff from her. But if Ffinch noticed the nuance, he did not attempt to expand on his previous answer.

'Sure. Laters,' he replied, returning to the sofa and switching the television on. Charlee glanced at him as she climbed the stairs but he was staring blankly at the wall to the right of the screen, in that way he had. His mind was clearly on more weighty matters than a rerun of the old spy movie *The Ipcress File*.

It wasn't far from the mews to Knightsbridge. However, by the time Charlee had bought two tracksuits, new trainers, a posh frock for the Gala Dinner and other things she thought necessary for the mission, she was exhausted. Ffinch had made her breakfast and then fetched an ancient motorbike from a garage across the cobbled yard, handed her a set of keys and told her to have fun. Typically, he'd roared off down the mews without telling her where he was going or when he'd be back.

Charlee was prepared to bet good money that none of his previous relationships had lasted longer than a few months - no, strike that, weeks - given his autocratic behaviour. Even if he appeared to have all the attributes most women found attractive in a man. He was undeniably sexy and good looking, a talented photographer and he came from a moneyed background, judging by the location of the mews. But that cut no ice with her. In her opinion, he came with too much baggage, too many issues to resolve. She didn't have the time to get to know him well enough to sort out his hang-ups, she had a career to forge and she couldn't let anything get in her way.

When he returned she would tell him that he took the whole 'I'm a lone wolf, don't bother me with questions, baby,' act a little too literally. And it wasn't attractive, well - not to her anyway.

Feeling suddenly rather lonely, she deposited the Harvey Nichols bags on the floor and wished that Poppy was here so she could show off her new clothes. Then she headed for the kitchen, poured herself a glass of Chablis, put the groceries she'd bought in the fridge and took her bags upstairs. After a quick shower, during which she dismissed the haunting image of Ffinch and one of his ladies getting up to no good in the same space, she dressed and then set about preparing pasta carbonara - her signature dish.

Her only dish if she was being totally honest.

When she next glanced out of the kitchen window, it was half past four and dark.

Walking back into the sitting room, she retrieved the Blue-ray of *Green Card* she'd bought and waited for Ffinch to come home. She imagined the scenario - eating pasta off their knees, drinking the bottle of Chianti she'd bought in Harvey Nicks, and watching a movie. The plot had a resonance for them and she envisaged them bonding over the DVD, maybe even shedding a tear at the end. Last night - apart from the secretive phone call, they'd got on pretty well together, and during breakfast it'd been the same - until he'd roared off on his bike without a word.

By seven o'clock Charlee had drunk more wine than was good for her. At seven thirty, after eating almost a full packet of grissini and with her stomach rumbling, she decided she'd have her meal. She was just about to make enough for two and plate Ffinch's up for microwaving later but stopped herself. No way was she playing hausfrau to his master of the hall when he didn't have the good manners to text her and say where he was. She'd lay even money on him being a reckless driver, he could be lying in A&E for all she knew, having come off his motorbike. She pushed the thought away and chastised herself for being overly dramatic.

Sitting cross-legged on the sofa, she ate her pasta slowly and time passed. She pictured Ffinch surrounded by pert nurses who, in her vivid imagination, wore starched aprons and caps not seen in hospital for at least thirty years. They'd be soothing his fevered brow, applying cool ointment to his grazes while she was ... Well, what was she, exactly? Worried about him or infuriated because he was acting like a total arse, and accountable to no one.

There was going to be some plain talking when he arrived home. This enterprise seemed designed to please only one of the partners.

At half past eight, the throaty roar of a motorbike reverberated through the mews and Charlee stiffened. Her mouth was set in a stubborn line, which, should Ffinch have the wit or the inclination to read her expression, would warn him that she wouldn't be playing ball tonight. The garage door slammed closed, the key turned in the lock and Ffinch entered looking the quite the man in his bike leathers and helmet. He pushed up the visor and sniffed appreciatively.

'Mm, that smells good.' He put the helmet on the stairs and un- · zipped his leather jacket to reveal a Polartec fleece over a T-shirt. 'What are we having?'

What are *we* having? Charlee almost choked on the last of her wine but kept her cool and smiled a bright, welcoming smile.

'Pasta carbonara with side salad and garlic bread,' she said, returning her plate to the kitchen. 'For pudding - chocolate cheesecake and raspberries. And the choice of wine this evening is Chianti Classico,' she called out from the sink, like this was Master Chef. Then she stuck her head round the kitchen door. 'You do know how to cook pasta carbonara, don't you? If not, this should help.' She returned to the sitting room, handed him a tatty old cook book, removed *Green Card* from the Blue-ray player and dropped it on the sofa. Then she took down her coat from the bentwood coat rack, scooped up the house keys and put them in her handbag along with her mobile phone.

For dramatic effect she checked her watch and then squeezed past Ffinch who was standing in the small space between the door at the foot of the stairs looking dumbfounded.

'You're going out?' he asked with all the disappointment of a man who'd clearly expected to eat a home-cooked meal prepared by someone else. 'Do you know what time it is?'

'Thanks, I do - and, actually, I'm running late. I'm meeting friends in the West End, so don't wait up. We can discuss the - what did you call it - the logistics, of how this is going to work over breakfast. If and when I return. Oh, and by the way, here's your homework - watch and learn.' She bent over the sofa, picked up *Green Card* and handed it to him. 'I will be asking questions.'

'You aren't going anywhere in that state.'

'I don't know what you mean,' she pronounced grandly, but rather spoiled it by hiccupping and wobbling slightly on her high heels.

Two glasses of Chablis and half a bottle of Chianti were swishing round in her stomach, as was apparent from her bolshie manner and the way she had almost gone head first over the back of the sofa. Grabbing her elbow, Ffinch hauled her upright and righted her as if she was one of those roly-poly toys found at the bottom of a budgie's cage. They were standing almost nose to nose, so close that Charlee had to lean away from Ffinch and squint up at him in order to focus.

She had to admit that he presented a beguiling picture, in spite of his furious expression. His hair was sexily dishevelled from wearing the helmet; he smelled of the cold night air, leather and aftershave. But what man wouldn't look good in bike leathers, Charlee pondered hazily, even one as boot-faced as Ffinch?

'You. Are. Going. Nowhere,' he said, breaking the spell. It was like rock, paper, scissors all over again, a battle of wills - but who would be the first to crack?

'I'll go where I like, and do what I like; and not you - nor anyone else - can stop me. So, I'll thank you to return my elbow. I'm going to need it for fighting my way to the bar.' She tried to wriggle free but he held her fast.

'You issue too many challenges, Montague, you know that. You push a man to breaking point, think you can deliver one of your cutting little remarks and -'

'And - what?' There had been a change of mood somewhere along the line. This didn't seem to be about him being late or her being drunk and refusing to come over all Nigella in the kitchen. It was about the interrupted kiss they'd exchanged in her father's study, the way his tongue had pushed seductively between her parted lips and how she'd relished the feeling - and wanted an encore.

'One of these days you'll go too far and you won't be able to talk your way out of trouble.'

'Well, let's just hope that you're around to witness my fall.' She was proud of the way she delivered that line. Eyes crossed, skin glowing, she removed Granny's ring and handed it to him. 'Here, put this in a safe place. I don't want it cramping my style. I'll let you know tomorrow if you'll be cancelling the announcement in *The Times*, too. And in case you're wondering, I am seriously pissed off.'

'Seriously pissed might be nearer the mark,' he observed snarkily. She pulled free of his grasp and almost broke several of his toes by accidently pitching forward in her killer heels. 'Well, okay, off you go and make a fool of yourself with all the other ladettes,' he mocked and pushed the door closed behind her with a booted foot.

Once Charlee was out in the mews, the cold night air stung her flushed cheeks and the echo of the door slamming ricocheted off the walls. Now, she wished she hadn't been so impetuous. She'd much rather have spent the night warm and secure in the mews, but she had to make her point. She was no pushover. When she reached the end of the mews, she headed for Sloane Square tube. She'd spend tonight in her freezing cold bedsit and return early tomorrow morning to lay down the rules of engagement.

They were equal partners and Ffinch'd better get used to the idea.

Next morning she walked down the cobbled yard blinking owlishly in the pale January sunshine. She'd slapped on extra make-up to hide the ravages of a hangover and a sleepless night spent fully dressed and wrapped in a duvet in her unheated bedsit. Letting herself into the mews with the set of keys Ffinch had provided, she half expected to find him still in bed. However, he was dressed and eating toast in front of *Sky News*, all bright-eyed and bushy-tailed.

'Morning, Charlee. Good night?'

'The best,' she said. 'Didn't finish until late.' She waited for him to ask where she'd gone and who'd she hung out with, but he didn't.

Typical.

'I watched your movie,' he said, pouring two coffees from the percolator.

'And?'

'I didn't cry if that's what you're asking,' he said, looking at her over the rim of his cup. His eyes were wary, showing he was unsure of her mood and taking things slowly. 'And I didn't need to ring for an ambulance, in case you're wondering.'

'Ambulance?'

'For my broken foot. You do remember stomping on it, I take it?'

'You manhandled me,' she replied, 'and got what you deserved.' Reaching over, she helped herself to a slice of buttered toast off his breakfast tray and bit into it. 'For future reference, I like thin cut marmalade.'

'Oh, I get it. You won't cook for me but you're perfectly happy to steal my breakfast?' Charlee could tell that he wasn't too annoyed and seemed in quite a buoyant mood. She wondered where he'd been, who he'd spent the day with which had resulted in him seeming so upbeat.

'That's about it,' she answered almost automatically as she tried to piece the jigsaw together. 'If you've learned anything from watching the movie you'd realise we have to know everything about each other in order to be convincing.' He raised an eyebrow at 'everything', and the look he sent told her that was never going to happen.

'And, another thing, how come you get to be Andie McDowell and I have to be Gerard Depardieu? I'm sure that France is very proud of him but - really?' He indicated his slim frame, newly washed hair and fashionable clothes with one sweep of his hand. Charlee couldn't help it, she giggled, even though she was still annoyed with him for his cavalier behaviour the previous evening.

'It's an allegory. You don't have to look like Gerard, you're much -' she didn't finish the sentence: better looking for one thing.

'Almost slipped up there and paid me a compliment, didn't you Montague?' Ffinch laughed at her discomfiture.

'You just have to be like him. Only make a better job of it. Sally and Vanessa will make those US Immigration officials look like Brown Owl and Akela once they find out we've become engaged. If we can fool them, everyone else will be a doddle.' She chewed at her - his - toast and sent him a covert look; it was plain that, without her, the plan to run a spoiler on *Mirror, Mirror*'s exclusive wouldn't get off the ground.

That gave her leverage and she intended to use it.

'Okay. Let's call a truce. I should have told you where I was going, that was wrong of me. It's simply that I'm used to working on my own. I'm not very good at being anyone's partner.' His face clouded over and Charlee suspected that he was drawn back to his abortive trip to Darien. It never seemed to be far from his mind. 'But you were out of the door before I could explain ...'

'I'm a hothead, I know it, but,' she took a deep breath, 'but, you see - I felt like I was reliving my teenage years. Taken for granted, sent on errands when my brothers were lounging around doing nothing in particular and being expected to run after them. It was a role that Mum was quite happy to play out, but I wasn't born to be anyone's handmaiden.' She sent him a fierce look and he held his hands up in a pacifying 'calm down, I get it' gesture.

'So, are we on? Are we a team?'

'I guess so.'

'In that case … would you put Granny's ring back on? It looked very lonely sitting on the bedside table next to my kindle last night.' He said it lightly but Charlee sensed that he'd come to realise that they needed each other. He needed her in the boot camp and she was desperate to get there and prove her worth. If last night's strop had led to this alteration in their relationship, it was worth a night freezing to death in her bedsit.

'Wh - what are you doing?' she asked as he slid off the sofa and got down on one knee.

'Getting into role. Finger,' he commanded and fetched Granny's ring out of his jeans pocket. Charlee glanced down at her engagement finger, which was sticky with marmalade and butter.

'Okay, but wait.' She stuck her fingers in her mouth and sucked them clean. That affected Ffinch in some fundamental way she didn't fully comprehend. He swallowed hard and his Adam's apple moved up and down as if his throat was suddenly dry. A slight flush spread across his cheekbones and, although his expression was bland, she suspected that he was relieved that she'd returned and the mission was still on. 'There.' She held out her hand and he took it in his.

'I should have done this properly first time round. Charlee, Charlotte, Carlotta - will you do me the honour of becoming my - temporary - wife?'

'Temporary, yes.'

She extended her finger and the ring slipped over her knuckle. When she'd tried it on the first time in her father's study, the ring had been cold from sitting in its velvet box. This time it was at blood temperature from being in his pocket and that felt much more intimate and unsettling. She shivered as the ring sat snugly under her second finger joint and - if the legend was true - connected straight to her heart.

They looked at it intently, each lost in their thoughts. Then Ffinch spoke, suddenly all professional and thorough, and broke the spell.

'You need to get showered and changed. I've booked us into a mate's studio for some photographs. You see, I have taken the DVD on board. He has all sorts of props, clothes, make-up, backdrops, etc. By the end of the session you'll believe that we really have been skiing in Val D'Isere or diving for coral in the Maldives.'

'Cool.' She smiled, getting to her feet. 'What should I wear?'

'Well not that all-in-one thing,' he laughed. 'Something smart but casual, you know the sort of thing. Half an hour? Don't worry about make-up, they'll take care of that at the studio.'

'This is it, isn't it?' Charlee said hugging herself, a big grin on her face. 'Us. Building our legend.'

Ffinch looked as if he wanted to say something dampening which would bring her back to earth, but apparently changed his mind. 'Yep, this is it. Now, go partner, get ready, we've a lot to get through today. And so as you know ...'

'Yes?'

'We're eating out tonight. I don't think my foot would withstand another assault.'

Laughing, Charlee took the stairs two at a time. She had questions, lots of them, but knew she'd have to curb her curiosity. Ffinch would tell her what this assignment was really about when he trusted her more.

She only hoped that she could wait that long.

Chapter Twenty-one
Green-Eyed Monsters

The next morning, Charlee and Ffinch took the lift to Editorial on the fifth floor of *What'cha!* in central London.

Charlee's hands were actually shaking as the doors pinged open and they entered the bright, open-plan office. Ffinch put his hand on the small of her back and rested it there, like Poppy reassuring one of her highly strung mares that she could take that fence and land safely on the other side. At Ffinch's suggestion they'd arrived fifteen minutes late and as they walked towards Charlee's desk, they ran the gauntlet of her co-workers. Once it was certain all eyes were on them, Ffinch dipped his head and kissed Charlee passionately before patting her on the bottom.

The office fell silent and all heads swivelled in their direction, like a flash mob version of *The Exorcist*.

'Catch you for lunch later, darling?' he asked, making his way towards Sam Walker's office.

'Of course, R - Rafa. L - laters,' Charlee replied in a strangled voice, sounding disconcertingly like Minnie Mouse with a stammer. Heart hammering and almost melting in a pool of lust after the unexpected kiss, she walked over to her desk. She hoped her co-workers would put her hectic colour down her being all loved-up and not anxiety at being found out.

The lift pinged and Poppy Walker walked out carrying two bottles of champagne and a huge bag of Kettle Crisps. She handed the champagne and crisps to the two post boys who'd travelled up in the lift with her and then sent them to the kitchen for glasses. Then she ran towards Charlee, waving her hands in the air and shrieking like a banshee.

'The ring. Lemme see the ring.' That was enough to break the spell which had fallen over the office and their co-workers rushed up to Charlee in a feeding frenzy to gawp at her left hand.

'That,' one of the male interns pronounced, 'is one serious piece of bling.'

'Bling?' an older female journalist sniffed. 'That, dear boy, is a fine piece of art deco jewellery, white gold with a square-cut diamond mounted on four sapphires cut from a single stone - if I'm not mistaken.'

'You're not mistaken,' Poppy put in, winking at Charlee. 'It's Ffinch's great-grandmother's ring, isn't that right, Charl?' Poppy widened her eyes and gave Charlee a significant look, reminding her that the game was afoot. They'd had a long heart-to-heart over the phone last night and Charlee now felt better prepared for what lay ahead.

'We could have chosen one from Tiffany's,' Charlee said, gathering her wits about her and slipping into role. 'But I think family heirlooms are more romantic, don't you?' She extended her hand obligingly, so the journos and interns could have a close look at the carbuncle.

'Just like Prince William and the Duchess of Cambridge,' one of the juniors swooned as the post boys handed round glasses of champagne.

'Hey, Montague,' one of the post boys said. 'When we last saw yer, you was waiting to be sacked. So what 'appened?'

'Not been up to anything you shouldn't, we hope.' His partner in crime patted his abdomen meaningfully. 'I think me uncle's got a shotgun if you need one.'

'To use on you, you mean?' Charlee quipped, and they all laughed.

'Like she'd tell you anyway,' Poppy said scathingly, handing round the tumblers of champagne. 'A toast - Charlee and Rafa.'

'Charlee and Rafa,' the others echoed, clinking glasses and relishing the moment.

A lowly intern landing Rafael Fonseca-Ffinch, what were the chances? As first days back after the Christmas holidays went, this one was exceeding anything anyone could have envisaged. They'd have plenty to talk about at the photocopying machine and in the Rat and Ferret after work.

'Thank you. It was all very ...' Charlee was about to say last-minute but stopped herself in time. 'Romantic.' There was a collective sigh from the younger women. 'The announcement should appear in *The Times* tomorrow, if anyone's interested. Rafa and I -' But she wasn't allowed time to say more because the lift doors pinged and Vanessa and Sally stepped out.

'We've got incoming,' the post boys chorused. Everyone scuttled back to their desks clutching glasses of champagne and even the post boys made themselves scarce. Only Poppy stood her ground, shoulder to shoulder with Charlee.

'Morning V,' she said, well aware that using an initial instead of her full name was guaranteed to antagonise Vanessa. 'Sally. Happy New Year.' She handed them a glass of champagne.

'What's all this?' Vanessa demanded frostily, looking round at the journalists who had their heads down behind their monitors, sipping at their champagne out of sight. 'Are we celebrating something? Does Chief know alcohol's being drunk so early in the morning?' she demanded, like she'd just taken the pledge.

'His idea,' Poppy drawled, topping up hers and Charlee's glasses. 'Which is to say - his and Rafa's.'

'Rafa?' Sally queried, forgetting herself and taking a sip of champagne. Vanessa gave them a steely look and put her glass down on Charlee's work station.

'Rafa?' she repeated. 'Rafa Ffinch?' she asked, as if there was any other.

'Yes,' Charlee put in, deciding it was time she joined the conversation. 'Rafa and I got engaged over Christmas.' She held out her hand, all the better to show off the diamond. 'It should be in *The Times* tomorrow, if they can fit us in. Otherwise it'll be in a day or two.'

'Fit you in?' Vanessa asked in constricted tones, massaging her throat with her right hand as if she was actually choking. Charlee reached into her bag and, magician-like, pulled out a silver picture frame. She polished it with her sleeve and made a great show of arranging it on her desk next to her pot of pens. The framed photo - one of several taken yesterday by Ffinch's 'mate', showed Ffinch in black tie, his jacket hooked over his shoulder on one finger and with his bow tie undone. Charlee was in an off-the-shoulder Grecian style evening dress and holding a helium balloon.

'Yes, it's been a *coupe de foudre* - taken us all by surprise.' Charlee gave what she hoped was a girlish laugh, but she was dead serious. If she couldn't convince Vanessa and Sally that she and Ffinch were love's young dream, what chance did she have with Anastasia Markova and the other bridezillas at the boot camp? 'And to think it all started in a skip ...' She paused for maximum effect, imagining for a moment she could hear Vanessa and Sally grinding their teeth. 'Although, to be fair, it started way before then and I have you to thank for that Vanessa.'

'Me?' Vanessa spluttered, looking as if she wouldn't give Charlee a paracetamol if it meant saving her life.

'Yes.' Charlee gave Vanessa and Sally a wide-eyed, innocent look. 'If you hadn't insisted that we acted as waiters at Rafa's book launch, I would never have bumped into him. We would never have discovered how much we had in common - journalism, a desire to travel, even to the most dangerous corners of the world, a sense of humour. Funny how these little twists of fate can have such an impact.' She breathed on Granny's ring and gave it a little polish on her jacket. 'Serendipity.'

'Oh my God,' Poppy said with such vehemence that they all jumped in their skins. 'I love that movie. John Cusack is beyond cute. I would never have let him get away so easily.' She looked so fierce and uncompromising that Charlee was glad Kate Beckinsale didn't work in Editorial, otherwise she would have feared for her safety. Vanessa, on the other hand, plainly had no idea what Poppy was talking about and looked as if her world had been turned on its head.

'I must have a word with Chief,' she said faintly, and made her way down the long corridor towards Sam's office.

'Ffinch is with him. They might not want to be disturbed,' Charlee said ever so helpfully. Vanessa skidded to a halt, swivelled round in her Manolos and gave Charlee a poisonous look. 'Just saying,' Charlee added, as Sally almost collided with Vanessa, who in turn glared at all three of them. Judging by Vanessa's expression she was feeling firmly out of the loop. They knew about things she didn't - like, the film *Serendipity* and the fact that John Cusack was - apparently - beyond cute.

A new world order was being established at *What'cha!* with Ffinch as its crown prince and Charlee its blushing, if not princess, bride. Ever astute, Vanessa had picked up the vibe but wasn't ready to make way for the Young Pretenders, yet. Time they were put in their place, her cold grey sweep of Charlee implied. She glanced round at the rest of the workforce who had popped their heads above their monitors and were watching silently.

'Thank you, Montague. Chief has never turned me away from his office and I don't imagine he's about to start now. Sally, with me, if you please. And as for the rest of you ...' The room was suddenly filled with the sound of fingers tapping away at keyboards and mice being clicked with such ferocity that someone needed to ring the RSPCA. Openly pleased that she hadn't lost her ability to strike terror into their hearts, Vanessa allowed herself a self-satisfied smile and teetered along the corridor as fast as her Manolos would allow.

The whole office waited for Sam Walker's door to open and close and then released a collective breath. Poppy high-fived Charlee and gave her a hug. The rest of the staff got to their feet, chanting: 'Go, Charlee. Go, Charlee'. Charlee grinned and allowed herself a modest bow before sitting at her desk and switching on her computer. After this, she didn't think she'd be exiled to the photo archive - ever again.

Times were changing at *What'cha!* and she was in the very vanguard of those changes.

Chapter Twenty-two
Sex, Lies and Telephoto Lenses

Fifteen minutes later, Charlee was poked roughly in the shoulder.

'Chief says you're to go in,' Sally spat at her. 'He and Rafa want to talk to you.'

'Thanks, Sal.' Charlee used the diminutive of her name to reinforce the change in their positions at *What'cha!* She thought of asking Sally to be a bridesmaid at the wedding-that-was-never-going-to-happen, but decided that might be taking the joke too far. Instead, she gathered her notebook and pen and made her way down the corridor.

Standing outside Sam's office, she remembered only too clearly the last time she'd been there. Then she'd thought she was about to be sacked. Now, here she was - less than two weeks later - 'engaged' to one of the most revered photographers in the business. It put a whole new spin on the concept of 'speed dating'; from zero to hero during the course of the Christmas hols!

Man - it felt good!

Pulling back her shoulders, she raised her hand to knock at the door and then paused. It was slightly ajar and she didn't want to barge in while Sam and Ffinch were deep in conversation. Her position wasn't that certain - just yet. She pushed the door further ajar, listening in on their conversation and trying to gauge when she should enter. Last time she'd seen Sam Walker, he'd been wearing an Emma Bridgewater apron and she'd helped him with preparing dinner. Back in harness, 'Chief' was quite capable of flaying the flesh off her bones with a cutting remark if she got above herself.

Rafa was speaking. 'Look, Sam, I'm not sure about this.'

'Oh, come on, Rafa - it's the best shot we've got. You land the story of the year, I run it and *What'cha!* gets all the glory. It'll be my last hurrah and double the price I can ask for the magazine. There could be a knighthood in it - Lady Daphne - imagine how that'd go down with the horsey set.'

'I know, but what about Montague? If anything happened to her, the Brothers Grimm would tear me apart, limb from limb.'

'Look, she's tough, smart and can carry it off. You're getting close, don't screw it up now, Raf,' Sam said in a tone that brooked no refusal.

'She's no fool, she's already beginning to suspect -' Ffinch began but Sam swept his objections out of the way.

'Last time I looked you're a man and she's a woman. Do I have to explain about the birds and the bees? Woo her, put so many stars in her eyes that she'll be blind to what's going on under her nose.'

'That's a tall order - I get the distinct impression that she thinks I'm a -'

The phone on Sam's desk rang and Ffinch's last words were lost. Judging this was an opportune moment to enter, Charlee knocked on the door and entered without waiting for Sam's usual, headmasterly 'co-ome' - or terse 'fuck off'.

'Charlee.' Ffinch frowned as she walked into the office, perhaps wondering how long she'd been standing there and what she might have overheard. 'You've got your notebook, good. There are a few details to finalise and then we're on.'

'That's great,' she said, smiling artlessly to allay his suspicions. 'What happens next?' she asked as Sam put the phone back on its charger.

'We're going to put it about that you and Ffinch are going off on a ...

what d'you call them, Rafa?'

'Minibreak,' Ffinch put in straight-faced, although she suspected that his lips were twitching. 'In a country house hotel, to cement our love, and to celebrate our engagement.'

'Country house hotel? Isn't that just a little bit too *Bridget Jones*?'

She recalled the conversation they'd had in this very office. 'I have no intention of working late, missing the last train back to town and staying over in some country house hotel with you. Or being shown to a suite of rooms which - surprise, surprise - have conveniently inter-connecting doors.' And his mocking rejoinder: 'Don't think you'd be able to keep your hands off me, eh Chelsea? I quite understand.'

'Why do we need to go anywhere?' Charlee foresaw herself being relegated to joke-girlfriend/comical-fiancée - a pawn, pushed and pulled this way and that by Sam and Ffinch. And she wasn't having any of it.

'We're not actually going any further than The Ship Inn, Thornham,' Ffinch explained. 'It's just a story we're concocting to explain why you and I have disappeared. In actual fact we'll be going undercover, initial-ly passing ourselves off as birdwatchers - to check out the salt marshes where the prospective brides go for their cross-country runs.'

Charlee was about to say that it all seemed a bit over the top just to get a few snaps of a dishevelled Russian model but she kept her coun-sel. Better they thought she actually was the lovestruck fiancée she'd been slated to play.

'The Ship Inn, Thornham? Never heard of it,' she said.

'It's close by Burnham Market or, to give it its nickname, Chelsea-by-the-Sea,' Ffinch put in. 'Lots of chichi shops and couples with black Labradors wearing Barbours.'

'You can get Barbours for Labradors now?' she asked, straight-faced. Ffinch looked about to explain that there should be an Oxford comma somewhere in the sentence, then he caught her eye.

'Very funny, Montague. Remind me not to tangle with a linguist in future.' Then he grinned and looked younger and momentarily free from the underlying strain that creased his forehead and had him pacing the living room floor during the night watches. His gaze rested on her for a few moments, consideringly, and Charlee flushed under his calm regard. Unbidden, her heart flipped over; but she put it down to excitement and anticipation of what lay ahead of them. 'You're getting a free holiday, a spa break,' he reminded her.

'A roll round in the mud more like it,' Charlee put with her usual asperity.

'So don't push it.'

'No, sir,' she saluted him. 'Or should that be sir - darling? I so want to get it right.'

'Okay you two lovebirds,' Sam said shortly. 'Get out of my office, you're putting me off my lunchtime pint. Go - make arrangements, work on your story, do whatever's necessary for the success of this venture. Just don't run up massive expenses or you'll be paying for them yourselves. Go!' he repeated as Charlee stood there clasping her reporter's notebook to her breast and Ffinch seemed lost in thought. 'Come back when you've got the spoiler - I want to run it as soon as possible. *Mirror! Mirror!* won't know what's hit it.'

He rubbed his hands together.

'Okay, Chief.' Charlee made for the door but then paused, expecting Ffinch to follow her. But obviously they had further business to discuss, business she wasn't party to. 'I'll go and tidy up my desk and put it about the office that -'

'Yes, yes, whatever.' Sam had already lost interest and wanted her gone.

Charlee walked back to her desk, sat down heavily, put her notebook and pen by the mouse pad and covered her face with her hands. She let out a long breath - there was a lot to think about and she needed to marshal her thoughts into some kind of order. Downing the last of her champagne, she made her way to the staff kitchen and put her glass in the dishwasher. Vanessa went ape if the work surfaces weren't kept clean and tidy. With everything else going on in her life right now, she didn't need Vanessa on her case, too.

Charlee spent a large chunk of the morning researching the north Norfolk coast around Brancaster and Thornham. She made it known that she and Ffinch were taking a minibreak in a country house hotel in Cornwall and left the bush telegraph to do the rest. At lunch time her colleagues kept passing her desk, demanding another look at the ring and asking some very personal questions.

'You're looking fabulous, Charlee,' one female intern said. 'You have a certain glow.'

'It's called fresh air and exercise,' she quipped. 'Almost a week in the country does that to a girl.'

'Surely you mean s-exercise?' another commented and they all laughed. 'You're having great sex, aren't you?'

'Of course she's having great sex. She's engaged to Ffinch - the man's sex on legs. Isn't he?'

'You might say so, but I couldn't possibly comment,' Charlee replied, concentrating on her typing with an air of mystery designed to keep them guessing.

'God, I'm like, so jealous, you know?' the first intern sighed.

'If I was engaged to him, I'd never let him out of my bed ...' someone added. 'We'd never get up, we'd order in food and champagne and ...'

'Those gorgeous grey eyes,' the first intern said, romantically. 'Or, are they blue?'

'Come-to-bed-eyes,' another female sighed. 'Although I'd settle for five minutes in the stationery cupboard, if the chance arose. Oops, sorry Montague, just kidding,' she said, realising she'd dropped a clanger.

'And his family's loaded,' someone else added prosaically. 'You've hit pay dirt, Montague. If you can hold onto him, that is.'

'I happen to think he's got a pretty good bargain, too,' Charlee said sniffily.

'Yeah, ri-ight,' they opined, leaving the words 'as if!' hanging in the air.

'Coming to Pret for a sandwich, Charlee?'

'No, I've got an article to finish for Vanessa, then we - Ff - Rafa and me, we're going home to pack and -'

'- have afternoon sex,' the girl at the next desk put in, comically popping her head over the top of her monitor, Muppet-like.

'You lot are obsessed,' Charlee laughed, thinking - 'little do they know'. The closest they'd come to amorous was the 'let's get it out of the way' kiss in her father's study and her standing on Ffinch's foot. 'But it's a possibility,' she said with a suitably dreamy expression whilst thinking - No Way, José.

'Lucky cow,' they chorused, meaning it as an accolade.

Vanessa and Sally came down the corridor and Charlee's co-workers scattered like ninepins, reaching for their coats and bags before Vanessa could invent some trumped up reason for them to work through their lunch break.

'Montague - a word,' she said imperiously and walked into the staff kitchen, clearly expecting Charlee to follow.

Sighing, Charlee pushed her chair away from her workstation. She would be furious if Sam had sent Vanessa to bring her up to speed on the assignment. That was Ffinch's job, he owed her that at least. Hadn't they said that the less people who knew about their plans, the greater chance the mission had of succeeding?

Entering the kitchen, she folded her arms and leaned against the doorframe, primed for a quick getaway.

'Montague,' Vanessa began, baring her teeth in what she obviously imagined to be a winning smile. 'Charlotte ... I've been a good mentor to you since you arrived at *What'cha!* have I not?'

There was only one answer to that question, Charlee thought, crossing her fingers behind her back. 'Yes, Vanessa.'

'And I've helped too, whenever I could,' Sally smiled, reached out and straightened Charlee's collar. It was only with the greatest of difficulty that Charlee stopped herself from flinching.

'I guess,' Charlee replied, wondering where this was going.

'So -' Vanessa brought her hands together and steepled her fingers, as if she was about to pray. 'We feel we ought to warn you.'

'Warn me?' Charlee felt as if someone had poured a jug of ice-cold water down the back of her neck. 'About?'

'Ffinch. The rumours.' Sally moved over to the sink and fired up the coffee machine.

'What rumours?' Charlee made an effort to pull herself together; repeating phrases like a simple-minded parrot would get her nowhere.

'His drug taking. What he was really doing in Darien. I mean, come on - taking his team deep into the rainforest and losing two of them in the process? How many people get captured by the Contras, held to ransom and live to tell the tale?' Charlee went quiet; these were the very questions keeping her from sleep.

'Go on,' she prompted, feeling strangely disloyal for talking about Ffinch behind his back - especially with two harpies like Sally and Vanessa. Then she remembered Sam's mocking 'put stars in her eyes' and Ffinch's economy with the truth and hardened her heart.

'They say ...' Sally and Vanessa took a step closer to ensure they weren't overheard. 'They say that the charity he's set up in Colombia ...' Sally's voice dropped to a conspiratorial whisper and racked up the tension.

'The one raising money to provide a hospital boat for the people who fished him out of the Amazon and nursed him back to health?' Charlee didn't want either woman to think that she was completely ignorant of her fiancé's backstory. 'What about it?'

'Just that it's a front for his other activities.' Vanessa paused meaningfully.

'What activities might those be?' Charlee asked, raising a skeptical eyebrow. Vanessa and Sally had shown no interest in her welfare before now, so why were they acting like her fairy godmothers all of a sudden?

'Gun running, drug smuggling, money laundering,' Sally ventured. She gave Charlee a pitying look which suggested that someone high on l-u-r-v-e, and grateful for being singled out by a man like Ffinch wouldn't see what was staring her in the face. That it was her duty as her superior - her friend - to point out these matters.'

'No-oh.' The premise was so ridiculous that Charlee burst out laughing. Ffinch, a money launderer, a gun runner and a cokehead? 'No-oh. Really, you've got it all wrong.'

'You didn't know Rafa before his trip to Colombia, did you?' Vanessa asked.

Charlee was forced to admit that was true. She'd heard him mentioned, of course, as if he was the best thing since organic, wholemeal Poilâne bread - but they hardly moved in the same circles. Ffinch was in the stratosphere while she was firmly anchored to earth.

'No, I didn't,' she admitted.

'He came back from South America a changed man. Mood swings, dark moments, lapses in concentration. He hasn't taken one photo since.'

Vanessa and Sally traded a look. If Charlee didn't know better, she'd suspect them of raining on her parade. But she dismissed the idea as ridiculous, even they couldn't be that mean - could they? Besides it couldn't be true about him not having taken a photograph since - he'd taken plenty of the Prince and Anastasia Markova on Christmas Eve.

'Well he would react like that, wouldn't he?' she snapped, deciding to put paid to their scheming. 'He's lucky to be alive and he knows it. It's bound to colour his view of the world.' Her nose began to prickle and her throat tightened as a wave of empathy washed over her. When she spoke her voice was rough with emotion. 'The book, and raising money for the hospital boat is his way of repaying his debt to the people who saved him, and at great risk to themselves.'

She turned away from them, and was about to say 'I don't have the time for this', when Vanessa made a grab for her sleeve.

'Ask yourself this, Montague. How many people actually escape the Contras, or live to tell the tale if the ransom isn't paid?' She raised her eyebrows to her hairline. 'How many?' she repeated for emphasis.

'I'm grateful for your concern but ... I've got to pack. So if you don't mind?'

'Of course, we just wanted to be sure that you know what you've taken on.'

Charlee detached herself from Vanessa's python-like grip and backed out of the kitchen before they could undermine her belief in Ffinch and her faith in her own judgment. She threw everything into her bag and hurried to the lift. Her heart was still beating madly when she reached the ground floor and stepped into *What'cha!*'s sunlit atrium.

Of course, Vanessa and Sally were pouring poison in her ear - she was smart enough to know that. They were jealous as hell that she had become engaged to Ffinch, even if neither of them had been in the running. However, once she was on the bus and heading back for the mews, she removed the piece of creased paper from the pouch at the back of her Moleskine diary and read through the list of forbidden topics again.

How many people actually escape from the Contras and live to tell the tale? Charlee didn't know; but she'd make it her business to find out.

Chapter Twenty-three
Forget the Bucket and Spade

It was a frosty afternoon and the sun was burning low on the horizon as Charlee and Ffinch headed for north-west Norfolk.

Charlee was glad of the excuse to slip on her wrap-around sunglasses against the glare because they concealed her expression. She'd spent two days brooding over her conversation with Vanessa and Sally. And, despite all best attempts, some of their poison had dripped into her ear and seeped into her brain. She glanced sideways at Ffinch as he drove along the twisting road from Fakenham to Wells-next-the-Sea. He looked buoyed up and exhilarated, more than was reasonable given that their mission was to catch a Russian supermodel with mud on her plimsolls.

What was she missing? She tapped her teeth with her thumbnail and drew her brows together in concentration.

'You're quiet, Montague. Why does that fill me with *dis*quiet?' Ffinch asked and, when she didn't answer, added, 'Anxious about the mission?'

'I'm worried that Anastasia might recognise me from the nightclub,' she prevaricated.

'Take it from me, she won't. She spends her life surrounded by her 'people' - gophers, hangers-on and the like. She probably wouldn't recognise her own sister unless she wore a name badge and carried a backstage pass.'

'Ouch. That was pretty cynical, even for you,' Charlee responded.

'Even for me?' Ffinch gave her words some consideration before asking with deceptive quietness, 'And what would you know about me?'

'Nothing. Absolutely nothing.' His words stung and Charlee returned to watching the bare fields sweep past, feeling cast down. Ffinch let out a breath and loosened the long scarf which he wore, muffler-like around his neck, as if he was suddenly too hot. Turning left at the junction, they skirted the top of Wells-next-the-Sea and headed towards Holkham.

'What would you like to know?' he asked resignedly, after a few miles of uncomfortable silence.

'Okay, bite my head off if you must, but I want to know what happened on your trip to Darien.' She turned in her seat to look at him. Like her, his expression was hidden behind sunglasses but she could tell from the way one corner of his mouth quirked in irritation that this information was being dragged out of him.

'It's something I'd rather forget, but it's something …' he paused, searching for the right words.

'Something you can't forget?'

'That's it,' he sounded surprised that she understood. 'Okay, long story short - I set out to take photographs while my research team took notes for the last chapter of my book. Chapter Ten - Darien.' He glanced at her and when she looked back at him, blankly, gave her a dark look. Charlee's crime was soon made plain to her. 'You haven't read the book, have you Montague? I might have known.' Although he made light of her indifference to his magnum opus, she could tell that he was smarting just the same.

'Come on Ffinch, be fair. When have I had time? It's been full on since we met at your book launch … '

'As if I could forget.' His tone seemed to imply that he would gladly forget every second of their contentious partnership, and that hurt. 'You strike me as the sort of person who recycles presents she doesn't want

- or value. Gives them to a brother, for example?' Charlee blanched; so he had seen his book on the kitchen table on Christmas Day and had been waiting for the right moment to bring it up. Oh, he was cute, very cute, and had her bang to rights.

'Never mind all that. You can give me another one,' she said cheekily. 'Carry on with your story.'

'Very well. I wanted to photograph the indigenous people of the rainforest - write about how the twenty-first century had impacted on their lives: trees being cleared for logging or cattle ranches, strangers bringing in viruses for which they had no immunity, guerrillas forcing them to work in the marijuana fields and using them as drugs mules.'

Drugs. Charlee glanced up, sharply. Maybe there was some truth in Vanessa and Sally's words. A photo journalist like Ffinch could pretty much go as he please, slipping over borders - his camera and passport his only credentials.

'Go on,' she urged. They travelled on with Holkham beach just visible through the trees, and, on their left, deer could be seen grazing in the woods behind a brick wall which marked the Earl of Leicester's land. But she couldn't afford to be distracted by the view; this moment might never come again.

'We set off, well prepared: guides, native speakers, two undergrads keen to help with my research. Two armed guards.' He let out a long breath, removed his scarf and unzipped his coat as if he was uncomfortably warm. 'Foolishly, arrogantly, I thought - with my father being Brazilian and my South American connections - I'd be ...' he struggled for the word.

'Safe?' Charlee supplied.

'Safe-r.' He stressed the last letter and shook his head at what he now perceived to be his folly. 'No one's really safe there.'

'You were wrong?'

'Very wrong. The first night we camped on the edge of the rainforest - it was a fabulous experience, listening to the animals calling to each other in the darkness. I couldn't wait to make contact with the indigenous people; it had all been prearranged through interpreters and the Ministry for the Interior. Then …' he paused. Plainly, recalling the moment it all went wrong was distressing. 'In the middle of the night - gunfire, chaos, confusion. We were dragged from our tents, roughed up, our belongings rifled - all the good stuff, cameras, mobiles and medicine, taken. Then they marched us through the rainforest. For days.'

'All your team?' She felt uncomfortable probing for more details, but in order to understand him, she needed to know everything that had happened.

'No, our armed guards and our guides disappeared into the jungle in the confusion. Or maybe that'd been agreed upon - as payment for alerting the kidnappers to our presence. Who knows? Only I, my camera crew and the two students from Colombia University were taken.'

'You were the cash cows,' Charlee put in. 'Europeans.'

'Exactly. The idea, I believe, was to hold us for ransom and when the money was paid they would release us.'

She frowned. 'You believe - don't you know for sure? Isn't that what the Contras do?'

Ffinch laughed harshly. 'Everyone says we were kidnapped by the Contras but the truth is less romantic and more prosaic.' He pulled a face at romantic, showing that he considered the notion ridiculous. 'We were kidnapped by one of the many illegal armed groups operating around the coca, marijuana and opium poppy fields. The Aguilas Negra - the Black Eagles - or the ELN, probably working in collusion with our native guides.'

'Ejército de Liberación Nacional - The National Liberation Army,' Charlee added, taking the opportunity to remind him that she'd studied Politics as well as Languages at university. He shouldn't underestimate her simply because of her current lowly position at *What'cha!* She was worth more than that. She deserved more than that.

'You've got the accent down to a tee.' He nodded his approval almost absent-mindedly. They were bowling along the road to Thornham but

Charlee knew that he was back in Darien. 'There was a problem with communication. The patois which the kidnappers spoke was so far removed from the Bogotá Spanish spoken by the undergrads and myself that we could barely understand them.'

They drove along in silence for several minutes while Charlee assimilated this information. She glanced over the low hedges and dun-coloured fields stretching towards the salt marshes where the sea was a black line on the horizon. The landscape perfectly suited their sombre mood.

'What happened next?' she prompted.

'It started to rain and didn't let up for days. They marched us through the rainforest stopping only to feed us basic rations or to let us sleep - while they smoked dope or chewed coca leaves. Elena was the first to fall ill. She was so young ...' his voice wavered, as if the memory was more than he could bear. Then he coughed to clear his throat and changed the subject, signifying that Charlee would learn no more that day 'The sea goes wa-ay out when it's high tide, then it gathers itself and rushes forward, like a mini tsunami. In certain places where the water is funnelled, it comes rushing in almost as fast as a man can walk.'

Hiding her frustration at the swift change of subject, Charlee looked where he was pointing. She wanted to know more about what had happened in Darien - not be treated to a learned exposition on tide tables. But she knew it was best not to push it.

Tides.

She sat bolt upright, remembering the conversation she'd overhead in the mews kitchen. What had Ffinch said ... Yes, the night of the high tide; I've checked the tide tables and the internet - twice. Stop worrying, it'll be fine. You'll be there? Good. No, she has no idea and that's how I intend to keep it ...

Charlee racked her brain but couldn't see the connection between high tide, a boot camp for brides, a Russian supermodel and a mysterious phone call conducted in Spanish in the middle of the night. One glance at Ffinch's closed expression showed he did not intend to elucidate further on the matter, or to return to the subject of his kidnapping. Sensing that, she slid lower in her seat and remained silent as the camper van ate up the miles. God, Norfolk was bleak, especially in the fading light of a January afternoon when the sun was setting, taking its meagre warmth with it. She was going to freeze to death at the boot camp. Fact.

But compared to the vicissitudes that Ffinch and his team had faced in Darien, freezing to death in Norfolk would be a walk in the park.

It was properly dark by the time they reached Thornham and The Ship Inn. As Ffinch parked the VW in the car park across the road from the inn, birdwatchers returning from the marshes with cameras and binoculars strung round their necks bade them good evening. They consisted mainly of retired couples in matching waterproofs, woolly hats and muddy boots. Ffinch took the heavier of their bags out of the back of the camper and left two smaller ones for Charlee to carry. Even so, she walked stiffly after the long drive from London and almost dragged them behind her.

'Have a care, Montague, those cases are vintage Louis Vuitton,' Ffinch said. Charlee couldn't tell if he was joking or not, that was the trouble with him. But she guessed that he was. He'd showed scant regard for material possessions during the short time she'd known him. It was as if he'd reached a place in his life where objects held no intrinsic value for him. But, maybe that was because he had - or could have - everything he wanted?

'You are such a poseur,' she said under her breath, but meaning it as a joke.

'I heard that,' Ffinch said, holding open the heavy door of the former smugglers' inn. 'Glad you've recovered your sense of humour and your enthusiasm for what we have to accomplish. I know you're on top form when you make plain your low opinion of me. I was beginning to think I would have to send for Sally to replace you, but you've bucked up and

- here we are.'

Charlee didn't have a low opinion of him, quite the reverse. Actually, the more she learned about what had happened in Colombia, the greater her respect for him. It was the knowledge that he was withholding information from her which was seriously pissing her off.

Didn't he know that he could trust her with his life?

They walked into the dark interior and Ffinch deposited their bags by the reception desk. A huge fire was burning in a fireplace which almost filled one wall of the square, flagstoned hall. Low lamps had been lit and people were strolling through into the low-ceilinged bars for their first drink of the evening. There was a nice buzz about the place; it was all very welcoming and just what Charlee needed. She let out a sigh of relief and her shoulders, which had been practically pinned to her ears all the way here, relaxed and dropped.

'Fonseca-Ffinch and Miss Montague,' Ffinch announced to the receptionist.

True to form the woman gave him a bright smile, almost purring as she handed over his key. She passed Charlee's key to her almost as an afterthought, but her gaze rested briefly on Granny's ring and her eyes widened. Then her polite, corporate expression fell back into place. But it was easy to tell she thought any woman who had the opportunity to share Ffinch's bed, but chose not to, was either a fool, a close blood relation - or Amish.

'Up the stairs and turn right. Your rooms are next to each other, as requested.'

'Thank you, Susanne.' Ffinch read the name on her lapel badge and gave her a smile that made her come over all unnecessary. 'And we are booked in for dinner?'

'A table for two at eight o'clock, Mr Fonseca-Ffinch.' She tripped over his name but then remembered to ask: 'Do you need any help with your luggage, madam?'

'I think we're okay. Can you manage, darling?' Ffinch asked, smiling down at Charlee like she was indeed his beloved fiancée.

'You know me, ever resourceful,' she retorted, adding 'sweetie.' The receptionist looked as if she was trying to puzzle out their relationship. Sweetie? Darling? Two separate rooms? Then, clearly deciding it was none of her business, she shrugged.

Ffinch led the way up the wide staircase with its faded tartan carpet and uneven treads. The old inn was so atmospheric that Charlee had no trouble imagining it as the haunt of smugglers who had navigated the creeks at high tide and landed brandy, tobacco and lace when the revenue men weren't looking. Was Ffinch a modern-day smuggler, she wondered? Vanessa's list of his alleged illegal activities echoed in her tired brain: gun running, drug smuggling, money laundering.

They reached a wide landing and Ffinch stopped by a rather battered door and turned towards her, jangling his key.

'This is mine - and that one, angel, is yours.'

'Thank you, hun,' Charlee replied in kind, although she felt like slapping him. And not simply because of the cloak of secrecy he and Sam had drawn over the mission - but, because of some other feeling she couldn't quite put into words.

'Permittez moi?' Taking the key from her slack fingers, he opened the door, picked up her cases and put them next to the bed. Charlee walked in and closed the door on him. She'd had quite enough of Señor Rafael Fonseca-Ffinch and wanted him to know it.

She leaned back against the door and surveyed her room. Unsurprisingly, it was decorated in a seaside theme with tones of navy-blue, white and red, coiled ropes, shells, and paintings of the marshes placed around the room for maximum effect. The bedside table lamp was lit, and there were water and tea-making facilities to hand. The bed, with its pale-grey tongue and groove headboard and patchwork quilt in navy and white, looked inviting. She walked over to the low window tucked under the eaves and looked across Ship Lane towards the marshes. Not that she could see much, however, it was almost a quarter to five and the last of the light had gone.

Drawing the thickly lined curtains against the January gloom, she dropped onto the bed, pulled the quilt over her shoulders and drifted off into a dreamless sleep. Half an hour later, she woke with a headache and a feeling of disorientation and loneliness. Since Christmas Eve, she'd stayed in her bedsit (twice), her parents' home, Ffinch's grand-parents' mews and now here she was in another location. In three days she'd be booking into the boot camp; small wonder she felt rudderless, adrift.

She threw back the coverlet and swung her legs out of bed. Maybe if she made herself a coffee and ate some of the biscuits on the tray, the sugar rush would help her to regain her equilibrium. As she waited for the tiny kettle to boil, she let her gaze wander round the room. It was then she saw IT. She leapt to her feet, all earlier feelings of disconnec-tion and detachment forgotten in her anger.

'Ffinch, you bastard ...'

Abandoning the tea tray she strode up to the interconnecting door between their two rooms and banged on it with her fists, like she was leading a police raid. The door opened and Ffinch stood in his jeans, stripped to the waist and with a towel draped round his shoulders.

'Christ on a bike, Montague - is there a fire?' he asked, slapping shaving foam from his cupped hand onto his cheeks. 'I would have thought it was the inn's place to inform us of an emergency.'

'You - you . . . ' She pointed at him, lost for words.

She found herself unexpectedly fazed by the sight of his naked torso, and couldn't help making an inventory of his salient physical points. Chest lightly downed with just enough dark hair to be considered sexy, deliciously tanned skin, slim waist, broad shoulders and -

'What?' he asked puzzled, as she seemed to have come to a com-plete stop. He wiped the newly applied shaving foam off his face with the towel and indicated that she should enter his room, but she hesi-tated on the threshold.

'An interconnecting door,' she choked out at last in constricted tones.

'So? It's an interconnecting door?'

'Don't you remember what I said in the office, before we went undercover in the skip?'

He gave out a tired, slightly exasperated sigh. 'Charlee - to be honest, you say so many things it isn't easy to distinguish one from another. What's wrong with having an interconnecting door? I thought it would make communication easier.'

'Communication? Ha! That's a new word for it?' Charlee spluttered, detecting his amusement and smarting. She had dug a hole for herself and he showed no inclination of helping her out of it.

'Lost me there, I'm afraid,' Ffinch said, walking through to the en suite bathroom.

'To recap . . .' Charlee was reluctant to cross the threshold in case it meant something. Like in a vampire movie where the heroine invites the creature into her house and there's no going back. 'I said - I have no intention of working late, missing the last train back to town and "staying over" in some country house hotel with you. Or being shown to a suite of rooms which - surprise, surprise - have interconnecting doors.'

'Oh that,' Ffinch laughed over his shoulder. 'And I called you Chelsea and said something about you not being able to keep your hands off me. Looks like I was right, doesn't it?' He started his shaving preparations all over again and Charlee knew that he hadn't forgotten one iota of their conversation. He was trying to wind her up - and succeeding.

'Why, you!' Forgetting her earlier resolution she marched across the threshold. She suspected, whenever this incident was recalled - and she had a gut feeling that it would be, and often - Ffinch would insist that she had broken the door down, marched into his room and -

And what, she wondered?

Standing in the middle of his much bigger room, she threw back her head and let out a groan.

'Look, make us both a coffee. And before you say anything, Montague, I fully acknowledge that you will be doing so as a huge favour to me. Because you're my partner and not because you're female and it's expected. Okay?' He shut the bathroom door with a deft backwards flick of his bare foot and went on to complete his ablutions in private.

Put that way, Charlee felt less like a faint-hearted feminist dead set against domestic duties and more like a complete idiot. Sighing, she switched on the kettle, checked out the pots of milk and his biscuit supply - which, incidentally, was better than hers. Clearly as senior partner, Ffinch had been accorded the best room. Finally, as the kettle boiled, he came back into the room wearing a hotel dressing gown over his jeans. Charlee cocked an inquiring eyebrow at the dressing gown and he laughed.

'The way you banged on that door, I'm taking no chances. If ravishment is on your mind, can I ask a favour? Can it wait until after dinner - I'm starving?' Charlee giggled and relaxed, acknowledging he had the power to infuriate her but could always make her laugh. She handed his coffee to him. He sat in the easy chair, crossed his legs and made a great show of arranging the folds of his dressing gown so not an inch of spare flesh was on view.

'Okay, knock it off, Ffinch. I was just -'

'Tired and emotional?'

'Hangry.'

'Hangry?' he asked.

'It's a word my brothers and I made up to express when you're so hungry that you feel angry. Never felt like that?' she asked, dunking a highland shortie in her coffee.

'Maybe, but not for food.' He looked at her with the now familiar, unblinking gaze which she fancifully imagined could see into her soul. A silence lengthened between them, not an uncomfortable one, but one loaded with emotions and expectations they both knew were best kept reined in. Then he changed the subject. 'Oh, I meant to say - we've made *The Times*. I picked up a copy in reception; I've left it open on the bed - take a look, guess we're officially engaged now.'

Charlee put down her coffee, walked over to the bed and picked up the newspaper he'd left open at hatches, matches and dispatches.

Mr R. Fonseca-Ffinch and Miss C. Montague
The engagement is announced between Rafael, son of His Excellency
Ambassador Salvio Fonseca-Ffinch and Mrs Richenda Fonseca-Ffinch
of Killiecrankie, Edinburgh and Charlotte, daughter of Doctor and Mrs
Henry Montague of Highclere, Berkshire.

The same heaviness of heart she'd experienced when Ffinch had shown her the mock-up of the announcement, overwhelmed her. It was as if they were making a mockery of love and it was wrong, somehow. Shaking her head free of the thought, she dropped the paper back onto the bed.

'So, the game's afoot?' she said in an attempt at levity.

'No shit, Sherlock,' he confirmed, drinking his coffee in one thirsty gulp. Charlee made as if to stand up. 'No, stay there; wait,' he commanded. Then he crossed over the threshold of the interconnecting doors and into her bedroom. She heard him running a bath in her en suite and she came over all hot and bothered. If he thought for one minute they would be bathing a deux and playing ducks and drakes, he'd better prepare himself for a disappointment.

After some time, he returned carrying a matching dressing gown to the one he was wearing. 'Dinner's at eight. I'll call for you at quarter to and we can have a drink in the bar. Don't worry - I'll use the proper door.'

Taking her hand, he guided her from his bedroom into her own and then softly closed the double doors and locked them.

Chapter Twenty-four
Keeping Up Appearances

True to his word, Ffinch knocked on her door at seven forty-five. Charlee paused and took several deep breaths before opening it. For reasons she couldn't as yet fathom, their relationship was undergoing a sea change. Everything felt different. As if here, on neutral ground, emotions and feelings had shifted up a gear and the dynamic had altered.

Ffinch knocked on the door for a second time and called her name.

'Coming -' Giving the room one last look, Charlee opened the door.

Ffinch was standing on the wide landing with his back towards her, looking over the bannister and down into the hall. He turned round, leaned back against the bannister and smiled. Adrenalin shot up from Charlee's solar plexus like a heat-seeking missile and exploded behind her breastbone. Taking a deep breath, she shrugged off the shiver of reaction that left her feeling weak and reminded herself this wasn't a date, it was a business arrangement.

Nothing more.

'You look ...' Ffinch appeared lost for words as he took in her cocktail dress in shades of blue, sheer stockings and high heels. 'Am I allowed to say lovely, or will that offend every feminist principle you hold? Will it make my compliment more palatable if I add that you're also the go-to civilian the local constabulary call upon when they have a particularly tricky door to batter down?'

'Very amusing Ffinch - let's settle for "don't we scrub up well".' Charlee's scornful expression hid her inner turmoil and the fact that she couldn't tear her eyes away from him. She gave him a second, more thorough look.

'I'll settle for that,' he said, giving one of his dry smiles. But there was a light dancing in his eyes and he seemed wired. Remembering Vanessa's caveat, Charlee wondered if he'd been snorting cocaine in the en suite bathroom as well as having a shower. 'Shall we?' He held out his hand, and, obviously sensing she had something on her mind, added: 'Keeping up appearances, remember?'

'Thanks for reminding me that I'm the pantomime fiancée,' Charlee wisecracked, but took his hand when he proffered it a second time.

They walked side by side down the wide staircase and into the hall where guests were having dinner by a roaring fire, with their black labs at their feet. Charlee's cocktail dress with its net underskirt and Ffinch's charcoal-grey suit, pale-grey shirt and coordinating dark-pewter tie drew admiring glances. The younger guests gave them looks of fellow feeling, while the older guests, remembering how it had felt to be young and in love, smiled at them. Feeling a complete fraud, Charlee returned their 'good evenings' and held onto Ffinch's hand tightly when she felt her courage was about to desert her.

They passed through the bar where young families were sitting down to their evening meal and progressed into the formal dining room where tables were laid with white linen, candles, glassware and heavy silver cutlery. A waiter checked their name in the reservations and then escorted them to a table where champagne was chilling in an ice bucket in a stand. He seated Charlee with great ceremony, shook out her napkin and laid it across her lap. Then she was given a large menu which looked like it'd been handwritten by the monks on Lindisfarne.

She chewed her lip in deliberation and read the list of starters several times.

'Don't go all girly on me, Montague,' Ffinch growled over the top of the oversized menu. 'I won't have my dinner ruined because you order a lettuce leaf topped by a pea, balanced on a spear of asparagus, and spend half an hour pushing it round your plate. This restaurant has a Michelin star - go for it, have what you want.' Then he returned to perusing his own menu.

Usually, Charlee had an appetite that would put a starving horse to shame and she was puzzled that he hadn't picked up on it, considering the meals they'd shared at the mews.

'I am a little hungry,' she confessed daintily. Ffinch's expression demonstrated that he wasn't buying her ladylike manners for a second.

'Good! Because, in two days you'll be existing on gruel and rice cakes - which aren't really cakes at all, by the way. I can see you sneaking off to the loos within an hour of arriving, with a Mars bar taken from the stash hidden under your bed.' Considering what she thought Ffinch got up to behind closed doors, eating forbidden chocolate seemed pretty tame.

'For your information, Ffinch, the menu at the boot camp is nutritionally balanced and prepared by an award-winning chef.'

'That'll be two rice cakes, then.' Ffinch apparently found the whole idea of her on iron rations vastly entertaining. She was just about to make some quip about him surviving on roots and berries in the jungles of Colombia, but stopped herself in time. 'Eat up our kid, you're at your auntie's,' he said in a cod Mancunian accent.

'Thanks, I will.'

The sommelier arrived at their table, opened the champagne and went through the ritual of offering Ffinch a thimbleful to check it wasn't corked. Then he poured out two glasses and walked away after draping a linen napkin over the ice bucket.

'Sam'll have a fit when he gets the bill for this,' Charlee said.

'Actually, I'm paying for the meal. And before you offer to pay half -'

'Believe me, I wasn't,' Charlee cut in, 'you're minted and I'm an impoverished intern. Besides, it's the very least you can do, to repay me for what I've had to suffer.' She looked at him over the top of her flute, waiting for his reaction. 'And what's yet to come.'

'That's true,' Ffinch acknowledged, holding his glass next to hers. 'Partners, Montague.'

'Partners, Ffinch,' she agreed, pushing to the back of her mind the thought that their partnership was one-sided. She wondered if he'd say more tonight over dinner; maybe share the rest of his story with her. They appeared to have reached a rapprochement and she didn't want to ruin it by forcing the pace.

Putting down his glass, Ffinch opened his wallet and brought out a piece of paper.

'You might need this.' He handed her the cutting of their announcement in *The Times*. 'When you're at the boot camp, I mean. I thought you could put it in the back of the photograph frame which holds the shot we had taken at our "engagement party". Put it on your bedside table to allay suspicion?' When she didn't respond, he appeared to run out of words and settled instead for sitting back in his chair, regarding her intently. Evidently trying to understand her swift mood change.

'Sure.' Charlee shrugged, determined not to make it easy for him.

Despite the splendour of their surroundings, the champagne and the delicious meal that was to come, Charlee's heart was heavy. She was conflicted; excited at the prospect of her first assignment, but provoked by Ffinch's refusal to divulge more than he thought necessary to ensure the success of the mission. In addition, she couldn't quite rid herself of the crazy notion that when she eventually met her future husband, this faux engagement would take the shine off her real engagement and ruin the moment.

It was a quixotic notion, but she felt as if they were deriding something she hadn't realised until that moment she held dear. Then she reminded herself that this wasn't real. And as for Ffinch, he was so far removed from the faceless man in her dream who flooded her heart with love, as to be almost a different species. She needed to toughen up if she wanted to be taken seriously. It was time for her to affect the world-weariness which he wore like a badge of honour.

She reached for the scrap of paper and their fingers touched briefly. Her skin was warm and soft but Ffinch's felt cold and dry, almost chilblained - reminding her that beneath his fading tropical tan there was a man recovering from dengue. The paper fluttered onto the starched tablecloth and Ffinch picked it up. He looked at her questioningly, apparently trying to figure out what was going through her mind.

'I'll keep it,' Charlee said, back in role and hiding her inner tumult. 'In case I forget what you look like, or why I'm here.' She'd promised Ffinch that she wouldn't go all mushy on him, and she'd better stick to her side of the bargain.

'I don't think you'll forget for a second why you're here, Montague. I simply meant as a means of establishing our credentials, our legend. Forget it.' She detected anger and impatience in his voice, as though he thought her some spoiled twenty-something who sulked when things didn't go her way. About a million miles removed from his two partners who hadn't returned to their feather beds at the end of the mission. His expression unfathomable, he picked up the cutting and put one corner to the candle. Charlee snatched it out of his hand, extinguishing the flame by pinching it between finger and thumb.

'Set off the sprinkler system why don't you? Deny me my dinner as they clear the restaurant and call the fire brigade. Not to mention have everyone in the restaurant thinking we're a couple of fruitcakes.'

'And aren't we? Maybe this whole thing is mad.' For a moment, Ffinch's guard dropped and Charlee panicked in case he was having second thoughts.

'If I knew what this whole thing entailed, I'd be able to make my own judgment, wouldn't I?' She paused, and with a very direct blue stare presented him with the ideal opportunity to fill her in.

'Concentrate on your starter, Montague,' he said. 'I hear that the Brancaster mussels are delicious.'

'Do you now?' Charlee raised her menu and hid behind it, frustrated. He'd been close, very close to letting his guard slip. Damn - maybe she should ply him with champagne and -

'Lower your menu, Montague. The cogs in your brain are whirring so fast I can hear them. I need to see your expression then I'll know what you're thinking. Don't take up the cloak and dagger business for a living, will you? You have one of the most expressive faces I've ever seen. You wear your heart on your sleeve.'

In spite of his earlier terseness it sounded like a compliment.

'You say it like it's a bad thing,' she came back with. 'Whereas you - why, I never know what you're thinking.'

'Then we complement each other, beautifully. Fire and ice,' he said, touching the rim of his glass against hers.

'Down the hatch,' she responded as the waiter came across and hovered with his Wi-Fi notebook ready to take their order and relay it to the kitchen. Then she put down her menu and with a heavy sigh gave Ffinch a loved-up look. 'You order for me, darling, you know what a Dithering Dora I can be.'

He gave one of his rare, quick smiles and raised her hand to his lips. 'Would Dithering Dora like mussels, steak, salad and a bottle of Rioja?'

'Oh, yes - and chips. You can't have steak without chips.'

'We serve twice-fried garlic hand cut chips rolled in parmesan, madam,' the waiter said politely.

'Twice-fried and rolled in garlic and parmesan, Pumpkin. How cool is that?' she asked.

'Garlic, darling?' Ffinch questioned as his thumb rubbed across the top of Granny's ring. 'Won't that be rather … unromantic?'

'Depends what you've got in mind,' Charlee gushed, batting her lashes at him. 'And not if we both have it.'

'Thank you, sir, madam.' The waiter gave Ffinch a fleeting, sympathetic look, as if Ffinch was holding a wildcat by the tail. Then the polite mask was back in place and he walked off to take the order from another table.

Ffinch let go of Charlee's hand. 'If you're going to behave badly, I'll have to order room service and confine you to barracks,' he said, but his lips twitched in amusement.

'You're one to talk - darling. Besides, aren't we supposed to be love's young dream and unable to keep our hands off each other?' Charlee drained her champagne glass like a thirsty bricklayer and the sommelier was at their side in a flash to refill it. 'I could get used to this,' she giggled, altogether more relaxed. 'I'm starting to feel rather chilled, if you must know.'

'Why does that thought fill me with alarm? Well, enjoy it, tomorrow we take off with a packed lunch to explore the marshes. I need to convince the staff and other birdwatchers that I'm a confirmed twitcher, and that my being on the marshes with my camera and binoculars is nothing out of the ordinary.'

'But, surely I'll be the one taking photos of Anastasia? Using my digital camera or iPhone?'

'Yes, I'm simply there for backup. In case ...'

Then he did his annoying thing where he cut himself off mid-sentence, as if he'd already said too much. Vanessa had said that since returning from South America Ffinch hadn't taken another photograph. Clearly that wasn't the case, so what was the truth? Then she thought, to hell with questions and answers, it was enough to drive one mad. Tonight was about enjoying herself; the real business would start tomorrow.

'In case what? The brides-to-be discover my stash of chocolate under the bed and an unseemly fight ensues?' But she'd left it too late to press home the advantage and Ffinch had control of himself.

'I'll station myself on the marshes,' he continued, as though the conversation was a run-on. 'Ostensibly, photographing the birds and wildlife while you and the other ladies thunder past.'

'Thunder past! Are you kidding? They weigh no more than a fly.'

'Okay, as you thunder past.'

'Thanks for that!'

'I'll be able to get some different shots of the group. If they get suspicious about your taking snaps, you can leave your phone at a prearranged spot and I can forward the photos to *What'cha!*'

'Won't I need my phone to keep in contact with you?' Charlee's brow creased as she considered the logistics of their mission.

'You won't get a signal on the marshes,' he replied with such certainty that Charlee knew he'd made it his business to find out. 'It's a dead zone for mobile phones. I only just get a signal here, or on the edge of the village. All contact between us will have to be made via a public call box.'

'If there is one,' Charlee said, pointing out another flaw in the plan.

'There is,' he said, eating his last mussel.

'You seem very certain.'

'I am.'

The last was said with such authority that Charlee didn't pursue the matter further. The waiter removed their plates and brought them lemon scented hot cloths to wipe their fingers. Then their steaks arrived and Ffinch tucked into his with all the relish of a starving man.

An hour and a half later after dessert, coffee and cognac, Charlee and Ffinch climbed the stairs to their respective bedrooms. Charlee was rather unsteady, a combination of vertiginous heels and the quantity of wine she'd consumed. She pulled a face and groaned, thinking of the hangover she would wake up with and the windswept salt marshes dashing ice-cold rain and sleet into her face. Ffinch walked up the stairs behind her, his hand resting lightly on her waist as if keeping a loving eye on her, whereas in reality he was holding her upright. Bidding the other guests goodnight, he whispered in her ear.

'Smile, for goodness sake. You look as if you're going to your doom, not a night of passion in The Ship Inn's best room. Stay in role.'

'I'm concentrating on my balance, if you must know, and,' Charlee whipped round as his words sank in, almost falling backwards into his arms. 'A night of passion, now hold it right there, mate. It'd take more than two glasses of champagne -'

'Half a bottle of Rioja, a sticky with your pudding and cognac with coffee - to do what? Floor you? Make the thought of sleeping with me more palatable?' Although he kept a straight face, Charlee detected banked down humour there.

'You didn't exactly drink Perrier water all night yourself,' she said, giving him a pondering look. Then the humour vanished from his eyes and was replaced by the sorrow that never seemed to leave him. It was as if he believed he had no right to happiness because he'd messed up big time and lost two of his team.

'Besides which,' he continued, as if she hadn't spoken. 'I haven't reached such depths of depravity or desperation that I have to get my date drunk before I can have sex with her.' Date? Have sex with her! The words leapt out at Charlee and she was about to make another cutting remark, but he hadn't finished. 'If I'd wanted to ravish you, Montague - don't you think I could have carried out my dastardly plan at the mews?'

'In Chelsea no one can hear you scream?' Charlee paraphrased, hiding that she was rather put out at discovering that he found her about as alluring as a wet fish.

'Exactly. Here we are - home.' They arrived at her door. 'Key?' She handed it over and he unlocked her door and put it back in her handbag. 'Okay, you get into bed, drink a huge amount of water and knock back some painkillers, that way you'll be fit for what I've got planned tomorrow.'

'Which is?'

'A yomp over the marshes when the tide's out.'

'Oh, God - I'm a dead woman,' she moaned, covering her face with her hands. 'I'll be sucked down some godforsaken bog and be found thousands of years later, perfectly preserved - like those leathery corpses in the Fens. That's if the vultures don't pick my bones dry.'

'Hm, I must consult *The Boys' Own Book of Fenland Birds*,' Ffinch said, now openly laughing. 'I don't remember vultures featuring widely in it.'

'Oh, shut up, Mr Smarty Pants,' Charlee said, giving him a push in his chest and starting to feel rather worse for wear. 'Goodnight. I won't be asking you in for coffee.'

'Goodnight, Charlee - you are priceless, know that? Sleep well, but remember - gallons of water and pain killers.' He leaned forward to kiss her on the cheek as a good fake fiancé should. At that precise moment, Charlee turned her face fractionally to the left and his kiss landed squarely on her lips.

'Oh,' Charlee said in surprise, leaning back against the door.

Ffinch didn't pull away or give an embarrassed cough, despite his earlier covert assertion that she wasn't his type. Instead, he leaned forward and deepened the kiss, unmistakably relishing the way their lips touched and their breathing became erratic. Then, just as Charlee felt herself floating above the uneven oak floor, two guests walked across the landing and he pulled back.

'Sweet dreams, Bunnikins,' he said softly, purely for their benefit. Charlee heard a rumble of laughter in his throat as he opened her door and pushed her gently, but firmly across the threshold.

The door closed. Charlee raised an unsteady hand to her lips, which were tingling. Just as they had done when, as child, she'd made a musical instrument out of a comb and greaseproof paper. Eventually the tingling stopped and Charlee walked into the bathroom to locate her painkillers. She stopped dead in the middle of the tiled floor as his last words penetrated the fug of her brain.

Bunnikins? Bunnikins!

She giggled. She'd never figure Ffinch out, not in a million years and felt suddenly sad that, after tonight, she'd have less than a week left in which to try.

Chapter Twenty-five
Look Out for the Vultures

C harlee woke in the middle of the night as hailstones hurled themselves at her window aided and abetted by a cutting wind off the marshes. She checked the time on her mobile phone - three a.m. Unable to sleep, she lay in the darkness expecting a hangover to manifest itself. However, apart from a raging thirst she seemed fine. She'd always had the constitution of a particularly energetic ox and it was standing her in good stead. However, deciding it was best not to take any risks, she swung her legs out of bed and headed for the loo for more painkillers and to rehydrate her liver.

It was then that she heard the other sound above the noise of the wind - a low moaning like someone in distress. It appeared to be coming from Ffinch's bedroom. What on earth was he doing in there? Conducting a black mass complete with animal sacrifice? Or maybe those Brancaster mussels were exacting their revenge. Wrinkling her nose at the thought, she put her ear to the interconnecting door. She couldn't just barge in, not after accusing him of engineering a have-it-away-weekend.

The moaning grew louder and became a muttering - and then she heard a name being called over and over. Taking her courage in both hands, she slipped her mobile into her dressing gown pocket, unlocked the door and peered into the darkness.

'*No. No. Elena. Elen-ah. Virgen santísima, ayúdanos. Cristo ayúda-nos. No dejes que Elena muera. Jesús, ten piedad. Por el amor de Dios, no dejes que se ahogue. Allesandro, ayuda!*'

Charlee stood listening as Ffinch relived the moment when he'd pleaded in Spanish with their captors to save Elena - and then turned to God, and someone called Allesandro when his pleas were ignored. She was overwhelmed by the need to go to him, to wake him from this nightmare and bring him comfort. Using the light from her mobile phone as a torch she negotiated her way across the room, allowing herself time to adjust to the darkness. His cries rang out afresh and she moved swiftly but silently to his side.

Charlee recalled reading somewhere that it was dangerous to wake people in the middle of a nightmare - or was that sleepwalking? She couldn't remember which. Glancing down at Ffinch, she saw that he was calmer now but she was reluctant to wake him and reveal that she'd seen him at his lowest ebb. He was a proud man, guarded, too - if he knew she'd been brought to his room by his cries for help, the fragile rapport developing between them would fracture.

He turned over and flung himself on his back, hands raised above his head and with his wrists facing outwards. Charlee let the eerie light from her mobile range over him, checking that he was okay but taking care not to wake him.

'Oh my God.' In the faint light she could just make out livid marks scarring the flesh on the undersides of his lower arms and wrists. She'd read that drug user's arms were marked with tramlines, but she'd never seen them for real. Her blood ran cold and she felt physically sick. Vanessa had been right when she'd accused him of gun running, drug smuggling, money laundering ... and more, besides.

Charlee took a step back from his bed, appalled.

How could she have got him so wrong?

Had she been so taken up by the idea of working with Ffinch the award-winning journalist that she hadn't thought it through properly? Or dug deeply enough to discover the truth? She swept the greenish beam of light over his bedside table - bottles of pills, prescription drugs with his name on the label. Maybe he was hooked on those, too? Frowning, she returned her phone to the pocket of her pyjamas and looked down at him, her eyes having adjusted to the darkness

Whatever had disturbed his dreams, his thrashing around and calling out seemed to have exorcised it. He was descending into the deeper reaches of sleep and his bare chest rose and fell rhythmically. For a moment the woman in Charlee took precedence over the journalist. She looked down at his bare chest, the delicate line of hair that led downwards - and wondered what lay beneath the duvet he'd almost thrown off the bed.

Did he sleep in the nude?

The thought sent lust scudding through her veins and her breath snagged in her throat. She placed her hand over her breastbone in an attempt to bring her breathing and her wicked thoughts under control. When she realised that her breathing had fallen into step with his - although her heart was still hammering away like a mad thing - she knew this man was getting to her. Overwhelmed by the need to peel back the duvet, climb inside that warm bed with him and ... she checked her wild thoughts and backed away from his bed.

If he caught her there, he would naturally assume that she'd come to compromise him in some ill-thought-out scheme to prize secrets from him. Tiptoeing, she retraced her steps back to her room and closed the interconnecting door. But this time, she didn't lock it. Instead, she fell into bed, restless and uneasy - wondering how one off-centre kiss and seeing him lying there naked and troubled had awoken unwanted feelings of yearning and desire in her.

Now it was her turn to twist the bedclothes into a knot as she pulled the duvet over her head and tried to go back to sleep. But sleep eluded her - for reasons that were only too clear to her!

The next morning, Charlee was outside The Ship Inn loaded down with birdwatching gear and looking a total wreck. After a sleepless night wondering what dark memories disturbed Ffinch's sleep and haunted his waking hours, she'd been practically comatose over the 'full English' - served at an eye-wateringly early seven thirty. Ffinch on the other hand looked ready for anything. And, to Charlee's oversensitive senses, seemed to be shouting rather than talking to her.

'The girl in reception said that a family of barn owls lives in the field across from the car park and can be seen quartering the fields, hunting for prey. It's a feature of the marshes apparently,' he added breezily. Then he peered at her in a critical fashion. 'Got out of the wrong side of the bed this morning, Montague?'

'As a matter of fact, no!' she snapped, hiding her blushes. Little did he know which side of whose bed she could have been climbing out of this morning! 'Couldn't sleep, that's all.' She left the sentence hanging to see if he'd mention his restless night. When he didn't, she continued grumpily, 'And, what kind of feckin' owls go hunting in the day? It isn't natural.'

'It's a common misconception that owls are nocturnal,' Ffinch read from an ancient copy of *The Boys' Own Book of Fenland Birds*. 'They are, in fact, diurnal - if you must know.' His eyes looked more grey than blue in the washed-out morning light and he had the appearance of a man who'd had a good night's sleep. Charlee suspected that he found her bad mood highly diverting - Little Miss Sunshine was finally having a cloudy day!

'Spare me the lecture, David Attenborough. I'm a country girl and have forgotten more about owls and other ... random wild creatures, than a townie like you will ever learn.' With a haughty toss of her head, Charlee hitched the rucksack containing packed lunch, bottled water and a flask of hot chocolate higher onto her shoulders and headed for the marshes. When it became plain that Ffinch wasn't following her, she swivelled round and stood with her hands on her hips.

'What now?'

'Wrong way, Montague. Follow me.' Turning on his heel, he headed for the village green without waiting for her.

'Baden-bleedin-Powell as well, is it?' Charlee mumbled under her breath as she followed close on his heels. 'Will you be giving me my sixer's badge for reading animal tracks?'

'Stop the mutinous muttering and keep up,' he called over his shoulder, apparently enjoying every moment of her bad mood. Fuming, Charlee followed at a trot, four of her steps being equal to one of his long strides. It was clear she would be shown no quarter this morning. Last night she'd wanted to climb into bed with him, today she had thoughts of a different nature running through her mind. Murderous ones. She'd always hated PE at school and her first foray as a serious journo was beginning to resemble a cross-country run more than the cloak and dagger mission she'd imagined.

They skirted the green and cut through a park full of static caravans closed down for the winter. Then they turned right and headed past some modern bungalows and older flint cottages overlooking the marshes. Ffinch stopped, raised his binoculars and pointed with his free hand, like a modern-day version of Millais's *The Boyhood of Raleigh*.

'Those are the old Coast Guards' cottages. They're rental properties now, but back in the day they had a perfect view of the marshes and the smugglers who tried to land contraband at high tide. Come on,' he urged, putting down his binoculars and striding forward with renewed vigour.

'Come on? Come on where precisely? Everything's either covered by water or feet deep in mud.' Charlee continued to complain as they skirted the village green where workmen were stacking reeds ready for thatching in the spring. They walked past a paper bank and towards the marshes. 'Oh, recycling bins - how picturesque.' Snarkily, she took a photo of the green and orange bins with her mobile phone, looking across the winter marshland where flocks of birds were coming down to feed now the receding tide made their feeding grounds accessible.

Ffinch ground to a halt and then whipped round to face her. 'Are you going to keep this up all morning, Montague? Whatever else I thought of you, I never thought you were a quitter or a whinger.'

'I'm not a whinger,' she protested. Then the telling phrase rewound and ran through her befuddled brain one more time: whatever else I thought of you. What did he mean? What did he think of her, exactly? 'Just tired, that's all. I didn't sleep well ... get off my case, Ffinch.'

'I'm not surprised with the amount of booze you put away,' he said cheerfully - all the more to goad her, Charlee presumed. 'Or was there another reason?'

'Such as?' Had he seen her creep in and out of his room and been feigning sleep? His expression deadpan, he raised an eyebrow and suppressed a grin. 'What, you mean that good night kiss? Mate - get over yourself.' She pushed him in the chest with both hands and he fell against the weatherworn fence which splintered on impact. 'I've had more passionate kisses from our two black labs, Teal and Marley. Although, admittedly, your breath didn't smell quite as strongly of doggy chews.'

For some moments he laid spreadeagled against the fence, the sloe bushes with their shrivelled berries doubling as his crown of thorns. Long, silent seconds stretched out and she took a step forwards, concerned that she had injured him.

'Ffinch are you okay? Speak to me for God's sake.'

She put the flat of her hand on his chest which was rising and falling in short, sharp breaths. Was he having a heart attack, or something? He looked young and fit, but she knew he was nowhere near the peak of fitness or health expected of a man in his early thirties. She started to unzip his waxed jacket and to rub his chest to ease his breathing. It took several seconds for her to realise that he wasn't gasping for breath - he was laughing.

At her!

'Why, you -' she raised her fists to pummel his chest but he caught them and held her fast.

'Tell me Montague, are your former boyfriends buried under the patio, having sustained fatal injuries in the course of romancing you?'

'Romancing me? What are you, some ancient minstrel? You'll be singing under my window next - For a man who doesn't believe in moon in June, roses round the door and happily ever after ... you have a very romantic turn of phrase.'

His lips twitched, then he sobered and sent her a straight look. 'You might think so, but believe me, no woman would want me - not if she knew what I was really like. What I've done.' The way he said it made her heart squeeze in compassion and with another emotion she couldn't identify. She asked herself the question she couldn't ask him - what had he done that was so terrible? A shiver coursed through her at his sudden mood change and the brooding look he sent over the marshes.

'I know what you're really like.' She sent him a fierce look, not allowing him to push her away physically or emotionally. He was just beginning to open up to her and she didn't want him to clam up. He was balanced against the fence, the weight of his rucksack making it difficult for him to right himself while he held onto her fists. He seemed in no hurry to let her go; meanwhile, she was imprisoned between his splayed legs. She felt no embarrassment at being so close and intimate; there was a part of her that knew, in spite of his warning, that she could trust him, with her life - if not her heart.

'And what am I really like?' he asked, pulling a self-deprecating face.

'Mad, bad and dangerous to know,' Charlee said with her usual flippancy.

Her knees were beginning to ache from holding herself away from him, so she relaxed and leaned against him. He was wearing double thickness walking trousers as protection against the wind, so if he did find her in the least bit arousing she'd never know. She blushed at the way her thoughts were running. Seeing him naked and vulnerable in bed last night had irrevocably altered her perception of him.

She shook away the wanton image, trying hard not to lose herself in the depths of his grey eyes; or to find his straight nose and the pensive, downward set of his lips appealing. He'd made it abundantly clear there was no place for sexual attraction in their relationship. And even if Sam Walker had commanded him to put stars in her eyes, he clearly had no intention of carrying out those orders. He was too honest - that much she knew about him.

'Mad, bad and dangerous to know,' he mused. 'Like Byron, you mean?' His straight dark eyebrows drew together and he dipped his head as he tried to read her expression.

'Just like Byron, except ...' she pulled up short.

'Go on - I'm steeling myself, Montague,' he remarked with a resigned but amused shrug. 'That particular genie isn't going to return willingly to the magic lamp. Say it. '

'Except. Oh, God - I wish I hadn't started this ...' She took a deep breath and rushed on, 'Except you probably wouldn't have sex with your sister.'

'Only - probably?' This time his eyebrows almost touched his hairline.

'Definitely,' she asserted.

'Thanks for the character reference. And, for the record, she was his half-sister.' Shaking his head at a further example of her off-the-wall observations, he asked reflectively, 'How did we segue from owls being diurnal, to incest, and nineteenth-century Romantic Poets? Only with you, Montague; only with you.' He gave her another measured look, apparently accepting that she was a total fruit bat - but his partner for good or ill. Charlee could tell that he found their conversation intellectually stimulating and enjoyed the badinage, as if humour could unlock those parts of him he'd closed off from the world.

'Good morning.' Two of the elderly guests from the hotel, similarly loaded down with walking sticks, binoculars and tripods, walked past them.

'Good morning.' Ffinch greeted them, as if it was nothing out of the ordinary for his fiancée to throw him into a hedge and then herself on

224

top of him. 'Lovely morning for it,' he added.

'It is indeed,' the wife pronounced, giving Charlee a 'good on you, girl' wink before walking on.

'Did you see that?' she gasped, finally pushing herself off him. 'She winked at me!'

'What? You think sex stops at sixty?' Ffinch asked.

'I'm trying very hard not to think about it. My parents are in their sixties. Urgh, don't let's go there.'

'Incestuous poets much easier to handle?'

'Much,' she agreed, brushing down her windproof jacket and adjusting the polar fleece bandana keeping her ears warm. It was shocking pink, but not as pink as her cheeks.

Head down against the buffeting wind, she followed Ffinch as he walked along the path hugging the outer margins of the marsh beyond the tide's reach. Eventually he came to a halt by a bench facing out over the marshes to the sea. He slipped off his rucksack, sat on the bench and indicated that she should do the same. Then he got out his flask and poured out two cups of hot chocolate.

'You know, The Ship is missing a trick,' he said as he savoured the hot drink.

'It is?'

'Yes,' he replied, raising his binoculars and looking towards Thornham Beach. 'Serving hot drinks in dark-green flasks with the hotel's logo on the side. How boring is that? You would have thought that Ninja Turtle flasks would have made it over here, eh Montague?'

'You are so bloody funny, Ffinch - not!'

Stifling the giggle that threatened to have her spluttering in her hot chocolate, Charlee relaxed and looked over the marshes. Now she was out of the wind and the sun had come out, they didn't look so grim after all. There was a stripped back beauty to them, she could see that, and the flocks of birds heading for the feeding grounds down by the shoreline ensured the view was an ever changing tapestry. And she had to admit, just sitting there, eyes closed, face soaking up the weak January sun, was the perfect antidote to the last couple of manic weeks. When she glanced at Ffinch he was still scanning the marshes through his binoculars, his cup of hot chocolate untouched on the bench beside him.

Why did she get the impression it wasn't the birds he was watching so intently?

'What's out there?' Charlee asked, slipping on her sunglasses against the almost overwhelming expanse of bright blue sky that filled three quarters of the landscape.

'The Wash. And over there you can see the wind turbines on the shoreline at Skegness.' Charlee followed his pointing finger and squinted at the distant shore where almost a hundred huge turbines were turning like quiet ghosts.

'No, I meant - what's out there that you find so interesting?'

'Just enjoying the view,' Ffinch said, sitting down and drinking his hot chocolate. 'We spent so much time abroad when I was growing up, staying with my Brazilian relatives on their coffee farm or on overseas postings. I don't know much about the English coast and I'm intrigued by it.'

Charlee felt excluded from his circle of trust, but she hid it well.

'Ditto. My father thought it was a good idea for me to practise my Spanish, Italian, Russian - whatever - in the country where it was spoken and booked our summer holidays accordingly. Mum didn't mind where we stayed as long as it involved sun, a five-star hotel with a pool and somewhere to stack her suntan lotion next to a pile of books. Thank God for the invention of e-readers, she always went over the luggage limit on books alone and father would go ape.' She knew she was gabbling but couldn't stop herself. 'The annoying thing is, as soon as the locals found out I was British, they wanted to practise their English on me.

'How is your Russian these days?' he asked, conversationally. 'Can you read and write it?'

'*Ya xorosho govoru po rysski.*'

'Which means?'

'My Russian is very good.' She sent him a calculating look. '*No mne interesno pochemy eto tak vajno vam.*'

'That doesn't sound complimentary. What does it mean, Montague?' he asked, clearly taking her shrewd look on board.

'But I can't help wondering why it's so important to you.'

'So you'll be able to understand what Anastasia says to her brides-maids and report back to Sam,' he said, as though explaining the rules of a board game to a child. 'What?' he asked as she jumped to her feet and stood in front of him, deliberately blocking the view of the marsh he appeared to find so engaging.

'Look, Ffinch. I don't know what's going on here but it's certainly more than photographing some anorexic models and reporting their banal conversations about how many calories are in a breadstick. Or spoiling *Mirror, Mirror*'s story, for that matter.'

Unfazed by her outburst, he put his binoculars down on the bench next to the hot chocolate and chose his next words carefully.

'Montague, that brain of yours is in permanent hyperdrive and it's quite exhausting if you must know. This story is Sam's way of easing me in gently after dengue fever; after - after everything that's happened, to - to me.' His voice faltered and Charlee felt guilty for voicing her suspicions, but only for a few brief moments. 'This is my therapeutic return to work, as recommended by the guys in HR - supervising a rookie, taking a few snaps ...'

'Pouf,' Charlee exclaimed dismissively. Ffinch hardly looked like someone who gave a stuff about what HR thought. However, there was a ring of truth in his explanation, but it wasn't the whole truth or anything approaching it, of that Charlee was sure. Turning away from him, she looked back at the wind turbines on the distant shoreline turning against the pale-blue winter sky.

'Charlee, this is Sam's last hurrah. If we get the scoop it'll not only steal the march on *Mirror, Mirror*, it'll put *What'cha!* in a strong position when he does come to sell.'

'I totally get that, but why is my being able to read Russian so important?'

'In case.'

'In case of what? Don't treat me like an idiot,' she said fiercely. She'd had a lifetime of her brothers denigrating and undermining her for their amusement and wasn't about to allow Ffinch to do the same. But he was already throwing the dregs of his hot chocolate onto the grass and screwing the cup back onto the flask.

'Look, Charlee,' he said wearily, getting to his feet and threading his arms through his rucksack. 'Your mission is to get photos of Markova. Concentrate on that. If, by listening to her conversation you should glean some information about -' he hesitated, her persistent lobbying apparently wearing down his resistance.

'About?'

'Her fiancé and his business dealings, then report straight back to me. No matter how inconsequential the details may seem. Only, keep it between us - don't even tell Sam; if you do well then doubtless you will be given something more deserving of your talents next time.'

'As your partner?' she asked, already knowing the answer.

'Possibly not. I - well, I've got unfinished business in Colombia which I must attend to.' She didn't like the way he said it, or how his expression darkened. Fear clutched at her heart and she forgot her anger and imagined him back on the trail of The Aguilas Negra - the Black Eagles. And never coming home …

'No, you mustn't,' she declared with sudden passion, grabbing his arm and shaking it in an attempt to make him see sense.

'I didn't know you cared, Montague.' Although he made light of her concern, he didn't shake her off - instead, he placed his gloved hand on top of hers and looked directly into her eyes. Walking in the cold wind had brought colour to his cheeks and Charlee caught a glimpse of the old Ffinch. How he must have looked before he'd set off on his research trip to Darien.

'I do care,' she said softly. 'As a friend and partner, I care what happens to you.' She gave him a fierce, 'don't try to push me away' look.

'Charlee, don't,' he said almost regretfully. 'I can't - it wouldn't be fair.' Removing his glove, he raised his hand and cupped her cheek. Charlee pushed her face closer into his palm and her eyes widened in response to his intense study of her face and eyes. A spark of sexual awareness arced between them which rocked Charlee to her foundations.

Perhaps, here on the salt marsh, where the wind sighed through the reeds and stirred the dried pods of the alexanders, they could be honest with one another. Confront those feelings which had been simmering beneath the surface since the book launch. Playing his pretend fiancée wasn't easy; the pretence was beginning to feel more real than the life Charlee had left behind. She was beginning to fall for Rafa Ffinch - for all his faults, irascibility and secretiveness. At the end of the assignment, when their partnership was dissolved, she knew that walking away from him would be the hardest thing she'd ever done.

It was time to redraw the line in the sand and use his blunt economy with the facts to armour herself against him. To hide her reaction to his touch, to him, she glanced down at the muddy earth at their feet and pushed a stone around with the toe of her spotty wellingtons.

'Back in Sam's office you told me not to go all mushy on you,' she reminded him. 'And I won't.' She pushed away from him although every instinct she possessed was telling her to throw her arms around him and keep him safe.

'For God's sake, Montague. That day I hardly knew you - apart from the fact you appeared just right for this post - ballsy, opinionated and capable of thinking on your feet. You came recommended by Poppy and Sam - but that meant nothing to me. I had to sound you out. I had to be sure, for both our sakes. Do you have to keep dredging it up at every opportunity? I get it, believe me; I know your feelings towards me. You said on that occasion you weren't looking for a life partner - and if you were, I was the last man on earth you'd choose.'

'Now who's dredging up the past?' she asked, moving over to the margin of the marsh.

'I think we know that I'm not your type,' he went on, as if she hadn't spoken. 'Though God knows who is. I have great sympathy for the poor schmuck who eventually takes you on; he won't know what time of day it is. Or what you're thinking from one moment to the next. And if I had wanted to start something,' he pulled a face at the expression, 'it would have happened back at the mews. But having my toes shish kebabbed by your killer heels and being left to starve because your post-feminist principles wouldn't allow you to make my dinner and keep it warm in the oven - made pretty clear your opinion of me.'

'Ha. See ... I knew you hadn't got over that.' Charlee turned back to him in triumph as she trumped his ace. This was less dangerous ground. This she could do. 'You should have come home at a reasonable time, not left me wondering if you'd come off your motorbike and was lying in A&E. I'm not one of your legion of girlfriends who would doubtless be only too happy to play house with you. And you're right - you're not my type,' she lied.

'Jesus, Charlee, don't spare my feelings will you?'

'I won't as, quite obviously, you haven't considered mine,' she said and then frowned. 'I can't remember what this argument is about any more, so let's move on.' She hoicked her rucksack higher on her slight shoulders.

'It was about us being partners; mates,' he ended the argument.

'Let's leave it there. If you want to risk your life in piranha-infested waters - that's up to you.'

'It certainly is.'

'Good.' Charlee went stomping off up the path, putting up a pair of wading birds whose long legs trailed behind them in flight. She heard her name called. 'Wot?' she rounded on him, glaring.

'Wrong way again Montague. Follow me.'

Ffinch coolly assumed the role of man-in-charge-of-an-ordnance-survey-map while Charlee fitted her smaller footsteps into the tracks he left in the mud and followed in his wake.

Chapter Twenty-six
Mates?

'Wait up, Ffinch, I want a sandwich,' she called out after ten minutes of trudging through the mud. They'd reached a second bench overlooking the marshes, so she swung her rucksack off, sat down and started to unwrap the packed lunch The Ship Inn had provided.

'Hangry?' Ffinch inquired, searching her face to see if it was safe to approach.

'Hangry,' she agreed. She was about to explain that low blood sugar wasn't the only cause of her anger towards him, but then changed her mind. Best to let the matter rest and get everything back on an even keel. Perhaps she could put her racing heart and sense of confusion down to a delayed caffeine buzz. She'd had little to eat at breakfast apart from a slice of toast and two double espressos.

'Mates?' he asked, watching her attack a ham and mustard sandwich.

'I guess,' she said, her mouth full of food.

Slipping off his rucksack, he perched on the back of the bench to give him extra height. He raised his binoculars and stared once more over the marshes towards the channels and gulleys revealed as the tide receded.

'Are we anywhere near the boot camp?' Charlee asked, taking a large swig from a bottle of mineral water.

'See where the vegetation is a deeper, richer green, and where some boats are moored? That's the beginning of the boot camp's territory. It stretches all the way to the Coal Shed and sluice gates at Thornham Staithe and out to the Wash.'

'Coal Shed?' Charlie frowned.

'You'll see when we get there. I want to walk across the marshes and down to Thornham Beach to familiarise myself with the lay of the land.' Noticing her curious look Ffinch went on to explain. 'I've thought of a few scenarios that might arise and I want us to be prepared for them.'

Excitement fizzed through Charlee's veins. This was what she'd been born for - adventure, derring-do, the scoop ...

'Such as?' She kept her tone level. She didn't want to come across as just another overexcited intern.

'I was thinking, say Markova suspected you of taking too many snaps of her. She might complain to the management and they might ask you to hand your phone over,' Ffinch said thoughtfully.

'That's a lot of mights, isn't it?' He nodded. 'So - what do you propose?'

'As a contingency - you inform me via the public phone of your itinerary for the next day and I'll station myself somewhere on the marsh and take the photos with my long range lenses as you all trot by.'

'I'm not sure why you can't do that anyway ...'

'We've been through all this, Montague. It's because we want detail for the column - what the bride-to-be's thinking, who's designing her dress, where they're holding the wedding, having their honeymoon. All the detail the readers of *What'cha!* expect - you know the score.'

'Moon in June, roses round the door. Got it,' Charlee said, getting in a little dig at the same time.

'Exactly. Now buckle up, you're in for a yomp over to Holme-next-the-Sea and then back to The Ship Inn for some chill-out time before dinner. What now?'

'Can we have dinner in the bar tonight? I mean, last night was great, don't get me wrong - but I would like to sit in the Smuggler's Retreat and absorb the atmosphere, listen to the locals, pick up the vibe. Now what have I said?' she demanded as Ffinch gave her an inscrutable look.

'You really are a conundrum, aren't you, Charlee?' His use of her first name showed that he'd consigned their spat to the past. The fine hairs on the nape of her neck stood to attention as if he'd trailed his fingers across them. 'You weren't fazed when I turned up in a vintage camper van on Christmas Eve, and genuinely seemed thrilled it had a Porsche engine. You settled right in at my grandparents' mews flat and didn't complain about the retro decor and offer to give it some kind of horrendous girlie make over. Now you're turning down a champagne dinner?'

'Well, I simply thought … there's only so much dressing up a girl can take.' She wanted to hear the second instalment of what had really happened to him in Colombia and instinct told her that he'd open up more readily in the Smuggler's Retreat with its low beams, dark walls and roaring fire.

'Okay, you're on,' he said in a light-hearted fashion. 'I didn't feel much like putting the old whistle and flute back on tonight, in any case.' Charlee laughed at his use of cockney rhyming slang.

'Lead on then, me old cock sparrow - and as we make our way down to the beach, let's work out our game plan - just in case anything does goes wrong. There is one good thing, though,' she added mischievously as she gazed out over the vast expanse of sea, marshes and reed beds, 'at least there aren't many hills in Norfolk.'

'I'll mention that to the tourist board, it'd make a great advertising slogan: Come to Norfolk for your holidays - it's so wonderfully flat!' Laughing, they made their way towards Thornham Staithe and the sluice gates which controlled the flow of water around the Coal Shed.

Mates.

Charlee was glad that Ffinch had told her to meet him in the bar at seven, sharp. She didn't think she could take another grand progress down the wide oak staircase and into the hall with everyone thinking them love's young dream. Turning right in the hall, she went into the low-ceilinged Smuggler's Retreat where she found Ffinch standing at the bar, his right foot on the polished brass rail and looking very much at home. As she approached, she heard him talking about the tides to someone whose flat vowels and nasal twang marked him out as Norfolk born and bred.

'Course, the most spectac-clear toides are later in the year,' the man was saying to Ffinch. 'But last noight's was quoite 'igh cause o' the full moon. In the old days, the smugglers would have landed their contraband and taken their chances with the revenue men. There's been murder, and worse, committed on these marshes,' he said, drained his glass and thumped it on the bar, meaningfully.

Charlee wondered what could be worse than murder but said nothing. Ffinch was unaware of her presence and she was happy to keep it like that. He signalled for the barman to refill his new-found friend's glass and swirled his whisky round and round in his tumbler without touching it.

'So what about the Thornham Boot Camp for Brides?' Ffinch asked.

'Lot o' daft women runnin' round loik idiots in my opinion,' the barman put in his two pennyworth. 'Moind you, in the summer you do get a good eyeful of posh tottie in skimpy shorts, tops and the loik - if you get my meaning.' He leaned forward and jiggled his hands up and down like he was weighing water melons. Then he summoned Ffinch to move in closer. 'The old owner sold out last year and those damned Ruskies took it over. They normally drink in the Lemon Tree on the main road where all the Londoners hang out. But they comes in 'ere occasionally, turning their noses up at moi best vodka and ordering champagne. We in't posh enough for 'em and they in't welcome.'

'Why did the previous owners move out?' Turning, Ffinch probed his new-found friend as the barman handed over his pint.

'They was getting old. Couldn't manage the big house no more - and the Ruskies offered them more than it were worth. Anyway - here's your young loidy waiting for you.' He gestured at Charlee with his pint glass, obviously keen to go join his mates who were setting up a game of cribbage by the fire.

'Charlee,' Ffinch greeted her, openly speculating how long she'd been standing there. 'What would you like to drink, darling?'

Charlee's insides turned to liquid at the endearment, momentarily forgetting that it was all part of the act.

'*Vodka-i zakyski iz menu. Ymerau ot goloda,*' she said with a flourish in Russian to cover her weakness. Realising what a brick she'd just dropped, she hurried on, hoping that the barman had poor hearing. 'Vodka - and the bar snack menu. I'm starving.'

'You can't be,' he said, glancing at his watch.

After their long walk to Holme-next-the-Sea, they'd ordered afternoon tea and Charlee had attacked hers with relish. In contrast, Ffinch had pushed his sandwiches and scones aside and drank gallons of strong black tea while poring over Ordnance Survey maps of the marshes, marking certain areas in black felt-tip pen - his face a study in concentration.

'I was always hungry when I was a child. My father said I had worms and threatened to mash up worm tablets in my dinner, like he did with the dogs. What, too much information?' She laughed at his expression. 'My dad's a vet, I'm a country girl at heart - get over it.' She took a bar snack menu and sat down at a small round table in an alcove well away from everyone. The ideal spot for grilling Ffinch over Colombia, later. 'Nothing prissy about me.'

'I had noticed,' Ffinch said rather dryly.

'You think that a little more priss is called for?' Charlee asked.

'Just a smidgeon,' Ffinch observed as he took his place at the table. 'You have a way of killing the moment, Montague, know that? Worm tablets, indeed. Just as well you're not my real fiancée.'

'How would a real fiancée act, then?' she asked, smarting at his tone. Playing the role of someone not held back by an excess of priss, she downed her vodka and slammed the shot glass down on the table. She managed to hide that her throat was burning and her eyes watering, but she'd made her point. 'Maybe I should have ordered a small, dry sherry in one of those old-fashioned glasses I saw back at the mews - what do you call them?'

'A schooner.'

'Well, Miss Prissy Pants wouldn't be much good to you on this occasion, now would she?' Charlee opened the menu, dismayed to discover that the catch in her throat and the hot tears misting her eyes had nothing to do with the vodka. 'Arranging flowers and knitting doilies won't be much use, whereas being able to read and write in six different languages might just be an advantage over the next few days.'

Ffinch said nothing for a few minutes as he read down the menu, clearly aware that he'd upset her but wasn't quite sure how. 'You're right, you are the woman for the job. And, by the way ...'

'Yes,' Charlie raised her head and looked at him.

'You don't knit doilies, you crochet them.'

He got to his feet and sauntered over to the bar to order. Although she almost hated him in that moment, Charlee was nonetheless aware how he drew glances from men and women alike. The men because they sensed his air of confidence and authority; and the women because he looked as if he'd just stepped out of a Rohan catalogue - straight leg black trousers, boxy shirt under a lightweight gilet and expensive looking trainers/walking boots. It took a lot of money to look so casually dressed and Charlee wondered about his privileged - if peripatetic - upbringing, which he never mentioned.

Apart from the aforementioned family coffee plantation in Brazil, she gathered that there was a strong highland connection, on his mother's side. Quite a mixture, that - fiery Latin and mystical, romantic highlander. When he returned from the bar with a bottle of wine and two glasses, she was unravelling the edge of her beer mat and staring into the blazing fire.

'Moving on from doilies to origami frogs?' he joked, joining her at the table.

'Oh, I thought a life-sized replica of the Taj Mahal ... seeing how we're celebrating our engagement. You didn't mention edifices to undying love on your list of forbidden topics. Did you?'

'No, I rather thought it was implied. And that goes for anything made out of matchsticks, too.' He looked up from his menu and sent her one of his slow, considering looks and then poured out two glasses of wine, holding his aloft. 'To undying love, boot camps, dodgy Russians and your first real assignment.'

'I'll drink to that,' Charlee replied and clinked glasses. After a few thoughtful sips, she took a deep breath and cautiously approached the elephant in the room.

'So, Ffinch, are you going to tell me the rest of the story? What happened after your captors marched you through the jungle in the rain for days on end?'

Ffinch put down his glass and let out a long breath, raking his fingers through his thick, dark hair. Then he rubbed at the scars on his wrists, as if they were suddenly in some way bothersome. In the light from the oil lamps and the log fire, his face was pensive and in shadow, his eyes immeasurably troubled and sad.

'Do you mind if I don't, Charlee? I will tell you one day, just not tonight. Talking about it drags me right back there and to everything that ... that happened and - well, tonight I just want to be. Can you understand that?'

'Sure.' Charlee shrugged and concentrated on the bar snack menu, hiding acute disappointment. But she took him at his word - if he said that he would tell her one day, then he would. 'I'm going for the rack of ribs with chips and salad, followed by sticky toffee pudding and home-made ice cream. Cheese and biscuits, too - if I have room. The thought of those rice cakes, early morning runs and being made to drink water drawn from the marsh is haunting me.'

She glanced at Ffinch who had his head bent over the menu, and wondered if he was even listening. She sighed, guessing that the elephant would have to stay in the room and do its best not to damage the furniture until he was in a more receptive mood. She just hoped that would be sooner rather than later - and before they parted company, for good.

Chapter Twenty-seven
The Whole Truth

Charlee woke in the middle of the night with a raging thirst and swung her legs out of the bed. She opened the bottle of water on her bedside table and glugged it straight down before heading for the loo. When she returned, Ffinch's voice reached her from the other side of the connecting doors, his cries much louder than the night before.

His moans grew more voluble and Charlee was worried he'd wake the hotel at this rate. Cautiously, she edged closer to the interconnecting doors and tried the handle. She hadn't bothered to relock the doors and neither had Ffinch. She pushed the heavy doors open and was in the middle of his room before she knew it. In a reprise of the previous evening, Ffinch thrashed around in bed, muttering incoherently in Spanish.

'*Dejadla en paz,*' don't touch her. '*Llevadme a mí en su lugar,*' Take me not her. And then a plaintive, heartbroken - '*Elena, primita,*' Elena, my little cousin.

When his cries rose in volume, Charlee rushed to his side. 'Ffinch - wake up.' Tentatively, she poked him in the shoulder but it had no effect. If anything, his muttering grew louder and she didn't need to be fluent in Spanish to understand what followed.

'*Cabrones ... hijos de puta. Allesandro ...*'

This time she leaned over his bed, took him by the shoulders in an attempt to shake him awake. 'Ffinch - Rafa ... it's me, Charlee.'

She let out a muffled shriek as Ffinch lunged out and grabbed her, although clearly still asleep. He dragged her onto the bed, rolled her under him and pinned her down as though shielding her from hurt and pain. Charlee began to panic; she'd read about a husband who'd strangled his wife in his sleep and had no recollection of it the next morning. Using all her strength she tried to push him off, but it was no good. Fearing for her safety, she took his ear between her teeth and bit down on it.

Hard.

'Wha - what?' he murmured groggily, waking slowly as if from a drugged sleep. It was apparent he had no idea of time or place - and was possibly mistaking her for someone else. This Elena person he kept mentioning, perhaps? In a dreamlike state, he nuzzled her neck and kissed along the line to her throat until he reached her lips. Charlee's moue of protest was lost as he kissed her with such thoroughness and passion that her heart snagged. She knew he was on automatic pilot - half-awake and half-asleep. She positioned herself more comfortably beneath him, savouring the kiss and the moment before she pushed him off. His right hand pushed questingly under her thin vest top and encircled her breast, while his other hand slid under her narrow buttocks and tilted her pelvis upwards and towards him.

But even as she writhed in delight at being kissed so comprehensively, in error, Ffinch swam to the surface and his eyes blinked open. Dazed, still lying on top of her, he pushed himself onto his elbows and looked down into her face.

'Charlee? What the fu - what are you doing in my bed, and -'

'Lying under you?' She finished his sentence as best she could, given that his full weight was pressing down on her. Acutely aware that he was naked apart from cotton pyjama shorts which did nothing to conceal the strength of his erection, Charlee experienced a weakening heat that left her feeling warm and golden - as if she'd been dipped in expensive, organic honey. Aflame with desire, she sighed and automatically began stroking his back lightly with her fingers.

It would be the easiest thing in the world, she thought, to shrug off her clothes and lie naked in Ffinch's arms. She wanted that more than anything. But she knew she couldn't give in to these pleasurable feelings, their relationship didn't allow for it - it wasn't part of the deal. Her fear of being throttled receded, replaced by a need to explain how she came to be in his bed in the middle of the night, and quickly too.

There being nothing else for it, she reverted to type. 'Gerroff me, will you!'

Ffinch, now coming fully to his senses and aware of his aroused state, rolled off her. He sat on the edge of the bed, reached down for a discarded pillow on the floor and pulled it across his lap. He then switched on the bedside light and remained there, silent and with his head bent forward and his back turned towards her. His skin was taut over his vertebrae and rib cage, and he looked painfully thin. Charlee longed to run her hand along the vulnerable curve of his spine and massage away the tension knotting his neck and shoulders.

'How did you - did we?' He spoke without turning round, still half-asleep.

'I heard you calling out in your sleep. I came into the room and tried to shake you awake, but you were deep under. Then you grabbed me and pinned me to the mattress.' Her cheeks flamed and she glossed over the part where he kissed her and she'd responded just a little too enthusiastically for someone who believed that she was about to be strangled.

'Did you bite my ear?' he asked, massaging his lobe and struggling to make sense of waking up in the middle of the night with Charlee lying beneath him.

'I did. But calm down, it wasn't meant as foreplay.' Charlee used sarcasm to cover up how instinctively her body had responded - was still responding - to his nakedness. Her breasts felt heavy and she wanted his hands back in place, working their magic. 'It was the only way I could wake you up. Sorry.'

'Yes, it's the medication, it zonks me out, but never mind all that. My ear hurts like hell. Have you severed it?' he demanded, as if using anger to cloak his reaction to finding her being in his bed.

'Oh, don't be such a baby.' Charlee tutted and pushed herself up into a sitting position, kneeling behind him to examine his ear. To her shame, it did look rather red and she could see the impression of two faint but definite teeth marks. 'I thought you might strangle me,' she explained somewhat lamely.

'Strangle you?'

'I read about this man, once -'

'Believe me, Montague, if I'd wanted to strangle you I would have done it before now - and in broad daylight.'

'Cheers!'

'Don't think I haven't been tempted.' There - normal service was resumed.

'Thanks again.' Charlee watched as he dragged his T-shirt off the back of the chair and pulled it over his head. Then he fetched the towelling robe off the sofa and slipped that over his makeshift pyjamas in a kind of double indemnity against her. 'Don't worry; I'm not going to leap on you - or under you, for that matter,' Charlee assured him snarkily, guessing what was going through his mind. 'Being pinned down in your bed in the dead of night doesn't make for a pleasant experience.'

'Didn't your mother teach you that you shouldn't enter a man's bedroom in the middle of the night?'

'There are a lot of things my mother didn't tell me,' Charlee said dryly. 'Anyway, I thought I was safe with you.'

'Because I'm not manly enough?'

'Stop fishing for compliments, Ffinch. I think you've established your credentials in that area, thank you very much.' She coloured, obliquely referring to his earlier state of arousal. Ffinch was a little taken aback by her response, and then he looked at her over his shoulder and grinned at her sauciness.

'Well, now that's established, you can go back to your room. I won't have the nightmares again. They usually only come once each night, when I'm in the REM phase of sleep.'

'REM?' Charlee queried, in no hurry to leave.

'Rapid eye movement, the phase of sleep during which dreams and nightmares usually occur.' He stood on the carpet looking at her expectantly, openly suggesting that she should return to her own room. Pronto.

'But, what if you start shouting again,' Charlee began, not entirely sure where she was going with this.

'Then you'll hear me and come in and bite the other ear.' He smiled, but the smile didn't quite reach his eyes. Evidently he was aware of what Charlee was proposing and doing his best to resist the candid invitation in her eyes.

She took a step closer. 'But, next time, I might be asleep and not hear you. Then the management would have to knock on your door and tell you to keep it down - as if we were indulging in noisy sex.'

'Is there any other kind?' he asked before he could stop himself. His frown and the faint flush along his cheekbones told Charlee that he wanted to call the words back. As the senior partner he probably felt that it was down to him to keep a lid on this ... attraction they felt for each other.

'Depends, doesn't it?' Charlee said casually and shrugged.

'On what?' Seemingly, Ffinch couldn't stop responding to Charlee's teasing, provocative words.

'On the man. The circumstances.' Boldly, she moved even closer to him. 'Don't push me away, Ffinch. Not tonight. We're partners. Doesn't that count for anything?'

'More than you know,' he said with a passion that surprised her. Then he passed a weary hand over his eyes. 'If we do - this - it'll ruin everything and our partnership will fall to pieces. I've seen it happen before - '

'With you? Is that why you always work alone?' She experienced a pang as she thought of him with other women in this very situation. Had he turned them away as he was now proposing to do to her?

'Go to bed, Charlee,' he said without answering her question. Charlee backed away from him and climbed back into his bed, which was still warm and smelled of his aftershave and a manly muskiness. 'I meant, your bed.'

'I'll just stay until you've told me the rest of your story and you're asleep. Then I'll leave, okay?'

'Very much not okay,' Ffinch demurred, taking a couple of steps closer to the bed. 'But I know enough about you to realise that you won't budge. So maybe I'll go to your room, instead ...'

'Look. You can trust me, I won't make you do anything that makes you feel uncomfortable. We'll just snuggle up in your bed together, like -'

'Babes in the Wood?'

'If you like. Or maybe more like Byron and his half-sister. Okay, that wasn't funny,' she apologised as she peeled back the corner of the duvet and patted the mattress invitingly. 'And, don't worry; I'll still respect you in the morning.' That, apparently, was a challenge too far for the alpha male in Ffinch. Shrugging off his dressing gown he leapt into bed, gathered her into his arms and pulled her up close.

'Don't start what you can't finish,' he whispered warningly, their noses touching. But Charlee wasn't afraid. Closing her eyes she went limp in his arms, the blood sang in her ears and her heart beat out an uneven tattoo. Ffinch groaned as though resigning himself to the inevitable outcome of their situation. He rolled her under him and started to kiss her with a slow thoroughness that made lust scud through her and her womb contract in anticipation of what the kisses might herald. Then, reluctantly, he put her from him, rolled over onto his back and flung his arm across his eyes as if to block out the enticing sight of her, all warm, rosy and inviting.

'Charlee - no, this isn't right. Go back to your room, for God's sake.'

'But I don't want to. I want to - to hear the rest of your story.'

'Okay,' he breathed, seemingly sensing she was not to be dissuaded. 'I'll tell you the rest of my story -'

'All of it?'

'All of it. Then you go back to your room. Deal?'

'Deal.' She held out her hand and he shook it, his expression making plain he'd made a deal with the devil. Charlee relaxed, took his arm and wrapped it round her shoulders and then snuggled into his side.

'Comfortable?' he inquired ironically.

'Very. Now, lights off - more atmospheric.'

'Not sure that's a good idea … okay; lights off.' He stretched out and switched off the lamp on the bedside table. 'Although I should warn you -' he paused.

'Yes?'

'I only have so much control, so don't push it. Although, to be honest, since -' he stopped and then rushed on, 'since Darien, I haven't …'

'Haven't?' Charlee pretended not to understand what he meant.

'Haven't wanted sex or …'

'Or?'

'Or found any woman capable of - arousing me. Happy now?' he asked in constricted tones, as if this confession was being wrested out of him. It was apparent, from the way his penis was pushing against the fabric of his pyjama shorts, that one problem had been dealt with tonight.

Charlee snuggled more closely into his side and sighed.

'Quite happy. But, just so as we're clear, I'm here for research purposes and to learn more about my partner - not sex.' She pressed her lips against his rib cage, his skin was warm and tasted slightly salty and she breathed in the scent of him. 'Just saying …'

'Glad we've cleared that up,' he said, his voice rumbling low in his chest and his words reverberating against her ear.

'I really want to know the whole story,' she said softly, encouragingly.

'And I'll tell you all of it. Maybe then you'll go scuttling back to your bed and leave me in peace.'

'Perhaps I will,' she agreed, 'or perhaps I'll stay the night.'

'Charlee, that isn't an option -'

'Okay. Story ...' she commanded. She slipped her fingers through his and squeezed his hand encouragingly. 'Go on, Ffinch, you can't re-nege on the deal now.' He took a shuddering breath and although she couldn't know for certain, Charlee felt sure he was staring wide-eyed in the darkness, remembering ...

'After marching us through the rainforest - soaking wet, eaten alive by bugs and battered and bruised - we finally made one of their base camps. They'd tied our hands together and fashioned a kind of leash through our bonds so they could pull us to our feet when we faltered. That seemed to amuse them,' he added grimly. 'I was fit and strong, as was Allesandro - the student from Bogotá University who was helping me. But Elena was only a slip of a girl.' He took a shuddering breath and Charlee filled in the gaps.

'Earlier, you cried out in your sleep: Elena, *primita*. Was Elena your cousin?'

'Yes,' he replied, his voice rough. 'A distant Fonseca relation, but a cousin nonetheless. I was reluctant to take her with us, but she pleaded with me - she said it would be an adventure and how she'd had enough of studying. That is why I hesitated before taking on another assistant -'

'Partner,' Charlee corrected.

'Okay, partner - if you must know. I didn't want the same thing to happen again.'

'But this is Norfolk, not Colombia. What danger could I possibly be in?'

'Danger comes in many forms, Charlee ...'

'Back to the story?' she prompted, sensing that he was about to get sidetracked.

'Very well. We stayed a few days at their base camp during which time I feared for Elena. Not simply because she was small and frail but because of the way they looked at her, and I was powerless to protect her. Do you have any idea how that made me feel?' Again his voice was rough, as though he found it hard to keep his emotions in check. 'But,' he swallowed hard, 'their leader at least had the sense to know they'd be fools to harm her.'

Charlee shuddered, knowing exactly what was on their minds. She pictured Elena, shivering in the humidity of the rainforest, growing weaker by the hour, Ffinch unable to follow every chivalric instinct he possessed. Involuntarily, her hand began stroking Ffinch's chest, slowly and rhythmically in order to comfort him. He almost seemed oblivious to her light touch, turning his head away from her in the darkness and continuing with his story.

'When the rain stopped and we could move on, they bundled us into three separate boats and headed up the Amazon. I heard them talking in patois and was able to make out - just - that their intention was to take us to their main camp and issue ransom demands for our release. Luckily, they didn't seem to realise how wealthy our respective families were. To them we were simply *hidalgos*: patricians, not *campesino*: peasants.'

Charlee thought that would have been obvious to anyone. With his height, fine features and bearing it was clear that Ffinch possessed the confident self-belief that education and wealth bestow. For a few moments he paused in his storytelling and laid his hand on top of hers, stilling her rhythmic stroking. Charlee felt the rise and fall of his chest, his heart beating fast and strong under her palm as he was transported back to a time and place he'd rather forget. But, she suspected, part of him was glad of this opportunity to exorcise the ghosts which haunted his dreams and waking hours.

'What happened next?'

'We - the three of us that is - fell ill. Feverish, sick - couldn't face food - started vomiting and couldn't get warm, no matter how many covers they threw over us.' As if reliving the moment, he was wracked by shivers. Charlee felt a shudder convulse his limbs, goose bumps pimpled the skin on his arms and legs and she drew the duvet over them, protectively. 'Long story short?'

'Yes.'

'We'd contracted dengue. In the end our captors decided that Elena wasn't worth the diesel needed to transport her to their headquarters. They threw her overboard before Allesandro and I realised what had happened. She was unconscious and sank like a stone. I jumped in after her, tried to swim to her - but my hands were tied. I called to them, to Allesandro -to save her. I held on as long I could and then slipped into unconsciousness, too. The boats carried on with Allesandro and -'

'And?'

'Well, you know the rest. It's well documented. The strong current pushed me up against a half-submerged tree, my clothes snagged on it and I was found by the Cat People who were out fishing. They took me to their village - hid me in spite of the danger to themselves and nursed me back to health. Well, an approximation of it.' Charlee felt his self-deprecating shrug.

'I'm so sorry,' she said and began to stroke his chest, his arms, his throat in order to rub life and heat back into his limbs. 'So sorry for what happened to you - and for all the stupid things I said about the Cat People on the night of the book awards.'

'You weren't to know. I goaded you that night, pushed you to see how far you were prepared to go; how capable you were of blagging it. I was auditioning you for this assignment, if you like, but you didn't know it.' She heard the smile in his voice. 'You passed with flying colours, Carlotta …' He rolled her name round his tongue giving it a Spanish intonation. He turned on his side until they were practically lying nose to nose. 'But now, I think you'd better leave, keep your side of the bargain. Otherwise …'

'Otherwise?'

'We'll end up making love and that's something I think we'd both regret.'

'Why?'

'Because after we've got our photos, and Sam's got his spoiler, I'm returning to Darien - I told you that out on the marshes. I have unfinished business there. I don't know how this will end.'

'But -' Just in time, Charlee stopped herself from saying, 'I don't want you to go'. She knew the last thing that would endear her to a man like Ffinch was to act like a clinging vine. 'Okay, one last kiss and then I'll leave you in peace,' she said resignedly, 'promise.'

They were still lying face to face and Charlee raised her left leg and hooked it round Ffinch's hip, pulling him towards her pelvis with her heel. Then she pressed her body against his, found his lips and started the kiss. Ffinch held out for as long as he could but then wrapped his arms around her, pulling her closer into his groin. Under the duvet the combined temperatures of their body heat soared and Charlee felt like she was the one burning with a fever. With a groan of capitulation, Ffinch lowered his head, pushed up her camisole and his mouth latched unerringly onto her nipple. For a few seconds they both stopped breathing as Ffinch began to tease and suck.

Charlee felt as if she was drowning.

'Rafa,' she said, cradling his head and urging him to suck faster, harder, her head thrown back against the pillows.

Her use of his first name was enough to call him back from the dream world into which they had descended. With a groan of regret, he covered her breasts with her camisole and pushed her away. Then he got out of bed, scooped her up as if she weighed no more than a feather and headed for the double doors. Before Charlee was aware of his intention, he kicked one of them open and dropped her unceremoniously onto her bed. Then without another word he turned on his heel, returned to his room and locked the doors behind him, leaving Charlee burning with unrequited lust and more than a little shame and mortification.

Chapter Twenty-eight
Will You Still Love Me Tomorrow?

Next morning, Charlee was waiting by the reception desk at nine o'clock sharp with her bags packed. Unsurprisingly, she'd slept badly and knew she couldn't face Ffinch after making such an exhibition of herself the previous night. Although she hadn't felt so at the time, she was glad that Ffinch'd had the sense and necessary willpower to call a halt to their lovemaking. If they'd become lovers she'd probably be feeling a hundred times worse.

'Your receipt and your taxi, Miss Montague,' the receptionist said smoothly. 'Was there anything else?'

'No - no. My,' she gulped down some air, 'my fiancé is staying on for a few more days. And -' she stopped herself. It really wasn't necessary to explain herself to the receptionist, who'd probably seen it all before in the line of duty. Charlee handed over her key and put her credit card receipt in her handbag. She'd need that to claim her expenses back from *What'cha!* at the end of the month. Then she slipped on her sunglasses and walked out into the cold, bright morning where a taxi was waiting with its engine running.

The driver put her bags into the boot. 'The camp, is it Miss? I take a lot of young ladies up there.'

'Yes, please,' Charlee responded dully, making it plain that she didn't want to talk.

He closed her door and she settled back for the short taxi ride, trying hard not to imagine Ffinch's reaction when he found the text she'd left on his phone. It explained that she was keen to get down to business, had left for the boot camp and would ring him at the first opportunity.

She needed time to reassess the situation and get her head round what had nearly happened last night. Maybe running round the marshes in a tracksuit would help her process her feelings for Ffinch and bolster her against him when they met again. She sighed as the taxi swung under the ornate gateway of Thornham Boot Camp for Brides, its cheesy motto picked out in cream and pink: Love is Never Enough.

Charlee groaned. She had an awful suspicion that apologising to Ffinch for going AWOL, no matter how she presented the case for the defence, would never be enough.

Thornham Creek Manor was set in extensive grounds overlooking the marshes. In scenes more reminiscent of boarding school than a weekend at a luxury spa, limos disgorged stick thin women onto the gravel drive and staff ferried their luggage into the house. Charlee's taxi driver deposited her and her battered M&S holdall on the drive and then left, wishing her well. Her suitcase came a very poor second to the other guests' Louis Vuitton, Mulberry or Smythson luggage and the staff studiously ignored her. Dragging her wheeled holdall over the gravel, Charlee noticed that the prospective brides carried their own vanity cases, hanging onto them for dear life/grim death. What did they contain, she wondered? Wraps of cocaine, syringes full of do-it-yourself Botox, amphetamines, appetite suppressants, monkey glands?

Tote bag slung over her shoulder, she walked into the house. The manor's former entrance hall was now a smart reception area and fitted out with a curved mahogany desk, low sofas and vases crammed with Casablanca lilies. An efficient-looking member of staff in a beauty therapist's uniform approached Charlee. 'Your name, madam?' she asked, her pen poised over a clipboard.

'Char - Charlotte Montague,' Charlee said, dropping her heavy tote bag onto the floor.

'Montague ... Montague. Ah yes, a member of staff will take your bags to your room.' She clicked her fingers and a young girl came scuttling forward. Charlee was surprised to hear her address the girl in Russian but had little time to reflect on it because two little dogs came rushing round from behind the reception desk and dived head first into her tote bag.

With all the thoroughness of canines trained in drug enforcement, the hairless pooches withdrew their heads from the bag, tussling over a king-sized Mars bar she had stashed there. There was a collective gasp from the therapists at the sight of the chocolate and shouts of '*Nyet - Yad. Yad.*' Poison, poison - as they leapt towards the ecstatic dogs.

'Sputnik, Laika.' A woman in a smart business suit came from an office behind the reception desk and scooped them up. She glared at Charlee. 'No food is allowed other than what chef prepares. Do you have further supplies?' For a few crazy seconds, Charlee thought the manager was going to hold out her hand and demand any chocolate bars she had stowed away. However, a great commotion in the entrance porch drew attention away from Charlee and towards the new arrival - Anastasia Markova, complete with entourage.

'Anastasia - *dobro pojalovat,*' the proprietress beamed a welcome, thrusting her dogs and the half-chewed Mars bar into the arms of one of the therapists. She dismissed Charlee with a curt nod and a member of staff handed her a large ziplock bag with her name written on it.

'What's this?' Charlee asked.

'For your mobile phone, camera and iPad, madam.'

'What? Now, wait a minute,' she protested, seeing her chances of getting the scoop on Markova disappearing along with the tools of her trade.

'Did you not read terms and conditions before you signed up for boot camp?' The assistant tutted, as though Charlee's was not the first act of rebellion she'd encountered that morning. 'They will be locked away in vault and returned to you at end of stay,' she said in thickly accented English. 'Our guests demand one hundred percent privacy.'

Damn! It was just as Ffinch had predicted. Now she'd be forced to get in touch with him, and -

'But, I wanted photos for the wedding blog I'm keeping,' Charlee said, thinking fast. 'I promised my girlfriends I'd keep them up to date with my weekend.' She gave the woman a girly pout and her eyes filled with tears.

'Photographs will be taken by us and passed onto you for purchase,' the therapist said, not giving an inch.

'Nice little earner for the boot camp, huh?' Charlee muttered and received a glacial stare. She glowered back - what was their problem? Didn't they understand the concept of customer satisfaction? God knows they charged enough for the privilege of staying at the boot camp.

'Photos will be taken by professional photographer on night of Gala Dinner when you and fiancé can pose in specially constructed romantic arbour.'

... specially constructed romantic arbour? Charlee gulped, that would go down really well with Ffinch - if he bothered to turn up. She rather suspected that by going AWOL she'd altered the terms of their partnership. Now she wouldn't be able to get any photographs of Anastasia and would have to face Sam Walker's wrath when she returned to London. Her expression must have been pretty glum because the assistant's face softened as she held out her hand for the bag.

'Ah, you are missing your fiancé, which is only natural. But think how romantic it will be when you see him in two days' time. Absence makes heart grow fonder, yes?' She gave Charlee a look which suggested that their reunion would be one long sex fest. Left with no choice, Charlee put her mobile, digital camera and iPad in the bag, zipped it up and handed it over. Just as well they didn't know about the bottle of vodka she'd squirreled away in her holdall. Sighing, she followed the girl with her luggage up the wide oak stairs and towards her bedroom.

Although her designated bedroom was well appointed with antique French beds, a pretty armoire, fresh flowers and fruit, and an en suite stacked with expensive toiletries, Charlee was less than pleased to discover she had to share. It was all too *Mallory Towers* for words. Next, she and her roomie would be having midnight feasts, investigating secret passageways by candlelight and thwarting smugglers.

All she wanted was to be left in peace to lick her wounds, get her head around her lack of photographic equipment and figure out how she could rescue the mission. And get Ffinch out of her head and stop thinking about him every sixty seconds. Standing hands on hips and giving the room one last despairing look, she noticed that her luggage had been placed at the foot of the least favourably positioned bed. In one last defiant act she marched over to her holdall, threw it on to the other bed and furiously unpacked - hanging her clothes in the armoire on scented coat hangers.

'Possession is nine-tenths of the law,' she said, moving her chair into the bay window and staring over the reed beds towards Thornham Beach. She could just make out The Ship Inn through the bare trees and her thoughts returned, predictably, to Ffinch. Pulling her knees up to her chin she sipped at a bottle of mineral water, which - according to the label - had been collected from 2,000 feet below the surface of the ocean off the Big Island of Hawaii.

Big Island? Big Deal.

Nothing made sense to her this morning, not $450 bottles of water, this luxurious room, nor the assignment. All she could think of was how badly she'd played it last night. Instead of standing her ground, she'd scuttled off like some frightened little virgin. Which she most certainly was not! Putting down the bottle of water, she buried her face in her hands and a moan of despair escaped as her traitorous body recalled the touch of Ffinch's hands on her skin, his lips on her breast. She had a dull, unrequited feeling between her legs and put her hand there, clamping her thighs together tightly and hoping it'd go away. She'd never felt like this over any man - and common sense told her that Ffinch was the last man on earth she should harbour these kinds of feelings for. Hadn't he made it perfectly clear that she was totally resistible? Dumping her on her bed like a sack of potatoes and locking the door behind him in case she should try to force herself on him twice in one night.

She was beset by a desire to leave the boot camp and return to The Ship Inn where she could make her feelings perfectly clear. She'd acted impetuously - nothing new there - but Ffinch shouldn't read anything more into her behaviour last night. It wasn't as if she was falling in love with him, for goodness sake. She straightened her shoulders; she'd come here to do a job and she couldn't let anything deflect her from that path All she needed was solitude and some deep breathing exercises to get her back on track. She sat on the bed cross-legged in the lotus position and starting chanting under her breath.

At that moment the bedroom door crashed open and a woman, well over six feet tall and looking exactly like a brick outhouse wearing a tracksuit, entered the room. She didn't introduce herself, simply looked Charlee up and down as if she was of no consequence. Then she jerked her thumbs backwards over her muscular shoulders and snarled.

'You. Leave now, Missy. Yes?'

'I beg your pardon?' Charlee said icily. She'd been pushed around enough in the last twelve hours without some former Soviet shot-putter getting in on the act, too.

'I say - you go, Missy. Come.' The Tracksuited-One reached up for Charlee's holdall on top of the armoire, threw it on the spare bed and began cramming Charlee's belongings into it.

'Stop. What are you doing? I'm calling the management.' Incensed,

Charlee untangled herself from the lotus position and an unseemly tussle ensued as she dragged her clothes out of the holdall. Just as determinedly, the Tracksuited-One stuffed them back in.

'*Ti angliiskaya blyad. Ybiraisys ot suda ili pojeleesh!*' the woman-mountain growled low in her throat. She grabbed Charlee by the arm and eyeballed her menacingly, their faces inches apart. Charlee reeled back from the fetid, sausage breath and collapsed on the bed in shock. Had she really just been called an English whore and told to leave the room or face the consequences?

Unable to let on that she'd understood every grunted syllable, she reached for the door handle. God knows what the thwarted shot-put champion of the Russian federation (circa 1966) would do if she disobeyed her a second time.

'That's it. I'm calling security.'

In the next moment she was picked up, thrown over the woman's shoulder in a fireman's lift and deposited unceremoniously on her bottom in the corridor. Pain shot up from her coccyx, along the length of her spine, jarred her head and her chin was thrust downwards. Forgetting that she was supposed to be blending into the background, Charlee scrambled to her feet and steamed back into the bedroom.

'Now, just a minute, Tamara,' she said, pummelling the woman-mountain's back with her fists.

'*Menya zovyt Valentina. Ne Tamara!*'

Charlee didn't care what her name was! All the sexual frustration left over from last night's interrupted lovemaking, being ignored by the boot camp staff and now this attack by a mad woman made Charlee lose it.

'Argh ...' With a grunt of effort, she pushed Valentina out of the way and then threw herself face down on the disputed bed and over her half-packed holdall. She was forced to cling onto the mattress as she was grabbed by the heels and forcibly dragged off the bed.

'*Ya slomau tebe sheu, angliiskaya blyad.*'

Charlee didn't doubt for a moment that Valentina wouldn't think twice about breaking the neck of an English Mother Fucker. But she wasn't giving in.

'Valentina. Stop!' a cool voice commanded from the door. Like a dog told to drop its bone, Valentina released her grip on Charlee's ankles and stood to attention. Charlee pushed herself backwards on her stomach, onto her feet and found herself staring straight into Anastasia Markova's anxious face. 'Are you alright, my friend?' she asked, straightening Charlee's clothing and glaring at the bull mastiff now filling the doorway.

'Yes - I suppose,' Charlee said, crossly. With some sharp words in Russian, Markova ordered Valentina to stand there and not to move without her express command.

'Valentina is my … minder, employed by my fiancé to keep the paparazzi at bay. She thinks she is sharing this room with me but she is not,' she added emphatically and Valentina winced. '*Nyet*. Do you understand, Valentina?'

'*Da*,' she said, giving Charlee a murderous look. Charlee winced at the thought of what Valentina would do if she found out who she really was. Then she turned her back on both of them and started to unpack her holdall and smooth out her wrinkled clothes.

'Don't,' Anastasia laid a gentle hand on Charlee's arm. 'Your clothes will be pressed and returned to you. Valentina - see to it.' She moved Charlee out of the way so that Valentina could carry out her orders. Then she went over, closed the door behind the massively proportioned Babushka and locked it before turning back to Charlee. 'Do you,' she inquired, 'have any more of those chocolate bars those disgusting little dogs were fighting over?'

'I do,' Charlee said cautiously, wondering if Markova was going to add insult to injury by grassing her up to the management.

'Then break them out, honey, because I am starving.'

Charlee gave Anastasia's slight frame a wondering look - would she be able to swallow a mouthful of chocolate without its passage down her gullet being painfully apparent? Grinning at the fanciful thought, she fetched a family-sized bar of Fruit and Nut out of her bedside table drawer, broke off a quarter and handed it to Anastasia.

'Enjoy. I have the feeling it's going to be a lo-ong weekend.'

Half an hour later, Charlee's chain store clothes were rubbing shoulders with Dior and Chanel in the armoire. She lay on her bed, watching in fascination as Anastasia unpacked cosmetics she'd only ever read about in glossy magazines; lotions and face creams with a SPF of 50+, guaranteed to hold back the ravages of time - their active ingredients containing caviar and gold. She guessed that her toiletries had better watch it, otherwise they'd be edged off the shelf in the middle of the night by their upmarket counterparts. As surely as Valentina had tried to eject her from the bedroom.

'So,' Anastasia stretched out on her bed, her long legs practically hanging off the edge, making Charlee feel hobbit-like by comparison. 'Now we put picture of our mens on the bedside table, yes? You first, Charlee.' She pronounced her name Sh-arlee and Charlee closed off that part of her brain which remembered how Ffinch had called her Carlotta, and she'd called him Rafa and ...

Okay. Stop.

Reaching into her tote bag, she took out the photograph of her and Ffinch at their 'engagement party', and her heart lurched. She knew it was as phony as Spam but Ffinch was still Ffinch and he looked almost edible in the photograph. She could feel the length of his body pressed up against her and remembered the moment when he'd almost lost control. She closed her eyes and shuddered, feeling suddenly bereft and longing for his touch.

He was right, she thought, nothing could ever be the same between them after last night.

Anastasia took the photo frame out of her slack fingers and gave it a professional once-over. 'You love him, yes; even a photograph of him. I can see why - of course - he is hottie? Is that the word?'

'It'll do,' Charlee commented, unable to stop her lips quirking.

Anastasia turned the photograph over and read the engagement notice which Ffinch had insisted Charlee fix to the back of the frame 'Your page in paper? Is romantic, very romantic.' She handed the frame back with a sigh. Charlee stood it on her bedside table, dragging her gaze away, but every time she looked at Ffinch her heart snagged in a way that was becoming all too familiar.

'Now you,' she prompted Anastasia when she seemed reluctant to open up the hinged leather photograph frame in her hands. Mouth drooping, Anastasia handed it over and Charlee stared down at the face of a man who was the personification of Mr Potato Head: bald head, no chin, hard little eyes and a cruel mouth.

'Is Yevgeny. He is very -' she struggled for the correct word.

'Kind?' Charlee supplied optimistically.

'Rich,' Anastasia supplied, taking the photo back. She turned it round so she couldn't see his face. 'What Yevgeny wants, Yevgeny gets.' She glanced at the door as if she suspected Valentina of listening at the keyhole. 'Like ...' she paused, perhaps wondering if she was being a little too free and open with her new best friend. 'This place.'

'You mean the boot camp?' Charlee kept her expression bland. She had the feeling, as she'd had on Christmas Eve, that Anastasia was lonely and uncertain of whom to trust. For the moment, she forgot all about her mission to get the dirt on the model and listened sympathetically to her story instead.

'Yes. He bought it last summer to add to his property portfolio and spends much time here.' She looked out of the window at the windswept marshes. She shuddered and pulled the cashmere comforter at the foot of the bed up and over her knees as if she was suddenly very cold. 'Sailing and exploring the marshes in his little boat when the tide is high, birdwatching perhaps?' She shrugged and her eyes took on a dead look as if she knew it wasn't her place to question Yevgeny. Or maybe she was remembering a time when she'd asked too many questions and he'd turned nasty.

With his hard, piggy eyes and mean expression, Charlee could imagine he was someone you crossed at your peril. She gave Anastasia a covert glance; surely she had enough money of her own? What hold did he have over her? She was drawn back to the 'engagement party' mock-up and her eyes lingered on Ffinch's face longer than she intended. Really, it was becoming an obsession with her!

'Why are you at boot camp?' Anastasia probed. 'This boot camp, I mean?'

'Well...' Charlee followed Anastasia's lead and pulled the blanket up from the foot of her bed and settled in for a girly chat. 'It's been a whirlwind romance, and Ff- Rafa, that is, adores me and can't wait for us to get married. Naturally.'

'Naturally, Sh-arlee, you are beautiful girl,' Anastasia said genuinely. 'Gorgeous hair and blue eyes - an English rose.'

'Thank you, Anastasia.' Charlee suppressed a smile. That was the first time that particular description had been levelled at her. 'Rafa is a civil engineer, an expert on building dams to generate hydroelectric power; green energy in some of the poorest parts of the world. He has a posting overseas coming up and wanted us to be married before he left. Apparently it's easier for me to accompany him as his wife, especially in countries governed by Sharia Law. I wanted to lose a few pounds before the wedding and remembered summer holidays spent in nearby Brancaster as a child, and I thought - why not?'

Anastasia took it all at face value and picked up the photograph.

'You can see how much you love each other. It is in the eyes. No?' She put Charlee's photo frame and her own side by side and sighed. The only thing Charlee could see in Mr Yevgeny-Potato-Head's eyes were greed and lust. She didn't want to think about him and Anastasia together.

There was a knock on the door and they both froze.

'Oh my God,' Charlee said, only half-jokingly, 'it's your killer bridesmaid, Valentina come to finish me off.'

Anastasia pushed the comforter off her legs and frowned at Charlee before she realised it was a joke. 'Silly gu-rl,' she laughed and made her way over to the door to unlock it. Then she turned on her heel. 'Sharlee, chocolate; hide, quickly, or we will be thrown out of camp, for sure.' She waited while Charlee stuffed the remains of the bar of Fruit and Nut under her blanket and then opened the door.

'Miss Markova,' the manager of the boot camp almost fell over the threshold in her eagerness to enter the room. 'Please forgive the mix up - Markova and Montague, a simple error; the girl in the office …' She gulped for air as she struggled to explain, holding up her clipboard for Anastasia to see. 'You should never have been shown to this room. You will be given a room on your own and your assistant, Valentina, will be given the room next to yours.' She clicked her fingers and a couple of chambermaids rushed in and started emptying the armoire of Anastasia's clothing.

Anastasia held up an imperious hand and made it clear that she didn't want to be moved. '*Nyet. Ya ne xochy pereselit' sya v drygyu komnaty.*'

'But, Yevgeny - your fiancé - was quite insistent that …'

'I will not move. But I will talk to him. I need telephone in room. See to it.' It was plain that the manageress wasn't pleased but she did as she was told and sent a minion scurrying for a telephone. '*Xotelos' bi poselit' sya zdes' i bit's Sharlottoi Montagye.* I will share with Sharlotta Montegyu, like Hogwarts? Yes?' She turned an appealing face to Charlee who thanked God for the universal appeal of Harry Potter.

'Exactly like Hogwarts,' she agreed, earning herself an evil look from the manageress.

'So, that is all?' Anastasia asked, dismissing the manageress. 'Go. Go. We do not wish to be disturbed,' she said with all the haughtiness of a czarina. She waited until she and Charlee were alone, sank down on the bed and explained. 'They are paid to spy on me by Yevgeny. As if I could get up to anything in this place.' She cast another despairing look over the marshes as if they were the Norfolk equivalent of the salt mines.

Forgetting her brief and ignoring the notion that she was developing Stockholm syndrome, only in reverse, Charlee put her arms around Anastasia's thin shoulders and pushed her thick plait of corn yellow hair out of the way. She gave her a hug and then sat back on her bed.

'It seems like neither of us wants to be here. But let's make the most of it and have some fun. What d'you say?'

'I say,' Anastasia appeared to give the idea her full consideration. 'Bring it on, Sh-arlee.'

Anastasia reached across the gap between their beds to high-five Charlee and accidently knocked over Yevgeny's photograph. She froze, sucked in her breath and looked around her, as if suspecting that the walls had eyes and ears and would report back to central intelligence.

'I prefer him that way,' Charlee said, hoping Anastasia would get the joke.

Anastasia went very quiet then she started to laugh - loudly and uproariously. She collapsed on the bed, drawing her knees up to her chest as tears of laughter ran down her cheeks. Taking that as a signal that Anastasia 'got her', Charlee fetched the chocolate bar from beneath the covers where she'd hastily stowed it. Then she produced a bottle of vodka from her tote bag, unwrapped the cellophane on two new tooth mugs and the party began.

Chapter Twenty-nine
The Runaway Bride, I Presume?

Charlee and Anastasia returned from a jog to Thornham Beach later that afternoon, sweating profusely and feeling the effects of a vodka and chocolate binge. Their room had been tidied up and, Charlee suspected, her belongings had been thoroughly searched before being returned to the wardrobe. A telephone handset rested on Anastasia's pillow and Charlee itched to contact Ffinch, but wondered how on earth she could engineer it without arousing suspicion.

Anastasia asked if she could have the first shower. Charlee guessed that she was used to working out in some swanky gym in Mayfair and getting muddy and sweaty on a coastal path was her idea of torture. Charlee was with her on that one! She watched as Anastasia, obviously used to the wall-to-wall nudity in communal dressing rooms, stepped out of her undies and pinned her plait on top of her head.

'We do not have our mans to dress up for tonight, but in two nights we have Gala Dinner and must look our best. Yes? Yevgeny will arrive tomorrow and go sailing with Natasha's husband, Paul. So maybe I won't see him until then.' She spoke matter of factly, making it plain that she preferred it that way. 'Sh-arlee - we had fun, as you said. Now rest; use phone and ring your Rafa ...'

'Are you sure?' Charlee asked. 'What about the manageress ...?'

'She will do what I say. But ...' Anastasia picked up her towel and gave Charlee a long look before continuing, acting as if she'd like to trust Charlee but wasn't sure. 'They will listen in to your call. Careful what you give away.' It was as much as Charlee could do to stop herself from stretching out towards the phone and ringing Ffinch there and then.

'Maybe I'll ring him, later; thanks.' She settled back on the bed with a stack of glossy bridal magazines provided by the management.

'Okey dokey, laters,' Anastasia replied.

Charlee waited until she could hear the power shower running, dropped the magazines on the bed and reached for the phone with a shaky hand. Rooting in her bag, she found Ffinch's mobile number and tapped it out - the signal was poor, but she felt certain she'd get through to him.

'Ffinch,' his voice came across clear and strong. Charlee's stomach lurched and when she tried to speak, she discovered that her vocal cords had tied themselves into a knot. 'Who is this?'

'Charlee,' she squeaked out after an awkward pause. Then it was Ffinch's turn to fall silent and she wondered what thoughts were running through his head.

'Ah, the runaway bride -'

His sardonic greeting and the fact that he'd answered the phone immediately, led Charlee to suspect he'd been waiting for her call. And, judging by his curt manner, felt he was owed an explanation for her bolting. Convinced that he was about to make another snarky comment, Charlee rushed on.

'I'm using the house phone, darling.' Her stomach flipped over at her use of the endearment which, given that he sounded extremely pissed off, was wholly inappropriate. 'You won't believe it; they've confiscated my phone along with my camera and iPad, which means I won't be able to update my wedding blog.' Charlee paused, hoping that he would get the message. 'Will you let the family know?'

'Oh, that is disappointing,' Ffinch said coolly, but she sensed his brain was in overdrive. 'I know how much reading your blog means to

Uncle Sam in his nursing home. It's the only thing that gets him out of bed in the morning' he added, simply unable to resist the wisecrack.

'I know,' she sighed. 'But what can I do?' Charlee stalled for a moment as she thought of hellfire and brimstone Sam Walker in a nursing home with a rug over his knees.

'Don't worry about it, sweetie, I'll have a new phone waiting for you when we meet again. Why don't you make notes for the blog and update it when we're home? I'll tell Uncle Sam and your legion of girlfriends that they'll have to wait a few days for the next blog post.' Only the sharpest ears and most suspicious minds would have picked up Ffinch's slight emphasis on 'new phone waiting for you when we meet again.'

'You are so understanding, Pumpkin,' she said with forced jollity. Had she imagined the longing in his voice over the word 'home'? The word transported her to the mews where they'd laughed and shared jokes over pasta and wine. Did he miss the easy friendship of those few days after Christmas as much as she did? The time before they became, truly, sexually aware of each other. 'I am getting plenty of ideas for my next post, which will be all about the boot camp and the fun I'm having. I'm doing Fartlek Training tomorrow morning, bright and early - can't wait to get back on the marshes. We're jogging towards Titchwell,' she added, hoping he picked up the vibe.

'That's good. Now, enjoy; make the most of your stay, the big day will be upon us before we know it.'

'I will,' she said, hearing his slight emphasis on big day and not quite sure what he meant. The Gala Dinner? Seeing each other again? The end of the assignment? Reluctant to bring the conversation to a close, she wanted to keep him talking, listen to his voice and feel close to him. She needed to explain why, in the middle of the night, she'd acted like a second-rate seductress and then scarpered the next morning. But she guessed that'd have to wait until the Gala Dinner.

'Laters.' There was a beep as Ffinch disconnected, then an answering echo as whoever was listening in on their conversation hung up, too. In the en suite, Anastasia turned off the shower and Charlee replaced the handset on the pillow. She lay back on her bed, with her arms folded behind her head. She was in last chance saloon and the fat lady was about to sing.

She couldn't afford to mess up a second time.

For someone who hated the gym at school and all forms of physical exercise, Charlee was awake surprisingly early next morning, all fired up for Fartlek Training. It was still dark and she lay in bed not wishing to disturb Anastasia who was snoring gently a few feet away from her.

Last night she'd had the recurring dream - the one where she walked down the aisle of the village church on the arm of her husband, heart bursting with love and euphoria. But when she glanced up at the man she'd be spending the rest of her life with, he was still faceless, and she woke up with a sense of loss. Would she ever feel that happy? At least her subconscious hadn't imprinted Ffinch's face on her mystery man. That really would prove that she'd lost it.

She was just drifting back to sleep when a none too gentle rap on the door brought her back to full consciousness.

'Fartlek Training this morning, ladies. Breakfast at seven thirty.'

Had the staff trained in a gulag somewhere, Charlee wondered ? Their technique lacked finesse and the exercises she'd observed them putting the other women through seemed better suited to a ninja training camp than preparing brides-to-be for the BIG DAY. Or what was coyly referred to in the welcome pack as the rigours of the bedroom. Urgh. That last thought stayed with her as she staggered into the shower and let the powerful jets of water wake her up.

The sky was lightening when Charlee and Anastasia - accompanied by the ever-vigilant Valentina - joined the other women on the drive in front of Thornham Manor. Charlee pretended to stretch out her muscles ready for a run, but was secretly planning how to dump Valentina and Anastasia without arousing their suspicions. Then the male instructor, wearing indecently sculpted running leggings and a sleeveless vest designed to show off his six-pack, addressed them.

'Ladies - we will be running as far as Titchwell. At the end of your run, we have arranged for an informative talk by one of the RSPB wardens on the rare marsh harrier and other Norfolk birds. ' A collective groan went up which was duly ignored by the instructor and his humourless colleagues. 'We will be running along the road in places where the path peters out. So remember to stay single file - and wear your high-visibility vests at all times.'

As she slipped on the lightweight Day-Glo vest, Charlee recalled Ffinch looking up vultures in his *Boys' Own Book of Fenland Birds* the day when she'd pushed him into the hedge. Would they ever be able to return to those days, or had her femme fatale act soured things between them for ever?

'*Prekrati soprotivlyat'sya Valentina.*'

Straightening, Charlee heard Anastasia advise Valentina to stop struggling as she guided the flimsy vest over Valentina's massive upper arms. Charlee knew that kind-hearted Anastasia felt mean at sidelining Valentina and planned to be more patient with her today - even if Valentina was Yevgeny's paid informant.

'Now, ladies, remember - Fartlek is about training the body to switch gear and use different muscle groups. It allows you to run at whatever distance and speed you wish, varying the intensity, and occasionally running at high intensity levels. Take your time to warm up; there are no prizes for torn ligaments or twisted joints.'

He fiddled with the stopwatch on his wrist and started down the gravel drive at a sensible pace. Pulling a comical face at Anastasia, Charlee followed on his heels with the fitter of the brides-to-be. Valentina was built for shouldering doors open, not running mini marathons across salt marshes, so Charlee seized the chance to leave them behind - and put Ffinch's contingency plan into action.

Last night, she and Anastasia had bonded over dinner, steering clear of the other bridezillas with their tales of rogue caterers, uncooperative florists and psychotic wedding planners. They'd stayed up well into the night, sharing their dreams and hopes and by the time they'd switched off their bedside light, had become firm friends. However, as she jogged out of the double gates and onto the marshes, Charlee's breakfast curdled in her stomach at the deceit necessary to keep Anastasia onside and learn more about her.

Sam would have called it groundwork. Charlee called it double-dealing and it didn't sit easily with her. Stiffening her resolve - she'd been sent here with the express purpose of getting the dirt on Anastasia and spoiling *Mirror, Mirror*'s exclusive - Charlee jogged along the margins of the marsh.

She couldn't afford to let misguided loyalty to a new friend distract her from carrying out the mission she'd been given. Added to that, she had to prove to Ffinch that she wasn't a complete airhead whose brains were located in her knickers.

Out of breath, face glowing in the cold January air, Charlee and the front runners reached Titchwell well ahead of the second group. Their instructor led them into a small café where they were served hot chocolate and nutrition bars which tasted like blocks of moulded sawdust. Charlee left hers on the table and decided to explore the hides overlooking the reed beds while she waited for Anastasia and Valentina to catch up.

Maybe she'd see one of the lesser-spotted marsh vultures which Ffinch had jokingly referred to. Smiling, she turned right and headed through a wild area where a wooden hide was hidden by foliage. The Fartlek Training had been vigorous and had succeeded in removing all feelings of pent-up sexual frustration. It filled her with new purpose, a determination to succeed and to make Ffinch proud to call her partner.

Inside the wooden hide it smelled of damp and mould, like an old garden shed, but Charlee was glad to be out of the cutting wind that was blowing straight from the Urals. Well, at least it would make Valentina feel right at home and might encourage her to get off Anastasia's case and let her enjoy her last week of freedom without fear of her every action being reported back to Yevgeny Trushev.

Charlee tiptoed over to the far side of the hide where a wooden flap dropped down and provided a window onto the flooded reed beds. A twitcher with a camera on a tripod was watching the reeds intently and hadn't moved since she'd entered the hide. She peered over his shoulder to see if anything was moving out there, but to her untrained eye the whole area looked dead, bereft of life.

She moved closer to the 'window', taking care not to bump into the twitcher or knock his equipment over. He was wearing the sludgy greenish-brown uniform beloved of marsh walkers and a black Polartec balaclava underneath a GANT baseball cap. They stood side by side for a few minutes without speaking and Charlee half-turned to go. In her opinion twitching came a close second to watching paint dry.

'You've forgotten your phone, love,' the twitcher called out to her. His voice was gruff, muffled by the balaclava which he'd pulled up over the lower half of his face.

'That isn't my phone,' Charlee replied, glancing down at the top of the range smartphone on the window ledge. 'Someone must have left it there, earlier.'

'I think you'll find it is your phone,' the man insisted, less gruffly this time. Instinctively, Charlee took a step away from him. What if he was some kind of weirdo who preyed on unsuspecting young women, offering smartphones instead of sweeties to lure them into the deserted reed beds and then - Urgh, that thought was way too weird, even for her. She shook her head free of it and made for the door, but the twitcher was already there and blocking her exit.

'Look, I should warn you,' she said, taking up a ninja-like stance. 'I'm one of the instructors from the boot camp and skilled in martial arts. I could snap your arm like a dry twig, so - get out of my way,' she snarled. He didn't budge. Instead, he lowered the bottom half of the balaclava and sent her a sardonic smile.

'Black belt in origami, was that?' he asked, removing his balaclava and baseball cap and sending her an exasperated look. 'Just take the bloody phone, Montague.' He reached out, caught her hand, and slapped the smartphone into it.

'Ffinch!' A tiny grenade of a bomb of joy exploded in Charlee's chest leaving an aftershock of happiness behind. 'Ffinch ...' she repeated in a more restrained tone. Last time she'd seen him, he'd dumped her unceremoniously onto her bed and locked the door behind him. And yesterday he'd snarkily referred to her as the runaway bride. It wouldn't do to be too pleased to see him. 'I thought you were some kind of birdwatching pervert! What are you doing here? How - how did you know I'd come into this hide?'

'I didn't. You told me that you were jogging to Titchwell and I took a punt on running into you. Don't worry, I've hidden another phone underneath the bench by the boot camp, the one overlooking the wind turbines. I've also stashed one in the hollow tree in the pine plantation near Thornham Beach in case your run took you in that direction. That's what we agreed, wasn't it?' He gave her a puzzled look as if waiting for a reaction, any response other than her stunned look.

'Mm, that's right.'

'And, here you are,' he continued evenly, his eyes never leaving her face. 'An expert in martial arts in under two days. Pretty good going, even for you, Montague.'

'Yes; here I am,' Charlee agreed, almost combusting under his steady regard. Ffinch, realising that he was still holding her hand, dropped it like a brand and stepped back from her. Charlee searched for some witticism; some smart alec remark which would re-establish her position as the go-to rookie and consign the hormonally imbalanced madwoman of the other night to the recycle bin. Using all her reserves of cool, she sent him a composed look.

Seeing him again, reinforced how much she'd missed him. There was so much she wanted to say; so much that she couldn't say. She settled instead for sending him a helpless look which acknowledged he'd been right all along when he said that nothing could ever be the same between them.

'Montague ... '

'Ffinch, I -'

Apparently sensing her inner turmoil, Ffinch took a step towards her and broke the tongue-tied silence. 'It might be a good idea to hide the phone, Montague? Before you leave?' he added, giving her a prompt to exit stage left.

'Of course.'

Charlee looked down at the phone, wondering where on earth she could hide it. Ffinch gave her close-fitting thermal leggings a professional once-over, clearly of the same opinion. His gaze lingered longer than was strictly necessary over the curve of her buttocks before he schooled his features. Blushing, Charlee stowed the phone inside her knickers just below the dip of her spine, pulling her top over the telltale bulge and rearranging her jacket.

'I hope you've set the ring tone to throb,' she said sternly. Then she realised what she'd said and rushed to cover up her double entendre. 'How's that?' she asked, turning round, dropping her hip and sticking out her bottom so he could check for phone-shaped bulges.

'In what sense?' he asked in a constricted tone.

'In the sense of: does my phone look big in this,' she said snarkily, hoping to return to their previous banter. The woman in her wanted to test Ffinch's breaking point, to see if he was as oblivious to the alteration in their relationship as his appearance suggested. But the professional in her knew that such behaviour was wrong on just about every level you could think of.

Rock - Scissors - Paper.

'It looks - okay,' he said. 'However, it's best not to test the willpower of a - how did you phrase it - birdwatching pervert.'

'Okay, so I shouldn't have implied you were a birdwatcher,' she agreed straight-faced, but didn't apologise for implying he was a pervert. Turning, she took a couple of steps closer, knowing that she had to say her piece. 'Look, Ffinch, before we're disturbed, I have a couple of things I need to say.'

'Go ahead.' He stowed his balaclava in his pocket and pulled the baseball cap down over his eyes, leaving Charlee with the feeling that he was struggling to keep things between them on an even keel.

'One,' Charlee let out a steadying breath. 'I shouldn't have come to your room, let alone climbed into your bed and - well - another man might not have acted so ... chivalrously.' She walked over to the open window, feeling sudden heat wash over her at the memory of his mouth on her skin. 'So, thanks for that,' she said diffidently, knowing that she hadn't wanted chivalry two nights ago. She'd wanted - well, she assumed they both knew what she'd wanted, it wasn't rocket science.

'Chivalrous? Is that what I was?' He pursed his lips, nodding thoughtfully as though the idea needed some consideration. 'It takes two to tango, Charlee. I wasn't a reluctant participant, believe me, I simply felt the timing was lousy. You've got to carve a path for yourself in the world of journalism - and I've got unsettled business in Darien.'

'Oh.' His 'it takes two to tango', made Charlee feel slightly better, although something inside her shrivelled when he mentioned returning to the scene of his dangerous expedition. 'And would you have told me this - the next morning, I mean - if I hadn't have bolted?'

'Most probably, but you didn't give me the chance, did you?'

'I acted like a fool.' He didn't contradict her.

'And the second thing?' he asked, looking through a crack in the door to make sure no one was coming along the path.

'It feels wrong to win over Anastasia's confidence just to pump her for some article Sam wants to write to spike his rival. I know, I know,' she raised her hand to forestall him. 'I need to man up if I'm going to survive in this game. It just feels - wrong. That's all.'

'Your scruples do you proud, Montague; however, we've come here to do a job and I can't do it without you,' he said, wearing his hard-bitten-photojournalist's hat. Then he stalled, as if he'd said too much. Charlee decided to press home her advantage before they were interrupted or he clammed up.

'Which brings me neatly to my next point. Get this - Anastasia's fiancée owns the boot camp. Doesn't that strike you as strange? Maybe it's a front for something else -'

'Such as?' he asked, his expression bland.

'I don't know. But there's something dodgy about him. About the whole set-up ... and I mean to find out what it is.'

'Someone's coming,' he said, cutting her speculation short. He removed his baseball cap, slipped the balaclava back on, pulling it up so only his gorgeous blue-grey eyes were visible. Charlee's stomach flipped over and a shiver of sexual awareness fizzed through her like champagne and replaced the heat which had earlier scorched her face. How could she have mistaken him for a birdwatching pervert? He looked every inch the sort of man any woman would be proud to call her lover. She sighed. 'You'd better go,' he warned. 'And, Charlee -'

'Yes?'

Ffinch looked as if he wanted to say more, but settled for: 'Take care.'

Charlee's heart swelled, but she hid her emotion behind a sassy grin and a throwaway remark. 'I'm a black belt, remember?' She struck a pose which Bruce Lee would have been proud of.

'In origami, I believe?' Then he returned to his camera and the reed beds where no birds sang. Dismissed, Charlee shook out her legs and arms to limber up for the jog back, knowing that Anastasia, Valentina and the other brides-to-be who couldn't keep up with the punishing pace would be shipped back to the boot camp in a minibus.

And that suited her. She needed to be out on the marshes alone so she could locate the spare phone and keep it as back up. It was just like the Easter egg hunts her parents used to organise in their orchard for

273

the village children, she reflected, as she walked up the path towards the café.

Except this was deadly serious and potentially dangerous - even if she hadn't quite figured out why - yet!

Chapter Thirty
He Who Must Be Obeyed

The arrival of Yevgeny Nikolayevich Trushev later that same afternoon sent the staff into a tailspin. Natasha the manager looked as though she expected to be sacked at any moment and Anastasia became increasingly nervous - although Yevgeny made no attempt to visit her. Only Valentina seemed happy that her boss was on the premises and delighted in sending Charlee and Anastasia 'just you wait and see' looks. As if their just desserts were just around the corner and she'd be the one dishing them up.

While Anastasia was taking her second shower of the day and preparing herself for Yevgeny, Charlee made the most of the opportunity to hide one of the phones at the back of the armoire, tucked into the buttoned-down pocket of a short, denim jacket. The other she held in her hand and looked at uncertainly. No way would she be able to get photos of Anastasia or anyone else at the boot camp without being blatantly obvious.

Sans photos, her piece on Anastasia was virtually worthless. What was she to do?

Standing in the bay window, she checked to see how many bars were visible on her phone. Two - one - then none; the signal came and went erratically. However, with Anastasia in the shower, Charlee thought this was a good time to ring Ffinch for advice.

Walking into the bay window and drawing the curtains behind her, she tapped out his number.

'Ffinch.'

'Ffinch, this isn't going to work,' she said in a rush.

'O-kay,' he said slowly. 'What do you suggest?'

'How about if you park the camper van by the Coal Shed and I persuade Anastasia to walk with me there - ostensibly to see the barn owls quartering the fields near the pinewood? You could draw the curtains and poke your lens through and get some close ups of her as we walk past? She won't be very muddied up, and she doesn't do dishevelled so the shots might not be what Sam's looking for. Her fiancé, Yevgeny, has just arrived, so I don't think we'll see her in a tracksuit again.' She realised that she was in danger of hyperventilating so she slowed down and hissed under her breath, 'Oh, this is bloody impossible.'

'Don't stress about it, Charlee, you've done your best,' Ffinch said in a surprisingly calm voice.

'I might as well leave tomorrow morning and forget all about the Gala Dinner. I've got enough info to run a background piece about Anastasia growing up in poverty in Odessa and how she was scouted by one of the agencies, whilst selling vegetables on the roadside by her parents' farm.'

'No. You're to stay the course.' His voice was sharp. 'Look, I'm going to drive round to the Coal Shed and park there for the rest of the afternoon. Meet me there, with or without Markova.'

'But how? It's easier to get a weekend exeat from boarding school than to walk out of these gates. Talk about the Gulag Archipelago,' Charlee complained as loud as she dared with Anastasia just out of earshot.

'You're resourceful, Montague, you'll figure it out.' Giving her no room for manoeuvre, he hung up.

Feeling dismissed, Charlee pressed her lips together and frowned. This morning in the hide she'd sensed a definite connection between them - as if he'd been pleased to see her. But perhaps a combination of the hormones and mild homesickness had dulled her perception. Evidently he had other things on his mind, things that took precedence over holding a rookie's hand.

It was a permanent state of affairs with him, she concluded, switching the phone to silent and stowing it back in her underwear. She was adjusting the curtains when Anastasia walked out of the en suite, a cloud of some delicious tangy, green scent trailing in her wake.

'That smells fab,' Charlee said. 'What is it?'

Anastasia shrugged. 'I don't know; Chanel 19, I think. I get given many things.' She walked back into the en suite and returned carrying a large bottle of shower lotion. 'You take,' she said to Charlee and put it down on her side of the dressing table. 'I have more; many more.' She frowned as if the thought brought her no comfort and Charlee felt a pang of empathy. Anastasia Markova had everything: money, beauty, an enviable career - and, okay, a fiancée who looked like Mr Potato Head - but she seemed desolate and suffering from low self-esteem.

That was something Charlee had never experienced. Maybe she should thank her brothers for making her stand on her own two feet and teaching her to shout loudest in order to be heard.

'I was going to walk to the Coal Shed. That place I told you of, and then down to the bench overlooking the fields where the barn owls can be seen,' Charlee said casually. 'Fancy coming with me?'

Anastasia stopped towelling and looked up at Charlee through tangled blonde hair - like a sad mermaid. 'Sh-arlee, you must understand, now Yevgeny is here I must be ready at all times.' Ready for what Charlee didn't need to inquire, bile rising in her throat at the thought of Anastasia being pawed by the Russian. How different things had been between herself and Ffinch the other night, the difference between having sex and making love.

'Forgive me for asking, Anastasia, but why do you stay with him? You've studied at a prestigious university, been on the front of every magazine and have your own money.' Anastasia's endless legs, long blonde hair, high cheekbones and slanting green eyes made her the highest paid model on the catwalk.

'My money must last me - and my family back in Odessa - all of my life, yes? Looks fade, men grow cold - I must have security ...' she tailed off, looking so forlorn that Charlee's heart squeezed with compassion.

'What about happiness? Love?' she asked, her own gaze slipping inadvertently to her and Ffinch's 'engagement photo'. She looked ecstatically happy in the photograph, but that was a sham too.

Anastasia shrugged. 'I choose security over love.' Her eyes took on a faraway look as if remembering cold winters back in Russia when there hadn't been enough food to go round.

'Properly managed your money could last forever,' Charlee said, not even sure if that was true. 'And you have many years on the catwalk and product endorsement ahead of you. Look at Cindy Crawford, still gorgeous, still earning. If being with your fiancé makes you unhappy, why don't you break off the engagement?'

Anastasia looked at her as if she was mad.

'Ah, Sh-arlee, how little you know, how little you understand.' If anyone else had said that to Charlee she would have reacted angrily, but she saw the mournful look in Anastasia's eyes and knew it was true. What did she know of sorrow, of never having enough? 'Yevgeny will never let me go.'

Dragging her fleece out of the wardrobe and slipping on her fur-lined boots against the cold, Charlee resolved - whatever it took - she'd help Anastasia find a way out.

'I've got to get out of the gulag for a while.' Her use of the Russian word made Anastasia smile. 'Catch you later?'

'Alligators, yes?' Anastasia used the phrase Charlee had taught her.

'In a while, crocodile,' Charlee high-fived Anastasia and left the room. As she took the stairs two at a time, Charlee told herself that it was the thought of an hour's freedom that put wings on her heels - and not that she'd be spending it with Ffinch.

The distinctive navy and white camper van was parked by the Coal Shed at Thornham Staithe. To Charlee's dismay, its dark-blue and cream gingham curtains were drawn. She was just about to walk away when the middle doors opened and Ffinch stuck his head out.

'Step into my parlour, Montague. Lively, if you please,' he added, looking over her shoulder to make sure they weren't observed.

'Making you the spider and me the fly?' Crazily, that thought made Charlee's heart beat faster. She climbed on board the camper van and Ffinch leaned across to shut the door. He took great care not to touch her, obviously deciding that grazing her breast with his elbow, however unintentionally, just wasn't on.

He indicated that Charlee should slide along the bench seat so she was sitting next to the window, then he squeezed between the bench and the table and joined her. It was surprisingly warm and intimate in the VW and Charlee was overwhelmed by a desire to turn the bench seats into a bed and spend all afternoon making love behind the gingham curtains. Putting the brake on her runaway thoughts, she hid the attraction she felt for Ffinch behind a sarcastic remark.

'Don't you think it's a bit obvious being the only blue and white camper van parked on the marshes in the middle of January, Ffinch?'

'Haven't you heard of hiding in plain sight, Montague?' he countered, clearly taken aback by her abrasive tone. 'I don't think I need you to tell me how to conduct an undercover assignment. Last time I checked, I was the award-winning journalist and you were the rookie elevated from filing copy and fetching lattes. Correct me if I'm wrong.'

'Don't spare my feelings, will you?' Then, thinking of another way to needle him, Charlee changed the subject. 'Bit cramped and stuffy in here, isn't it? Why don't you invest in a Winnebago?' she asked, dissing his beloved camper van. Ffinch crossed himself as if warding off the evil eye.

'She didn't mean it,' Ffinch said, stroking the side of the van lovingly and patting the woodwork. Charlee wished that he was stroking her half as sensuously! Burning with sexual frustration and feeling overheated as lust burned through her veins, like a flame along a dynamite fuse, she peeled off several layers of clothing. When she emerged from pulling her sweatshirt over her head, her eyes met Ffinch's and the tension ratcheted up another couple of notches. Although he gave no outward show of it, Charlee sensed that he felt the pull of sexual attraction between them as keenly as she did; he simply had greater reserves of self-control.

As they sat staring at each other, eyes wide open, pupils dilated and their breaths coalescing in the steamy atmosphere, the whistling kettle came to the boil and condensation dripped down the windows. Charlee felt that the muggy environment in the VW summed up exactly how she was feeling!

'Ah, tea,' Ffinch said as though it was the most marvellous invention in the world. He made two mugs of builders' tea and poured a slug of spirit in each for good measure. Then he reached across to the door where a tin marked SWEET THINGS was jammed tightly into a built-in spice rack. Removing the tin, he put it on a table which took up half the width of the camper van. 'Chocolate Hobnobs, your drug of choice I believe? Help yourself; it might help to restore your blood sugar levels - in this mood you look capable of murder.'

His wry expression showed he suspected he was top of the list.

'Manna from heaven - biscuits.' Suitably distracted, Charlee tipped a handful of biscuits on to the pixie-sized table. She dunked one in her tea several times and then took a large swig of the alcohol-laced tea, coughing at the strength of it.

'Had your fill of rice cakes and lentils, Montague?' Ffinch returned to their former verbal jousting, as if deciding that was the best way forward. Keep it light; keep it professional; keep their minds above their navels. 'No Markova, then?'

'She's on standby in case Mr Potato Head wants sex. Gross, in my opinion,' Charlee said, spitting crumbs all over her fleece. 'Not sex per se; just sex with him,' she added in case Ffinch thought she'd turned celibate after the other night. He looked at her consideringly over the top of his mug and drank his tea, as if taking it as read that she - they- both enjoyed sex.

'Mr Potato Head? I assume you mean Yevgeny Nikolayevich Tru- shev, one of the richest men in Russia.' Wisely, Ffinch steered the con- versation onto less contentious subjects.

'And one of the ugliest,' Charlee added, reaching for her second bis- cuit.

'You don't find power and wealth an aphrodisiac, then?'

'Should I?'

'Lots of women do,' Ffinch observed as he chose a biscuit. 'Markova must, otherwise why is she marrying him?'

'I think she's more frightened of him than in love with him,' Charlee said, putting down her mug. 'Since his arrival, the boot camp has been on high alert. I was able to slip away because I'm too insignificant to show up on the radar. Trushev, on the other hand, is treated like he's royalty and Anastasia his crown princess. Odd, don't you think?' She stirred her tea with a battered, crested silver tea spoon. 'With them being Russians, I mean. Considering they went to all that trouble to slaughter their royal family in the cellar at Yekaterinburg.'

'You know your history,' he observed, dunking another biscuit in his tea. It went quiet as they both gave weight to what she'd said. 'Mon- tague - I can hear those cogs whirring. Spit it out.' Charlee was happy to oblige. Processing her thoughts into theories made her concentrate on something other than Ffinch's grey eyes and the senses stirring combination of expensive aftershave and manly muskiness that car- ried to her every time he shifted on the bench seat.

'Okay. Doesn't it strike you as strange that a Russian oligarch should (a) establish a boot camp for brides in Norfolk and (b) send his fiancée there in the middle of winter when she could stay in any number of spas in exotic locations around the world? I thought oligarchs bought football teams and owned racehorses, not gulag-like boot camps. Then,' she paused for dramatic effect, 'he gets here, ignores aforementioned gorgeous fiancée and makes plans to go night fishing with the manageress's husband. Weird, huh?'

'Night fishing?' The casual way in which Ffinch asked the question was at odds with how still and alert he appeared. He poured more of the fiery liquor into their tea and Charlee wondered if she'd be capable of jogging back to the boot camp. Removing her gloves, she cupped her hands round the mug for warmth. Reaching behind him, Ffinch located a patchwork quilt in shades of blue and cream and wrapped it round her shoulders. Charlee shivered as his fingers grazed the nape of her neck. 'Better?'

'Better.'

'You were saying ...'

Still smarting from his comment about her place in the office hierarchy, Charlee was keen to show that she was capable of more than filing and dog walking.

'Anastasia told me they often go night fishing when the tide is at its highest. But, they can't go out tomorrow night because it's the Gala Dinner,' she said, her voice slowing. She stalled, recalling the conversation she'd overheard in the mews kitchen and gave Ffinch a searching look. 'What aren't you telling me, Ffinch? This isn't about Anastasia and spiking *Mirror, Mirror*'s exclusive, is it - if it even exists?' She slammed her mug down on the table with such force that Ffinch winced. 'So give.'

'That table had to be sourced specially, you know. So careful with it -'

'I don't give a flying fuck about the table,' she exclaimed hotly. 'I know that you and Sam have been using me like some kind of - of Trojan Horse to get you into the camp. What I haven't figured out is why, but give me time and I will. Don't bother to deny it, Ffinch; I know you well enough to tell when you're lying. And, judging by your expression, you have no intention of letting me in on the secret, have you - partner?'

'When it's all over, you'll be told everything,' he said, maddening Charlee even further.

'When what's all over?' Charlee was so vexed she felt like hitting him - or - or, damaging his beloved camper van.

'I've said too much …'

'You haven't said anything, that's my point. Oh, here,' she thrust the mug at him. 'I don't need you, your tea, your biscuits - or the crumbs from your table, come to that. I'll find out for myself.' She got to her feet, replaced her outdoor clothing and tried to squeeze between his knees and the tiny table. But he pushed her back down onto the bench seat.

'You will not find out for yourself, Charlee; it's too dangerous,' he growled.

'Pah!' Charlee waved a dismissive hand in his direction.

'Seriously, Charlee, I mean it.'

'Then take me into your confidence.'

'I can't, not yet. In our business, plausible denial counts for a lot,' he explained.

'What does that mean, exactly?' She turned to face him.

'It means that if you don't know what's going on you'll be able to lie all the more convincingly when questioned.'

'Questioned? By whom - Mr Potato Head, or the bridesmaid from hell - Valentina?'

'Valentina?' Now it was Ffinch's turn to look puzzled.

'See, you don't know everything.' Charlee slid over the bench seat and managed to manoeuvre herself between him and the table. Un-expectedly, he jerked her into his arms and onto his knee, tipping her back and cradling her, his eyes ranging over her face.

'Don't go poking around, please. Just once, do as you're told.'

'Told?' she asked, annoyed.

'Asked,' he amended. 'I know you too well, Carlotta.'

'It's going to take more than calling me Carlotta to put me off the trail - Rafa.'

'Seriously, Charlee, it could be dangerous. I - I don't think I could bear it if anything happened to you.' Did she imagine it, or was there a catch in his voice?

Touched by his concern and that he was man enough to show it, her heart missed several beats before continuing in its usual rhythm. She examined his face minutely - saw the flaws on his skin, the unexpected flecks of gold in his eyes. 'What could possibly happen to me?' she asked, shivering at the thought of danger stalking the boot camp.

'Just be careful, that's all,' he said cryptically. Then he brought his head closer as though he wanted to kiss her, badly. 'When this is over …' he breathed.

'Yes? What about when it's all over?' she prompted as Ffinch, apparently thinking better of his desire to kiss her, let her go.

'Nothing. You'd better go,' he said through gritted teeth as though it cost him to release her.

Charlee sent him a frustrated look that acknowledged that returning to the intimacy they'd shared the other night would be sheer madness. But neither could she deny how lying in his arms made her skin tingle and her stomach flutter as though a thousand butterflies had taken up residence. The genie had escaped from the bottle two nights ago and was in no hurry to return. It would be easy to surrender to the wildness pulsing through her veins, blot out the rest of the world and succumb to passion in this curtained-off, intimate space.

The very thought made her giddy.

If she'd been Ffinch's real fiancée and separated from him for weeks, she knew he wouldn't waste time night fishing when time could be spent more engagingly in bed. That made her doubly suspicious of Yevgeny's motives and what he was up to at the boot camp. It also reminded her that she was here to do a job. Gathering herself together, she wriggled and slithered along the bench seat until she could stand upright.

Questions had to be answered, reassurances given and truths told. Until that happened she couldn't give in, she had to be strong. Without turning round - knowing that simply looking at him would weaken her resolve - Charlee stepped out of the camper van.

A couple of schoolboys sauntered round from the back of the Coal Shed carrying a six-pack of cider and sharing a cigarette. They took one look at Charlee emerging from the camper van and shouted: 'Doggers!' at them. Then they choked with laughter as though they'd just said something witty.

'What did you say?' Charlee demanded fiercely, her eyes sparking fire. She took a couple of steps towards them, her expression making plain that they'd picked the wrong afternoon to try their brand of adolescent humour on two strangers. 'Repeat it, you little shit.'

'Nothing, missus, nothing!' Clearly believing her deranged, they dropped their cigarettes and high tailed it across the car park towards Thornham. Charlee made as if to chase after them and then stopped, unsure what she would do if she caught up with them. Shouting at them had released some of her pent-up tension and when she looked over her shoulder at Ffinch he was standing by the side of the camper van barely concealing his laughter.

'She has a black belt in origami you know,' he shouted after the boys. 'You've had a narrow escape. '

Still smarting from his unwillingness to tell her anything more about the investigation, Charlee didn't appreciate him laughing at her expense. Smoothing out her tracksuit, she glared at him, let out a loud 'huh,' and headed back to the boot camp with as much dignity as she could muster.

To her credit, she didn't look over her shoulder to see if he was watching her.

Chapter Thirty-one
A Storm in a Samovar

When Charlee returned to her room, it looked like a tornado had passed through it scattering debris in its wake. Anastasia's possessions had been removed and the armoire doors were gaping wide. Charlee had half expected it, but the untidy room and the fact that she probably wouldn't be permitted to talk to Anastasia made her feel unutterably sad. They'd developed a rapport over the last two days and she already missed her exotic room-mate. The only consolation was that she could now use the mobile phone to get in touch with Ffinch without being overheard.

Mobile phone!

She rushed over to the armoire where her denim jacket was lying on the floor. Unsurprisingly, when she searched the pockets for the spare mobile phone it was missing. Damn. Had she been rumbled as an undercover journo? Or did they think she'd hidden the phone so she could ring her boyfriend in secret?

Boyfriend! She let out an almost Gallic pouf and shrugged her shoulders. Whatever their relationship was, she could hardly claim to be Ffinch's girlfriend - thorn in his side might be a more accurate description. Sighing - she seemed to do a lot of that lately - she started to tidy up the bedroom. The first item she picked up was the framed photograph of their 'engagement'. Turning it over, she noticed that the cutting from *The Times* was missing.

She frowned and searched for it on the floor but it was nowhere to be found.

Now she was intrigued. Why had Anastasia's people considered it worth their while to remove a seemingly innocuous piece of paper? To check her out, maybe? Deciding she'd better act like a bona fide fiancée whose room looked like it'd been professionally turned over, she marched downstairs. Better start complaining before the management put the mobile phone and the cutting from *The Times* together, googled Ffinch's unusual surname and started to ask some uncomfortable questions.

She pinged the bell on the reception desk impatiently and the manageress and her sidekick came out of the back office. 'Yes?' she asked, putting her hand over the bell to prevent Charlee ringing it again.

'My room's been virtually ransacked by your staff when they moved Anastasia Markova out. If you think for one moment I'm going to act as chambermaid and tidy up their mess - you are much mistaken.' Charlee leaned across the desk and stared boldly into the manageress's boot face. 'And if I find anything missing when I return to my room, I'm calling the police.'

Stepping away from the desk, she folded her arms and waited.

'I was told that you'd gone for a walk on the marshes, Miss Montague. You have returned earlier than expected. Give me one moment.' She spoke to her sidekick in Russian, the gist of the conversation being that everything was to be put back exactly as it had been before.

'*Konechno ,vse doljno bit polojeno obratno, kak eto bilo.*'

'*Daje telefon?*' the girl asked.

'Everything but that,' Natasha said firmly. 'The telephone which you overlooked, Miss Montague, was found by a member of staff moving Miss Markova's things. The battery was flat and the phone was bleeping in your pocket.' Charlee knew that to be a lie; Ffinch had ensured that both phones were charged before stashing them away. 'It will be returned to you at the end of your stay.'

'*Ona pozvonit v policiu?*' the girl asked, sending Charlee a worried glance.

'There's no need for the police, is there Miss Montague?' the manageress said silkily. Her cheekbones slid upwards in a smile that didn't quite reach her eyes. 'This has all been a misunderstanding, a storm - as you English say - in a tea cup?'

'Or, as you say in Russia, a samovar?' Charlee replied impertinently, letting the manageress know she couldn't be intimidated.

'Quite.'

'And Anastasia?' Charlee inquired.

'Naturally Miss Markova's fiancée wants her close to him and we are happy to accommodate their wishes,' the manageress said.

Their wishes? Charlee didn't think Anastasia's wishes came into it.

'Come, Miss Montague, you should be pleased. You will no longer have to share a room, no? Please - go into the sitting room, read lovely bridal magazines and drink tea. Your happy day will be here soon, yes?'

Feeling that she'd protested enough, Charlee graciously inclined her head. The manageress clapped her hands and spoke in rapid Russian to a couple of minions who headed upstairs. Then she led Charlee towards the sitting room where a roaring fire, a stack of glossy magazines and a cup of Earl Grey were waiting.

After dinner, Charlee sat in the bay window staring into the darkness across the marshes, her knees under her chin. She'd seen nothing of Anastasia during the meal and had been informed that Miss Markova and Yevgeny Nikolayevich were dining in private. The bedroom felt empty and she was glad that she would be returning to London after tomorrow night's Gala Dinner.

She imagined herself back in her shabby bedsit, which smelled of sardines, and typing up her copy story on her laptop. Copy? What copy? This was fast becoming the-scoop-that-never-was.

Demoralised, she reached into her tracksuit bottoms and pulled out the mobile phone. She checked it for a signal and then sat looking at it consideringly. She longed to talk to Poppy, to Ffinch, to anyone - but she daren't risk running the battery down. It had to last her until tomorrow night when she and Ffinch met up. What was he doing now, she wondered? Watching TV in his room after a calorie-laden meal at The Ship Inn, she bet!

Hearing noises on the gravel drive below her, Charlee looked down and saw a group of boot camp instructors, kitted out SAS-style in dark clothing and Polartec balaclavas, hauling a couple of motor boats onto trailers and then out of the main gate and towards the marshes. She guessed that was Mr Potato Head going fishing and wished him well. It was a freezing cold night and frost was already turning the trees silver under a gibbous moon. Perhaps, she mused, it reminded him of Siberia or wherever he'd been born. She frowned - did Siberia have salt marshes or salt mines? Geography had never been her strong suit.

Beset by a sudden desire for company, Charlee decided to go downstairs and join the other brides-to-be in the sitting room and pretend enthusiasm for everything that accompanied getting married these days. Preparing herself for yet more chatter about cupcakes on stands versus traditional fruit cakes, she locked the bedroom door behind her. What did it matter that your wedding cakes consisted of rounds of different cheeses or that the chocolate fountain had seventy per cent cocoa solids for dipping marshmallows into?

Surely, the only thing that mattered was that you were marrying the right man. One you not only fancied the pants off, but who made you laugh and who would bring you mugs of hot chocolate and painkillers when you went down with the flu.

A few hours later, she was back in the bay window watching the lights out on the marshes. But these were no will-o'-the-wisps, it was the fishing expedition zigzagging across the narrow channels and returning to the boot camp. Perhaps that's what night fishing entailed, she thought, and went on to wonder what one caught on the marshes in the middle of January. For a night fishing expedition there appeared to be much to-ing and fro-ing, she reflected.

Bored, she turned her attention to watching the moon rise in the east where it hung like a searchlight in the sky, illuminating the marshes. There was a timid scratching at the door and when she opened it, Anastasia was standing in the corridor looking furtively over her shoulder.

'Anastasia!' Charlee exclaimed joyously. 'I've missed you. Come in, come in. I have wodka,' she joked, pronouncing as Anastasia had done.

'No Sh-arlee, I cannot stay. I have skipped away from Valentina while she is on toilet.' There was a pause as they struggled to keep that particular image out of their heads. 'I have present for you.'

'Present?' Charlee asked, puzzled. 'I don't need a present, your friendship is all I ask,' she said. And, in a moment of epiphany, she knew she wouldn't be writing any article that hurt Anastasia, destroyed her reputation or ruined her wedding. Even if she had chosen to marry Mr Potato Head. What Sam would have to say about that, she'd worry about later; what Ffinch would have to say about that, she'd think about much, much later! After this debacle, language school, translation services or teaching would be a worthy, alternative career.

Anastasia stood in the half-opened doorway, looking too spooked to venture further into the room. She called Charlee over and then pushed a smart washbag into her hands. Puzzled, Charlee unzipped it and discovered that it contained expensive toiletries and a business card with Anastasia's personal phone number and email printed on it.

'Sh-arlee, I know it was you outside nightclub on my hen's night - when prince was there. Yes? I remembered your funny, spiky hair and friendly blue eyes.'

What had she said to Ffinch before she'd embarked on this mission: she's no airhead ... she'll remember me from outside the nightclub? What had he said: she probably wouldn't recognise her own sister unless she came with a name badge and a backstage pass. She'd take great delight in pointing out to him how wrong he'd been after she'd been 'let go' by Sam Walker for dereliction of duty.

But, for now, she had to explain. 'Anastasia, I have to tell you ...' Charlee struggled to find words which would excuse her double-dealing.

'There is no time. *Vi govorite po rysski?*'

'Yes, I speak Russian,' Charlee said, glad she could drop the pretence at last.

'*Vi mojete prochest kirillcy?*' Anastasia asked, somewhat desperately.

'I can read Cyrillic script, too, of course - but I don't understand ...?'

'You are my way home, Sh-arlee. But it is dangerous and you must take care. Take present. Sweet Sh-arlee.' She took a step into the room and hugged Charlee, her eyes brimful of unshed tears. 'You will not let me down.'

Then she was gone.

Perplexed, Charlee flopped on the bed and unzipped the bag. She put Anastasia's business card in the expanding pocket at the back of her Moleskine diary next to the now redundant list of questions. Then she tipped the toiletries onto the bed and rooted through them. They appeared nothing out of the ordinary, apart from being astronomically expensive. She turned over a bottle of Chanel 19 eau de parfum and then absent-mindedly squirted herself with some.

Zipping up the washbag, she placed it on her bedside table next to the photograph of Ffinch. She longed to ring him, but curbed the instinct. What could she say to him? 'I've been given a bag of toiletries which have a significance I do not understand. Anastasia Markova not only knows that I can speak and read Russian, but has identified me from outside the nightclub on Christmas Eve.'

He'd most likely go apeshit. Much better to keep quiet until she knew exactly what she was dealing with.

What exactly Anastasia expected from her.

Chapter Thirty-two
Don't We Scrub Up Well?

The following day, huge catering vans arrived at Thornham Boot Camp for Brides and disgorged their contents. There were about two dozen brides-in-the-making staying at the camp and tonight their fiancés would join them for the Gala Dinner which included such delicacies as lobster, foie gras and elaborate ice sculptures now being carefully removed from the refrigerated vans. Most of the fiancés would be staying at nearby inns or B&Bs and bright and early tomorrow would collect their future brides in order to allow the chambermaids to prepare the rooms for a new influx of guests.

Charlee was desperate to meet up with Ffinch on the marshes but every time she rang his phone it went straight to voice mail. Maybe he thought that if he didn't speak to her, she wouldn't be able to ply him with more questions - or chicken out of the Gala Dinner. For want of something better to do, Charlee decided to get away from the brides-to-be who were all a-twitter at the thought of seeing their fiancés that evening and loudly discussing their outfits. What would they say if they knew her true relationship with Ffinch?

She hoped that a brisk walk to the pinewood plantation near Thornham Beach to retrieve the spare mobile stashed in the hollow tree would blow away the cobwebs and settle her nerves.

'No, Miss. Return to the house please,' she was told firmly by a member of staff as she tried to pass through the gates. 'Lunch is being served early due to preparations for the Gala Dinner this evening.'

'Are there no training sessions on the marshes?' Charlee asked, recognising her as one of the female trainers from yesterday's Fartlek run.

'The staff have to get things ready for this evening. See?' She pointed over to other instructors who were helping to unload battered stainless steel trolleys from the catering vans. 'You can use the swimming pool in the conservatory or the gym if you wish to exercise. After lunch, complimentary spa treatments will be offered so that all ladies can look their best for the photographic session later.' She sounded like she was quoting a line she'd memorised from the boot camp flyer.

'Sounds more like Crufts than a Gala Dinner,' Charlee muttered, starting back for the house. She imagined herself as Peg, the sassy Lha-sa Apso in *Lady and the Tramp*, and Anastasia as a long-legged borzoi tipped for Best of Breed. Ffinch would be an Irish wolfhound, grey and secretive, looking down his long aristocratic nose at them and giving nothing away.

'I've got to get out of this dump,' she thought. 'I'm going barking mad.' Then she laughed at her unintentional pun and walked into the house. The last thing she saw was a group of men carrying a wrought iron arbour, festooned with plastic roses out of one of the sheds. That had to be the specially constructed romantic arbour mentioned when her phone had been confiscated two days earlier. Somehow, she couldn't imagine Ffinch willingly posing under it or having his photo taken with her.

Another argument. Another tussle of wills.

A lousy day just got a whole lot worse.

After an energetic swim, Charlee spent the rest of her time packing and getting ready for the Gala Dinner. When Ffinch arrived, she was going to demand that he take her home. Her mission had been accomplished (or rather - not accomplished) and there seemed little point hanging around the boot camp, where it was beginning to feel like the party was already over.

As she walked downstairs into the reception area at seven o'clock, Charlee knew she looked good. She'd spent half an hour artfully teasing her layered blonde hair into shape. Her faux Herve Leger wrap dress fitted where it touched. Heavily made-up eyes, underlined in blue kohl, gave her a dramatically different look from that usually achieved with a flick of a mascara wand and hastily applied lipstick.

Whatever happened this evening, Charlee Montague was ready for it!

Despite that confident assertion, her hands had been shaking as she'd fastened on her earrings and matching necklace and replaced Granny's engagement ring. She'd kidded herself that the tremulous fluttering in the pit of her stomach was connected to her failure to write a hatchet piece on Anastasia; the arrival of Trushev, and the feeling that the boot camp was on a war footing. It was unconnected, she'd assured herself for the hundredth time, with the fact that she'd be seeing Ffinch in less than fifteen minutes.

She stepped off the last tread of the Victorian staircase and glanced round at the other brides-to-be in the foyer waiting for their fiancés, whose cars were being valet parked. There was no sign of Anastasia or Trushev, but she'd half expected that; she couldn't see him mixing with the hoi polloi. They'd probably dine in private and tomorrow morning Anastasia would be whisked away in a bulletproof limo and Charlee would never see her again.

Neither was there any sign of Ffinch.

Was he being fashionably late? Or would he simply choose not to turn up and she'd be left Little Millie-No-Mates, a jilted bride for everyone to laugh at? Just as the other couples were making their way through to the dining room and the clock struck the hour, the door opened and Ffinch was blown in by the wind gusting off the marshes.

He looked totally wired. His eyes shone, his cheeks were a healthy colour courtesy of the stinging wind off the marshes. The same north wind had ruffled his dark hair and he appeared to have shrugged off the air of melancholy that dragged him down. She'd like to think that his air of animation and excitement was connected to escorting her into dinner. But she rather suspected this wasn't the case.

Brushing a leaf off the sleeve of his dinner jacket, Ffinch paused on the threshold, shot his cuffs and commanded the room. Charlee's heart beat faster as he walked towards her and it was as if she was viewing the room through a soft focus lens with Ffinch in the centre, sharp and clear, and everything else blurred and out of focus. The chatter of the other guests was like a faraway buzzing in her ears. Feeling suddenly shaky, she gripped the newel post at the bottom of the staircase.

Ffinch was at her side in a heartbeat. 'Are you okay, Charlee? You've gone deathly pale.' His voice was full of concern and he caught her hands. 'You're burning up.'

Which was strange because she felt icy cold!

'Yes, I'm fine. A couple of dodgy Brancaster mussels, nothing more,' she lied, patting her midriff by way of an explanation. 'I hope you didn't think I'd gone all weak-kneed at the sight of you,' she glowered, hiding her inner turmoil.

'The thought never crossed my mind,' he grinned. 'But you have to admit, we do scrub up well. No, I'll amend that - I scrub up well; you look amazing, Montague.' His eyes widened in appreciation and his second, more thorough glance made her go weak at the knees again.

'You don't look so bad yourself, Ffinch,' she said as he appeared in no hurry to release her hands. Charlee glanced round the room which had now swum back into focus. 'The bridezillas are watching, we are supposed to be engaged, remember? I think,' she swallowed hard and bowed her head, 'that you're expected to kiss me. But, don't worry - I have no plan to break down your bedroom door and ravish you once we're back at the mews.'

Although Charlee had striven for a snarky, sarcastic tone to under-line that she was immune to him - even the scrubbed up version - her words had the opposite effect. Hectic colour scorched a trail from her burning ear lobes and scarlet face down and over her décolletage.

'You disappoint me, Montague,' Ffinch came back with, his arm snaking round her waist. 'I was actually looking forward to being ravished for a second time in forty-eight hours. And we do have our reputation as The Doggers of Thornham Staithe to live up to.' That made Charlee laugh and she relaxed, just as his hold on her tightened. She gasped in surprise as he pulled her closer, moulding her body into his and squeezed the breath out of her.

'Wh - what are you doing?' she demanded.

'Playing my part - and remember, this kiss was your idea, not mine.' His mouth pulled back in a quirky half-smile as he brought his head closer. His eyes a heady combination of amusement and desire, he added, dryly: 'The things I have to do in the line of duty.'

And then he kissed her.

As show kisses went, it was pretty convincing and had all the required elements.

They avoided clashing noses and teeth, eyes remained closed and sweetness, which they drew from each other, set their pulses racing. When the kiss went on for longer than was necessary for demonstration purposes, Charlee felt duty bound to end it. After all, she was the one who had asked for it in the first place. She opened her mouth to say just that, but Ffinch - evidently mistaking objection for invitation, prolonged the demonstration.

Two nights ago, he'd called a halt to their lovemaking but now he whispered her name against her lips. When their tongues met, it felt completely natural for Charlee's hands to span the space between his shoulders and draw him closer and prolong the contact. And they might have gone on doing just that if a member of staff hadn't banged the dinner gong with unnecessary force, evidently anxious to have all the guests seated.

'QED,' Ffinch said breaking off, his sangfroid regained and back in role.

'What?' Charlee asked, dazedly shaking her head.

'Come on, Montague, you - of all people - should know your Latin.'

'*Quod erat demonstrandum*,' she translated automatically. 'That which is proved by demonstration?' Moving away, she smoothed out the wrinkles in her constricting dress and got a handle on her runaway senses. Was that all the kiss had been? A show to make their legend more convincing and them appear a bona fide, loved-up nearly-weds? She bowed her head to hide her hurt and disappointment and then pulled herself together. Of course that's what it was - what else could they be to each other?

This was all an act. Which bit of that didn't she understand?

'Sir, madam,' a member of staff holding a camera approached them. Charlee's heart stopped for a minute. Had they been rumbled and were about to be asked to leave?

'Yes?' Ffinch asked, his imperious manner making the young woman with the camera draw back briefly.

'Your photographs.' She pointed her camera lens towards the wrought iron arbour which had been erected in one corner of the large reception hall. Photographic lights and a paper backdrop showing a landscape Capability Brown would have been proud of, set the scene.

'Oh, I don't think -' Ffinch started to say, but a look from Charlee made him change his mind. 'Our legend,' she mouthed, 'remember?' and he appeared to change his mind. 'Very well, but be quick about it.' As the photographer adjusted her lights and other props, Ffinch pulled Charlee into his side in a seemingly loving embrace. 'What are you doing?' he whispered against her ear, his lips brushing her temple. 'Us being photographed could compromise the mission,' he began, but Charlee forestalled him.

'What mission?' she hissed back at him. 'I've done what's been asked of me, and more. If you won't level with me, then you'll have to take what comes your way. I'll find out for myself just what's going on … Oh, sweetie, you're holding me just a little too tightly,' she said as his hand tightened on her wrist. 'How would you like us?' she asked the photographer, breaking free of Ffinch's vice-like grip.

'If madam would sit in the chair - and sir, if you would stand to the left and rest your hand on your fiancée's shoulder? That's great. You are the most photogenic couple this evening; so I'll take some extra special shots, at no additional expense to you. Something to look back on, to remember this night.'

'I don't think I'll be forgetting in a hurry,' Ffinch said dryly, and laid his hand on Charlee's shoulder when she took up her position on a button-back Victorian armchair. 'When will the photos be ready, we have to leave early, and -'

'The presentation packs will be ready after dinner. Now smile and say: biscuits.' Ffinch and Charlee complied. 'If your fiancée could look up at you, sir - and if you could take her hand and look down on the engagement ring?' When the photographer wasn't looking, Charlee and Ffinch grimaced and then set up the pose. As they waited for the shot to be taken, Charlee realised that tomorrow she'd hand Granny's ring back to Ffinch and he'd set off for Darien. It'd be left to her to explain to the staff at *What'cha!* how - after a weekend together - she'd realised they weren't suited and had called off the engagement.

There'd be knowing glances and whispered: 'She couldn't hold onto a man like Rafa Ffinch.' 'What was she thinking?' 'He chose to return to a place where he'd nearly died in preference to remaining engaged to Montague.'

Ffinch spoke and broke her dream. 'What about copies of the photographs, should we want them?'

'You have full copyright on the photographs and can reproduce them at will, it's inclusive,' the photographer explained. 'Okay, all done. Would you like to go through to dinner?'

Charlee sent Ffinch a sharp look. 'Worried that Interpol might track you down, Ffinch?'

'Interpol?' Ffinch gave a guilty start and laughed just a little too loudly. 'Darling, you have the most vivid imagination.'

Charlee frowned. Sally and Vanessa had implied that Ffinch was a drug smuggler, gun runner and God knows what else, but the more she got to know him, the more preposterous their accusations seemed. Yet - the tramlines on Ffinch's lower arm and wrists which she'd picked out by the half-light of her mobile phone, marked him as a user. Then there was the secrecy over this project and his part in it. How much of the truth was being kept from her? She gave a frustrated tut and Ffinch sent her a searching look.

'Last time I eat mussels,' she explained, patting her stomach.

'Food poisoning, Montague? Why am I not buying that? You have the constitution of an ox - you said so yourself.' Now it was his turn to send out a: 'what's going on in that fevered brain of yours,' assessing look. 'Shall we, Pumpkin?' Charlee took his arm and went into the dining room just as the amuse-bouches arrived.

The night wore on but Ffinch hardly said a word during the five courses. He appeared preoccupied, on edge, and kept glancing at his watch or looking over his shoulder into the darkness beyond the windows.

As if he was waiting for something.

Or someone.

Chapter Thirty-three
Zero Dark Thirty

At eleven o'clock the tables were cleared and the nearly-weds returned to the reception area to collect their commemorative photographs while the dining room was made ready for dancing. Ffinch showed little interest in the photographs so Charlee went over to the table and picked up the wallet herself. The disco was announced and, as Paul Weller's 'You Do Something to Me' played, several of the brides-to-be exclaimed it was their choice for the 'first dance' at their wedding and led their fiancés onto the floor.

'At our wedding reception,' Charlee said loudly to the couple nearest to them, hoping to shake Ffinch out of his introspection, 'we're dancing to "I Like Big Butts and I Cannot Lie". Like the couple whose wedding video went viral on YouTube? Isn't that right, Rafa?' she asked provokingly. But Ffinch, alternatively glancing out of the window or down at his watch, didn't rise to the bait.

'Hmm, that's right,' he mumbled. 'Come on, let's dance.' Taking the photographs out of Charlee's hands, he tossed them onto the coffee table and then led her onto the dance floor. The slow, insistent beat of the song matched the blood beating thickly through her veins as Ffinch pulled her into his arms.

'I love this song,' she said almost to herself, resting her head on his shoulder and closing her eyes.

'Charlee ...' Ffinch said quietly, but in a tone that ensured he had her full attention.

'Yes?'

'At the end of this song, I want you to go quietly to your room and pack ...'

'We're going home? Tonight?' she asked, pulling back from him. 'Thank God, I'm sick of this place.'

'Yes. But listen, you must be ready to leave at a moment's notice. And maybe not by the front door, either. Are you up for that?' He whispered in her ear and a heady mixture of excitement and old-fashioned lust lanced through Charlee and goose bumps pimpled her skin.

This was more like it. This was what she'd been waiting for ... the real deal!

'Yes. But, Ffinch, what -'

'No time for questions. Soon, everything will become plain.' With the greatest reluctance, he pushed her away from him as the music ended. Then the DJ chose another romantic track. Charlee turned on her heel, picked their presentation pack off the coffee table and without a backward glance headed for the downstairs cloakroom. Then she made a sharp right and walked quietly up the servants' staircase to her room hoping that no one had noticed. Once in her room she changed into tracksuit, fleece and trainers and packed everything she owned into her zip-up holdall.

Then she dragged her chair over to the window - and waited.

By midnight, when Ffinch hadn't appeared, Charlee wondered if she ought to ring him, but some sixth sense told her that a phone call might jeopardise whatever he was engaged in and she put the phone down and waited. Then, at half past midnight the central heating switched off, the last fiancé drove away and the boot camp settled down for the night. On the drive below Charlee's window, catering vans were loading up with the empty stainless steel trolleys which had transported the food for the Gala Dinner. They trundled awkwardly over the drive, their wheels almost buckling as they dug into the pea gravel.

Dragging a blanket off her bed, Charlee draped it round her shoulders to ward off the cold. In spite of her state of excitement, she nodded off, briefly. When she jerked awake around one fifteen, the catering lorries were getting ready to leave. Curiously, the security lights which normally picked up every movement outside Thornham Manor, had been switched off and the vans were getting ready to make their way down the drive - also with their lights off.

Getting to her feet, Charlee threw off her blanket and moved closer to the window. Below her, Natasha, the boot camp manager - wrapped in a quilted coat with a fur collar turned up against the wind - was standing next to a stocky man with a bull neck.

Mr Potato Head! Charlee clamped her hand over her mouth and moved back into the shadows. Luckily, they hadn't seen her; they were too preoccupied watching the last of the catering vans loading up and getting prepared to leave. Charlee let out a frustrated sigh. Whatever Ffinch had thought was going down tonight, clearly wasn't. On top of that, he was nowhere to be seen and it didn't look like she'd be leaving the boot camp until tomorrow morning. Without bothering to undress, she flopped down on her bed with a huff of annoyance and lay in tracksuit and trainers watching the full moon climb slowly, hypnotically, up and over the window's Victorian glazing bars. Lulled by its inexorable progress and with a feeling of anticlimax, Charlee fell asleep. She woke moments later when small pebbles clattered against her window. Rushing over, she found Ffinch, dressed in birdwatching gear and wearing a black balaclava, throwing pebbles up at her. He signalled for her to open the window.

'Charlee, get your things. We've got to get out of here, fast!'

At that moment, the whole frontage of Thornham Manor was illuminated by the full moon and the intermittent blue flashing lights of police cars. Then the previously silent marshes were pierced by wailing police sirens and barking dogs.

'What's going on?' she demanded.

'No time for all that, now. Throw down your belongings and then lower yourself out of the window.'

'Lower myself out of the window? Are you kidding? It must be at least a twenty-foot drop. I'll kill myself or break an ankle.'

'Man up, Montague. It's only about fifteen feet if you lower yourself out of the window, hang on by your fingertips and then let go ...'

'Fifteen feet? Hold on by my fingertips! What's going to break my fall? Oh, I see, you are!'

'I'll catch you, no problem. Just as well you didn't have that second helping of profiteroles, though,' he joked, clearly in an attempt to boost her confidence. His tone made plain there was no time for debate. 'Come on, Carlotta - you can do it.' This time his voice was soothing, cajoling. Charlee threw out her holdall, coat and handbag, climbed over the window ledge and dangled her legs. It was a long way down.

'Ffinch, I can't ...'

'I'm not leaving without you, Montague. We're partners, remember?'

'Ha. Now he remembers?' she asked the moon, sarcastically.

'Trust me. I wouldn't let anything bad happened to you,' he said softly, looking up at her. Then, tearing off the balaclava, he changed tack. 'Just get your arse over that window ledge, Montague, turn around and lower yourself down and then hang on by your fingertips. On my count of three - let go.'

Charlee had been chosen for this mission because she was a gung-ho, up for anything kinda gal. Now was the time to prove it. Taking several deep breaths and then exhaling, she did as commanded. Holding on by her fingertips, she dangled from the window ledge, her arms almost pulling out of their sockets.

Suddenly she felt afraid. 'Ffinch ...' she wailed as loudly as she dared, feet dangling in thin air.

'I'm here. I'll catch you, darling. On three - One. Two ... Oof.'

Charlee was so surprised to hear Ffinch address her as darling without his usual sarcastic inflection that her grip slackened, she let go of the window sill and gravity exerted its pull. She scraped and banged her knees against the brickwork on the way down, fell into Ffinch's outstretched arms and then landed in a heap on top of him. Expertly, Ffinch rolled her over and ran his hands over her to ensure that nothing was broken. Charlee considered that he lingered just a tad too long over the curves of her breasts and hips, but seeing as she found the examination quite pleasurable, she didn't protest.

'You are bloody marvellous, Charlee. Know that?' Pulling her onto her feet, he jerked her into his arms and gave her a relieved, if none too gentle, kiss. He looked as if he'd like to say more but knew this was neither the time, nor the place. Instead, he picked up her holdall, coat and handbag, and stood ready for flight.

'Oh, my back.' Charlee stretched out her bruised spine and flexed her arms.

'You okay?'

'Think so,' Charlee stammered, winded and still reeling from the kiss. Ffinch grinned at her in the moonlight, his grey eyes alight with excitement - more animated and alive than she'd ever seen him. Charlee realised that this was the old Ffinch standing before her. The one who hadn't led an abortive expedition to South America, lost two research assistants to the Black Eagles, had nearly died and was haunted by recurring nightmares.

She liked the transformation.

'I think we may have put Romeo and Juliet into the shade, don't you Montague?'

'I don't recall him asking her to leap off the balcony,' Charlee said pertly.

Ffinch laughed and kissed her again, as if he couldn't get enough of her. Then all at once he became businesslike. 'We have to get through the gardens unseen. The Vee Dubbya is parked on the darkened slip road that leads to the caravan park, the one we took a short cut through. Remember?' he asked over his shoulder, edging them round the side of the house, using its bulk to conceal them. 'Keep your head down, Montague, we're not out of the woods, yet,' he commanded, grimacing at the unintentional pun. Holding her hand, he led her at a crouching run across the parterre and into the spinney.

The police sirens and flashing blue lights were getting louder as more officers arrived, and Charlee fancied that above the shouting and screaming, she'd heard the pop-pop of hand guns.

'Why are we running away from the police? We haven't done anything wrong,' she began breathlessly. Then she thought - or should that be, I haven't done anything wrong?

'I've got the scoop on Trushev, on what's really been going on at the boot camp. I've tipped off the police and they've stopped the catering vans leaving. The food trolleys are full of uncut heroin, fresh from Colombia. I've given the police all the evidence they need to convict him, he won't wriggle out of their grasp this time. I - we, need to get back to London and break the story before other journos beat us to it.'

'Colombia? Heroin?' Charlee whispered. 'I don't get it ...'

'I'll explain in the van on the way home,' Ffinch said, leading the way through the undergrowth. He paused for a moment as their eyes met over his use of the word 'home' and they nodded at each other. Then he pulled her forward and didn't allow their pace to slacken until they reached the camper van and were driving out of Thornham as if the wild hunt was on their tail.

Chapter Thirty-four
Home is Where the Heart is

A round half past three Charlee woke up, stiff, cramped and uncertain of where she was and … had she just been kissed?

'We're home, Charlee.' The note of longing in Ffinch's voice
made Charlee wish this was their home and they were returning to it
after landing the scoop of the century.

'What time is it?' She struggled to gather her wits about her as
Ffinch parked the camper van in front of the garage doors and waited
for her to climb out.

'Almost four a.m.; you've been asleep for hours.' Charlee gave an
extravagant yawn and stretched her arms above her head. Her slim fitting T-shirt rode up, exposing her midriff to Ffinch's appreciative gaze.
Insanely, considering that he'd seen a lot more than that a few nights
ago, she felt shy and pulled it down.

'Sorry, I should have stayed awake and kept you company.' Had she
snored and dribbled slack-mouthed all the way back from Norfolk?
She hoped not!

'I was quite glad of the breathing space, actually. I have things to
sort out now the police have their evidence and Trushev in custody,' he
added with a note of satisfaction.

Sickness lodged in the pit of Charlee's stomach and her breath
snagged. Now that they were on his home turf the balance of power

had subtly shifted. They were no longer two journos with a common goal, enjoying (almost) equal status. She'd reverted back to being the rookie; albeit one who'd helped expose a massive drugs bust, befriended the villain-in-chief's girlfriend, leapt out of windows and dashed back to London in the middle of the night.

Ffinch was the hero of the hour and had his copy to file before anyone else broke the story. If she was really lucky he might let her proofread it for typos. And what had she got to show for her time, apart from a bag of upmarket toiletries?

Zilch. Nada. Jack Shit.

And her mobile, iPad and camera were languishing back at the boot camp.

'Yes, I have things to think over, too,' she said, not wanting to be left out. But what those might actually be, escaped her at that moment. Slithering out of the camper van, she walked stiffly to the front door and unlocked it - she guessed she'd be returning the spare set of keys along with Granny's ring tomorrow. As she disarmed the alarm, she wondered if Ffinch would change the code once she'd left, just in case she morphed into a crazed bunny boiler, unable to accept that their 'engagement' was over.

Argh - why did these extreme thoughts keep popping into her head? And at this time of the night, too? Tomorrow, Ffinch would coolly thank her for everything, drop her off at her bedsit after breakfast and that would be that.

Hasta la vista, baby ...

When Charlee pushed the door open, the mews was warm and welcoming. The sitting room smelled of polish and there were fresh flowers in the tiny hearth, placed there by Ffinch's tame Mrs Mop who'd worked her magic in their absence. Charlee bet there would be milk, bread and butter and a ready meal of some variety in the fridge. She shut her mind to the state her bedsit would be in after lying unoccupied since the day after Boxing Day. It wouldn't just smell of blocked drains and sardines - as per usual - it would smell as though a Japanese whaling fleet had taken up permanent residence in the kitchen.

'You make the coffee, Charlee, and I'll carry the bags upstairs,' Ffinch said, closing the outside door and making her jump.

'Coffee, right, yeah.'

'Make it a large pot, double strength, something tells me I won't be sleeping tonight.' Charlee's heart sank as she noted his use of the personal pronoun - what'd happened to we, all of a sudden? She stood without moving and then Ffinch spoke again. 'You okay, Montague?'

'Yes, just tired.' She gave an extravagant yawn. 'Coffee. Fully leaded. Coming up.'

She returned to the sitting room some time later carrying a tray of coffee, Mrs Mop's home-made cake, a bottle of cognac and two glasses. Ffinch was on the floor leaning back against the sofa, one knee raised and viewing photos through his expensive digital camera. Charlee took up position behind him on the sofa, looking over his shoulder as the slideshow played. She resisted the urge to run her fingers through his mussed up dark hair, lean forward and drape an arm casually across his shoulder; breathe in his unique body scent. Kiss his neck.

It was time for plain talking … even if it was the middle of the night. There might not be time tomorrow when he drove her back to her bedsit. Taking a deep breath, she placed her hands on her knees and plunged straight in.

'Ffinch, don't you think I deserve to know exactly what's been going on?'

'I was going to tell you on the journey home but you fell asleep,' he teased, half-turning towards her.

'Stop playing games. I want answers - now!'

Ffinch put his camera carefully to one side, poured two mugs of coffee and then took up residence on the cube-like footstool, facing her. He sent her one of his considering looks and then said: 'I guess you've earned the right, so fire away.'

Charlee had been expecting another of his 'need to know' speeches and was taken aback by this sudden willingness to divulge all. Marshalling her thoughts into some kind of order, she began.

'First of all, why was it necessary for me to attend the boot camp? From what I saw, you could have got what you wanted and informed the police about Trushev without my help.'

Ffinch nodded. 'You're right. My original intention was to enter the boot camp at night and gain access to the files on their computer. The police felt they had enough information to raid the boot camp - but without written evidence Trushev could still come out of this unscathed. You were my backup plan, my Trojan Horse. If I couldn't gain entry through a window or door - conveniently left unlocked by you - the Gala Dinner would provide me with a second chance. I planned to slip away during the dancing while everyone was preoccupied and go through their files.'

'So the whole story about photographing Anastasia and spiking *Mirror, Mirror*'s exclusive was just so much ... smoke and mirrors?' she asked quietly.

'Yes and no. Okay, don't give me that look, I'll explain.' He reached over for a slice of cake. 'After what happened in Colombia I was too ill to travel home immediately. The authorities in Bogota wanted to find the kidnappers almost as much as I did and called me in for a couple of debriefing sessions.'

'I can imagine that your kidnap and two researchers being killed did nothing for their tourist industry,' Charlee said dryly, earning an encouraging look from him.

'Quite. I managed to do some preliminary digging around during my convalescence and discovered that the trail led from Colombia to England where the drugs were processed and then sold on the street. The whys and wherefores I couldn't figure out, because every time I got closer to unravelling that particular Gordian knot, I ended up with a dead end.'

'So, how did you make the giant leap connecting Trushev to drug smuggling and money laundering?'

'A lucky break. I kept coming across his name when I was planning my trip to Darien. He'd set up a number of foundations in Colombia to educate poor children and give them a better chance in life. I didn't buy into the whole 'philanthropic Russian businessman helps street children in Bogota,' for a moment. Why travel halfway round the world to help orphans when you could just as easily have helped children in your own country? In Belarus, for example, where the fallout from the Chernobyl disaster continues to claim lives.'

'Good point. Anastasia told me about the charitable foundation she'd set up in Odessa to provide playgrounds and green spaces for orphaned, disabled and deprived children. Yevgeny could have concentrated his efforts there.'

'Exactly,' Ffinch said. 'Although in a way he has. He's twinned his foundation with hers, giving him the perfect excuse to travel between Colombia and Russia without arousing suspicion. When one is on a humanitarian mission - and greasing palms along the way - paperwork and visas have a tendency to get passed through on the nod.'

'I can't believe that Anastasia's been party to any of this. She's a good person ...'

'Maybe you're suffering from a kind of reverse Stockholm syndrome?' Ffinch suggested, delicately reminding Charlee of her place in the pecking order. 'It's when ...'

'I know what it is, thank you,' she snapped and then continued in a more conciliatory tone. 'It's when victims of trauma or kidnapping sympathise with their captors.'

Ffinch nodded. 'Only in this case you've done the reverse and bonded with Anastasia, which has clouded your judgment.'

Charlee ground her teeth but kept her peace knowing she couldn't afford to give vent to her anger before she'd heard the entire story. 'Go on,' she urged.

'This next bit is conjecture and I will admit that I lack documentary evidence. I'm pretty certain that the money raised selling drugs on the streets is used by Trushev to purchase white goods: fridges, washing machines, freezers. The white goods are then shipped to the former

Soviet Bloc where they are sold, the money "laundered" and used to finance further expansion of the poppy fields in Colombia.'

Charlee let out a long, slow whistle. 'A drugs triangle? That's some theory - but with nothing to back it up … that's all it will remain.' She shrugged her shoulders and Ffinch nodded.

'I know; that's why it was so important to get into their office. There was bound to be some documentation lying around …'

'Somehow I don't think Natasha and Trushev would be that careless. I mean, really?' Now it was Charlee's turn to imply that he was being naïve. Ignoring her sardonic aside, Ffinch continued with his story.

'I want to nail Trushev and his gang. Not only do they flood this country with cheap heroin, they force the indigenous people of the Amazon Basin into slavery and use them as drugs mules. Their way of life is vanishing along with the rainforest and I want to do something about it.'

'I get it,' Charlee interjected. 'This is your way of repaying them - and honouring Elena and Allesandro's memory. ' She wanted to make clear that she understood his need for closure - for revenge, even. Maybe, once he achieved both, the nightmares would end, too.

Ffinch nodded, openly pleased that she was on his wavelength.

'My original trip to Darien was twofold. To write the last chapter in my book but, more importantly, to follow the drugs/money laundering trail I'd uncovered - wherever it led. That's when I became unstuck.' Pulling a self-deprecating face, he rubbed at the marks on his wrists and lower arms reflexively, an unconscious reference to his kidnap. Charlee now understood that those marks had nothing to do with tramlines or shooting up; they were the result of his being tied up by the Aguilas Negra.

'So that's why the proceeds of your book are going to the Cat People,' she said with a flash of insight. He rubbed the scars again and nodded. Her heart went out to him and she wanted to close the gap between them and kiss the lesions on his wrists until they stopped aching. But she held back; there were still elements in this story that she didn't understand, hadn't had explained to her.

'Exactly. What I didn't know, and had to be certain of before I involved the police, was how the drugs came into the country. Trushev is rich and powerful, his money can buy him anything he wants - information, friends in high places and immunity from prosecution.'

'I see.' Charlee realised that by witnessing Trushev and Natasha supervising the loading of the drugs into the catering vans she'd put herself in danger. But she said nothing to Ffinch; she preferred to keep a lid on that - for now.

'Of course, the boot camp is ideal cover for his smuggling activities,' Ffinch explained. 'It's close to Lowestoft and Harwich where big ships can drop anchor and offload drugs onto smaller vessels out at sea. It's right on the marshes, which conveniently flood at high tide several times a year, enabling dinghies and smaller boats to go night fishing.'

Charlee was ahead of him.

'But in reality, ferrying the drugs backwards and forwards? Of course; those were the lights I saw on the marshes. I thought them highly suspect at the time.' Although she despised Trushev, she acknowledged that he ran a well-oiled operation. 'But how does he get the drugs out of there and sent to factories to be processed and ready for selling on the streets?'

'The Gala Dinners are key to the whole operation. Food is brought into the camp by a Kings Lynn catering company owned by one of Trushev's associates and the drugs are taken out of the boot camp in empty food containers. Neat, huh? All I needed was to persuade the UK authorities to look into my suspicions about Trushev. Luckily, I had the Colombian Narcotics Squad on side; they corroborated my story and convinced the Met it was time to act.'

He picked up his mug, drained it, poured himself a fresh coffee and sipped his cognac. Charlee, suspecting this was going to be an all-night session, followed suit.

Ffinch continued. 'When you mentioned the night fishing expedition yesterday in the camper van, I knew that the Gala Dinner would be our last chance of catching them red-handed until the next high tide in early spring. If they'd suspected the authorities were onto them they'd have abandoned the boot camp and we'd be back to square one.'

Charlee blushed; she'd been too consumed with lust in the steamed-up camper van to be fully aware of what she'd said to him. But she did remember the conversation she'd overheard in the kitchen.

'The first night I stayed at the mews, I heard you in the kitchen speaking fluent Spanish. It was the middle of the night and you said you were talking to your rellies in Brazil.'

'And you said - they speak Portuguese in Brazil, not Spanish. I should've known then that I wouldn't be able to pull the wool over those baby blues of yours, Montague.' Although he said it like it wasn't meant as a compliment, his eyes locked with hers and she felt suddenly warm.

'Go on,' she urged, keeping him - them both - on track.

'You'd overheard me talking to my contact at the Colombian Drugs Agency who was working alongside officers from the Met at that point,' he explained. 'We had to keep things under wraps right up to the last minute, because corruption is rife and,' he looked at her, the truth suddenly dawning. 'Oh my God, Montague! You thought I was part of the drug smuggling cartel, didn't you?'

'Well not exactly. But you have to admit, you are very secretive.' She didn't want him to know that Sally and Vanessa had poured poison in her ear, implying he was involved in drug smuggling and money laundering - and that she'd fallen for it. They'd been jealous that she'd landed Ffinch and, uncertain of her own position, she'd allowed herself to be manipulated by them.

How could she have been so stupid?

'Actually, I'm not secretive by nature, but over the course of this investigation I have had to be. Trushev is a wily character and has paid informants everywhere.' Charlee immediately thought of the woman-mountain, Valentina. Maybe one day over a glass of wine she'd tell Ffinch about their wrestling match, being dumped unceremoniously in the corridor and rescued by Anastasia. 'Unless he's caught red-handed he'll try and wriggle out of this and say that the boot camp staff were running the operation without his knowledge.'

'But -' Charlee tried to assimilate everything Ffinch was telling her.

'But, nothing - the staff would take the rap for him, believe me. Twenty years in Pentonville with your nearest and dearest being looked after by Trushev is preferable to polonium in your coffee. Or, a prick on the leg with a syringe concealed in a rolled up umbrella.'

Charlee laughed. It all seemed a bit too James Bond to be real, but judging by his expression, Ffinch was deadly serious.

'Okay, back to me,' she said, pointing at her chest. 'Why did Sam spin me a line about getting photographs of Anastasia and ruining *Mirror, Mirror*'s exclusive? I'm guessing there is no exclusive; you wanted me in the camp as your - your mole, and you and Sam dreamed up a fake assignment to make it appear legit? Feel free to correct me at any time.'

'Look, Charlee . . .' He put down his cognac, crouched on the floor in front of her and took her hands in his. 'You're a natural - bright, inquisitive and can do the maths. When two and two add together and make five, a journo's antennae start twitching. And you're more intuitive than hacks who've been in the business for years. But, as I explained in the Vee Dubbya yesterday afternoon, you were able to act innocent because you were innocent. They didn't suspect a thing, although in the end we didn't need to use you.'

'Plausible denial - you said - I get it now.' She snatched her hand back. Then she remembered Anastasia. 'But that's where you're wrong, Anastasia remembered me from outside the nightclub on Christmas Eve.'

Now it was Ffinch's turn to falter. 'She did?'

'Yes! But don't worry; she's looking for a way out of her engagement with Trushev and she thought I might provide it.'

'How?'

'That's the bit I haven't worked out yet.' She was just about to give

Ffinch the lowdown on her conversation with Anastasia: 'Shar-lee you are my way home', but stopped herself. What had she meant by that? 'Probably just wishful thinking on her part, she seems terrified of him.'

'Rightly so. Anyone who crosses Trushev has a way of disappearing, I'm glad I got you out of there.' He returned to the footstool and concentrated on swirling the cognac round in his cut crystal balloon. 'I couldn't bear it if anything happened to you, Montague, know that?' he said, his voice suddenly rough.

'After what happened to Elena and Allesandro, you mean?' She faltered, unsure of the significance of his words. 'You mean you wouldn't want to lose another partner on your watch?'

'I think we both know what I mean, Charlee. It's time we were completely honest with each other in this respect, too.' Putting his glass on the coffee table, he dragged the footstool closer until their knees were touching. He reached out for her hands again, but Charlee wasn't about to fall for his blandishments or lose herself in his storm-grey eyes.

'Let's be honest by all means,' she said with a catch in her voice, twisting Granny's ring round on her finger. 'Tomorrow it all changes … I return to my bedsit. Back at *What'cha!* I revert to being the girl who fetches the lattes and gets sent to the photo archive.' She didn't want to think about the speculation which would arise from her and Ffinch breaking off the engagement. 'You'll write the story, get the glory and then move on. Isn't that how it works? How it all ends?'

'Charlee, I've never had a partner before so I'm not sure how it works.' He released her hands and raked his fingers through his hair, doubt clouding his eyes. 'I thought you might know.' He smiled uncertainly and leaned towards her.

'Me?' Suspecting he was about to kiss her, she drew back. There was no future for them; and it was best that she didn't surrender to the hormones which were screaming out: 'kiss him, you fool'. She was tired, had downed too many brandies and it was time to beat a hasty retreat. 'Goodnight, Ffinch.' She got to her feet and walked round to the back of the sofa, pausing at the foot of the stairs. 'And you wanna know the really sad bit? I didn't get to speak Russian, after all.'

She walked heavily up the stairs, leaving him staring into his brandy.

Chapter Thirty-five
A Fish Called Wanda?

Valentina picked Charlee up and hurled her into the marsh. The tide was on the turn and dragged Charlee with it, thick reeds fastening round her legs and pulling her down, down into the brackish water. Gasping for breath, she surfaced. Trushev was laughing at her from his boat while Anastasia sat on a stool combing her hair and regarding her reflection in a hand mirror - an unlikely Lorelei of the marshes.

'Anastasia,' Charlee called out as she went under the murky waters again.

'Sh-arlee, you did not use cosmetics I give you - and now you drown,' Anastasia sighed, shaking her head as if there was nothing she could do to help.

'You know too much,' snarled Valentina. 'Drown, English bitch.'

'You have seen too much. *Ti slishkom mnogo videla,*' Trushev agreed, piggy eyes glittering in the moonlight. '*Seichas ytoni.* Now you drown.'

'Ffinch, Ffinch - where are you?' Charlee called out as water filled her throat and closed over her head. The next time she surfaced, she was in the middle of a wide, fast-flowing river swimming alongside a group of cats with bones through their noses. Trushev's boat had been replaced by a larger vessel and dark-skinned men wearing crossed bandoliers on their chests and smoking thin cheroots were laughing at her struggles.

'*¡Más le vale nadar, señorita, si no quiere que se la coman las pirañas!*' They seemed amused by her dilemma - swim in the fast-flowing river and maybe drown, or be eaten by piranhas. The cats didn't look too happy, either.

'Ff-iii-nch,' she called out. 'Help me.'

Strong arms caught her and lifted her out of the water. She started thrashing about, trying to escape her latest tormentor. But she was held fast and ...

'Charlee. Charlee, wake up. You're having a nightmare. It's Ffinch - I'm here, darling.'

And so he was, sitting on the edge of her single bed and holding her in his arms - pushing her wet, sticky hair off her forehead. Charlee freed herself and rubbed her eyes with the heels of her hands.

'Where - what?' she stammered, disorientated.

'You were calling out in Russian and then Spanish, and -' Ffinch wasn't allowed to finish his sentence because Charlee gripped his arm.

'You just called me darling!'

'Don't think I did.' Ffinch drew his eyebrows together, appeared to consider the idea and then dismissed it as preposterous. 'That would seriously compromise our professional relationship.'

'I guess it would,' Charlee agreed dully, not sure if he was joking.

'Want to tell me what your nightmare was about?'

'I was drowning ... in the Norfolk marshes and then the Amazon. Ffinch, it was horrible - Trushev was there, and then the Aguilas Negra and,' she puckered her brow, 'cats, lots of cats.'

'Cats?' He gave a theatrical shudder, patently trying to make light of her fears and help her to relax. 'Russians, bandits and swimming cats - that's some dream, huh?'

'And Anastasia was a mermaid, combing her long hair and she said: "you did not use cosmetics I give you - and now you drown".'

'Cosmetics. A girly dream, then,' he teased, 'apart from the amphibious cats.'

'Yes. Think I'd better lay off the brandy before bedtime.' She gave a weak smile and as her heartbeat returned to normal she relaxed in his arms.

'Was I in your dream?' Ffinch asked, making out that the answer was of little consequence to him.

'I think it was you who fished me out of the Amazon before the piranhas put me on the lunch menu. Or maybe,' this time she gave him a considering look, 'you were the one who pushed me in? To get me out of your hair?'

'And why would I do that, exactly?' he asked, sending her an uncomprehending look.

'Because I'm a pain in the arse?' she suggested, willing him to contradict her.

'You are that and more. But I don't want you out of my hair.'

'Out of your life, then?'

'Nope. Not that, either.'

'Oh!'

'Oh.' His look implied she just didn't get it, but that he was prepared to wait until she did.

'You don't?' she repeated, feeling very uncertain but buoyed up by the smile he didn't bother to hide.

'I don't.'

'Ah, then …'

'Yes?' His eyes were warm as he waited for the full impact of his words to sink in.

'This conversation is pretty monosyllabic, even for this time of the night.' She found it hard to breathe and was afraid of dropping her defences and revealing the true extent of her feelings for him. Just in case she'd misread him and got this all wrong.

'Maybe, that's because neither of us is saying what's really on our mind?'

'Which is?' Now it was Charlee's turn to wait.

'Charlee ...' Ffinch began, choosing his words with care. 'Okay, forget I even spoke. Silly o'clock isn't the time for confessing one's hopes and desires.'

'Desires,' Charlee said under her breath, moving away from him. She knew the lines her thoughts were running along. Now she'd got over the terror of her nightmare she longed to scramble back under the thick duvet and invite him into her narrow bed, curl into his back with her arms round him, holding him so close he'd know she'd never let him go.

And yet - tomorrow, if she read the signs right - they would sever their partnership. And, much as her body yearned to make love to Rafa Ffinch and keep the memory forever - her brain counselled caution and an instinct for self-preservation held her back.

'Okay, forget I spoke,' he said, his voice rough. 'Come on, you can sleep in my bed - no need to raise those eyebrows, Miss Prim and Proper ...' Although they knew after the episode at The Ship Inn that she was neither of those things. 'You need a good night's sleep and this bed was designed for a child or a small adult and you are neither of those.'

'Thanks!' Charlee said, feeling suddenly the size of Valentina, the woman-mountain. Jokingly, Ffinch flexed her arm and felt along it for newly developed muscles - the result of her internment at the boot camp.

'Don't fish for compliments,' he laughed at her affronted expression. 'We both know you're gorgeous, sexy; everything a man could desire.' Charlee was taken aback by the depth of emotion in his voice. Wrong-footed, she stammered the first thing that came into her mind.

'Fish. Did you have to mention fish! It was a toss-up in my dream which got to me first, the piranhas or the cats,' she gabbled. Her teeth started to chatter and her whole body reacted to his passionate words as though she'd been plunged into a pool of icy water. If they'd become lovers a couple of nights ago it would have been a 'let's act on our impulses' kind of thing. But now they really knew each other, had been tested under fire and shared so much, Charlee knew exactly what she'd be walking away from if things didn't work out.

One night of love might be enough for some women but it would never be enough for her. Not with Rafa Ffinch. It was safer not to travel that road and better to be left wondering what might have been, rather than knowing for certain what could never be. Tomorrow, taking her leave of him and returning Granny's ring would take all of her reserves of courage and her willpower - and she didn't think she could bear it.

'Ah yes, the cats.' Ffinch, unaware of the thoughts racing through her head, adopted a mock-learned tone and spoke with a strong Austrian accent. 'Your subconscious was probably thinking about the Cat People and wove felines into your nightmare, Fraulein. This is a psychological phenomenon commonly linked to young females.' He laughed at her expression and then reached out and pushed her fringe out of her eyes for a second time, as if he wanted to read her expressive blue eyes. 'What else lurks in the darkness of your subconscious, Fraulein Carlotta?' His voice was warm and seductive - as if his thoughts were running on the same trajectory.

'Nothing Dr Fonseca-Ffreud needs to know,' Charlee said in her usual robust fashion. 'And - just so as you know, this Fraulein won't be swapping beds, thank you very much. You'd have to stick your long legs through the bars at the foot of this bed to fit in. Most uncomfortable,' she said in the brisk tone of a ward sister.

Looking down at the aforementioned long limbs, she realised that he was naked apart from his pyjama shorts. She'd bet even money that he slept in the nude and had dragged the shorts on when he'd heard her cry out. That thought alone was enough to make her stop shivering and become feverishly hot.

'Don't think I'm giving you the choice,' he added, returning to the subject of their sleeping arrangements, 'because I'm not.' Scooping her up, he carried her through to the master bedroom as though she was hollow-boned and light as a bird.

The bedroom was dominated by a king-sized brass bed, the head and footboard of which was fashioned into an intricate lover's knot.

'Yes, I know, some bed!' Catching her expression, he gave a sheepish grin and laid her gently on it. 'It's a bed made for lurve,' he said in a Barry White growl which made her laugh. 'Granny and Grandpa are such romantics - even if they are now in their mid-eighties. They had it made to their specifications back in the day and it underlines a simple fact.'

'Which is?' Charlee asked, expecting another one of his bone-dry witticisms.

'Once a Fonseca chooses his woman, he never lets her go.' He said it in passionate Latino-style but with such quiet force that Charlee's breathing arrested and her blood sang in her ears.

Had Ffinch chosen her? Was this his way of telling her that he'd never let her go?

'Ffinch, I'm not sure that I - that we - should ...' She couldn't bring herself to finish the sentence.

'I'm not certain either, so let's concentrate on getting a good night's sleep and talk about it in the morning. I can't decide if I'm exhausted after the raid on the boot camp and by all that's happened over the last couple of days - or exhilarated at the thought of Trushev getting his just desserts. But having you in my bed, Carlotta - well, that evokes a different set of emotions altogether.'

'Oh.' Charlee was back to responding in monosyllables. Then, she threw caution to the winds and let her instincts take over instead. Moving over to the right-hand side of the bed she peeled back the sheet and blankets and sent him a look of such open invitation that he couldn't fail to understand her meaning. But, just in case -

'There's no point in you squashing up in that tiny bed when there's room for a pony in this one. It's mega-comfortable, too.' She bounced up and down on the mattress, pulled the covers up to form a yashmak and then regarded him over the top. Her eyes were shining but her heart was thudding in case he rejected her.

'I had a new mattress installed when I returned from Colombia, memory foam with posture springing, in case you're interested.' Ffinch acted as if concentrating on practical matters would stiffen his resolve to leave further discussion until morning. 'I did wonder about sharing the bed with you and was about to suggest it - with a bolster down the middle for modesty's sake, naturally. But, with your recent fitness re-gime I figured you'd probably scale the bolster in no time and I'd be at your mercy.' Ffinch looked at her, his eyes shining and full of laughter. Then the humour in them vanished and was replaced by something deeper and more intense. 'It's pointless in any case,' he finished, 'isn't it, Carlotta?'

Charlee knew he was right, resistance was futile.

There was an inevitability about their becoming lovers which was almost karmic. It'd been there since the book launch, waiting to be acted upon. However, events, emotional baggage and simply being in the wrong place at the wrong time had prevented that from happening. Now all practical problems had been overcome, leaving them with just their collective hang-ups to deal with. Ffinch's guilt over his inability to save his research assistants; Charlee's desire to prove to her family that she was deserving of their respect and should be allowed to live the life she desired.

Now it was time for them to open up and be honest with each other. As if reaching the same conclusion, Ffinch drew back the blankets and climbed in beside her.

For a moment, their breaths snagged and their hearts beat to the same tempo. Then Ffinch pulled Charlee into his arms and kissed her with a thoroughness that made stars burst behind her closed eyelids. She gave herself up to his kiss, acknowledging that this was what she wanted; what she'd wanted from the moment she'd first set eyes on him.

Ffinch drew back from the kiss and broke the spell.

'So,' he said, lying on his side and propping his head on his hand, 'fish. You were saying?'

'Fish?' Charlee asked, dazed and breathless. She wanted to rip her pyjamas off and press her breasts up against him, exactly as she had done that night back at The Ship Inn. Flesh against flesh; her warm skin heating his cold limbs.

- And he wanted to discuss fish!

Really?

'It's important to get the details right, Montague. As a journalist you should know that,' Ffinch said, straight-faced and severe. 'What colour were the piranhas?'

'What?' Charlee asked, throwing herself on her back and frowning at the ceiling in frustration. 'I didn't bother to look; they were fecking fish, what more can I say? Ffinch - if this is your idea of foreplay, then -' she began but he cut across her.

'Were they red bellies, golden, or black piranhas?'

'Does it matter?'

'It does, it's one way of ensuring ...'

'Yes?'

'That one of us keeps a lid on this.' He nodded towards her and then his face broke into a teasing grin to show that he was ragging her. 'Looks like it won't be you.'

'I can be strong-willed, I'll have you know,' she sniffed, pretending affront.

'So if I was to do this,' getting to his knees he straddled her and rolled up her pyjama top as if it were a field dressing. The gentle swell of her breasts was revealed and so, too, was her hectic breathing as her rib cage rose and fell. Her heart hammered so loudly she felt he must hear it banging against her ribs. 'You could resist?'

'Easy-peasy,' Charlee retorted. Although her voice was cracked and her throat dry she refused to close her eyes - or give into the craving to wriggle seductively beneath him, inciting him to make love to her. Instead, she looked him boldly in the face, meeting his challenge without giving an inch.

'How about ...'

Lowering his head, but keeping his body weight off her, he pushed her pyjama top aside. Then he bent his head and kissed a trail from her taut stomach to her right breast before taking its erect nipple in his mouth and sucking gently.

'Not a p-problem,' Charlee said in strangled tones, her womb contracting in response to the gentle teasing and her whole body rigid in anticipation of the pleasure that was to come. Ffinch raised his head and looked down at her, his eyes drowsy with desire, his skin flushed.

'But, say - for the sake of argument - I did this,' he pulled her top over her head and threw it onto the floor. Then, with her breasts fully exposed, he spreadeagled her hands above her head and curled her fingers round the framework of the lover's knot. Now that she was completely at his mercy, he lowered himself once more and kissed her with mounting passion, exploring the soft contours of her palate and mouth with his tongue. Charlee released her grip on the rail and wrapped her arms around him. Ffinch stopped his kisses and looked into her face. 'I don't call that resisting, do you?' He returned her hands to the headboard.

Rolling off, he knelt by her side, slid her pyjama bottoms down until the waist band was level with her pubic bone and preserving her modesty - just. Then, keeping his eyes on her face, he slid his hand below the rolled down pyjamas and his fingers found where she was warm and eager for his touch. Charlee arched her back as his finger entered her vagina and he began rhythmically stroking the sensitive flesh in a way that was almost too pleasurable. Then, slipping his other hand beneath her, he pulled her closer and kissed her with a mastery that took away the remains of her self-control.

Charlee was desperate to let go of the headboard, but every time she removed her hands, he replaced them. 'Ffinch, stop teasing,' she begged. 'You're killing me.' But he was unrelenting and shook his head.

'Montague, you can dish it out but you can't take it back. You've teased me from the instant I set eyes on you and you've held me in thrall ever since.'

'I have?' she asked, sending him a dazed look, wondering why he was wasting time talking. And why - Mother of God - he had stopped the delicious, rhythmic stroking of her clitoris.

'You have,' he said decisively, then went on. 'You've made me suffer - three weeks, or more, of foreplay - leading up to this moment.' She gave a moue of protest when he withdrew his hand and sat back on his heels enjoying the sight of her naked and in his bed. 'Tossing your head, blue eyes sparking fire, unleashing an arsenal of sarcastic remarks, like little darts. Do you deny it?' His words were harsh but his voice was gentle and there was an almost bemused light in his smoky eyes. As if he found the idea of them finally becoming lovers surreal, yet completely beguiling.

'I don't deny it. Do your worst,' she challenged, wriggling beneath him and inflicting a torture of her own. Ffinch groaned and his penis pressed against her abdomen. That was all the signal Charlee needed. She exchanged places - her straddling him. 'I won't insist that you hold onto the headboard,' she said turning over his wrists and looking at the livid scars there. 'But, let me kiss away the pain, remove the bad memories.' Dipping her head, she kissed along each scar, trying to imagine what he'd gone through in Colombia. Tears filled her eyes and her heart squeezed in compassion - maybe it was best that she never found out.

'This torment is much worse,' Ffinch said. 'I think I should ...' He pushed her gently to one side, reached into the bedside drawer and ripped open the foil packet of a condom with deft fingers.

'What happened to just holding each other and sleeping?' Charlee demanded. As Ffinch unrolled the condom over his penis, she tried to block out how many women he'd made love to in this vintage bed. That way madness lies ...

'I think we've gone past the point of no return, don't you, Carlotta?' Ffinch paused, as if needing to be sure this was what she wanted. Charlee nodded, pushed him back onto the bed and helped him wriggle out of his pyjama shorts and threw them on the floor with her clothes.

Suddenly shy, she reached over and put out the bedside light so that her blushes were hidden by the friendly darkness. She ran her hand along the length of his inner thigh and upwards to his groin, felt where the hair grew coarse and springy round the shaft of his penis. 'No more talking,' she said.

'Not even about fish?' he teased, his voice gruff.

'Especially not about fish,' she said, and then it was her turn to kiss him. 'Although I never did get a chance to speak Russian, at the boot camp I mean.' Then she whispered the words she didn't have the courage to say to him in English. Not yet. '*Ya lublu tebya.*' I love you. '*Ya xochy tebya.*' I want you. '*Ti nyjna mne.*' I need you. In the dim light issuing from the en suite bathroom she could read his puzzlement as he struggled to understand what she'd said. 'Although ...'

'Yes?' he asked, his hands reaching out for her, seemingly tired of prolonging the moment.

'There was one fish you forgot to mention. In *A Fish Called Wanda*, John Cleese speaks Russian and - Ffinch! Mmwph.' He flipped her over onto her back, placed his hands beneath her buttocks and tilted her pelvis upwards. Then he gently but insistently pushed inside her. For a moment they lay perfectly still, revelling in the intensity of the feeling. When their hearts stuttered back to life, Ffinch began moving rhythmically, surely; banishing all thoughts of fish, fictional or otherwise, from her mind.

'Ffinch, oh my God, don't ...'

'Don't what?' he asked, all innocence. As if he didn't know.

'St-st-stop,' she stammered.

Instinctively, she pulled up her knees, wrapped her legs around him and drew him deeper inside her, her muscles gripping and releasing his penis in time to the slow rise and fall of his body. Ffinch reached for the bedrail, grasping it so that he could control the rhythm and then, taking one last look at her flushed face, bent his head and teased her nipples with his mouth and tongue until Charlee could take no more.

Behind her closed eyes there was only darkness. However, as Ffinch released his hold on the bedrail and placed his hands underneath her to intensify her pleasure, the shadows were replaced with a golden light that seemed to emanate from inside her head.

'R-Rafa' she murmured as his questing fingers sought for and then found the swollen mound of her clitoris and began stroking it - faster; ever faster.

'Yes, Carlotta?' he whispered. 'Now?'

A voice which Charlee barely recognised as her own shouted: 'Now - now - now.' In response, Ffinch quickened his pace, found her lips and kissed her with an ardour that left the physical world behind.

'Rafa ... I ... don't stop, don't - don't stop.'

Charlee lost her grip on reality as wave after wave of golden pleasure rippled through her. She held onto her breath until she felt Ffinch's answering pulse deep inside her and then she released it on a long sigh.

'Carlotta,' Ffinch gasped, lying spent on top of her. After a moment or two, he withdrew and flopped onto his back. He pulled her into his side and kissed her neck. 'That was -' but words failed him. 'Carlotta, speak; are you okay?'

'More than okay,' Charlee acknowledged, snuggling into his side. 'I would say that okay is an understatement,' she began, suddenly beset by the urge to talk. 'It was ...'

'Montague?' Ffinch whispered, lover-like, in her ear.

'Yes, Ffinch?'

'Shut up.'

'Yes Ffinch,' she gurgled, threw her free arm across his chest and held onto him as if she would never let him go.

Later, Charlee heard the loo flush. She propped herself up on her elbows and saw Ffinch leave the en suite and pad across the carpet to the window. He opened the top half of the plantation shutters and looked down into the cobbled yard below. He glanced over his shoulder, saw she was awake and beckoned her over.

'Charlee, come and look.'

She dragged the coverlet off the bed, wrapped it round her and joined him at the window. Removing the coverlet from her shoulders, Ffinch positioned her so she was standing closest to the window and he was behind her. Crossing his arms over her breasts, he pulled the coverlet round them like a cloak and rested his chin on her head.

'It's snowing,' she exclaimed, watching as the flakes danced this way and that under the light streaming from a heritage Victorian street lamp. Then she began to chant under her breath. 'White bird feather-less flew from paradise, onto the castle wall. Along came Lord Land-less, took it up handless, rode away horseless to the king's white hall.'

'What was that?' he asked.

'An old riddle my grandfather taught me to sing when it snowed. This is perfect,' she declared as they watched the snow settle on the winter pansies and tiny cyclamen in the window boxes across from them.

'No - you're perfect,' Ffinch whispered. He kissed the line from her shoulder to her ear, cupping her breasts in his warm hands and teasing the nipples with his thumbs.

Charlee revelled in his touch and leaned back against his chest, her legs seemingly unable to take her slight weight. 'I'm not perfect. Far from it,' she admitted, turning round to send him a loving look. His face was pale in the false light and, in that moment, Charlee knew for certain it was the face of the man she loved. The man she wanted to spend the rest of her life with. She wished with all her heart that the snow would maroon them in the mews and they'd be forced to stay in bed to keep warm. Making love until they had no strength ...

Then reality kicked in.

They lived in central London, fat chance of that happening.

'They do say,' Ffinch observed, as though he'd awoken from a pleasant daydream, 'that practice makes perfect. Let's put it to the test, Carlotta?' Dropping the coverlet on the floor, he scooped her up and laid her down on the old-fashioned brass bed which encompassed their world, and did just that.

Chapter Thirty-six
Kettle and Pot

Charlee stretched luxuriously and then winced. She ached in places she hadn't even realised were places until now. She blushed to think what she and Ffinch had done to warrant those aches. She spread her limbs starfish-fashion in the wide bed and wished that Ffinch would hurry out of the shower so they could begin all over again. She'd never experienced the level of skilled lovemaking they'd shared last night nor given such an unfettered response to any man. Ffinch had whispered encouragement in her ear and urged her to take the lead and she'd responded wholeheartedly, delighting in making him gasp with pleasure at her touch.

It was all quite different to the quick fumbling in narrow college beds with the few undergrads she'd slept with. Boys who couldn't hold themselves in check and came in a rush, whereas Ffinch - in the words of the song - had a slow hand and knew how to delay gratification until she felt scorched by their lovemaking.

She glanced at the clock; it was almost noon and she was ravenously hungry. She would shower and then, as planned, she and Ffinch would grab some lunch before heading to *What'cha!* to bring Sam up to speed. She twisted Granny's ring round on her finger and then kissed it; didn't look like she'd be making her excuses at *What'cha!* for breaking off their engagement, after all. She was filled with sudden joy, knowing for the first time the feeling of being wanted, of belonging to someone who cared for her.

'Come on, sleepy head,' Ffinch said as he walked back into the bedroom towelling his hair. 'Your turn.' Charlee's insides liquefied at the sight of him with a bath towel wound round his slim hips. She sat up in bed and sent him a smouldering look, making it clear what was on her mind. 'Don't look at me like that, Carlotta, it's more than a man can bear and we have things to do this morning.'

'Better things?' She revelled in her power to make Ffinch temporarily forget their mission to bring Trushev to justice. Just as she was reaching out for her pyjamas, the phone rang. Ffinch answered it, tutting at the interruption.

'Ffinch.' He listened intently as someone on the other end rattled on. 'How the fuck did that happen? Don't give me that -' Grim-faced, he flopped down on the edge of the bed. Hurriedly slipping on her PJs, Charlee tried to make sense of the snatches of conversation she overheard. 'Someone fucked up, and it wasn't me. Do you have any idea how long this took to set up? The risks that some people have taken?' He glanced over at Charlee and sent her a worried look.

She sat cross-legged, leaning against the headboard, and waited for the phone call to end. Eventually he hung up, tossing the phone onto the bed in disgust. Getting to her knees, Charlee shuffled forward and knelt up behind him, massaging his taut shoulders.

'What's happened?' She raked her fingers through his wet hair and kissed the nape of his neck. Last night she'd learned - among other things - that Ffinch liked being touched, which suited her just fine because she loved touching and caressing him.

'What's happened?' Ffinch repeated. 'I'll tell you.' Kissing the back of her hand he walked over to the wardrobe and started rooting out clothes and underwear. Absorbed, Charlee watched as he dropped the towel and stepped out of it, unaware of the strong response to seeing him naked evoked in her. Shaking her head free of errant thoughts, she focused instead on what Ffinch was saying.

'When they raided the boot camp, Trushev wasn't there - and the staff are prepared to swear under oath that he hadn't been there over the weekend. None of the guests interviewed could attest to seeing a man answering his description. Looks like he'd been tipped off and had left hurriedly with his girlfriend.'

Ffinch sent her a steady look which implied she'd been taken in by Anastasia Markova. Charlee went very quiet and thought carefully what to say next. Something precious was slipping out of her grasp and she wanted this resolved quickly so they could get to *What'cha!*, give Sam the story and get on with their lives.

'Ffinch,' she said slowly, not sure where she was going with this and considering every word. 'I don't understand - I saw Trushev and Natasha underneath my window supervising the loading of the vans.'

'Are you sure? What time was this?' His tone was urgent and his attention swung back to her.

'It was about quarter past one, I think. What I don't understand, if the police were at the end of the drive waiting to raid the vans, how come they didn't see Trushev leave?' She paused and the tumblers all slotted into place. 'He left via the marshes, didn't he?'

'That would explain it. I told the police that Trushev was a wily bastard and they'd need to post men everywhere. But I got the impression they'd had enough of an interfering journo and wanted to do their own thing, and get the kudos for netting Trushev. "Leave it to us now, lad," were their exact words as I recall. Like an old episode of *The Bill*.'

Charlee walked into her bedroom to collect her toiletries and when she returned, Ffinch was pulling on his leather flying jacket, biker boots and shoving his phone and wallet into his messenger bag.

'Where are you going?' she asked and then felt like kicking herself. She didn't want to come across like a clingy girlfriend who needed to know where her man was every second of the day. Ffinch looked out of the window, barely seeming to register her question.

'I have to see what I can salvage of this ... fiasco.'

'Ffinch - haven't you - we, done enough?'

'Enough?'

'They've got their haul of drugs and ...'

'Charlee.' He came over and gripped her by the shoulders. 'You don't understand -'

'I think I do,' she said, shrugging free, 'but enlighten me, anyway.'

Clearly missing the edge to her voice, Ffinch dutifully explained. 'Trushev is Mr Big. He'll live to fight another day, set up a different distribution centre. I - we've - achieved zilch. Simply made his supply chain stutter to a temporary halt; nothing more.'

When did *we* suddenly morph into *I*, Charlee wondered?

'Are you crazy? We've foiled an attempt to transport heroin to a factory where it would've been cut and sent onto the streets. The haul must be worth at least thirty million. What more can we do?'

'I can - I don't know ... go back to Colombia, gather more evidence?' Charlee's heart and spirits plummeted; surely they didn't have to go over this again?

'Not a good idea. Look, I understand you're doing this for Elena and Allesandro, but don't you think survivor guilt is clouding your judgment.'

'Survivor guilt?'

'Last night, you accused me of having Stockholm syndrome, only in reverse. It's the same difference.' That didn't come out right. Shaking her head, she sought how to rephrase the sentence, but Ffinch, eager to be gone, was already picking his bike helmet and gauntlets off the floor.

'I haven't got time to discuss it right now. We'll talk this through when I get back.'

'Will we, indeed?' For the second time that morning, Ffinch failed to register her clipped tone. He wandered over to the window and manoeuvred the louvres on the shutters so that they admitted more light. Snow was still falling in fat, heavy flakes, muffling the sound of London traffic and the sky was the same bruised grey as his troubled eyes.

'The snow's lying; London will have ground to a halt so I'm taking the bike. There are some people I need to see ...' His voice trailed off. 'I want you to stay put, start writing up your copy. Use my laptop; we've both got a story to tell. When I return, I'll know what can be salvaged from this disaster and then head over to *What'cha!*'

He seemed to have forgotten she was there; he looked as if he was planning to go off-piste without consulting her. Charlee shot him a furious look. She wasn't prepared to play the part of the tame girlfriend who did as she was told by the alpha male, no matter how gorgeous. This was her mission, too, and it was time she reminded him of the fact.

Then, in a flash, a solution suggested itself to her, one which would save the day and their embryonic relationship. Eager to share it with him and to have him acknowledge that she was still part of the team, she put her hand on his arm.

'Ffinch, we can contact the police and tell them I saw Trushev and the manageress supervising the loading of the vans. Gather evidence - testify against him in the witness box; send him down for thirty years.'

Warming to her theme, Charlee saw headlines in 30 point Times New Roman:

ROOKIE REPORTER PUTS RUSSIAN BEHIND BARS.

Ffinch grabbed her by the shoulders and shook her none too gently in an attempt to dislodge the foolish idea from her mind. 'Charlee. Promise me, whatever happens, you won't do that. No, don't give me that look; I know exactly what's going through your mind. No one - I repeat, no one - called to testify against Trushev has ever made it to the witness box.'

'What do you mean?' Fear clutched at her heart but she took a deep breath and presented a brave face. She wasn't about to give up on her idea, no matter what he said. That's who she was, wasn't it? Stubborn, block-headed Charlotte Montague. It would take more than a night of earthmoving sex to alter that.

'They've all met with "unfortunate accidents" of one sort or another.' The headline in Charlee's head was replaced with a new one, accompanied this time by a grainy photograph of a body bag being taken away in an ambulance.

ROOKIE REPORTER VICITIM OF HIT AND RUN - Police say there were no witnesses to the incident which occurred in Chelsea during the early hours of Saturday morning.

'The police will protect me …' Charlee said. Even to her ears, her words didn't ring true. She wished now that she hadn't made such an impetuous offer but didn't feel that she could back down. Not if the alternative was Ffinch returning to Colombia to gather fresh evidence to nail the Russian. During his last trip he'd been lucky to escape with his life; next time he might not be so fortunate.

She tried to imagine life without Ffinch but the thought was so unbearable that she pushed it to the back of her mind. She had to convince him that her plan would work.

'You think the police could protect you? And what would happen after the trial, always supposing that he was convicted? I'll tell you. You'd have to disappear into a witness protection programme, assume a new identity - drop off the radar, forever. You'd never see your family and friends again. You'd never see me again - we could have no future together.' He delivered the last sentence quietly and without emotion, but his eyes pleaded with her to show sense.

Charlee didn't know which would be worse. Never seeing him again because he was dead; or never seeing him again because it would put her life in danger. But what would her life be worth, in any case, if she couldn't spend the rest of it with him?

Then Ffinch delivered the *coup de grâce*. 'Trushev has a long reach. Even from prison he'd be able to organise people to find you, to kill you. He wouldn't rest until you were dead.'

'Ffinch,' Charlee laughed to show she thought he was exaggerating.

'Charlee, I mean it.' He folded her in his arms like she was the most precious thing in the world. 'Please, for me; just once in your life, do as you're told - asked,' he amended, finally sensing the resistance in her. Holding her at arms' length, he tilted her chin and looked down into her face. 'You aren't a rebel without a clue any longer, Charlotte Montague, you're a fully fledged journo. Act like one; start on that copy and wait for my return. And don't answer the door to anyone, I'll let myself in.'

Then he kissed her roughly, passionately, as though they'd never see each other again in this world. After that he put her from him, gathered his gear together and left without another word. Taking the stairs two at a time, he slammed the front door behind him and double-locked it. A few minutes later the sound of his motorbike revving and sliding over the snow-covered yard reached Charlee. She ran to the window to look for him but he had gone, leaving tyre tracks behind him in the virgin snow.

Rebel without a clue?

That stung - even if he'd sugared the pill by adding she was now a fully fledged journo. Fully fledged … didn't that mean she was ready to fly the coop and go it alone? She'd spent years breaking free of the shackles of her family interference; she didn't need someone else telling her what she could, or could not, do.

Especially someone she was trying to save from himself.

Chapter Thirty-seven
Partners ... in Crime

C harlee dragged her holdall over the snow-covered cobbles to where a taxi was waiting to take her back to her grotty bed-sit. Bedsit - the very word made her shudder; her lodgings had been virtually unoccupied since just after Christmas and would be freezing cold. In fact, she wouldn't be surprised if a light came on the instant she opened the door. Grimacing at the cheesy joke, she made her way over to the taxi where the driver helped her with her cases. She was so preoccupied with the idea of testifying against Trushev and stopping Ffinch from returning to Colombia that she hardly noticed the winter wonderland they travelled through.

Snow flurries had turned the Royal Borough of Kensington and Chelsea into a fairy kingdom, glittering with frost and the twinkling lights of the upmarket shops. She was also becoming increasingly concerned over Ffinch's eventual reaction when he discovered she wasn't safe and secure in the mews, typing up her copy.

What copy, she wondered resentfully? Some girly piece about what Anastasia wore at the boot camp, the make-up she preferred and her wedding plans? Ffinch meanwhile would be commissioned to write about how he'd busted a Russian/Colombian drugs ring on the Norfolk marshes. Single-handed.

She might get an acknowledgement at the foot of the column - if she was lucky.

She was so eaten up by the unfairness of her situation that she was surprised when the taxi pulled up outside her bedsit. Tipping the driver, she dragged her belongings up the flight of stone steps and into the hall, where she met another resident laden down with shopping.

'Charlee-ee, long time no see,' the other woman greeted her and they exchanged a few pleasantries. 'Belated Happy New Year.'

'You, too. I've been staying with friends,' Charlee explained away her absence.

'Have you heard? The Bastard Landlord is putting up the rent and has turned down our request to have the night storage heaters replaced with a proper central heating system.'

'Bastard,' Charlee agreed automatically, opening her letter box and removing a sheaf of envelopes and junk mail. She felt detached from the real world of final demands, unheated flats and no money left at the end of the month. Three days posing as a boot camp bride and one blissful night in Ffinch's arms had changed all that.

'I'd heard you moved in with a hot new man. Engaged, even. Is it true?' The woman opened the inner door with her key and they trudged up the filthy stairs together. 'Must be, if the bling is anything to go by,' she observed, staring goggle-eyed at Charlee's wedding finger.

'Bloody hell,' Charlee exclaimed. 'Granny's ring!'

'What is it?' They'd reached the landing and were about to peel off and go their separate ways.

'I - I've just realised, I've got something that doesn't belong to me. Something I should have given back. Oh - never mind. Catch you later.'

'Laters,' her neighbour agreed, shooting her a curious look.

Charlee knew how it must look - she disappears, her post mounts up and no one sees hide nor hair of her for weeks. Then she turns up in the middle of a blizzard sporting the Koh-I-Noor's lesser cousin amid rumours of where she'd been, what she'd been up to. Good thing she paid her rent by direct debit or The Bastard Landlord would have had her belongings out on the street and a new tenant in situ.

But - the ring - how could she have been so absent-minded? Simple - because it felt part of her and she'd rarely had it off her finger since Ffinch had placed it there on Boxing Day. It didn't take a genius to work out that, given the course of action she'd taken, all bets were now off. Ffinch would want his great-grandmother's ring back in the family vault. Pronto. She should have left it behind on the mantelpiece with a note explaining her behaviour, at the very least. This was the second time she'd bolted and, knowing Ffinch as she did, there wouldn't be a third.

But she wouldn't think about that right now, she'd dump her stuff in the bedsit and contact the police as per her original plan. After that, she'd ring Ffinch and try to explain … She pushed the door closed behind her, using her bottom. As expected, the bedsit was freezing cold and smelled of drains and tinned fish.

'Least of my worries,' Charlee said to the untidy space formerly known as home.

In her heart, home was Ffinch's mews off the King's Road where they'd made love like newlyweds before falling into a sated, exhausted sleep. But, it only felt like home because he lived there. Without Ffinch the million-pound mews reverted to prime Chelsea real estate badly in need of a makeover.

'God help me, what have I done?' she asked the empty bedsit, then answered the rhetorical question: 'I've just walked out on the man I love because I'm pig-headed, obstinate and can't be told.' Even by her impulsive standard, Charlee knew she'd messed up. Big Time.

She didn't need it spelled out that Rafael Fonseca-Ffinch wasn't the kind of man who came chasing after errant girlfriends. The next time she heard of him he'd be halfway to Colombia and there'd be a letter from his family solicitors requesting the return of the family heirloom, at her earliest convenience.

She let out a frustrated: 'Bugger,' and kicked a floor cushion across the room.

Here she was, back in Grotsville - cold and miserable and already missing the shabby comfort of Ffinch's mews. But this bedsit, like her decision to leave when Ffinch had asked her to wait for his return, simply underlined her pathological stubbornness. She could easily have commuted from her family home to *What'cha!*'s offices but had valued her independence too much to live at home. She could have shared Poppy Walker's pied-à-terre in Kensington and lived the myth that they were characters from *Sex and the City*, but felt Poppy had done enough for her.

Feeling thoroughly annoyed with herself, she dragged her holdall over to the futon and started sorting through her dirty laundry. It was all so far removed from the blissful night she'd spent with Ffinch that her throat tightened and her vision blurred.

Blinking away her tears she removed the remains of a giant bar of Fruit and Nut, a quarter bottle of vodka and the bag of posh toiletries Anastasia had given to her from her holdall. The photograph she and Ffinch had posed for under the rose arbour fell out of her dirty washing and landed face down on the stained carpet so she picked it up and dusted it off.

'Oh, Ffinch, what have I done?' She kissed the photograph, checked her mobile just in case he'd messaged her (he hadn't) and then unscrewed the lid on the bottle of vodka.

'To love!' she toasted, taking a swig of it.

The fiery liquid burned a path down her throat and made inroads on her empty stomach. She ate a square of chocolate as a chaser and then felt sick. For want of anything better to do, and to take her mind off what a hash she'd made of everything, she tipped Anastasia's toiletries onto the futon. She sorted through the contents in the hope of finding a tube of something expensive which would banish the blues from her heart and the dark circles from her eyes. One of the tubes had been sealed up with sticky tape. This struck her as odd; somehow, she couldn't imagine Anastasia cutting the end off an empty tube to get out the last bit of make-up.

The tube felt strangely heavy and when she removed the sticky tape it became obvious that something had been rammed inside it. Something other than two-hundred-dollar face cream. Intrigued, Charlee wiped her snotty nose across her sleeve, poked inside the tube and winkled out a data stick.

'What the -'

She remembered her last conversation with Anastasia: 'You are my way home, Sh-arlee. But it is dangerous and you must take care. Take present. Sweet Sh-arlee ... You will not let me down'.

Rushing over to the kitchen table, she fired up her ancient laptop and inserted the data stick in the USB port. 'Come on, come on,' she coaxed. The machine whirred and complained, unhappy at being left unused in sub-zero temperatures for almost a month. Then - bingo! The drive opened and revealed a number of sub-folders labelled in Cyrillic script.

Anastasia's desperate: '*Vi mojete prochest kirillcy?*' and her reassurance that, of course, she could read Cyrillic script, made sudden sense. But what was contained in the sub-folders? Charlee left-clicked: a spreadsheet opened and when she scrolled to the bottom her eyes widened in amazement.

'Holy Shamollee.' A frisson ran through her as surely as if Lenin's ghost had just walked over her grave. She copied the contents of the data stick onto her hard drive, backed it up on iCloud and then removed the stick and kissed it.

Two hours later, Charlee's intercom buzzed and she picked up the phone with a trembling hand.

'Who is it?' Like, she didn't know!

'Ffinch,' he said tersely. 'Who were you expecting - The Household Cavalry?'

'Come up.' Charlee put the phone back on its cradle.

Ffinch sounded mad; madder than mad, actually. She knew she'd have some explaining to do before he collected Granny's ring and walked out on her for the last time. She glanced over at her laptop and took a deep breath. Maybe she could turn this round with a bit of quick thinking.

A peremptory bang on the door announced Ffinch's presence. Charlee opened it and ushered him in. 'Leave some paint on the door, won't you,' she said, faking anger. He stepped across the threshold with a thunderous expression but looking every inch the sexy biker in his leathers. Her stomach flipped and it had nothing to do with vodka or Fruit and Nut bars.

'Coming from the door-batterer of The Ship Inn, I'll take that as a compliment. Which part of "Start writing your copy and wait for my return" didn't you understand, Montague?'

'Look, I can explain. I don't like being ordered about, okay?' She felt flustered, wrong-footed and knew there was no justification for her behaviour other than mule-headedness.

'I get that. But, your bloody-mindedness could have proved danger-ous. How can I protect you when I don't know where you are?'

'I don't need your protection.' To her surprise, she discovered there was something immensely appealing about being looked after by the man she loved and … She pulled herself up sharp, knowing she had just set the course of feminism back a hundred years.

'I think you do,' he said, equally obstinate.

'So, I have a baby in the back of the wagon while you ride off into the sunset scouting for Indians?' she demanded, playing out her part.

'Baby? What on earth are you talking about?' His eyes widened as the implication of her words hit home.

'Calm down, I meant it as a metaphor,' she said crossly and then blushed, too. Unless she was prescient she wouldn't know if she was pregnant so soon after making love. Especially when they'd pretty much used a packet of condoms to prevent that happening.

'A metaphor?'

'Don't worry, I know what you've really come for.' She marched over to the sink, squirted some washing up liquid into her palm, rubbed her hands together and then twisted off Granny's ring. 'You want this, don't you?' She hoped that he didn't hear the catch in her voice or detect the sheen of tears there.

'I do.' He took the ring, returned it to its blue velvet box and then put the box in the pocket of his flying jacket. Having had the wind well and truly sucked out of her sails, Charlee crashed down on the kitchen chair.

'You've got the ring. Just go,' she said, resting her elbows on the table.

'There's something else,' he said, sending her a dark look from beneath furrowed brows.

'You've got a bloody cheek, Ffinch. Who do you think I am - Wonder Woman? I haven't had time to write up my copy yet,' Charlee said with some asperity. 'I'll email it to Sam tomorrow.'

'Montague.' Ffinch crossed the sticky carpet in his heavy biker boots, took her by the hands and pulled her to her feet. 'Don't be so bloody obtuse -'

'Obtuse!'

'Yes, obtuse. I've come for you?'

'But,' Charlee was confused. If he'd come for her, why had he taken the ring back?

'Last night, I told you that once a Fonseca has chosen his woman, he never lets her go.' Somehow, he made the statement sound passionate rather than arrogant.

'Yes you did, but -' He put two fingers on her lips to silence her.

'Remember the night of the Gala Dinner, when I kissed you? *Quod erat demonstrandum*? Coming here, hot on your trail to ask you to come home is my way of demonstrating, of showing that - '

'But, Ffinch,' Charlee interrupted, 'nothing has changed - you're returning to Colombia and I'm back to exercising Vanessa's rat on a rope.'

'Charlee, I was caught on the hop this morning. After last night's escapades at the boot camp; driving through the night; making love

- energetically, and more than once as I recall.' Charlee blushed at his forthright manner. 'Not to mention being flattened when you dropped on me from a great height. I was exhausted. Not thinking straight. You were right; I've done my bit, now it's down to the police to do theirs - hopefully, more thoroughly next time. Trushev is down by almost thirty million after last night's seizure and the money invested in the heroin isn't his alone. He'll have some explaining to do to his drugs cartel and, with a bit of luck and a following wind, rough justice will punish him more effectively than British justice could ever hope to.'

'So,' she said slowly. 'You aren't returning to Colombia?'

'I'm staying here, with you. Well - not here with you, you understand. I think the overwhelming smell of damp and sardines would get to me after a while. I want you to move into the mews with me. Come live with me and be my love, as the poets have it.'

'So, why did you ask for the ring back?' Charlee demanded, wanting boxes ticked, i's dotted and t's crossed. She couldn't afford to get this wrong.

'Because it wasn't offered to you in the right spirit and you accepted it under false pretences. I want to right that wrong. Charlee, I only need - want - you,' he said passionately. 'You've turned my life on its head, helped me confront the past and deal with it. You've shown me that I can stop feeling guilty for what happened in Darien and live a decent life. I've never met anyone quite like you. I love you, Charlee and I want -' He paused in the middle of his passionate speech and sent her a perplexed look. 'Are you listening to any of this?'

'Yes! No - wait.'

'Yes. No. Wait?'

'I know I'm not making sense but now I know that you're not returning to Darien, I have something to give you.' She turned the laptop round so Ffinch could see the screen. 'Ffinch - the scoop of a lifetime!'

'It's in Russian,' he said, confused by the Cyrillic script and her lack of response to his passionate speech.

'Correct, but luckily I can translate. This,' she pointed at the spread-sheet, 'contains everything the Crown needs to put Trushev and his associates behind bars for the rest of their lives. Names, bank account, drugs consignments, payoffs ... it's all on the data stick.' Ffinch edged closer to the screen as if fearing the evidence would vanish in a puff of smoke. 'Without the key players, his drugs cartel will collapse; I will be safe and Anastasia will have her way home.'

'But how?' She handed over the data stick and he held it in the palm of his hand as if it was made out of solid gold.

'Anastasia. She wanted a way out of the relationship and the only way she could achieve that was to put Trushev behind bars. I'm guess-ing that he threw the laptop containing this information into the creek the night he escaped, destroying all the evidence. Or so he thought.'

'Charlee. Oh my God. You are magnificent and I love you.' Leaving the laptop on the kitchen table, he came across and kissed her rough-ly.

'You do?'

'I do. I said so earlier but you weren't - '

'Because of this?' she asked, pointing at the spreadsheet. She needed to be sure, very sure, before she gave her heart unreservedly.

'No, you idiot. Because I love you and because ... you're brave, fun-ny, sexy, exasperating, pig-headed, annoying ...' He rained little kisses on her face as he delivered each adjective.

'Can we just stick to the more flattering stuff?' she demanded, giv-ing him an arch look and moving out of his reach. There was one final thing she had to say. 'I may have given you the data stick, but without my knowledge of Cyrillic script - or getting in a linguist - you have no hope of using it. We're partners, Ffinch; equal partners, every step of the way. Deal?' She spat on her hand and held it out to seal the con-tract. Regarding her with complete admiration, Ffinch took her hand and turned it over, then he kissed the back with an old-school courtesy that sent her legs wobbly again.

'Partners,' he agreed, looking as if it would take just the slightest bit of encouragement for him to take her on the low-slung futon.

As much as she wanted that to happen, Charlee held out and stated her terms. 'Montague and Ffinch.'

'Ffinch and Montague,' he argued, his eyes alight with love and mischief. 'And, while we're on the subject of names, do you think you could bring yourself to call me Rafa? Considering the fervour with which we made love last night, I think it's time we progressed to using first names. All this Ffinch and Montague business makes me feel like I'm back in boarding school.'

'And you may call me Carlotta. I rather like that. It makes me seem exotic, different.'

'You are exotic; and as for different, I can say with some certainty that there's no woman in the world quite like you,' he said with feeling.

'I'll take that as a compliment, shall I?'

'It was meant as one. Now, back to business. In exchange for the data stick … Granny's ring.' He retrieved the ring from the blue velvet box. 'Fonseca-Ffinch, campaigning journalists, it has a certain *je ne sais quoi*, wouldn't you say?'

'Just like Brad and Angelina in *Mr and Mrs Smith* …' Charlee said, her blue eyes sparkling.

'… Only without the cache of weapons in a secret room under the garage and with fewer rooms being trashed.' Laughing, he held the ring between thumb and forefinger and quirked an eyebrow at her. 'Unless your feminist principles prevent you from taking my name? The choice is yours, Carlotta.'

Wordlessly, for no words were necessary, Charlee stepped forward and slipped Granny's ring back on her finger. She curled her fingers into her palm in case he, or anyone else, tried to take it from her.

'I choose you, Rafa,' she said and walked into his arms.

'Then I am, without doubt, the luckiest man on earth. Home, Carlotta?'

'Home,' she agreed.

Chapter Thirty-eight
High Tide and Summer Solstice

A delicate knock on the door woke Charlee from a wonderful dream of her and Rafa swimming in a turquoise sea along with a school of dolphins. She was sure there must be some Freudian significance to the dream but it escaped her for the moment. Her mother entered with a tray of coffee, toast and a bright red gerbera in a vase. Bringing up the rear was Miranda, wearing one of George's old shirts over cut-off jeans. Charlee rubbed her eyes, it was early and maybe she was still dreaming.

'Mum?' she said, sitting up in bed. Her mother had never brought her breakfast in bed, not even when she was a little girl and ill with the flu.

'We thought, being as this would be your last breakfast as an unmarried girl, we'd serve it to you in bed.'

Unmarried girl? Her mother made it sound like she was the last ugly daughter left at home and they were lucky to have someone take her off their hands.

'Thanks,' she said and put the tray on the bedside table. Then she looked at them pointedly, willing them to leave. She didn't want them spoiling the day with their nonsense, tears and emotional stuff. The church and the Rev Trev were booked for eleven o'clock and she didn't want to rush. 'Was there something else?'

'Do you mind if I sit down, Charlotte? Now that I'm pregnant I find myself exhausted at the slightest effort.'

'Like walking along the landing from your bedroom?' Charlee asked, straight-faced.

Miranda and George had just had their twelve-week scan and been reassured that everything was good to go for a Christmas baby. Although she was still as thin as a rail, Miranda had taken to wearing oversized shirts in lieu of maternity clothes and had copies of the scan printed to hand out to relatives and friends. Charlee suspected that it was going to feel like a lo-o-ong pregnancy.

'Charlotte,' Barbara Montague snatched her daughter's hand before she could pull it away. She patted it and her eyes filled with tears. 'My baby girl,' she glanced over at Miranda and their faces took on soppy expressions. 'Such a big day for you. For us all.' Charlee laughed, it was a bit late for her to be coming over all motherly.

'I'm ready for it, so if you wouldn't mind leaving me alone I'll finish my breakfast before Poppy and Anastasia get here.' She reached out for a slice of toast and started to chew at it but her mother and Miranda stayed put.

'I do think that you could have asked Barbara and me to help you get ready, Charlotte. We are family, whereas the other two -'

'Are my best friends,' Charlee said, cutting Miranda off in mid-gripe. Then she muttered through clenched teeth, 'and can be guaranteed not to drive me mad on my wedding day.' She swallowed her toast and drank some coffee before continuing more diplomatically. 'Miranda, you couldn't help because you would exhaust yourself, and Mum - you have to supervise the church and the cars, etc. I think I can get dressed on my own, don't you?'

'I suppose so,' Barbara said, dabbing at her eyes with the edge of her dressing gown. 'Just one more thing ...'

'What now?' Charlee asked.

'Just to warn you, to say that ... wedding night ... men can ... it can all be ...' Barbara and Miranda exchanged a look and Charlee blushed to the roots of her fair hair. Surely, even her mother wouldn't deliver a Sex Ed lesson on her wedding morning?

In spite of everything that had happened at the boot camp, their headline-breaking scoop and Charlee living permanently at the mews, Barbara couldn't quite let go of the notion that her daughter was still twelve years old. Charlee folded her arms across her chest and adopted a mutinous expression until they got the hint and stood up. Miranda pressed a hand into the small of her back like she was eight months pregnant. Barbara paused on the threshold and turned back with a woeful expression.

'Was there something else?' Charlee asked, hoping there wasn't.

'Just ... relax and give in gracefully, Charlotte.'

Charlee nearly choked on her toast. They were acting like this was a Jane Austen novel and she'd never been alone with a man, let alone ... Little did they know she'd been giving in disgracefully to Rafa Ffinch as often as twice a night for the past several months. The mere thought of Rafa and their lovemaking sent squadrons of butterflies fluttering in her stomach.

'Thanks Mum,' she said, desperate to get rid of them. 'Miranda. That was very ... uplifting.' Dismissed, the two women exchanged a look of fellow feeling and left.

When they closed the door behind them, Charlee let out a squee of excitement and then glanced over at the white linen bag hooked over the wardrobe - her wedding dress. There'd been a tussle over that, too, her mother wanting the full meringue and Charlee demanding something more befitting a country wedding.

If she'd had her way, they'd have sloped off to Chelsea Register Office and got married like a couple of sixties film stars, with only Poppy and Anastasia to act as witnesses. But Rafa had insisted on doing everything according to time-honoured tradition. He was his parents' only child, and felt that he couldn't cheat them out of the wedding. Charlee acquiesced, knowing she would happily have jumped over the broom and forgone all this brouhaha as long as it meant they would be married and stay together, forever.

'Shar-lee, you look beautiful,' Anastasia said, as Poppy - in her role as chief bridesmaid - fastened the simple wreath of flowers on Charlee's head. The garland of flowers had been Anastasia's idea and she'd trimmed it with ribbons which streamed down Charlee's back, giving her wedding outfit an almost Ukrainian look.

'Fabulous, Charl,' Poppy agreed and the two girls stood back to get the full effect. Much to Charlee's relief, Poppy and Anastasia had bonded over a mutual love of horses and the countryside. It seemed an unlikely match - a girl from Odessa and one raised in the Home Counties - but somehow it worked.

'Flowers,' Anastasia handed Charlee a hand tied bouquet which picked out colours in the ribbons and the blue in Charlee's eyes.

'Ring,' Poppy said, holding out her hand for Granny's ring which Charlee removed, reluctantly. Poppy wrapped it in some scented tissue paper and then put it carefully inside her silk reticule to return to Charlee after the ceremony.

'God, you two are so bossy,' Charlee complained, stepping forward to give them both a hug. Then she composed herself. 'You can tell my father that I'm ready.' For the first time that morning her voice quavered and she took in a deep breath. Poppy and Anastasia had sent Barbara, Miranda and Charlee's four brothers off to church about fifteen minutes earlier. All that remained was for the four of them to walk the few hundred metres along the lane to the village church.

Her bridesmaids gave Charlee one last, satisfied look.

Her cream silk and taffeta dress was ballerina length but with a longer fishtail at the back, the whole dress was underlaid with a stiff net petticoat which kept the hem off the floor. The bodice, tight-fitting and sewn with tiny seed pearls, had a shawl collar which perfectly suited Charlee's slim shoulders. At her throat was the string of pearls Rafa had given to her before leaving for the Walkers' house the previous night. They'd been nestling in a heart-shaped red velvet box for many years and Rafa's mother had had them cleaned and restrung for her son to give to his bride.

As Poppy and Anastasia helped her to slip on cream leather ballet flats, Charlee took a deep breath, closed her fist round the pearls and whispered: 'I love you, Rafa Ffinch.' Then, without a backwards glance, she closed the door on her childhood, forever, and followed the girls downstairs to join her father.

The Rev Trev was standing at the side door to the church almost beside himself with anxiety when the four of them reached the church's lych-gate. The Montague brothers, Rafa's Fonseca cousins and two of Anastasia's minders were arguing with a group of paparazzi and holding them at bay. Rafa had suspected that a few might turn up at the wedding of the two reporters who'd smashed a drugs ring and - more importantly for the Sundays - had chosen Yevgeny Trushev's supermodel girlfriend for a bridesmaid. As for Trushev - he'd seemingly vanished into thin air soon after the drugs bust at the boot camp and hadn't been seen since. The smart money was on him lying somewhere on the bottom of the North Sea wearing concrete wellies, a present from the drugs cartel whose money he'd lost.

'My, my, my,' the Rev Trev stammered, shaking Henry Montague's hand and then mopping his forehead with his surplice. 'I didn't realise just who would be at the wedding; I mean - Ambassador and Mrs Fonseca-Ffinch. Why did no one warn me?'

'Well, they are Rafa's parents,' Poppy pointed out.

'I should have asked the bishop to officiate.' He fingered the silken edge of his stole, clearly believing that he'd dropped a clanger.

'I wanted you, Rev Trev,' Charlee said sincerely, laying her hand on his arm. 'This church and all my friends and family. Not some crusty old bishop who'd no doubt feel obliged to preach a sermon to a captive audience when everyone is desperate to get to the champagne and canapés.'

'Quite,' her father said with finality. 'Shall we? Boys!' He waved the Montagues and the Fonsecas forward. The men were standing goggled-eyed at the collective loveliness of Poppy (who the Montague brothers had previously thought of as a horse-mad teenager in jodhpurs and smelling slightly of manure); and Anastasia - who looked tall and love-ly in a matching deep-blue satin dress overlaid with cream lace.

The ushers and the Rev Trev slipped away and after a few moments the organ struck up 'The Arrival of the Queen of Sheba'. Charlee and her father stepped over the threshold and into the church. The congre-gation got to their feet and tried their hardest not to glance over their shoulders as the bride processed up the aisle.

Charlee was oblivious to it all. The colours, the scent of dust and hymn books undercut by roses and lilies, the light streaming through the stained glass window and the choir waiting for the first hymn. Her attention was focused on the red carpet leading to the nave where a broad-shouldered man in a morning suit was waiting. The man she loved above all others. For a moment she faltered, lost step with the music, and then she was by Rafa's side and he was looking at her as if all his Christmases had come at once.

'I love you,' he mouthed, making Charlee's heart flip over and her hands shake so much that she feared she'd drop her bouquet. Smiling, but feeling a little unsteady, she handed it to Poppy. Henry Montague took a step back because Charlee had declared she was no man's prop-erty to be 'given away'. She'd given herself to Rafa and that was enough. There was a general rumble as the congregation sat back in the pews and the ceremony began with the time-honoured words:

'Dearly beloved, we are gathered here today ...'

Rafa searched for Charlee's right hand, linking his fingers through hers. The words of the marriage service echoed round the tiny church and on the longest day of the year, in high summer, Charlee and Rafa were wed.

A huge marquee had been erected in the Montague's orchard. Char-

lee and Rafa stood in the receiving line as friends and family shuffled past amidst kisses and well wishes. Rafa's Brazilian cousins waited
their turn and then solemnly kissed the back of Charlee's hands before
turning their attention to Rafa, slapping him on the back and digging
him in the ribs.

They wished him a bawdy night of love (in Portuguese) and said
how they envied him having the lovely Carlotta in his bed. Charlee
laughed and Rafa whispered to his cousins that Charlee spoke fluent
Portuguese and had understood every word. They fell over themselves
apologising but Rafa waved them away.

'I agree with all of your sentiments. I am a lucky son of a -' Charlee
dug him in the ribs as an aged aunt, wearing what looked like a lopsided turban, stood in line to give them a whiskery kiss. Rafa caught
Charlee's hand and pulled her closer into his side, whispering what he
was going to do to her when they were alone. Charlee, storing up her
mother's 'give in gracefully' comment for later, pretended outrage at
what he was proposing.

'Ladies and Gentlemen, be upstanding for Mr and Mrs Rafael Fonseca-Ffinch,' Charlee's father said, and they took their place at the top
table amid applause from the assembled guests.

Later on, after the first dance - which was not 'I Like Big Butts and I
Cannot Lie' - Charlee cornered Rafa and demanded to know where
they were going on honeymoon. A trip to establish the Elena and
Allesandro Foundation for Street Children in Bogota (with a generous donation from Anastasia) had been arranged for the near future.
Fitted in, that is, between interviews about their coup on the marshes
- once the case was no longer *sub judice* - and after-dinner talks to raise
money for the foundation. There was even word of them co-authoring
a book based on their experiences.

Life was good.

But that all lay in the future. Tonight, was just about the two of them. Charlee had been instructed to pack a holdall with some casual clothes. Puzzled, she'd obeyed. Anastasia and Poppy would pack her suitcases with her trousseau and drive them to the airport in two days' time when she and Rafa would fly off to somewhere 'hot'.

That was all he'd tell her, for now.

At four o'clock, Rafa's navy-blue and white camper van was waiting on the drive, tied up with yards of white ribbon which was finished in a large bow over the nose. Some wag had stuck their names onto the windscreen - Carlotta and Rafa - and they laughed, remembering Christmas Eve when Charlee'd suggested the selfsame thing and Rafa hadn't found it in the least bit funny.

'Shall we, Mrs Fonseca-Ffinch?' Rafa asked.

Realising she was still holding her bouquet, Charlee turned her back on her friends and family and tossed it in the air. To everyone's bemusement it was caught by the ancient aunt wearing the lopsided turban. Tutting, Miranda snatched it from her and handed it back to Charlee for a second attempt (which was probably unlucky) but no one seemed to mind. There was a great whoop as it was caught by Poppy Walker this time. Was it Charlee's imagination or did her brother Tom sidle closer to Poppy's side?

Amid tears, kisses and ribald comments in Portuguese, Charlee and Rafa climbed into the VW and drove down the lane and towards the M25.

'Where are we going?' Charlee asked, but Rafa wouldn't be moved.

'Wait and see,' he said. 'You won't be disappointed.'

Charlee put her hand on his right thigh and gave it an affectionate squeeze before moving it higher. Rafa put his hand over hers and held it there so he could concentrate on his driving. Charlee suddenly burst out laughing.

'What?' he asked.

'I was just thinking of the old joke. You know - the one where a woman hitches a lift off a complete stranger and then reveals that she's a witch. The man doesn't believe her until …'

'She puts her hand on his knee and turns him into a lay-by?' Rafa stole the punchline. 'That joke might be truer than you imagine, Carlotta,' he added with a cryptic smile.

'What does that mean?' Charlee asked, settling down for the magical mystery tour to where they would be spending their wedding night.

It was almost ten o'clock when they drove into Thornham but, on the longest day of the year, it was still light. Ffinch made his way past The Ship Inn, so clearly they weren't staying there, and towards Thornham Staithe and the Coal Shed. He pulled up on the hard standing, where other camper vans were parked for the night, watching the sun setting over the pine plantation and waiting for the highest tide of the year to maroon them, temporarily.

Charlee got out stiff-legged. 'Rafa Ffinch, are you telling me that we're spending our first night as man and wife in a camper van on the Norfolk marshes?' she demanded, hands on hips.

'I am,' he said unrepentantly, 'and you only have yourself to blame.'

'I do?'

'Remember the afternoon when you came along the edge of the marshes from the boot camp?' He climbed out of the van and joined her over by the sluice gates, looking towards Thornham Beach.

'I do. You had the curtains closed and were having a brew up, as I remember. I was doing all the hard work; all the dangerous stuff while you were dunking a tea bag and reading the paper, at your ease.'

'Hardly at my ease.' He turned her round so she was leaning against the fence, wrapped his arms around her and gave her a passionate kiss. 'I watched you coming along the path and I knew then that I would never willingly let you out of sight - or my life.'

'You were so grumpy that afternoon,' she said, pulling away from him slightly. 'I felt like walking out of the van and leaving you to stew. It didn't occur to me until later that you might not turn up, might leave me in the lurch.'

'I was grumpy,' he admitted, 'but I'll never let you down, Carlotta. I give you my word.' Oblivious of the other campers who were sitting outside their vans enjoying the longest day of the year, he kissed her again, and then grinned. 'Sexual frustration.'

'What about it?'

'A bad case of it. I kept cursing myself for being noble and returning you to your room two nights previously. That afternoon, I wanted nothing more than to convert the back of the van into a bedroom, draw the curtains and -'

'I felt exactly the same,' Charlee laughed at the memory. 'But I thought you were mad at me because I hadn't managed to get any photographs of Anastasia.'

'At that point, Carlotta, I would have exchanged the mission's success for half an hour in the Vee Dubbya with you.' He sent her a passionate look, his eyes appearing almost wolf-grey in the long twilight.

'Half an hour? Hardly worth taking one's clothes orf in the middle of January for a quickie,' she joked. 'Mind you, it was so cold that day we would probably have had to put clothes on to make love.' As they remembered the moment when their partnership had almost been severed and the number of times when they'd subsequently made love, Rafa kissed her again.

'Just as my resistance was reaching its lowest ebb you stormed out and those two schoolboys shouted 'dogger' at you, and -'

'I glared at them - wild-eyed - and put a hex on them. They were so scared they dropped their ciggies and ran off towards The Ship Inn and Thornham.'

'They must have been mind readers, although I really don't regard lovemaking as a spectator sport. Might scare the horses.'

'Me neither, so why ...' Charlee nodded towards the other camper van owners. By now they'd seen the ribbon bedecked VW, the remaining balloons and streamers tied to the roof rack and an old pair of gardening boots fastened to the back bumper. They sent Charlee and Rafa knowing smiles and then looked at each other, remembering their own wedding nights.

'I tried to book the marshes just for us, so we could relive the moment and bring it to a more … satisfactory conclusion,' he teased. 'But The Ship Inn said no one had tried to prebook the car park before and that such matters were out of their control. In fact, overnight camping here is strictly *verboten*.' Charlee looked worried for a moment and Rafa grinned at her. 'Carlotta, you've smashed a Russian drugs cartel, I've been kidnapped by the Aguilas Negra and left for dead, do you really think a traffic warden with a ticket machine holds any terrors for me. For us?' He made his way back to the camper van.

'You're right,' she agreed, following him round to the side of the van and waiting patiently while he opened the double doors.

'Okay, first things first,' Rafa said, suddenly practical. 'We make the bed. Then we break out a couple of camping chairs and watch the sun setting behind the pine trees and the tide coming in. Evening,' he greeted a couple who were parked close by in a massive RV.

'Evening,' they returned the greeting. 'We come here every year for the solstice. It's an annual pilgrimage for us.'

'Cool,' Charlee said in a friendly but firm voice, that made it plain they wanted to be left alone. She helped unload two chairs and a table, then they made the bed and Rafa pulled the champagne out of a cool bag. She lit a large citronella candle to keep the vicious midges at bay and took her place at the table. Although she'd eaten and drunk her fill at the wedding breakfast she wasn't about to turn down a glass of fizz on her wedding night.

'Tomorrow night we are staying at The Ship, in the very room where you tried to seduce me and very nearly succeeded. I thought you might appreciate a return match. Then we travel south for our proper honeymoon. Why are you smiling?'

'Does that mean tonight is our improper honeymoon? I quite like the idea of that!'

'I thought you might,' Rafa said. 'Now what's amused you?' he asked as Charlee downed her champagne, took one last look at the perfect sunset and held her hand out to Rafa.

'Something mother said this morning when she tried to deliver a sort of garbled Sex Ed lecture and a warning about wedding nights. '

'Bit late for that I would have thought,' Rafa observed, and received a punch on the arm for his pains.

'She said I should give in gracefully.' Charlee blushed as she repeated her mother's outmoded advice. 'I thought I'd give in disgracefully instead.'

'Amen to that,' he said, leading her into the camper van and drawing the curtains around them. 'It's the longest day of the year and, therefore, the shortest night. I don't think we should waste a single moment of it, do you, Carlotta? I want you naked - in my bed - and wearing nothing but the Fonseca pearls.'

And for the first time in her life, Charlee was happy to do as she was told.

Also by Lizzie Lamb
Tall, Dark and Kilted

Fliss Bagshawe longs for a passport out of Pimlico where she works as a holistic therapist. After attending a party in Notting Hill she loses her job and with it the dream of being her own boss. She's offered the chance to take over a failing therapy centre, but there's a catch. The centre lies five hundred miles north in Wester Ross, Scotland. Fliss's romantic view of the highlands populated by Men in Kilts is shattered when she has an upclose and personal encounter with the Laird of Kinloch Mara, Ruairi Urquhart. He's determined to pull the plug on the business, bring his eccentric family to heel and eject undesirables from his estate - starting with Fliss. Facing the dole queue once more Fliss resolves to make sexy, infuriating Ruairi revise his unflattering opinion of her, turn the therapy centre around and sort out his dysfunctional family. Can Fliss tame the Monarch of the Glen and find the happiness she deserves?

Read the first three chapters of Tall, Dark and Kilted on Amazon Kindle http://t.co/jKpB4WMM4F

Some reviews for Tall, Dark and Kilted:

"If you fancy a bout of total escapism with some serious sexiness thrown in, this book ticks all the boxes."

A note from the author

If you have a dream - go for it.
Life is not a rehearsal

With Scottish, Irish, and Brazilian blood in her veins, it's hardly surprising that Lizzie Lamb is a writer. She even wrote extra scenes for the films she watched as a child and acted out in the playground with her friends. She is ashamed to admit that she kept all the good lines for herself. Luckily, she saves them for her readers these days. Lizzie's love of writing went on hold while she pursued a successful teaching career, finishing up as a Deputy Head teacher of a large primary school. Since deciding to leave the profession to realise her dream of becoming a published novelist, Lizzie hasn't looked back. She wrote Tall, Dark and Kilted – which echoes her love of her homeland in every page, not to mention heroes in kilts - and published it. Lizzie loves the quick fire interchange between the hero and heroine - like in old black and white Hollywood movies - and hope this comes over in her writing.

For her second novel: *Boot Camp Bride* she's had enormous fun researching VW camper vans, the Norfolk Marshes and the world of journalism. Not to mention falling in love with delicious hero - Rafael Ffinch.

Acknowledgements

Thank you for purchasing Boot Camp Bride. It has been a pleasure to write and I hope you enjoy reading it. I have quite a few people to thank, so I hope you'll bear with me.

First -Mrs Hood of Lenzie who has spread word of my writing to the Antipodes and never once complained about the postage (much). Sorry, Maggee, not even a 'wee murder' in this one. Better luck with number three.

I won't be able to open this book without thinking of Joan and Roger Bushby who put their caravan at Thornham at our disposal and where the idea of this novel was originally conceived. A return visit on a high tide weekend with as many friends as we can muster is called for now the book is finally published. Also, Susan Greet (1951 - 2003), who was much in my mind as I wrote Boot Camp Bride because it was lovely Sue who first introduced us to North West Norfolk.

I must also mention all the readers/writers/friends and followers on Facebook and Twitter who spurred me on to finish Boot Camp Bride by demanding - in the nicest way possible - a date when they could download it off Amazon. See - I've done it!

Next, I need to come clean and admit that I don't speak Russian, Spanish or Portuguese - but I know people who do. So many thanks to RNA member Maureen Stenning who put me in touch with her Russian daughter-in-law Vera Stenning who double-checked every-thing. And to Penny Brindle (RNA/NWS) who helped with the Russian translation, too. Another RNA member, Sarah Callejo corrected all the Spanish and Suzy Turner verified my Portuguese. You are the best - thank you!

In order to produce the best manuscript possible, I have employed two proof readers. I owe my dear friend and RNA member Jan Brigden a special big thank you for help with editing The paperback and kindle version of Boot Camp Bride were formatted by the excellent Jane Dixon-Smith (http://www.jdsmith-design.com) Thanks also to beta readers Miss Davies of Edge Grange and The Beekeeper who gave excellent advice, removed extraneous plot strands and reined in my wilder flights of fancy.

I wouldn't have reached this far without the support, expertise and knowledge of the Romantic Novelists' Association - in particular: Katie Fforde, Margaret James, Freda Lightfoot and Amanda Grange. Not to mention the talented writers in the Leicester Chapter, which continues to go from strength to strength, with many new titles, published each year.

And I can hardly leave out my co-conspirators and best mates: Adrienne Vaughan, June Kearns and Mags Cullingford (aka The New Romantics 4) who have taken this journey with me. Check out their new novels at back of Boot Camp Bride.

And finally, I cannot sign off with mentioning Alison Parr - the inspiration for Anastasia Markova. The similarities between them are quite remarkable - if not downright spooky.

But I owe the biggest debt of thanks to Bongo Man - who, quite simply, is all my heroes rolled into one and better than all of them. I couldn't have done any of this without his help, support and practical advice. As for the parrot - if he's good, he could have a starring role in the next one. Maybe.

I'd love to hear from you so do get in touch

email: lizzielambwriter@gmail.com
Facebook: www.facebook.com/LizzieLambwriter
twitter.com/@lizzie_lamb
website: www.lizzielamb.co.uk

The New Romantics4 blog: www.newromantics4.com
twitter.com/@newromantics4

Novels published by The New Romantics 4

Lizzie LambTall, Dark and Kilted
Boot Camp Bride

Adrienne Vaughan A Hollow Heart
A Change of Heart

June Kearns An English Woman's Guide to the Cowboy
20's Girl, The Ghost and All That Jazz

Mags CullingfordLast Bite of the Cherry
Twins of a Gazelle

If you've read an enjoyed our books, please leave a review on Amazon or GoodReads. Look out for new books from The New Romantics 4, autumn 2014.

Made in the USA
Charleston, SC
15 May 2014